WOLFBLOOD

WOLFBANE SERIES: BOOK 2

CELIA HART

Celia Hart LLC

Wolfblood
Wolfbane Series: Book 2
by Celia Hart

Copyright © 2022 by Celia Hart

All rights reserved.

Edited by Corbeaux Editorial Services
Cover design by Emily's World of Design
Chapter heading artwork by Studio Saturno

Print ISBN: 979-8-9864024-2-0
E-book ISBN: 979-8-9864024-3-7

CONTENT WARNING

These content notes are made available here so readers can inform themselves, if they want to. Some readers might consider these "spoilers." If you don't like spoilers, look away. You've been warned.

- **Bad language**: strong and frequent, including hate speech and slurs

- **Sex**: several fully described and explicit sex scenes, including cunnilingus and fellatio

- **Violence**: several graphic and explicitly violent scenes, including torture

- **Other**: alcoholism, attempted rape, car accident, death, depression, domestic abuse, drug use, fatphobia, homophobia, mention of suicide, murder, panic attacks, pregnancy

If you'd like more information on any of the above content notes prior to reading, please reach out (celia.hart.author@gmail.com) and I will be happy to elaborate so that you may make a fully informed decision before choosing to turn the page!

For my parents, who gave me blood, raised me with tough love, pushed me to succeed, and I hope will never open this book.

Chapter 1

Talia

Dead. Killed in cold blood. The only person in the world I loved was taken from me, her heart ripped from her chest, leaving a gaping hole behind. The red splatter staining the wall of the bedroom indicated it had subsequently been thrown as if it were nothing more than a rotten fruit. Even through the acrid smell of blood, I could still smell him. *He* was the one who did it.

He came almost every week, sometimes several times a week, going back years. In fact, I could not recall a time when *he* did not exist in my consciousness. He had always been obsessed with my mother. Now his smell invaded her bedroom; he couldn't have left long ago as his rancid stench lingered, burning my nostrils and poisoning my stomach.

I crawled over to my mom, tears pouring from my eyes, blurring my vision. I clutched her cold, soft hand in mine, unable to let go. Maybe if I held it long enough, she would just wake from this nightmare, her vibrant brown eyes showing themselves again. Even as I thought this, I knew it was hopeless as the very faint scent of death and decay entered my nostrils. In a matter of minutes, she was already dead.

I gasped for air in agony'. My tears turned to sobs as footsteps sounded in the hallway, becoming louder as they approached until a piercing scream penetrated the air.

I couldn't bring myself to move from my position as a group formed around me. All I could hear were muddled voices, their words blending into something incomprehensible as I squeezed my mom's fingers. Sturdy hands abruptly grabbed me around the waist and pulled me toward a warm body, breaking my grip. I thrashed back, trying to get back to my mom.

"Get her out of here," Madam Coco's deep, raspy voice commanded as the man carried me out of the room, holding my arms down while I kicked my legs, screaming,

I cried out in desperation, "Mom!" Another man grabbed my legs and carried me downstairs into my bedroom, a tiny room the size of a closet in the basement.

The two men dropped me on my bed and stood above me, staring, with their arms crossed. "Talia, I'm sorry to do this. You have to be quiet, or we'll have no choice but to force you. Please don't make us." Hugo touched my shoulder gently.

"It's my mom." I looked at the man, who had become one of my closest friends over the last couple of years, through my tears. "What are they going to do to her?"

He avoided eye contact with me, shuffling his feet and fidgeting with his hands. "Please, Talia," he pleaded with me.

"Please, Hugo. What are they going to do with my mom?" I implored louder.

He shook his head. His fellow bouncer, Tyrone, stayed silent, exhibiting a pitying frown.

"Hugo, please tell me." Tears tumbled down my cheeks.

"I'm sorry, Talia. They have no choice. They're going to dispose of the body. We can't go to the police about this. You know that. Please cooperate, Talia. If you don't—"

He didn't have to say it. I knew what would happen. Because the entire operation was completely illegal, things were always swept under the rug. Sex wasn't the only thing sold here, and I didn't know the complete product listing, I just knew that if you needed something illegal, this is where you came, be it drugs, weapons, or something else entirely. It wasn't far from Calabogie, Ontario, a ski resort village, and an unsuspecting location for such an operation. Just far enough from Ottawa that it was isolated from the city but close enough to make the trip to fulfill one's desire.

But I knew that *he*, the sick, murderous asshole, was not from Ottawa. No, *he* was like my mom and me and knew our secret. *He* lived deep in the forest where humans did not go. But close enough to come here regularly, to get his fix—his fix being my mom. Yes, all the women here wanted regular clients, but *he* was not like other regulars. He had evil eyes, irises so dark that they were indistinguishable from the pupil. He was sadistic. He regularly left injuries on my mom. And while the brothel banned bad clients, my mom would never report him, for reasons that eluded me, and allowed him to keep coming back. Yes, she healed quickly, but she still felt the pain. She'd told me he paid well—better than all the others.

I looked up at Hugo through my tears. He was also like us, but he lived in a werewolf community that he called a pack, unlike my mom and me. I let the tears roll down my face quietly, getting the message that I needed to keep it down. Hugo nodded at Tyrone, who left. Once the door shut, Hugo sat down next to me. He was a big, muscular man with darkly tanned skin. We'd dated in the past, which eventually ended in heartache for me. Hugo was not the boyfriend type. I tried to be friends with benefits until I realized that sleeping with him caused too much pain—he'd made it clear he'd never be able to give me what I really wanted. But he was one of my only friends, and I couldn't stand the idea of not having his company anymore. He was able to explain things to me about being a werewolf, things my mom never wanted to explain. She had abandoned that part of her life years ago, denying that it was within her, a part of her, and she tried to convince me to do the same.

"Talia," he said softly. I reached for his hand but he moved it, giving me a friendly pat on my back. "I'm sorry."

"What will happen now?" I asked, trying to keep my voice even.

"They're going to call the cleaners in. Afterward, you can collect whatever you want from the room. But, and I'm sorry to be the one to tell you, you will have to leave. Madam Coco won't keep you around unless you—"

"Unless I start working here," I finished his sentence.

He looked at me sadly. "You should find a pack. I know your mom was against it, but a pack will take you in and protect you. They'll help you get on your feet. Come to my pack, the Pine Forest Pack. I'll ask the alpha to accept you in."

"That's where *he's* from, isn't it?" I glared at Hugo, sickened by the idea of living in close proximity to my mother's murderer.

"Yes." He sat next to me in silence, staring at the wall of my room. After a beat, he continued, "I don't have any other ideas. But your mom must have had a pack before she came here. Did she ever tell you which one?" He looked at me meaningfully.

"I don't know. All I know is we're not in Canada legally."

"Maybe it was in the US. There are some packs just over the border."

I considered this idea. Could I have been born over the border? A knock sounded, interrupting my thoughts. Hugo got up to answer it, revealing Tyrone with his arms crossed. He gave a quick nod. Hugo returned the nod and let himself out, closing the door behind him.

I tossed and turned for several hours while my stomach churned and my throat burned with anguish. I'd drift in and out of sleep, thinking it had all been a nightmare only to realize that I was, in fact, in a living nightmare.

The next day, a knock jolted me awake. When I didn't answer, the knock got louder. I forced myself up to unlock and open the door slightly before falling back into my bed, still exhausted from the restless sleep. Hugo walked in and put his hands out to help me up. When I didn't take them, he said, "Come on. There's not much time before they get rid of everything." And then I remembered the most crucial thing.

He walked with me upstairs to the main floor. We walked past the lounge area where clients would come to meet the courtesans into the hallway with all their bedrooms—to my mom's bedroom. Her body was gone; all the evidence had been removed. It was as if she had never existed. An emptiness pierced my soul. The wall which had been stained red the prior day was now white, her shattered heart taken away. My mom was completely gone. Gone without a trace, not even giving me the option to say goodbye.

I held my tears at bay as I ran to the same wall that had been stained the day prior and tilted the framed picture to uncover a hidden hole. I quickly reached in until my hands found the familiar shoebox. But as I pulled it out, I realized something wasn't right—it was uncharacteristically light.

My heart sank as I threw off the lid. I fell to my knees. It was all gone. Someone had found it and stolen our life savings. They had taken every dollar and didn't leave even a single loonie or toonie behind. Fresh tears rolled down my cheeks. A situation I didn't think could get any worse had turned into a living hell.

And I knew—it had to have been Madam Coco. There was no way she'd have let the cleaners have free rein of the room without her watchful eye following them intently as they worked. *Fucking greedy cunt!* It wasn't enough for her to exploit my mom throughout her life—she had to do it after her death too.

Hugo came over and knelt next to me. "What's wrong?"

"It's all gone. All the money's gone. All the money we had saved so we could finally leave is gone." I sobbed, wrapping my arms around him, needing something to hold on to.

"Shit. Do you have anything?" Hugo gently pulled away, shortening a hug I wished would have lasted longer, and lifted my chin so he could look into my eyes.

I shook my head. Maybe I had a twenty in my wallet, maybe some loonies and toonies, but certainly not more than that. Anything extra we made we put into this shoebox. I put my face in my hands and sobbed, feeling more alone and lost than I ever had in my life.

After some time, Hugo patted my back and said, "We don't have much time. Is there anything else you want to take from here?"

I looked around and felt my heartbeat in my throat. My mom didn't have any real valuables. Either way, I just wanted her back. Everything else was just stuff.

I walked out of the room, Hugo following. His footsteps sounded behind me as we made our way to my bedroom. Once inside, I sat down on my bed and looked up at him. "Hugo, if I ask you a question, can you please promise to answer it and answer it honestly?"

"Yes, anything." He sat down next to me.

"Can you please tell me how to kill a werewolf?" I reached for his hand.

He pulled his hands away, immediately clenching them into fists and squeezing his eyes shut. Then he turned to me and said, "Listen, Talia, I know why you're asking, but I wouldn't be a friend if I didn't tell you not to even fucking try. You won't be able to kill him. He's very well trained—better trained than me. Even I would never pick a fight with him."

"Just answer the question, Hugo," I demanded, becoming irritated.

For a few moments we sat in silence, in a staring competition. I glared at him and he finally gave in and sighed. "There are a few ways. The most common way is to remove an essential organ, such as by beheading or tearing out someone's heart or lungs. Simply injuring the organ doesn't work, as werewolves can just heal. But removing it completely is a guarantee for death. Another common way is poisoning by wolfsbane. Our pack sometimes shoots darts filled with wolfsbane at enemies to get it into their bodies quickly. But you can also die from eating it or if it's pushed into an open wound."

"How can I get my hands on wolfsbane?"

He shook his head and said, "I can't help you with that. I'm sorry. I refuse to help you get yourself killed." He got up and walked out.

Maybe Hugo wouldn't help me, but I did live in a place where illicit items were obtained. There was someone who could help me. After all, this had been my home for all twenty years of my life—at least as long as I could remember.

Chapter 2

Talia

The following day, Madam Coco summoned me to her office. As soon as I entered, I was met with the familiar scent of old lady perfume and cigarettes, the smell now more nauseating than it ever had been in the past. I tried not to breathe it in too much, becoming enraged with each breath. I forced myself to stay calm, digging my nails into my palms, barely able to look at her.

She was a tiny woman, petite and always sporting a tan—her skin taking on a leathery appearance from spending so much time in tanning beds over the years. I wasn't sure of her exact age. If I had to guess, I'd say late fifties or early sixties.

She gestured to a chair in front of her desk, barely looking up at me, flipping her long, platinum-blonde hair behind her shoulders as I entered. I took a seat. She casually played with thick rings on her fingers. She loved jewelry and was always draped in it. *Bought using my mom's body and desperation.*

After dragging the silence out for far too long, she said, "Talia, *ma chérie*, you know how much I've always cared. I took your mother in when she had nothing. I was practically a mother to her myself, grooming her from nothing to become one of my best employees. That's why this is so hard for me." She pushed her bottom lip forward and shook her head. "But if I make an exception for you, I have to make an exception for everyone. I allowed you to live here as I do with all children of our girls. But now that your mother is no longer employed here and paying your rent, we can no longer house you. Of course, I'm not a monster, and I won't put you on the streets today. You have a week to find housing, and I expect you to be gone by next weekend. We need your room to accommodate others who are bringing in revenue."

I stared at her openmouthed, not knowing what to say. When I didn't respond, she began speaking again. "Of course, we do have an opening now, and I can't deny you're a beautiful woman. If you chose to work for us, you'd get a much larger room. Plus, you are young, and the pay is quite good for someone your age." She smiled and looked at me meaningfully.

Madam Coco's eyes didn't leave mine, waiting for my response. After turning different options around in my head, none that I knew Madam Coco would ever agree to, I forced myself to reply politely although she didn't deserve the courtesy. "Thank you for the offer, Madam Coco, but I will be out of my room before next weekend."

She nodded and turned her attention to something on her desk.

I took a deep breath and continued, "But I do have one favor to ask. Can I please have some wolfsbane?"

She looked back up, meeting my eyes, studying me, and cocking her head to the side. While she was human, Hugo told me that she knew about our kind. He and my mom were not the only werewolves she employed. "What do you need wolfsbane for?"

"It's personal." I wasn't telling her shit.

"What form do you want it in?"

"What forms does it come in?"

"The two most common are dehydrated and a concentrated liquid—usually we sell the liquid form in darts."

"I'd like the liquid form."

"I can get it, but it will cost you."

"How much?"

"It's twenty dollars for half an ounce. Thirty if you want it preloaded into darts."

My body tensed and I saw red at her audacity to charge me after she had just stolen my life savings just the day prior. I took a deep breath, forcing myself to remain calm as I made the abrupt decision to confront her. "I've already paid you."

Her lip lifted on one side, an evil glint in her eye. "What do you mean, Talia?" she asked, her voice even and clearly calculated.

"There was $3762 in the wall of my mom's room. That should more than cover a few darts, and I believe I'm owed change."

"I don't know what you're talking about." She rolled her eyes. "And even if I did, your mom died with debts to her name—she owed me rent for both your rooms, and the cleaners I had to hire due to her client's unfortunate behavior weren't exactly cheap, eh?"

I gasped and almost projectile vomited, her words bringing bitter bile to my throat.

"Additionally, I fronted her this month, helping her with her little habit."

Tears threatened to fall again, but I forced myself to stay strong. I took several breaths, resigning myself to the fact that there was no good way for this to end. I needed a week to figure out where I was going. The alternative was a screaming confrontation that ended with me on the streets with barely a penny to my name. I finally choked out, "Okay, let me see how much money I have, and I will get back to you." I wondered how much I'd be able to scrape together and if half an ounce would be enough to kill.

"Before you go, let me give you this." Madam Coco pulled a folder off her desk. "'They're your mom's papers." I took the folder from her and walked out of the office.

When I was far enough away, and in an area without cameras, I kicked the wall, satisfied with the hole my foot left behind. Madam Coco could use the stolen money to fill it.

I threw open the door to my bedroom and dropped onto my bed, tears forming in my eyes again. While I had grown up in a messed-up place, it never felt so bad when I had my mom in my life. It was the two of us against the world. When the world was dark, my mom would wrap her arms around me and kiss my cheeks over and over again, leaving behind red lipstick stains. "My Tali," she would whisper as I'd inhale her familiar scent that had brought me so much comfort over the years.

I was about to grab for the folder to go through it when a knock sounded on the door, distracting me from my thoughts. "Yes?" I shouted.

"It's Hugo. Can I come in?" the voice on the other side of the door replied.

"Come in," I responded, sniffing back the tears brimming my eyes. He opened the door and sat down on the bed, my thin mattress dipping under his large muscular frame.

"Here, this is for you." He shoved a bunch of bills into my hand.

"What's this for?" I asked, my eyes widening.

"It's not much, but it's what I had to spare. You know I support my mom and younger brother. But I'm worried about you, Talia. Please let me know how else I can help you." He grabbed me into a hug, his strong arms and warm body bringing me some much-needed comfort.

"You've done enough," I mumbled, my heart swelling at the kind gesture. Even if Hugo could never be to me what I wanted him to, he was a good man and a good friend. I normally wouldn't have even accepted the money from him, but I now had a goal overriding any decency and politeness I'd normally show.

"Why don't you stay with me, eh? I can get you into the pack, at least temporarily, until you get back on your feet. They don't like rogues, but I can speak with the alpha."

"What's a rogue?" I asked.

"It's a werewolf without a pack. They smell differently, almost unpleasant. I think they smell that way to warn packed werewolves away from them. Most rogues live in their wolf forms and become more and more feral and savage the longer they stay in that form, so they can be dangerous and unpredictable if you come across them."

"Do I smell like that?" I asked, sitting up and studying him.

"Yes, but I've gotten used to your smell now. I almost don't even notice it anymore."

"Oh," I replied, considering this new information. I hadn't realized that I smelled unpleasant to other werewolves. I wondered if that was part of why Hugo never wanted anything more.

"Come with me. Where else do you have to go?" he asked, wrinkling his brows.

I looked away from him, considering his offer. I was about to decline when an overwhelming warmth spread through my body, and I smiled to myself at how brilliant it would be. He lived in the same pack as *him*. It would make my plan so much easier. Hugo had told me in the past that they guard the borders. But if I were already in, I wouldn't have to worry about that, eh? "You're right," I replied. "If you don't mind, I'd like to stay with you until I can save enough to move out."

"Of course, Talia. I'll speak with the alpha as soon as I can." He gave me a quick pat on my shoulder, then got up and walked out, a pep in his step. In my mind, I was skipping too. The only motivation I had to move forward now was finally seeing *his* lifeless body, limp on the ground.

My eyes then fell on the folder sitting on my desk. I instantly grabbed it and ripped it open. Inside, I found an American passport that I opened and noted was long expired, with a picture of my mom in her younger years, around the age I was now. She looked almost identical to me in the picture—the main difference being her eyes. She was always impressed that I somehow ended up with blue eyes when hers were brown. I continued flipping to find my birth certificate from a town in Vermont. Behind it was my mom's birth certificate from a different town in Vermont. Hugo was right. We did come here from over the border.

I quickly looked up both towns on Maps. They were close to each other and not far from the Quebec border. While I didn't have a passport, I could always just cross over in my wolf form through the woods. Maybe there was a pack in that area, just as Hugo had theorized. I could look for it and maybe I could even find my father, a faceless man I'd always wondered about. *I could finally get some answers.* What brought my mom to Ontario? How did she end up as a sex worker?

Determination within me, I counted the money Hugo brought me. Between that and what was in my wallet, I had $120—enough for four darts. I didn't know how much it took to kill, but I hoped it would be enough.

Chapter 3

Talia

Upon finally succeeding in taking every last penny from me, Madam Coco came through and handed me a box with four darts inside. I'd deliberated on it for a while but eventually concluded that the darts were a much more efficient tool for infiltration and worth the extra cost. I didn't even bother thanking her or saying goodbye, relieved that I'd never have to smell the disgusting mix of old lady perfume and cigarettes, or hear her raspy smoker's voice, again.

A few days later, on a warm Thursday in mid-August, Hugo drove me to his pack. We stopped at the entrance and exited the car, then we were brought to a small room. The werewolves who escorted us there wrinkled their noses at the sight of me, and I realized it must be my rogue smell. I let out a deep sigh. When we were waiting alone, I asked Hugo, "Is the smell really that bad?"

He rubbed the back of his neck and said, "No, they're exaggerating. It's just a little unpleasant."

I nodded and wondered if he was just being polite. It wasn't long before a very tall and muscular middle-aged man entered the room. I could instantly sense he had a superior presence and was likely someone high up in the pack. He sat down across from me at a table and made himself comfortable, making me believe this was not too uncommon an occurrence.

"Hello, I'm the beta of the pack. And you are?" He looked at me, squinting his eyes.

"Talia," I replied, studying him. He had a friendly face, with kind eyes, a scruffy beard, and a pleasant scent. But the way he spoke, he was all business.

"We don't normally allow rogues in, as I'm sure you know. Your kind is not exactly predictable."

I nodded even though I didn't know, and he spent the next hour interrogating me. Yep, all business. Hugo chimed in constantly—something I was thankful for because I didn't feel much like talking. He pleaded my case that I was homeless and needed his help, pulling the damsel-in-distress card. In the end, the so-called beta must have decided I was harmless and had good reason for being there because he let us through.

"We did it!" Hugo celebrated as we headed back to his car. I wondered how many people had been rejected in the past, and how common of an occurrence a stranger entering a pack really was. As we passed through the gates, I turned my attention to the surroundings. I'd never seen a pack before and was fascinated by the small community in the middle of the woods. I was even more intrigued by how uniform it was—all the houses were built in a similar log-cabin style, like a cute little village in the middle of the forest. I felt as if I'd stepped into a fairy tale. The downtown area was even cuter, with cobblestone streets and stone storefronts. Rivers ran along roads, with homes lining ponds. I could only imagine how breathtaking this place would be during the winter when snow would cover the abundance of pine trees and the many bodies of water would freeze over.

Hugo's home was located on the outskirts of town, overlooking a pond in his backyard. He let me in and hung his head a bit, his eyes downcast. "It's not big, but it's home. We don't have a spare bedroom, so I put a blow-up mattress on the floor of my room. I hope you don't mind."

"I don't mind at all," I replied, thankful I had a place to stay. Although, I couldn't help feeling a bit stung that he wanted to keep our sleeping arrangements separate. My recent loss and pathetic state made my loneliness only more painfully noticeable, and I couldn't help but harbor a desperation for love.

He showed me around, and I was in awe. While it was not a large house, it was cozy and much more than my mom and I ever had. I wondered why she never brought us to live in a pack. All this time, we could have had something like this. "This is amazing," I professed.

When we entered the living room, we found his mom in wrinkled sweats with matted hair, hypnotized by the TV.

"Mom, this is Talia." Hugo brought me over to her.

"Oh, hello, Talia." She turned to me for a moment before bringing her attention back to the TV, clearly not interested in the visitor to her home. I was taken aback and couldn't help but notice how aloof she was compared to my own mother who had always been so warm and inviting, even while she suffered depression throughout her life.

Once we were in the privacy of Hugo's bedroom, he said, "I have to apologize about my mom. She may come off as rude but don't take it personally." He slumped his shoulders, his whole face downcast. "I never told you this, but a few years back, my dad was a firefighter in Greater Madawaska. A house in town caught fire, and a child was caught inside. They'd pulled the mother out, but she was hysterical, screaming for her son. My father ran in trying to save him, but he never made it out. They say he exhausted his air supply and got stuck somewhere in the house's interior, right before the whole house collapsed. They never found his body. Probably because werewolves turn directly to ash from burning." His eyes were red as he blinked. He took a deep breath and continued, "Anyway, my mom never recovered from the loss. She's now too depressed to do much and definitely not work. That's why I support her and my brother."

"Wow, Hugo, I'm so sorry. I had no idea." Tears trailed down my cheeks at his confession, the feelings from my own mom's death rushing back to me. I leaned forward to hug him, putting my head against his chest. He wrapped his arms around me in return and I inhaled his familiar scent. I allowed the tears to fall freely, soothed by the steady drumming of his heartbeat. I rubbed his back, feeling empathy for his situation. He had also lost a parent, and all this time, I had no idea. No wonder he had been so good to me—we now shared a harrowing bond.

"Why didn't you ever tell me?" I choked out, my throat burning, realizing now that perhaps we'd never been as close as I thought we were.

"I didn't want to talk about it." Hugo sniffed, pulling apart. "Goddess, look at us. We're so pathetic, eh?"

"You're not pathetic. You're taking care of your family, and now you're taking care of me too. You're one of the strongest people I know. You must be in so much pain, but you hold it together for everyone else." I sighed, wishing that things could have been different between us. "Until you told me that story, I would have never even guessed that you'd experienced loss."

"It's no big deal." He rubbed his neck humbly. "Here, why don't we have some ice cream, eh? It always makes me feel better." He led me into the kitchen. As he rummaged through his freezer he said, "This ice cream is from Pine Forest Dairy, the pack's dairy processing facility. That's how the pack pays for everything. It's a huge operation." He finally pulled a pint out of the freezer triumphantly. "I always keep some on hand. It's needed around here." He gave a small smile but I noted the sadness behind his eyes.

After we finished eating, Hugo took me for a walk to show me around the pack. He lived on the outskirts, so it took us quite a bit of time to get to the downtown area. People gave me odd looks as we passed by them.

Hugo leaned over and whispered, "The beta sent an email to the pack to let them know we're hosting a rogue, so don't worry. They'll be too polite to say anything to you."

I nodded but decided it would be best if I stayed out of the public areas moving forward and perhaps mostly confined myself to the woods.

After walking around for some time, I asked, "So, where does *he* live?"

Hugo knew who I meant and my aversion to using his real name. He shifted a bit and wouldn't look at me, staring straight ahead as he continued with his tour, pretending like I hadn't just asked anything.

Becoming enraged about being ignored, I shouted more forcefully, "Tell me!"

Suddenly, Hugo stopped, becoming immobile, his head turned with eyes pointing. I followed his gaze to a large chalet-style house at the center of town. He then shook his head and asked, "How did you do that?"

"Do what?" I asked.

"You just almost forced me to answer your question." He searched my eyes.

"I did?" I asked. "What do you mean?"

"I didn't want to answer your question, but when you shouted, it was like I couldn't help myself. Something compelled me."

"Oh," I replied. "I don't know."

Hugo had to work most afternoons and evenings, leaving me behind in his home. I didn't mind and, in fact, preferred the solitude. It left me time to mourn my loss and reflect on my past—make peace with the fact that I had so many questions that I would never have answers to now. My mom had preferred to never tell me anything. When I'd try to push her, she'd become shifty, sometimes breaking down into tears. In the end, I'd decided to just give up. Her past was a closed door to me.

When wandering the house, I tried to speak to Hugo's mom a few times, finding the idea of us just ignoring each other while living in close quarters awkward, but she'd mostly give one-word answers, her eyes glued to the television. She rarely changed her clothes, and she clearly didn't shower much either by how strong her scent was. His brother was a teenager and wasn't home much, mainly at school and with his friends. I never made friends in school, being too ashamed of where I lived and what my mom did for a living. It was better just to keep to myself. I did have a boyfriend during my junior year of high school. We mostly hung out at his house. He eventually wanted to know more and more about me, see where I lived, and meet my mom. So, I broke it off, knowing he probably would have dumped me once he found out anyway.

After that, I began sleeping with different bouncers they hired at the brothel, deciding it was safe—they already knew who I was and what my mom did. Madam Coco loved hiring attractive and muscular men for the job. And they loved giving me attention. A few months after I graduated from high school, Madam Coco hired Hugo. That was about two years ago. We started out as friends, eventually became lovers, and turned back into friends again. Since then, I hadn't been with anyone else. I was still a bit stung from the rejection and decided men were too much of a liability. Sure, I sometimes felt lonely at night, but—well, it was just better this way.

Either way, I now had more important needs that overrode anything else. I wouldn't sleep soundly until *he* was dead.

In the evenings, while Hugo was gone, I'd make the long trek to the chalet, sticking to the shadows of the trees. For several weeks, I kept my routine, always holding my switchblade and darts close by, waiting for the perfect opportunity. Because I knew how well trained and powerful my mom's killer was, I knew I'd have to find a way to catch him unawares because there was no way I'd ever be able to overpower him. Even being tall as I was, he still towered over me, and his body had to be at least three times the mass, most of it pure muscle. No, he would not be easy to take down, but my overarching need for revenge overpowered any fear I should have had.

For weeks, I'd watch the windows from afar—hopefully, far enough away they wouldn't catch my scent—figuring out where everyone slept and planning how I'd enter the house once I was ready. He lived there with his wife, a middle-aged woman. They also seemed to have two grown children. One was a woman, and the other was a very attractive, muscular, blond man who I found out from Hugo was the alpha. I'd sometimes inadvertently catch his scent, which seemed to mix itself with the most spellbinding cologne. I'd never smelled such a luxurious, masculine, sexy cologne before. What was it? Maybe something outrageously expensive from The Bay. I loved inhaling the scent when my nose would catch it. Sometimes I'd catch it in the woods where I was hiding after he'd been there earlier in the day, and I'd put my nose to the ground, trying to inhale as much of it as I could.

It was a week into September when the perfect opportunity finally presented itself. One Friday night, when I knew Hugo wouldn't be back until the early morning, I spent the evening in the woods behind the house, watching. It was a very dark, cloudy night, the sky pitch-black. I was thankful for my night vision. While I never spent much time in my werewolf form, it provided some handy benefits.

That night, *he* got in a fight with his wife, and I keenly observed as she turned the lights on in another bedroom before pulling the curtain closed. The light stayed on in that room for at least another hour before it went dark. The night was crisp and cool, and *he* opened his own window, presumably to get some air. Almost immediately, a plan began clicking into place. I brushed my fingers along my switchblade—I'd just have to cut through the screen, which would be easy enough.

Adrenaline pumping through me, I waited long after the light went out in his bedroom. It was imperative for him to be out cold when I entered. It wasn't far-fetched to believe that he would do to me exactly as he had to my mom. When enough time seemed to have passed, I forced myself to wait a little more. I had one chance and it had to go perfectly.

When I felt satisfied it was safe, I crept my way into the backyard, mentally begging my heart to stop beating so loudly. I snuck closer in the shadows until I reached the pine trees lining the back of the house, probably for privacy. Clearly they hadn't realized how easy they were making my job. I hoisted myself onto the lowest branch, using every muscle to steady myself as I climbed, trying to keep the branches from moving, practically holding my breath so my panting wouldn't be heard. My whole body was wet with sweat by the time I reached the top from both anxiety and from the workout I'd had to do to keep the tree still.

Finally, I made it to his window. Balancing myself on a branch and leaning against the house, I sliced through the screen as quietly as possible, thankful the blade I had was so sharp and created minimal noise. He had a huge window, so it was close to the ground, allowing me to pad across the floor of his bedroom very quietly.

I was in. He was snoring loudly and alcohol permeated the air, comforting me that he was completely out. I pulled the darts out of my back pocket, a smile on my face. A warmth spread through my body at my luck. This was much easier than I was expecting, as if someone had been watching out for me.

I quickly removed the protective coverings from the darts and crept closer. He let out a loud snore as his stale and putrid alcohol breath blew into my nostrils. *God, his breath stinks.* I almost dry heaved but forced myself to focus. Knowing there wasn't much time, I'd have to be quick. Choosing the easiest target, I stuck one dart into his exposed arm.

My heart jolted when his eyes shot open in shock, locking instantly with mine as confusion played across his face. "Bianca?" he choked out, and I was taken aback for a moment at the mention of my mother's name. My body tensed and heat flushed through my body, my need for revenge amplified.

"No, her daughter!" I roared. Not giving myself any more time to think, I promptly stuck in another. That must have shocked him into clarity because, in seconds, he was out of bed, lifting me off the floor as if I weighed nothing, grasping me tightly, my arms pinned against my body. *Fuck!*

Before I lost my chance, I stuck the last two darts into his leg as that was the farthest my arm could reach at that point. And all I could do was pray that they worked quickly. He growled and threw me up against the wall, violently slamming my body against it so hard I'm pretty sure drywall shattered. I fell to the ground, my back throbbing. I was certain it was now stained black and blue.

He pulled back his arm, ready to punch me, and I wondered if it was over. But then, a miracle happened. Instead of swinging his fist at me, he brought his hands to his throat.

Blood sputtered out his nose and mouth as he coughed out choking noises, gasping for air, his eyes bugging out as they stayed locked on mine, desperation on his face. He soon fell to his knees, letting out a whimper. Acting on impulse, I quickly got up, pulled my blade out of my back pocket and shoved it into his back, forcing him to collapse on his stomach while his arms flailed like a helpless rag doll. And then he was gone, blood flowing freely from his back and face.

I glanced at him, about to turn around and leave, when the door flew open. A man with dark eyes and dirty-blond hair looked down to the ground at his father and then slowly up at me until he locked his eyes with mine. And I stopped—the world stood still, time halted. It was as if we were the only two people left on earth.

Every nerve in my body pulsed with desire. My lips parted, desperate with need to feel his on mine. I couldn't help but be drawn to his brawny frame, the thin fabric of his T-shirt revealing his clearly well-defined chest and broad shoulders. My inner thighs tingled and my breathing deepened. My hands lifted upward against my will, now with a mind of their own, reaching for him. I could already imagine how his skin and muscular body would feel under my fingertips.

I felt both a tenderness and lust I never had before in my life, and it was almost as if I could sense all of his feelings—shock, despair, shock, lust, shock. We both spoke at the same time. "Mate!"

I quickly covered my mouth and came to, realizing the situation before me. I had just killed his father, and he knew. Overwhelmed, and without a second thought, I shifted into my wolf, tearing all the clothes I was wearing, and jumped out of the window, running into the dark night.

Operating on instinct and adrenaline, I sprinted out of the pack's territory. I had just been caught red-handed killing the man's father, and deep in my gut, I knew the sentence for that was likely death. Even as a part of me hesitated, something scratching deep within me, tugging me back to that wonderful-smelling man, I ran. I knew I had to run.

So that's what I did. I ran into the woods and didn't look back.

Not knowing where else to head, I decided to find my way to Vermont. Maybe I could find my mom's old pack and get some answers. I wasn't sure where to go, but my wolf was taking over now. In my wolf form, I had a much better sense of direction than as a human. I knew to head southeast. I'm sure I'd find signs along the way to point me in the right direction. And if I got hungry, I could hunt.

As I ran, I realized it was much nicer being in this form, and I wondered why I'd never embraced it much before. It was nice running on instinct rather than logic and emotion. My problems started to fall away. I was free. It was just me and the wilderness. Maybe I would prolong my trip and really bond with this new part of me that I'd never bonded with before.

And that was what I did. I spent about a week and a half running in the woods until I found the town my mom's birth certificate was from. During that time, I became one with nature, enjoying exploring the wooded areas and taking long swims in brooks, rivers, and lakes, preferring to travel by water rather than on land when the weather was nice.

After arriving at my destination and exploring the town of my mother's birth, I discovered a pack deep in the woods, noticing that wolves were guarding the border from a distance. I began observing, walking parts of the border, trying to figure out whether I should approach or not. I knew I would eventually, but I always liked to take my time with things, preferring not to be rash and reckless with my approach to anything. Well, besides sleeping with all the bouncers, I suppose. And that was when I felt myself becoming warm, recalling all those memories vividly, suddenly wishing I was back in the brothel to experience them all over again, back in the days before Hugo became a cockblocker. It had been a long time, and I was very alone in the woods.

Chapter 4

Blake

One afternoon, well into September, a mindlink for Luke and me came in while we were in the office together.

"*I smell a rogue in my patrol area.*" Jack's voice spoke in our minds. Luke and I both looked up at each other and instantly got to our feet.

"*Be right there,*" I mindlinked Jack back. We both rushed outside, quickly shifted into our wolf forms, and sprinted over. When we got to him, Jack led the group in tracking the scent, inhaling the unpleasant aroma that had clung to the dirt and ferns just outside our territory. Rogues usually weren't a big problem. It was just a matter of making it clear to them that this was pack land and that they should move away from the area. Every once in a while, we'd encounter a problematic rogue, one that had spent so much time in its wolf form that it became feral and refused to shift, occasionally attacking us. Those rogues were dealt with differently. But hopefully, this would just be the standard, run-of-the-mill, confused rogue.

We followed the scent to a rocky hill that turned into a mountain, continuing up some rugged terrain. We dug our sharp claws into the stone, making our way up quickly and efficiently, stopping at a plateau partway up. Resting on the ledge, looking over the forested land, was a she-wolf with thick, dark-brown fur and icy-blue eyes. The three of us instantly surrounded her as she got up onto her four legs, turning to face us. She slowly moved her head, making eye contact with each of us one by one, her face emotionless.

Unable to communicate in my wolf form, I shifted into my human one and stepped forward. "Please shift so we can speak," I said.

The wolf looked me up and down.

When she didn't shift after a few seconds, I spoke again, more loudly. "Shift now, or we'll force you to shift." She didn't move or make a noise so I continued, "If you don't shift peacefully, we are not afraid to attack, and you're outnumbered."

Her eyes locked with mine, and after a moment, she finally shifted into her human form. She got up from her crouching position and moved toward me on her long legs, her voluminous, dark hair blowing in the wind. She was actually quite beautiful and had an elegant gait. I thought to myself, she was not at all like other rogues I'd met who'd normally been quite bedraggled and always seemed to have something a bit off about them, clearly growing wild throughout the years of sticking to their wolf form.

As she came closer, I realized that something about her seemed very familiar, but I couldn't place where I'd seen her face before. She came nearer and eventually touched her palms to my chest, tracing them down to my stomach, inching lower. Recognizing what she was doing, I pushed her hands off me and backed away. "Stop! Don't do that!" I used my alpha aura in shock.

She moved back toward me, and my mouth fell open in disbelief that my aura hadn't worked on her. Although she wasn't part of my pack, it should have at least temporarily immobilized her. She fluttered her long eyelashes a bit and said, "You like to work out, eh?" Her eyes traced my entire body. She put her hands out again, reaching for me, and I reflexively grabbed her wrists, holding them away from my body. What was with this rogue?

"Luke, Jack, grab her!" I commanded. They both shifted, and each took one of her arms from me. Once they had her in a firm grip, I asked, "Why are you here?"

"I want you," she replied.

"You want me?" I asked, running my hands through my hair.

"Yes, I want you so badly. I want to feel your cock inside me."

I almost choked.

"Wow, she's exactly your type, Blake." Luke chuckled.

I gave him a hard stare and turned back to her. "That's why you came here?"

"No, but now that you're here, that's what I want," she replied, shaking her hair out in a seductive manner and thrusting her chest forward, putting her not-so-modest breasts and erect, light-pink nipples on display. I froze, flustered by her behavior, and she soon threw her head back, exposing her neck and parting her full lips, letting out a soft pant.

I blinked a few times and quickly gathered myself. "You need to leave. This is pack territory, and you're a rogue," I said sternly, not allowing myself to be distracted by her antics.

"No," she replied, just as sternly.

I shook my head in frustration and looked between Jack and Luke, who were continuing to hold her arms as she put on her show. "Let's bring her down." I was baffled. I'd never met a rogue that came on to me like this before. The two of them pulled her with them as they moved back toward the path we'd come up. We hiked back down the mountain in our bare feet, careful to stick to the path, me in front, and the other three behind.

"You've got one very nice butt," she said.

Luke and Jack both snickered, flustering me once again.

I turned my head and said, "That's enough! Keep your thoughts to yourself!"

"You've caught him at a bad time. A year earlier, and he would've been much more receptive to the commentary." Jack laughed. "But I can't disagree with you."

"You too, Jack!" I gave him a quick glare.

Once we made it to the bottom and got back to the patrol station, we put shorts on and gave a T-shirt and shorts to the rogue. I called over some juniors to take her from me and bring her to the cells overnight, perplexed by her behavior. I was hoping a night in a cold cell would sober her up to act more appropriately, and then she could explain why she was trying to seduce me, or whatever she was doing, and why she was here.

The two juniors came over. They balled their hands into fists and stopped far from where we were standing. "Good afternoon, Alpha, Beta," one of the juniors, Jimmy, said, looking between Luke and me, almost groaning, with a pained look on his face.

Not understanding why the two juniors were acting so strange, I started speaking to them. "Can the two of you please escort this rogue to the cells? She is acting very odd, and I'm hoping we can have a normal conversation tomorrow morning."

"Alpha, I'm sorry, I can't," Jimmy choked out, pleading with his eyes.

"I can't either." The other junior, Chad, backed away, flinching.

"Why the fuck not?" I shouted, irritated by two juniors refusing my orders.

"Alpha, she's in heat," Jimmy replied.

"What?" I looked at Luke and Jack. They both shrugged. "That can't be. Why isn't it affecting me? I'm not marked."

"I don't know, but it's affecting me," Jimmy said, his neck and shoulders stiff and forehead creased.

"It's affecting me too." Chad looked as if he was in agony as he squeezed his eyes shut.

"Okay, leave now. I'll find others," I replied. They both let out deep breaths and instantly sprinted away. "What the fuck?" I looked at her. "Are you really in heat?"

"Heat? Like a cat?" she asked.

"Do you feel really horny right now?"

"God, yes," she replied.

"Do you have a mate?"

"A mate?"

Did this rogue know anything? "Have you met anyone that you felt an instant connection with like they were your soulmate or a love-at-first-sight-type feeling? Perhaps you even said the word *mate* when you met them?"

She seemed deep in thought as she considered my question. After some time, she replied, "Yes, I guess I did. But I don't ever want to see him again. His father is evil."

"Fucking Artemis. Why don't I sense it?" I spoke more to myself than to anyone else. I turned to Luke. "If she's in heat, maybe we should just take her back to the packhouse and keep her there overnight. It's probably not safe to leave her in a cell in this state. Also, not much privacy—since I'm sure she's going to want to, well, take care of her needs."

"I'm not sure Lucy would be happy about me bringing home a rogue, especially with a baby in the house. Jasmine would probably have something to say about it too. I mean, the rogue's all over you."

"What should we do then?"

"Is there another house we could bring her to?" We both turned and looked at Jack.

"Why are you looking at me?" he asked, then groaned. "I hope I'm not going to be your heat babysitter moving forward. The last time was pretty fucking awkward as it was."

"Okay, let's not talk about that!" I quickly responded.

"Agreed," Luke chimed in. My neck prickled in discomfort. I'd never told Luke that story, and I wasn't about to start telling him now. I wasn't sure how much Jasmine may have told him. There was still a lot of tension between Luke and me when it came to Jasmine, so we'd made a silent agreement to speak of her as little as possible.

I did plan to move her into the packhouse as my mate and luna eventually. But it was still a very delicate situation, considering that Luke was her fated mate and ended up choosing her best friend as a chosen mate over her. Jasmine and Lucy were still not on friendly terms, and it wasn't clear if they ever would be again.

"You can babysit me," the rogue moaned out, licking her lips.

I sighed. "Jack, I promise I will return the favor. Anything you want."

"Anything?"

"Not a threesome."

Jack laughed. "Look who got his sense of humor back finally."

"I wouldn't mind a threesome," the rogue said.

"Fuck! Look what my sense of humor just did." I groaned.

She tried to inch her way back over to me, struggling to pull her wrists free of Jack and Luke. "Please, I want you so badly. I'm so wet. It's like a waterfall on my thighs," she cried out.

"Fucking A."

"Why aren't you interested? Most men are," the rogue choked out with emotion, pleading with her bright, feverish eyes.

She bit down on her bottom lip as I stepped closer. As she looked up at me, I noted there was a sadness in her eyes. I realized her eyes reminded me a lot of my own—the same very icy shade of blue. I softened toward her and asked, "What's your name?"

"Talia," she replied as a tear slid down her cheek.

Her tear imparted some compassion in me toward her. "Don't take it personally. You're only doing this because you're in heat now, and you won't feel like this tomorrow. Normally it would affect me too, and I have no idea why it isn't. You are clearly a very attractive woman. But I have a girlfriend I love very much, and I would never cheat on her. In fact, I'm planning to propose to her soon."

"You are?" Luke jerked his head up at me and blinked a few times.

I nodded.

"Fuck, man, well, good luck." He looked down at the ground. The air was thick with tension.

The rogue whimpered.

"Okay, let's take her to my car." Jack sighed. Luke nodded and turned to walk with Jack, pulling the rogue along with them. We put her into the back seat, and Jack drove away.

Once Jack's car disappeared into the distance, Luke and I returned the shorts we'd borrowed to the patrol station and shifted back into our wolf forms, sprinting back to the packhouse. After we found our clothes and dressed, before we went inside, I stopped Luke. "Is everything okay? Is me proposing to Jasmine bothering you?"

"It's fine," he replied, in a voice that indicated it was not fine at all.

"It's obviously bothering you," I pushed.

"Blake, it's fine. Just let it go," Luke replied, his jaw tense.

"What, you didn't want her, but you don't want anyone else to have her?" I demanded.

He sighed. "Well, it would be a whole fucking lot easier if the person she ended up with didn't live in the same house as me."

"What am I supposed to do? I love her, Luke."

"It's fine. We'll figure it out." He patted me on the shoulder and walked inside.

Chapter 5

Alexander

Well, that was an interesting way to meet my mate, to say the least. It almost wasn't surprising when it happened. Okay, it was very unexpected and shocking, but I'm also one of those people who attracts drama and crazy situations. Needless to say, it is never a dull day in my life, and I never run out of stories to tell at parties.

So, it was almost expected that I wouldn't meet my mate the normal way. Most people meet their mates at a party or a café, they lock eyes from across a room, they go to the same park one day. You get the picture—there are hundreds of normal ways to meet a mate. Of course, I'm the one that meets my mate at my father's murder scene, my mate being the number one and only suspect. If it weren't so disturbing, I'd laugh about it. The Moon Goddess clearly has a sick sense of humor.

Granted, my father was not exactly in the running for father or, heck, person of the year. But I'm not quite sure what crime he committed that deserved murder. Okay, okay, there have been many times I've wanted to murder him myself. But it's something completely different when a stranger does it, eh?

Although murder aside, she was quite captivating. She was tall and beautiful, with very long brown hair that blew seductively in the wind coming through the window (objectively, it probably wasn't that seductive, but it *felt* seductive). And, oh man, those eyes. It was like they could see into my soul. They were the most distinct shade of blue. Granted, I knew nothing about her, but physically she was perfect—exactly my type.

And then she was gone. I could sense fear permeating the air around me as she jumped from the window, tearing all her clothes. I stepped forward, past my father's corpse, far too captivated to bring my attention to him. All I could do was stare out the window as she disappeared into the dark night. I turned back around and knelt down to pick up her clothes, now just scraps, before bringing them to my nose and inhaling her intoxicating scent. A moan escaped my lips as I did so, the scent was so enchanting and sensual. It was the same scent I'd caught in the woods behind the packhouse, not knowing at the time what it was. I finally understood what people meant when they talked about the scent of a mate. It was tons better than all my other favorite scents: fresh laundry, cinnamon buns, cookies fresh out of the oven, freshly cut grass, new car smell. I'd be willing to never smell any of those things again in exchange for smelling her scent every day for the rest of my life.

My sister and mom caught me in the act as I inhaled my mate's clothing scraps. Clearly, that was not the correct reaction for stumbling upon my father's murder. My mother screamed—the correct reaction.

"What the fuck?" Sara, my sister, gasped as she walked into the room and squatted next to our father. A large puddle of blood had formed by his face, seeping out from his mouth and nostrils. She pulled a dart out of his arm and smelled it. "Wolfsbane," she said.

"How ironic," I responded.

"What?" She looked at me, confusion on her face.

"Well, it was his idea to use wolfsbane darts in battle. It's pretty ironic that that's how he dies in the end, eh?"

"Did you do this?" She glared at me. "Did you kill Dad?"

"What? No!" I replied in shock. Although, that must show how good our father-son relationship was for her to accuse me of that. "Anyway, if I did kill him, it wouldn't be using darts."

"Who did this? Did you see them?" she shouted at me.

"Yes," I replied. My mom shrieked.

Sara looked over at our mom and sighed. "Stay here," she said, going to my mom. She helped my mom get up and led her out of the room. I did as commanded and didn't move from the place where I was sitting, inhaling the scent of my mate again. Goddess, she smelled amazing.

After some time, Sara returned. "Who did this?" she demanded.

"I don't know," I replied, my thoughts returning to the beautiful mystery woman, sighing to myself.

"But you said you saw them."

"I did, but I'd never seen her before."

"Her?"

"Here, smell this," I said, handing her a clothing scrap.

"Rogue," Sara said, looking evil as she sniffed. As she said the word, I instantly recalled that one of our pack members had asked to bring a rogue into the territory as a temporary living situation thing. It seemed innocent enough at the time. My beta, a man I trusted with my life, had checked her out and approved her moving here.

"I think I know who it is. Or at least who brought the rogue here," I said.

"Well, what are you waiting for? Let's go get them!" She shot up, looking ready to kill.

"Under one circumstance. The rogue is mine, and nobody touches her but me." I looked fiercely at Sara. I couldn't exactly have someone killing my mate. And Sara was not someone who hesitated when it came to killing. She took far more after our father than I did.

"I'm not promising that," she replied.

I grabbed Sara by her arms, holding her in place, staring into her eyes. "She's mine, and if you touch her, I will banish you from the pack." I glared at her.

"Are you fucking serious?" She looked shocked, struggling to free herself from my grasp. Sara was tough, but she wasn't as strong as I was.

"Yes, 100 percent. You lay one finger on that rogue, and you are dead to me. She's mine to do what I want with. So you better fucking promise that you will hand her over to me alive and in one piece."

"Fine!" she cried as I tightened my grasp on her arms.

"Promise me now," I demanded. I wasn't usually like this with my sister, but I felt very possessive of my mate, and I couldn't trust that my sister wouldn't take matters into her own hands if she got to her before I did. My hands were tightening around her arms—any more and I'd likely snap her bones.

"I promise!" she screamed in agony.

I let her go. "Good, now let's go find her." I led Sara to Hugo's house. He wasn't someone I knew well. We were a few years apart in age, and he wasn't one of my warriors. During our drive over, I mindlinked the senior warriors on duty to see if any of them had spotted a rogue leaving the territory. One of them mindlinked me back a couple of minutes later to confirm that a rogue had sprinted out of the territory. *If the rogue comes back, grab her, and put her in a cell immediately,* I mindlinked all of the senior warriors.

It was around two in the morning when we banged on the door of Hugo's house. His brother, Rocco, answered it groggily, his eyes shooting open in shock to see the two of us standing there. "Alpha, how can I help you?" He straightened up.

"Where's Hugo and the rogue?" I asked.

He widened his eyes. "Not here. Did something happen?"

"Stay here." I used my alpha aura on him, forcing him to stay put as Sara and I pushed past him to search the house. It was a small house and a quick walk through all the rooms. His mom was shocked to see us, waking when we entered her room, but I quickly commanded her to stay still until I left.

"No fresh scent anywhere in the house. Neither of them was here recently," Sara reported.

"Hugo is at work. He works until four or five on Fridays normally," Rocco said once we stepped outside.

"Where does he work?" I asked.

"A brothel near Calabogie."

"I know it," I said, looking at Sara. "You're free to go." I turned to Rocco, undoing my alpha aura. We got back into the car and drove just over a half hour to get to Hugo's place of work. I was familiar with it as that was where we got our wolfsbane darts supply, which would explain how the rogue was able to obtain them.

We stormed in to be greeted by the brothel's madam, clad in a leathery dress clinging to her bony figure. I'd met her once before. Normally my father picked up the supply, but I'd gone with him a couple of times to become familiar with the operation.

"Mr. Adalwolf." She nodded at me. "Here without your father?"

"My father is dead," I replied. "Which is why I'm here. One of your employees is likely responsible for his murder."

She gasped. "It can't be!"

"Yes, it is. Now, if you don't mind, I'd like to speak to Hugo Bernardi immediately."

"Of course," she replied, nodding at a couple of men behind her. We waited until they brought him over to us.

"Alpha," he said, looking at me, appearing shocked to see me.

"Come with us quietly and we won't make a scene," I said. He nodded and followed us outside. We walked across the parking lot, over to where I was parked. After checking to see no one was around, I asked, "Where's the rogue?"

"Back at my house," he replied.

"We just checked your house, and she wasn't there. Now, I'm going to ask you again, and you better answer. Where is the rogue?"

"I honestly don't know if she's not in the house. I can call her if you'd like." He pulled out his phone and showed that he was calling her, putting the phone on speaker so we could hear. It rang and went to voice mail.

Hi, you've reached Talia. Sorry I missed your call. Leave a message after the beep!

"Let's take him to the cells for interrogation," I said, turning to Sara. We each grabbed an arm and threw him in the back seat. We drove to the pack jail where I chained him to a wall.

"Okay, start talking," I said once Hugo was chained in place. "Where is the rogue?"

"I don't know. I'm sorry, Alpha. She's staying with me and will probably return later tonight if she's not there now."

"I have reason to believe she won't. Now, where would she have gone otherwise? You must know her well if you were keeping her at your house." I pulled out a knife, threatening him with it. I wasn't opposed to torture. I had been trained by both my father and my university in the art. While it wasn't my preferred activity, it was effective for getting answers.

"I honestly don't know. Her mother is dead, and she doesn't have a father. I think I'm her only friend. Alpha, may I ask why you are looking for her?"

"She killed my father."

"Fuck." Hugo's chin trembled and muscles tensed.

I brought the knife closer to him, making a shallow cut in his neck so that blood trickled down it. "Now I have reason to believe you may be involved."

"Please, Alpha. If you kill me, my mom and brother won't have anyone to support them."

"Maybe you should have thought about that before you brought a murderous rogue onto our territory."

"I didn't think she was capable of murder—I swear. And I never would have assisted her in any way. In fact, I advised her against it."

"But you knew she wanted to kill my father, eh?"

When he didn't answer immediately, I shoved the knife into his thigh. He screamed in agony as I withdrew it. I waited for him to begin healing and stop screaming. "Now, tell me the whole story, and don't leave anything out."

"Alpha, I'm sorry. It was a mistake. But you have to know something. Your father killed her mother."

"What!" I roared. "Tell me the whole story now!" I bellowed using my alpha aura. I probably could have done that from the beginning, but, okay, there was a part of me that may enjoy torture just a little bit. Especially after the murder of my father.

"Talia's mother was a sex worker at the brothel where I work. Your father was her number one client and, from what I understand, had been going to see her for years, possibly decades. Talia was raised in the brothel'. I became friends with her after I was hired as a bouncer. A couple of weeks ago, Talia discovered her mother's corpse, with her heart ripped out, and your father's scent was the only other scent in the room. Based on the scent, that he had just been in to see her, and the way that Talia's mother was killed, there is no question it was him who did it. Talia was kicked out of the brothel and had no other place to go, so I offered for her to stay with me until she could get back on her feet. She did ask me how to kill a werewolf and I replied honestly, but I also told her that she'd more likely get herself killed than accomplish what she wanted to do."

"What the fuck?" Sara gasped. "Dad was going to a brothel regularly?"

"Well, it explains a lot. Like where he disappeared to on his nights off and why he always smelled like rogue when he'd get home," I responded, then turned back to Hugo. Using my alpha aura, I asked, "Where did she get the wolfsbane darts?"

He looked at me, eyes widening. "I don't know."

"Where is she?" I asked using my alpha aura again.

"I don't know." He let out a long, low sigh and, in an emotion-choked voice, asked, "Are you going to hurt her when you find her?"

"None of your business," I replied.

"Please don't hurt her, Alpha," he pleaded with me.

"You have no right to ask anything of me. You brought danger into the pack, and you're lucky I'm not banishing you. I think it's best if you stay in the cells for now. And you better pray to Artemis that we find her because otherwise you might find yourself rotting in here."

He nodded sadly at me. Sara and I unchained him and led him into a cell, locking the door. I nodded at the guard on duty as we exited.

"Well, I guess that leaves only one option," I said, looking at Sara as we walked back to the car. "You are our best tracker."

"My pleasure," she said, grinning.

"But my directive stands. You better bring her back alive and in one piece."

She rolled her eyes and said, "Fine. Why do you get to have all the fun?"

"Because I'm the alpha."

Before going into the packhouse, we walked into the backyard, sniffing the area. Her scent led us to a small purse that was left in the woods behind our house. I picked it up to find a small wallet and cell phone inside. The cell phone was locked, so I wasn't able to open it, but there was a picture of her with her mom on the lock screen. The two of them looked very alike, like sisters. I opened her wallet to see there wasn't much in it. She didn't even have a driver's license. There wasn't much money in it either, just a few loonies and toonies.

Sara left me and headed into the woods, hot in pursuit of my mate's scent. She returned over a week later, empty-handed. "This rogue bitch loves to swim," she whined.

I returned to the cells to visit Hugo. "Well, we weren't able to track your rogue friend," I said. "Any ideas on how to find her?"

He sighed and said, "I don't know. I honestly have no idea where she could have gone. Maybe you can go through her things in my bedroom. Maybe it will give you a clue as to where she went. We did speak about her joining a pack. I mentioned that her mom may have been part of a pack before she came here. If I had to guess, I'd say that may be where she went."

"Any idea where her mom's pack was?"

"I'm not even sure if her mom was part of a pack. The only thing I know is that Talia's not from Canada. She told me she's not here legally."

"Well, you better start coming up with some more ideas. You don't get out of this cell until we find her. But thanks for the tip on the pack." I walked out of the jail heading straight for Hugo's house. Just as he suggested, I searched his room. I found a backpack inside with different notebooks and books. Pulling everything out and going through it all, I came across a folder with an American passport and two birth certificates. Bingo!

Chapter 6

Talia

After feeling so hot and desperate, I woke up late the next morning and found myself back to normal again. I recalled in agonizing, anxiety-inducing shame to everything that had happened the day prior. What had come over me? Thinking back, I couldn't lie. The man who approached me on that mountain was very hot. He was even better built than Hugo, and Hugo was very fit. He was the type of man you only ever saw on a fitness magazine cover, and half the time they were probably airbrushed anyway.

But ugh, the shame. I'd totally come on to him and he completely rejected me. I'd never experienced something like that before. Most of the men I approached were more than willing to take me up on my offers. Then after he shoved me in the back of the car, I realized that the blond man who drove me here was actually quite attractive as well, being so tall and muscular. He rejected me too. He told me he was gay, so I suppose it made sense. He brought me into a bedroom, and I stayed there the rest of the day and night, too ashamed to leave, and finding comfort in being in a warm bed after almost two weeks in my wolf form, sleeping on the forest floor.

I tiptoed out of the bedroom, looking around. A man with brown hair was sitting at a desk in the living room and turned around at the sound of me approaching. "Ah, you're awake!" he said. "Now I finally get to meet the lady who was trying to get my mate to bat for the other team." He chuckled. "I can't lie, he could have done worse." He winked.

"Sorry about that," I mumbled.

"Hey, no worries. Are you hungry?"

"I'm okay," I replied, not wanting to be a burden, especially after they offered me a place to stay when they were originally planning to put me into a jail cell. At the time I didn't even think twice about it, but now, in a more stable state of mind, I realized where I could have spent the night.

"Okay, here, I have some clean clothes for you. You seem like you're about the same size as Jack's sister." He handed me a bag.

"Thank you." I nodded, grateful for the hospitality.

He then got up and said, "Come this way. Let me get you a towel so you can take a shower and get dressed." He led me into the washroom and pulled a towel out of the linen closet. I couldn't believe how nice and hospitable this man was being. "My name's Tyler by the way."

"Talia," I replied. When I stepped inside the washroom, he closed the door behind me. While I'd gone swimming during my run over, it had been a while since I'd properly bathed or shaved. Unfortunately, I wasn't going to be able to take care of the shaving part today, but I could at least finally take a warm shower. After I stepped out and dried myself, I opened the bag Tyler had given me to find leggings, a tunic, and sandals. I threw the outfit on. It was weird wearing clothes without underwear, but I didn't have much of a choice.

I came out of the washroom to find Tyler back at the computer desk. He turned to look at me and said, "The alpha's on his way over to talk to you. Feel free to make yourself at home until he gets here. Would you like me to put the TV on for you?"

"No, I'm fine," I replied, sitting down on the couch.

"I heard you came on pretty strong to him too." Tyler smirked.

I put my face in my hands, putting two and two together, realizing the man I'd aggressively tried to seduce was on his way over now.

"Hey, don't be embarrassed. That guy is hot. Unfortunately, he's also my sister's boyfriend, and that whole 'being straight' thing. But a man can dream." He gave me a playful smile.

"I made a complete fool of myself." I moaned, crumpling into the sofa, tears brimming my eyes. I was far from home, in a strange place, without my mom. I couldn't help myself as I started crying.

Tyler came over and sat down next to me. "Hey, don't cry. You were in heat. You couldn't help yourself and he knows that. He's just coming over to talk to you."

I sniffled, trying to suck the tears back in, using the bottom of the tunic I was wearing to wipe the water from my face. I was, again, embarrassing myself, crying on some stranger's couch. "I'm sorry. I've just gone through a lot recently," I said.

"Don't be sorry. It happens." Tyler gave me a reassuring smile. "Just sit here and relax. I have to work but the alpha should be here soon."

I did as he said, deep in thought. I kept reaching for my phone, then realizing that I had long forgotten it in Ontario, in the woods behind the chalet house. I had absolutely nothing but the clothes from a stranger that I was wearing.

After some time, the doorbell rang. Tyler got up from his office chair and opened the door, greeting the alpha as he entered. I couldn't even bring myself to look, feeling so much shame about everything that had happened the prior day. I stared down at my feet as I sensed him sit down on the adjacent part of the sectional.

"Hey, Talia, I just want to talk to you," he said softly. I looked up, locking eyes with him and noticing his eyes looked quite similar to my own. "Can you please just let me know what you're doing here?"

I took a deep breath and let it out, deliberating on what to tell him. Realizing this might be my last chance to plead my case and finally get some answers, I decided to be forthright. Feeling pain in my chest as I spoke, I said, "My mom died recently, and I found out she's from the area. I thought maybe she used to live in a pack around here. I just wanted to find out more about her past because she never told me anything." A tear trickled down my cheek as I was overcome with sadness again. When he didn't say anything, I said, "I'll leave if you want me to. I didn't mean to cause trouble. Just please don't put me in the cells."

"Do you have somewhere to go?" he asked. I shook my head, looking down. "Where did you come from?"

"I'd rather not talk about it. It doesn't matter anyway. I'm not going back."

"You said you met your mate yesterday. Where is he?"

Suddenly a feeling came over me that I should be with that man, a deep longing. I crossed my arms across my stomach, pain from within emerging from the knowledge that I was away from him. I shoved the feeling away. "It doesn't matter. I'm not interested in him."

"I see," he replied. "Are you planning to reject him then?"

"What do you mean? Isn't it clear I rejected him since I ran away?"

"I meant formally."

"Formally?" What was he going on about?

"It seems you don't know much about being a werewolf." He stared into my eyes. "Did you grow up in a pack?"

"No, I didn't," I replied.

"Okay, well, then I should probably explain a few things to you. First of all, if you don't reject your mate, and you stay far from him, you will become weak over time now that the mate bond is in effect. You will also continue going into heat every month. That's what happened to you yesterday. And you will need to stay away from unmated males when that happens, as it is very hard for male werewolves to resist when they sense you're in heat."

"It didn't seem hard for you to resist." I glared at him.

"Honestly, I don't know why that was. For some reason, I couldn't sense it in you. I've definitely sensed it in others before, and, trust me, it is not easy to resist, especially if the woman is coming on to you." He chuckled. "I'm still impressed with myself that I resisted when my girlfriend threw herself at me while she was in heat. She wasn't my girlfriend at the time, hence my resistance. But damn, that was the worst blue balls of my life." He smiled to himself, clearly lost in his memory. After a moment, he turned to me, his face taking on a more serious expression, and asked, "Where'll you go if you leave the pack territory, Talia?"

"I don't know. I'll figure it out I guess," I replied.

"You're not going to just throw her out with nothing, are you?" Tyler spoke up. "Talia, if you have no place to go, maybe you should stay here until you can figure it out. Jack might be annoyed, but I'll talk to him. I don't like the idea of throwing a lady out on the street. And, Blake, maybe her mom used to be part of this pack. If so, we should find out why she left."

Blake looked at Tyler, shook his head, and sighed. "No, I can't put this on you and Jack. I've already asked Jack for too many favors. Talia, why don't you come stay at the packhouse for now? We have plenty of room. Do you know anything about babies? Maybe you can help my beta's mate out with her pup. She's having a hard time. The baby had colic for three months and she's apparently still not sleeping through the entire night now."

"I don't know anything about babies, but I can try to help," I replied, unsure of the idea but also with no place to go. At least it seemed he'd left everything that happened the previous day in the past. I didn't know if I'd ever stop feeling ashamed of what had happened.

"Okay. Do you have anything that you need to take with you?"

I shook my head.

"Okay, well, let's go then," he said, getting up. I followed him out to his SUV. He opened the door for me and helped me into the car. He was very polite. We drove in silence.

I looked around as we drove realizing that this pack looked much different than the one back in Ontario. This pack was not so uniform. It was more like a regular town with regular houses. It wasn't anywhere near as majestic as Hugo's pack. Blake pulled into a lot on the side of a very large house. He came around to open my door and help me out. He looked at another car that was in the lot and said, "Looks like Luke's parents got in earlier than expected." We walked to the front door, which he opened for me and let me in.

He then began walking me around, giving me a tour. This house was humongous. I'd never been in such a huge house before. Suddenly a blonde girl around my age came down the stairs and said, "Why do I smell rogue in here?"

"Hi, Lucy," Blake responded. "This is Talia, she's going to stay with us for a while."

"Hi," she replied. She stared at the two of us and then said, "Blake, can I please talk to you?"

"Yes?" He raised his eyebrow at her.

"In another room."

"I'm busy right now. We can talk later."

She huffed and walked away. It seemed like they may not be on the best terms.

He was about to lead me up the stairs when an older man came out from down a hallway. He stopped in his tracks and stared at me. "Bianca?" he gasped. My heart almost stopped at the mention of her name.

"Bianca's my mom," I replied in shock, my heart racing. "Do you know her?"

"Bianca's your mom?" he repeated. "How old are you?"

"Twenty," I replied as he came closer.

"Your eyes." He stepped even closer, his eyes boring into mine, making my muscles and heart quiver. Who was this man?

"You knew her mom?" Blake asked.

"Blake, she has the same eyes as you and your father," the older man said. "Do you remember Bianca? You were probably three or four when she left."

Blake gave the older man a blank stare. The older man looked between the two of us.

"Blake, I think this girl might be your sister."

Blake turned to look at me, his eyes squinted in concentration, and gasped. "That's why the heat didn't affect me!"

"What?" I asked, completely dumbfounded.

"The heat. It didn't affect me, remember? That's why. Because I'm your brother. I can't believe it!" His eyes were now wide open, staring into mine.

"How can you be my brother?" I asked.

"Have you ever met your father?"

"No, actually," I replied. "One of the reasons I came here was to see if I could find him."

"Well, my—our father wasn't exactly a good person. He's dead now, and you're lucky you don't have to have the displeasure of meeting him." He turned back to the older man and asked, "So, I take it that Bianca was one of my father's mistresses?"

"Yes," the older man replied, sighing. "She was young too. Her father was a warrior and died in battle when she was a junior in high school. Her mom committed suicide a year after losing her mate. James offered

Bianca a job as a nanny at the packhouse after she graduated from high school. He took a liking to her, and she got pregnant a year later."

"Let me guess, he banished her?" Blake clenched his fists, his nostrils flared and brows furrowed.

The older man shook his head slowly and said, "It was your father's way. I was the one who drove Bianca to a women's shelter that took her in."

"You're my brother?" I studied Blake and my whole mouth took on a bitter taste as I began dry heaving. "God, I feel sick."

"Are you okay?" The older man reached out, touching my arm.

Blake started laughing and said, "She may have felt a bit too much brotherly love yesterday."

"Oh God," I moaned, suddenly very light-headed. "I need to lie down."

Blake grabbed my arm and led me to the couch, helping me sit down. As soon as my butt touched the cushion I fell back, covering my face with my hand.

"God, could I have done anything more disgusting? What is wrong with me?" Tears threatened to fall as I recoiled, repulsed with myself.

"Is she okay?" The older man came over.

"Yeah, she's fine. Just let her rest," Blake replied, sitting down next to me. When the older man walked away, he said, "Talia, we can just pretend it never happened. Although it is a pretty funny story." He chuckled. "My own sister trying to seduce me. How's that for a meet-cute?"

I started dry heaving again.

"Hey, it's okay. You didn't know. Let's forget it happened. But, holy shit, I have a sister." He grinned, his eyes shining, clearly delighted by the news.

"Who was that man?" I asked. Something about his demeanor made my skin prickle.

"That's the former beta, Alfred, Luke's dad. Luke was one of the guys who was with me yesterday. He lives in the packhouse here with me, and he's my beta. Do you know about alphas and betas?"

"Kind of. I stayed in a pack with my friend for a couple of weeks before I came here, and I met the beta. But I don't know more than that."

"He's my second-in-command. I give the orders and my beta oversees the logistics."

"Are there gammas, deltas, epsilons too?" I asked, trying to recall what I'd learned of the Greek alphabet a while back.

"I've heard some packs have gammas and deltas, but ours doesn't. It's just Luke and me. We both live in the packhouse. Luke lives here with his mate and daughter, and I'm just on my own for now. But I plan to make my girlfriend my mate officially soon, and then she'll move in here too." He beamed. "I'll introduce her to you tonight. She'll be coming over for dinner with her family for the autumnal equinox after she gets out of training. She recently became a warrior in preparation for eventually becoming my luna."

"Luna?"

"It's like the female version of an alpha. The alpha's mate is the luna."

"Oh, I see," I replied.

"Anyway, let me show you to your room," he said getting up and holding out his hands to help me up. I followed him as he led me upstairs. He quickly pointed out the beta floor as we passed, the sound of a baby crying resounding. "The beta's daughter is just as desperate for attention as her mother," he commented.

Once we got to the alpha floor, he showed me the private alpha living room and common washrooms. As we walked the hall, he suddenly stopped and shook his head. "I have a sister!" he exclaimed. "Goddess, I still can't believe it. I guess I always knew you were probably out there, but for you to actually show up. Damn."

"Damn," I echoed, my chest tightening, trying to make sense of everything.

"Damn," he said again. We locked eyes, both letting out an awkward chuckle, which somehow put me just a little bit at ease.

Then he led me into a guest bedroom. "Make yourself at home," he said with a polite smile. "I have to work but feel free to walk around. There's a TV in the alpha living room, and if you get hungry, there's food in the kitchen. You can just help yourself." He turned to leave, giving me one last glance before he disappeared.

I sat down on the bed, looked around, and sighed to myself. I was having a hard time processing everything. I was also hungry, not having eaten for almost twenty-four hours at that point. After pacing the room to quiet my racing heart, I made my way back down the stairs, recalling where he said the kitchen was. Luckily, the house had a mostly open floor plan, so it wasn't too difficult not to get lost.

I looked around the packhouse again as I headed toward the kitchen, feeling almost as if I were in a trance. In just a month, everything changed and my whole life had been flipped upside down.

Chapter 7

Jasmine

As soon as the bell signaled the end of training for the day, I caught the girls in my group snickering together. I looked up to catch them whispering with their heads turned toward the bleachers, where I spotted Blake sitting, waiting for me.

"Daddy's here," I overheard one of the girls say.

I rolled my eyes at the jab, telling myself how childish they were. But, in reality, it stung—my transition to warrior had not exactly been easy. It felt like high school all over again, maybe even worse. I mean, we all try to pretend we're past that whole "need to fit in" thing once we become adults, but then when you don't, it's like you're back there all over again. Even my old high school nickname, PJ, that my classmates would use to taunt me for being "Perfect Jasmine" had been resurrected. Salt in the wound.

It all started because Blake wanted our training schedules to be identical, making the argument that I was going to be his luna and therefore I should train with the alpha. I was totally on board, eager to prove myself. When I first started, I bought all new sneakers and workout clothes, and I'd look forward to each morning when he'd come pick me up with two travel mugs filled with hot coffee. It seemed like I'd finally gotten my life back on track. However, not long after Blake and I started training together, I had a huge reality check.

First of all, most warriors start straight out of high school. While, at twenty years old, I wasn't exactly an old geezer when I started, I'd definitely missed the prime bonding window. The thing is, our pack had only even begun allowing women to become warriors ten years ago, so the group was small and tight-knit, and it was a bit like missing rush I suppose.

Second of all, Blake kept talking me up during training all the time. He'd turn to the trainer and say something along the lines of, "Did you see that perfect kick?" I can't lie, it was super sweet and I still got butterflies when he'd smile at me approvingly. But, hey, this was training, and we weren't exactly supposed to be flirting. Not that he was really flirting. But it didn't look good. And he was the alpha, so he got away with it, appropriate or not.

To make matters worse, the trainers were afraid to ever go as hard on me as they did on everyone else with Blake's imposing presence. I mean, who can blame them? You don't exactly want to be yelling in the alpha's girlfriend's face with him right there watching. I loved how he cared about me, but I also wanted to prove I could be a good warrior on my own.

The whole thing basically made me look even worse than a teacher's pet—I became the friggin' alpha's pet! Alyssa, who had been in my class in school and was never nice to me even then, quickly informed everyone of my old nickname, and now I was PJ all over again. I ended up in tears one night, pleading for Blake to stop training with me. He finally understood when I told him I had to show everyone I was a good warrior in my own right and he, very begrudgingly, backed off.

But, of course, the damage had already been done. Now I was trapped. It made Blake so happy to see me as a warrior, so I continued to follow my training schedule and put in my best effort. But it was soul crushing. All the other girls would hang out together during lunch and after training, and I was never invited. When I really wanted to torture myself, I'd scroll through their Instagrams to see what they'd been up to. There were constantly pictures of them hanging out and doing different things together. Clearly, my invitation had gotten lost in the mail.

I tried to push the anxiety from my mind as I walked over to Blake. His face instantly lit up. As soon as I got close enough, he pulled me against his body, bringing his mouth to mine. I completely gave in to the kiss, all my feelings for him rushing forward and my problems forgotten. At least I had Blake. Even if the days were challenging, feeling his arms around me always cheered me up. I deepened the kiss, full-on making out with him, pushing my tongue into his mouth, desperate to taste him. Today had been especially challenging, and all the pent-up stress was coming out now.

He pulled away, smiling down at me. I brought my hand to his stomach, gliding it under his shirt, feeling his abs. "Do we have time?" I asked, trying to look as seductive as possible. Hopefully, I wasn't too gross and sweaty from training all day.

"Mmm." He closed his eyes, bringing his hand to my hip. But then he suddenly opened them again. "Actually, there's something I need to talk to you about."

"What? You'd rather talk? Are you still Blake?" I teased, giving him a playful punch in the arm.

He chuckled and took my hand, bringing me back toward the bleachers, and pulled me down to sit next to him.

"What is it?" I asked, peering into his piercing blue eyes and rubbing my fingers along the calluses on his hand.

"So, remember how I told you about my father and how it was rumored that he'd banished various mistresses throughout the years?"

I nodded.

"Well, one of them has appeared—well, her daughter I should say."

"Her daughter? You mean—?"

"Yes, my sister."

"Oh my Goddess." I gasped. "Where did she come from?"

"I'm not actually sure. She wouldn't tell me."

"How do you know she's your sister?"

"Well, she apparently looks just like her mother, and Beta Alfred recognized her. She also has the same eyes as me."

"But are you sure?"

"Yes, I am."

"How?"

He rubbed his neck and looked away. It seemed like he might be hiding something from me. He turned back to me and, avoiding the question, said, "I'd like for you to meet her. She'll be coming to dinner tonight and I'll introduce you."

What was he hiding?

"Okay," I replied. "Well, I better get home and shower then. My parents and I will be over after the service."

"Perfect." He smiled, pulling me in for another kiss. He then walked me to my car and kissed me again before I got in. I hesitated to let him go, pushing up against him, relishing in how nice his warm, muscular body felt against mine after another hard day of training, but eventually I sighed and pulled away so I could have time to get ready.

I quickly showered as soon as I got home. They had let us out of training an hour earlier than usual today for the autumnal equinox. A service was going to be held at six, so I was thankful for the extra time I had to get ready. It allowed me to put on makeup and curl my hair. My parents pulled into the driveway at five thirty, and we headed out fifteen minutes after that.

Because it was a holiday, the pews were fuller than usual. Even Lucy's family attended holiday services. I wasn't really looking forward to dinner tonight much. Blake and Luke were hosting a family gathering at the packhouse, and that now included my family as well as Lucy's. Between the way things were with Lucy, Luke being my ex-mate, my brother, Tyler, being my father's secret love child, and the tension between my parents and Lucy's parents, it was not exactly a gathering of the Brady Bunch. However, a grin spread across my face and my heart thumped at the thought of meeting Blake's sister. I looked over to where the alpha and beta families normally sat and instantly spotted Blake sitting with a very tall girl with long brown hair. I recognized the dress she was wearing as one of Lucy's. Was that his sister? I craned my neck to try to get a better look.

After the service, Blake left with Luke's family and the tall girl before I got a chance to approach them. My parents stayed behind, as usual, to gossip. Lucy's mom gave me a quick squeeze on my shoulder as she slipped out with her own family.

Jack and Tyler hadn't come.

I wasn't the only one being ostracized in the pack. Jack and Tyler were the first openly gay couple that had ever lived in our conservative, religious pack, and consequently, people did not exactly welcome them with open arms. I appreciated that Tyler moved here so that he could have a relationship with me now that we had finally met, but I also felt horrible about the way they were treated. Jack had always been really popular in school and around the pack, so it was a huge blow and reality check when so many people's attitudes toward him changed.

We had noticed signs popping up in people's yards that read Take Back Vermont. I initially had no idea what it meant. I had to Google it to learn that it was a political movement from over twenty years earlier, starting before I was even born, that was triggered by a law establishing civil unions for same-sex couples. I couldn't believe that pack members were resurrecting such an old campaign. Although, I supposed, in our pack this was now a new issue.

When my parents and I finally arrived at the packhouse, everyone else was already there. Blake greeted us at the door, shaking both my parents' hands and leading them inside. He then turned to me and kissed me on the cheek. "You look stunning tonight, Miss Alpha. I can tell you've been working out." He winked at me. It was true—I had become much more toned than I ever was before from all of the training.

He asked my parents what he could get them to drink, leading them over to where a drink station was set up. I grinned to myself at how adorable he looked showcasing all the soft drinks available. I had no idea how he did it, but Blake had completely charmed my parents, and they had actually lightened up a lot since Blake and I started seriously dating. I mean, they weren't exactly at the same level of relaxed as Lucy's parents, but they had come a long way from how they'd been a year earlier.

"Hey, Jaz." Tyler came over and pulled me in for a hug.

"Nice to see you," Jack said, doing the same. "How's joining the ranks going?"

"Well, you know, they're kicking my ass, being the newb and all." I gave a small laugh, not wanting to make it obvious how much it was affecting me.

"It'll get better," he said, giving me a reassuring smile and a pat on the shoulder, clearly well aware of the actual situation, being a warrior too. "You haven't gone on any missions or been to battle yet. That's usually when the bonding happens."

"Yeah," I replied. "I'm ready and eager!" I may have said that a little too enthusiastically. Damn, I was a terrible actress.

"Ready and eager?" Tyler raised his eyebrow at me. "C'mon, Jaz, we both know you hate it."

"I don't hate it . . ." My voice trailed off.

"Why don't you just go back to school?" Tyler asked.

"I completely destroyed my GPA during the fall semester last year. There's no going back now." I laughed, trying to play it off like it wasn't a big deal. "Anyway, Blake wants me to be his luna, and I want to give it a try."

"But Blake's mom isn't a warrior. I'm sure he'd understand if you told him being a warrior isn't for you. And I can't believe you're even stressing about your GPA. After you graduate and start working, it won't even matter anymore." Tyler and I had gotten close since he'd move to my pack, and I kind of hated how well he could read me now.

I knew what he was saying, but it did matter, to me at least. I'd never gotten anything but a 4.0, and it made me feel sick every time I thought about how badly I'd screwed up.

"Hi, Tyler." My dad came over, smiling at my brother, and patting him on the shoulder. My dad was trying to build a relationship with him now after years of not being a part of his life. "How's it going?"

"Pretty good, Drew," he replied. "How are things with you?"

"Same as usual. How's your mom doing?"

"She's good. She's planning to come visit over Thanksgiving."

"That's great. Let her know I'd like to catch up with her when she comes into town again."

"I will. I'm sure she'd like that."

I glanced over at Blake, noting he was deep in conversation with my mom. He somehow, miraculously, got my *mom* to like him. It was pretty crazy.

Before long, we started being corralled to sit at the table. I had to pass by Luke on my way. "Hey, Jasmine." He nodded at me awkwardly. "Thanks for coming." He gave me a small smile.

"Hi, Luke," I replied, forcing myself to smile back at him. A sharp pain pierced my chest. Blake's mom seemed to think it would go away once Blake and I finally marked each other, but for now, it made things really awkward and painful, for me at least.

Blake stood at the head of the table and pulled out a chair on one side of him once I approached. The tall girl I'd seen sitting next to him at the service was seated on the other side. Being much closer to her now, I realized she smelled like a rogue, which was not the most pleasant scent. I also noticed what Blake meant about her eyes. Her eyes did look very similar to his, that same piercing shade of blue. My parents took their seats, my mom sitting down next to me, and my dad next to Tyler.

I looked around the table. Thank Goddess the packhouse dining table was huge because it was a very big group. Besides Kyle and Emma, who had gone to Emma's family's autumnal equinox celebration, and Blake's mom, who was seemingly working tonight, everyone else was here. There were almost twenty adults seated at the dining room table, and a separate kids' table had been set up for Luke's nieces and nephews.

Once everyone was settled in their seats, Blake tapped on his glass, signaling for everyone to be quiet. He stood up and began speaking. "Hello, everyone. Thank you for coming to the packhouse tonight to celebrate the autumnal equinox. It's always nice being surrounded by family, whether by blood or by friendship. Speaking of family, I want to introduce someone to everyone. Up until a couple of days ago, I was an only child, and I just recently discovered that I have a sister. Everyone, please welcome Talia to the extended family."

"Sister?" Jack gasped. Luke broke out in a coughing fit. I turned to Talia who winced and hurled her face into her hands. When I looked up at Blake, he was glaring menacingly at both Luke and Jack. It had been a while since I'd seen him look so threatening. And then I realized he was mindlinking them. What was going on? I practically got whiplash as I tried to figure it out, eyeing everyone's reactions.

"Welcome to the family, Talia." Beta Alfred broke my concentration, putting up his glass of wine with an amiable smile on his face.

"Yes, welcome!" His mate, Robin, did the same.

"Welcome," my dad echoed, putting up his glass of apple cider.

"As another long-lost sibling, it's great to have you as part of the family." Tyler gave her a friendly smile, lifting his glass.

Everyone else started repeating the same sentiment. Blake sat back down and squeezed Talia's shoulder. "Don't worry, it's fine," he said.

"What's fine?" I asked.

"Talia was just nervous about meeting everyone. And as you can see, everyone is being very welcoming," he replied. Blake was definitely hiding something. "Anyway, Talia, this is my girlfriend, Jasmine, who I was telling you about. She saved my life, both literally and figuratively, and is the reason this pack has an alpha." He smiled down at me and pushed a piece of hair behind my ear. My heart raced at the gesture.

"Nice to meet you, Jasmine." She glanced over at me, nervously twirling her hair.

"Nice to meet you too," I replied, giving her a friendly smile. "So, how did you find Blake?"

"It's kind of a long story, but the short version is that my mom never told me anything about her past, and I only recently found out that we were both born in Vermont. So, I came here to see if I could learn more about her and maybe meet my father."

"Where's your mom?"

She looked at me sadly. "My mom passed away recently."

"Oh, I'm really sorry," I replied, surprised by the information and instantly softening toward her. Blake hadn't mentioned that to me. Had he known? While Blake acting strangely had initially made me suspicious, her expressive eyes couldn't hide the genuine pain she clearly felt. And, I realized, they really were similar to Blake's eyes. Perhaps that was why I could read them so easily after the many hours I'd spent mesmerized by Blake's beautiful eyes and memorizing all the expressions they made.

"Talia doesn't have anywhere to go, so she'll be staying at the pack-house for a while," Blake chimed in.

"Will you be joining our pack?"

"I haven't decided yet," she replied.

"Well, you are certainly welcome to." Beta Alfred, who was sitting on the other side of Talia, leaned over.

Luke's oldest sister then came over and tapped Talia on the shoulder. "Hi, Talia. It's so nice to meet you." She pulled her in for a hug. "I'm Peyton and I knew your mother quite well. She was only three years older than me, and she used to live in the packhouse. So, if you ever want to learn more about her, I'd be happy to talk to you. You look so much like her, it's eerie."

Soon everyone began passing around food and eating. My parents joined in conversation with Blake and me. Talia stayed quiet and kept her eyes on her plate, clearly feeling out of place.

When we were well into dinner, Blake's mom came in wearing her scrubs. She waved hello to everyone and walked over to Blake, kissing him on his head. She then looked up, locking eyes with Talia. Our side of the table went quiet as she began to lose color from her face. "Bianca," she gasped.

"Mom!" Blake got up pushing his chair back. "Shit, I should have told you."

"You didn't tell your mom?" Beta Alfred, who was normally calm, suddenly stood, puffing his chest and glaring at Blake. The entire table was now quiet, staring at the scene unfolding. He got up and took Luna Sienna's arm, leading her out of the room.

"That was really stupid, Blake," Robin snapped at him, getting up to follow. Lucy's baby started crying. This set off Luke's sister Lauren's baby as well. They both got up, trying to comfort them and walking into the living room.

"Fuck," Blake said and followed Robin. The rest of the table was left in shock, not saying anything.

Breaking the silence, Peyton's mate, Ryan, said, "So, how 'bout them Red Sox?"

That elicited some nervous laughter from the group.

"We should start cleaning up for dessert." Lucy's mom got up, grabbing for people's plates on her side of the table.

"Absolutely." My mom got up in agreement and started doing the same on our end. Everyone followed suit, getting up to help, moving everything into the kitchen. I got up as well and looked toward Talia who was left sitting there, spacing out.

"Hey, are you okay?" I waved my hand in front of her face.

She shook her head, coming out of a daze. "Oh yeah, I'm just really tired. I think I'm going to go lie down." She got up and headed toward the stairs. There was something that seemed off about her. She didn't seem harmful, but the rogue scent activated some instinct inside me, provoking me to want to keep my distance from her as if there was a danger in being around her.

After we cleared the table and put out desserts, Lucy and Lauren rejoined us with their babies, having calmed them down.

Peyton stood up and said, "Everyone, tomorrow is Asher's first birthday, so Lucy very generously made a cake for him. We thought it'd be nice to celebrate tonight while everyone is here."

"It's also Jasmine's birthday in a couple of days." Lucy smiled at me. "So, I made two cakes."

My mouth fell open, and I instantly covered it with my palm. Lucy barely spoke to me anymore. As I moved my hand from my mouth, all I could think to do was awkwardly smile. Was this maybe her way of extending an olive branch to me? My breath bottled up in my chest, and I clung to some small fraction of hope that maybe one day things wouldn't be so broken between us.

"Mom, can you help me bring them out?" She looked to her mom, who got up and walked to the kitchen with Lucy. Moments later, the two of them emerged, Lucy holding a dinosaur cake for Asher and her mom holding an elaborately decorated cake with French macarons and a small pink champagne bottle sticking out of it for me.

Everyone sang "Happy Birthday" as Lucy's mom placed my cake in front of me, with twenty-one slim sparkler candles on top of it. "Happy birthday, dear Asher and Jasmine!" everyone sang out, "Happy birthday to you!"

"Now make a wish!" Lucy's mom said to me, making me recall a year ago when I wished for something that never came true. But this year I had more hope. As I blew out the candles, I thought, *I wish I could have female friends again.* I let out a small laugh, thinking about how pathetic I'd become lately, then looked over at Peyton and Ryan who were helping Asher blow out the candles on his cake. My chest warmed with that same hope I'd felt moments earlier.

"Damn, I missed it." Blake's voice sounded behind me. I turned around to face him and he leaned over, smiling, and whispered in my ear, "I think I know what you wished for," then winked at me.

What did he think I wished for?

"But don't say it or it won't come true." He was now so close to me and smiling at me so earnestly I wished I could kiss him, but my parents were very present and I wasn't exactly ready to show that part of me to them yet . . . or ever.

Knowing we'd have to keep our hands off each other until later, we both sat down, and Lucy's mom grabbed the cake from the table, bringing it to the other end to cut it up.

Beta Alfred entered with Robin and Blake's mom. "Where did Talia go?" he asked.

"She was tired, so she went to lie down," I replied.

"I see," he responded, pulling out Talia's seat for Blake's mom. "Well, maybe you can meet her tomorrow. It's probably better that way with less of an audience."

She nodded in response and sat down.

"Happy early birthday, Jasmine." Blake's mom gave me a friendly smile. "I heard it's a big one this year. Twenty-one? I hope my son has something special planned." She elbowed Blake playfully.

"Of course I do," he reassured his mom and then winked at my parents who were sitting next to me. The rest of the night seemed to go pretty smoothly.

After we cleaned up, everyone began heading out. I walked over to Lucy, who was sitting on the couch with her baby. "Hey, Lucy, thanks for the cake. That was really nice of you, and it was really good." I gave her a polite smile. The gesture was lovely, especially considering we weren't on the best terms.

"You're welcome." She returned the smile.

As I walked back toward the crowd, Blake came up from behind and wrapped his huge arms around me, pulling me toward him. I couldn't help but smile as I turned to face him and inhaled his familiar scent. "You're not going anywhere until I give you your pre-birthday gift," he said.

"And what's that?" I asked, looking up at him through my lashes. He grinned at me, his blue eyes glistening with mischief.

His stubble brushed against my ear as he leaned his face close to mine and softly said, "It's a surprise, but I'll give you a hint. I have to take that dress off to give it to you."

My stomach quivered, and my thighs tensed, wanting nothing more than to receive Blake's surprise.

"It's a nice dress, but it would look so much better on the floor of my bedroom."

Goddess, I was wet, already imagining everything Blake was planning for the evening.

"Are you ready to go, Jaz?" My dad's voice jolted me from my fantasy, car keys in his hand and a purse slung over my mom's shoulder, totally ruining the moment. Nothing to dry me up like the desert more than them showing up!

I glanced at Blake sadly, wishing I could stay longer. "Yeah," I said glimpsing over at my parents, then looked back at Blake. "See you tomorrow?"

"See you tomorrow," he replied, looking as if he were hesitating to say more. Then he approached my dad, putting out his hand to shake it. "Thank you for coming tonight, Drew." After giving my dad a hearty shake, he leaned in to kiss my mom on the cheek and said, "Nice to see you as always, Miriam."

"It's unfortunate we didn't get to know your sister much tonight. Maybe another time," my dad said.

"I'm sure you will. After all, my family is your family."

I lifted an eyebrow in response. My dad smiled at Blake and patted him on the arm, then turned to head out.

"Bye, Miss Alpha," Blake sang out as I followed my parents. I turned to wave goodbye to him.

After we began driving, my mom said, "Well, I guess that confirms the rumors over the years about Alpha James were true."

Chapter 8

Talia

Well, that was really awkward. Scratch that—the whole day was really awkward and uncomfortable. I should make a list of all of the uncomfortable things that happened since I got to this place:

1. I tried to sleep with my brother.

2. I tried to sleep with a gay man.

3. I found out my father is dead. Still not sure how he died, but maybe I can find out.

4. I found out that my mom was a nanny mistress at only eighteen years old.

5. I found out why my mom got banished from the pack—and it was because of me.

6. The two men who witnessed me seducing my brother, who I now know are named Luke and Jack, know that I tried to seduce my brother. Will they tell other people? How many people know now?

7. Oh, right, my brother has a girlfriend. Does she know? What does she think?

8. This blonde girl who lives here, Lucy, is a bitch. She keeps calling me *the rogue*. Blake forced her to give me a dress to wear for tonight. I really didn't want to wear it, but I didn't have much of a choice.

9. I still don't have any underwear or bras. And I don't have any money.

10. Oh, and I met the widow of my father tonight. She could not have looked any less pleased to see me. The whole table went quiet. I wanted to throw up. I'm glad I was able to sneak away.

Blake seemed eager for me to just go along with everything as if it was totally normal for his long-lost sister to just show up out of the blue. He actually seemed pretty nice, but I almost felt like he was not addressing the messiness of the situation, just assuming things would work out.

I had two competing thoughts in my head. The first was that I wanted to leave. I was uncomfortable here. This was not my home, and I was overwhelmed by meeting so many people who were connected to my mother. But then my second, weaker, thought was that I wanted to stay and learn more about my mother's past and accept my brother into my life. I'd never had any family besides my mom, and she was gone now. My brother was my last chance at having any sort of family on this earth, and he seemed eager to welcome me with open arms.

When I awoke the next day, I took a shower and dressed back in the leggings and tunic from the previous day. It was either that or the dress. I then walked downstairs to get something to eat. Upon entering the kitchen, I came face-to-face with the older man, Beta Alfred, and his wife, who had introduced herself as Robin yesterday, feeding a baby in a high chair.

"Good morning, Talia." He smiled at me in greeting.

"Good morning," I responded politely.

"Have you met my granddaughter, Libby, yet?" Robin asked.

"Briefly," I replied.

"What can I get you to eat?" Connie asked me. She was a kind lady in her fifties and told me she had been the packhouse cook for over ten years the previous day.

"I'll just have some cereal," I replied, not wanting to be a burden. She opened a cabinet with different cereal choices, and I reached for some Rice Krispies. Connie then grabbed a bowl, spoon, and some milk out of the fridge, which she placed in front of me.

"Coffee?" she asked.

"Sure, thank you."

She went to fill a mug for me. "Cream? Sugar?"

"Just black is fine."

"Just like James and Blake," Beta Alfred remarked, smiling at me. Connie dropped the mug in front of me and walked out of the room after I thanked her.

I took a sip and then realized this might be my chance to learn more about my father. "You knew my father well, right?"

"Very well. I grew up with him in this packhouse. He was practically a brother to me."

"What was he like?"

Robin sat down next to Beta Alfred as he spoke. "He changed a lot over the years. When he was young, he was quite amusing and charming, a lot like Blake when he's in a good mood. He was very handsome—I think every girl we went to school with had a crush on him. But once he began taking on more responsibilities as the alpha, he changed. At first, it was gradual—he was more irritable and withdrawn. I think the responsibility of leading the pack was just too much for him. But then his father sacrificed himself in battle to save his life, and it was like he completely changed overnight."

"Wow," I remarked.

Beta Alfred nodded and continued, "The two of them had always been close, and his father was a true mentor to him when it came to leading the pack. After he died, I believe James felt like he had to bear the burdens of the whole world on his shoulders alone.

"He went down a dark path. He lashed out at his friends and became promiscuous, causing a lot of mischief around the pack. He was self-destructive. After every battle we fought, he became more and more despondent. He did eventually mature, but he stayed hardened. The old James that I had grown up with had vanished.

"He eventually met his mate right before he turned forty. We were all hopeful because he seemed to finally cheer up. We started seeing bits of the old James. He smiled and joked again. When Sienna got pregnant with Blake, he was ecstatic. He couldn't stop talking about his heir to everyone. He may never have really shown it to Blake, but he did love him. Unfortunately, his good spirits were short-lived. We went to battle again a couple of years after Blake was born, and it was like all the good was undone. His old demons returned and never left again. That was the same battle that your mother's father, your grandfather, died in."

"How did Ja—my father die?" I asked.

Beta Alfred's face took on a downturned appearance, and he gave a sad sigh. "He died a little less than a year ago. Our pack was attacked by another pack waging war on us, and he sacrificed himself to save Blake's life, just like his father did for him."

"Really?" I jerked my head back. "How did he do that?"

He shook his head, looking down at the table and I got the idea that he was hurt by the loss. I wondered if I should be asking so many questions.

After a beat, he replied, "He jumped in front of a wolf that was attacking Blake. Instead of beheading Blake, the wolf beheaded him."

"Oh, wow," I said, blinking and trying to digest what I was being told. I had not expected such a graphic description of what happened. "I'm surprised that Blake doesn't seem upset about his death at all."

Robin closed her eyes and shook her head. "Blake never had a good relationship with his father."

"James had a very difficult personality. While he meant well with how he treated Blake, his execution wasn't very good. He was a complicated man." Beta Alfred let out a deep breath. "Sometimes people try to do what they think is best, but they don't understand how it's coming off."

We all sat silently, reflecting, as Blake walked in and interrupted our thoughts. *Speak of the devil!*

"Good morning," he said looking around. "Ah, Talia, just the person I wanted to see."

"Good morning," I replied, looking at him curiously.

He rubbed the back of his neck and said, "Obviously the introduction to my mom didn't go very well yesterday, but I'd like to introduce you to her properly today. Would you mind if we went by her house this morning?"

"Your mom won't mind?" I asked, recalling how upset she seemed yesterday.

Beta Alfred cut in. "It's not easy for her, especially since you look so much like your mother, and obviously those were not pleasant memories for her. But you are Blake's sister, and Blake is her son. So, she'd like to have a relationship with you now that you're here."

After considering, I agreed. It's not like I had a busy schedule. At this point, it was either sit around the packhouse or do whatever Blake had planned for me.

"Then, later, I asked Jasmine to come by. It's her day off, so she agreed to take you shopping so that you can have some clothes for while you stay here."

"But I don't have any money." God, I felt pathetic.

"It's on me. You're family now. And what kind of brother would I be if I didn't take care of my sister?"

"I can't accept that!"

"If the tables were turned, I'd like to believe you'd do the same for me," he said. "Anyway, if you don't want to accept it as a gift, you can look at it as a favor, and you can return it to me one day."

Connie came back into the room. "Breakfast, Alpha?" she asked. "The usual?"

He nodded at her.

After we finished eating breakfast, Blake took me to his mom's house. It was a pretty short walk from the packhouse. When we arrived, his mom smiled at me in greeting. She had a very warm smile that extended to her whole face. I could instantly tell she was a good person. Her eyes, on the other hand, looked sad. I wasn't even sure how exactly I could tell they were sad. And then, after a few moments, it clicked. They reminded me of my own mother's eyes—a haunted look of something gripping her that she couldn't shake off.

"Hello, Talia." She put her hand out to shake mine. I extended my own hand and she had a surprisingly firm handshake. "Thanks for coming by. Why don't you come sit in the kitchen, and I'll bring over some tea?"

"That'd be great, Mom." Blake wrapped his arms around her as she patted his back and kissed his cheek, and I instantly understood they had a close relationship.

After Blake's mom laid everything out, she took a seat at the table with us. We all made small talk for a bit. It was mostly Blake and his mom that held the conversation with me just giving short answers when asked something. I was thankful that they didn't expect more than that from me because I wasn't in the mood for talking.

Then, during a pause, his mom abruptly said, "Yes, you definitely have the same eyes as Blake and James." She nodded, looking between the two of us, then let out a deep sigh. "You also look so much like your mother. How old are you, Talia?"

"Twenty," I replied and blinked a few times, wondering what else to say. What did you say to someone who was looking at the product of an affair her husband had with someone that was barely an adult at the time?

"Talia's mom passed away, so I want to help her get back on her feet." Blake gave me a friendly smile.

"I'm sorry to hear that," Blake's mom replied. "Talia, I'm going to be honest with you. It's not easy for me for you to come here. But none of what happened is your fault, and you are more than welcome to stay in our pack as long as you want, or permanently if you decide to join us. If you ever need anything, I am here to help as well. I know I may not seem it, but I am happy that Blake was able to meet his sister and have a relationship with her now. Family and pups are very important and valued by werewolves, even if they come from unorthodox circumstances."

"Dad didn't value them," Blake added with a bitter tinge to his voice.

His mom sighed again. "Blake, I do agree your father did a lot of hurtful things. But he wasn't all bad. Yes, he hurt me a lot, and I probably let him get away with more than I should have. But he was always a good leader and put the pack ahead of all else. He helped a lot of families throughout the years. While that may not count for everything, it does count for something." She then turned to me and said, "Talia, I want you to understand that your father was a very complicated man. He went through a lot in his life that didn't change him for the better.'"

"Mom, you always defend him."

"He was my mate, Blake. I understand him better than most people." She picked up a napkin and dabbed it to her eyes. "I still miss him. The mate bond makes it easy to forgive and hard to forget."

"Mom, are you okay?" Blake asked, touching her arm in a loving gesture.

"I'll be fine, Blake. Thank you for bringing Talia by so I could meet her, but don't let me keep you from what you were planning to do today." She then turned to me and said, "Don't be a stranger, Talia. My door is open."

I reflected on our conversation as his mom walked us to the front door so we could leave, thoughts swirling around in my head, especially about how Blake's mom had spoken about her mate. While I kept trying to push my own so-called mate from my mind, he did keep popping back in. She wasn't wrong. It did seem difficult to forget about a mate.

On our walk back, Blake said, "Our grandmother, our father's mom, lives not far from here with the Autumn Moon Pack. They have a mental hospital there. After my grandfather died, she apparently went crazy and was committed. Losing a mate can do that to someone. She's old now—getting close to ninety. We also have an aunt who joined another pack to be with her mate. But she became estranged from my father at some point, probably because he was such a dick."

"Maybe losing all of his family caused him a lot of pain and that's why he acted the way he did," I said to Blake, imagining how hard it must have been to lose both your parents and your sister. Just losing my mom was painful enough.

"It's not an excuse. He terrorized my mom and me, the two people he did have and never lost. I hate him for not even taking into consideration all of the women he banished over the years because he couldn't keep his own dick in his pants." Blake's eyes took on an ominous, evil appearance. They almost reminded me of *his* eyes. I instantly understood that Blake was not someone you ever wanted to mess with.

Not long after we returned to the packhouse, Jasmine showed up. Blake's whole face lit up as soon as she walked in. He pulled her close to him, kissing her as if he were starved. I could tell he cared a lot about her. My own heart dropped as I was reminded of Hugo. I longed so much for him to feel that way about me. I wondered if anyone would ever feel that way about me.

Then another thought popped back into my mind—of my so-called mate. I had only glanced at him for a few moments before I disappeared, but I couldn't forget how he looked, standing there in a thin T-shirt, his muscular arms straining against the sleeves. His mouth was agape as he stared at me, a closely trimmed beard lining his well-defined jaw, and a thick head of brushed-back, wavy, dirty-blond hair atop his head. It was the type of hair I could spend hours running my hands through, and I could just imagine how scruffy it would look after spending time in bed together.

Ugh! Why was I thinking about him? I never wanted to see him again. He was *not* my mate.

"Thank you for taking Talia shopping, Jasmine. Here, take my credit card and buy whatever she wants." He handed a card to her. Jasmine slipped it into her purse.

"Did someone say shopping?" Lucy appeared from the stairs.

We all looked at her, no one saying anything.

"If you're all going shopping, I'm coming with you. I finally have a babysitter, and I need to get out of the house. Let me get my purse!" she said running back up the stairs.

"What?" Jasmine appeared dumbstruck, blinking rapidly.

"Maybe she's coming around," Blake said. "You have my permission to kick her out of the car and strand her on the side of the road if she gets too annoying." He chuckled.

Great, the blonde bitch was coming with us.

Chapter 9

Talia

Once Lucy was ready to go, we headed outside to Jasmine's blue Jeep Wrangler Sport. I pulled my seat forward so that Lucy could climb into the back seat. When we were all buckled in, Jasmine pulled out of the lot and sped out of the pack territory. We drove about an hour to Burlington, Vermont to go to a shopping mall that was located there.

Lucy dragged us to Victoria's Secret first. I was relieved since I did need bras and underwear big time! I looked around and decided to settle for the cotton panties since they were the best deal at five for thirty dollars. It was pretty pricey, and much more than I normally spent on underwear, but I wasn't sure if I'd end up anywhere else that sold underwear. I quickly grabbed five pairs.

"You should get something sexier than that." Lucy came up behind me. "They have some really cute lacey thongs over there." She pointed over to a display.

"These are fine," I replied. It's not like I'd be wearing these for anyone anyway. I'd already embarrassed myself enough trying to get laid. Jasmine came over to hand me a shopping bag to put them in.

I walked around looking at all the bras. They were so expensive. I felt bad indulging, especially since I wouldn't normally spend so much on myself.

"How about this one?" Jasmine pulled a simple bra off the wall, showing it to me.

"Goddess, Jasmine, can you pick anything more old lady?" Lucy chuckled.

"That one is fine," I said. It was beige and looked like it would work with most outfits. I went over to find my size and threw it in my bag.

"Are you going to buy anything for Blake?" Lucy asked Jasmine.

"What?" she replied, giving Lucy a blank look.

"You should give him a little birthday surprise." She winked. "Here, I have the perfect idea," she said walking away.

"Maybe you should get two bras," Jasmine suggested. I hesitated, not wanting to spend too much money.

"It's okay. One should be fine," I replied.

"How long will you be staying?"

"I don't know." I sighed.

"Get another bra. It's okay. You don't know how long you'll be here, so you should have at least one more." I bit down on my lip and grabbed the same bra in black.

Lucy came back over holding the slinkiest little lace teddy and held it up to Jasmine's body.

"Stop, what are you doing?" Jasmine slapped it away.

"I'm doing Blake a favor."

"And what favor is that?" Jasmine snapped, backing away from Lucy and narrowing her eyes at her.

"Giving him something other than granny panties to look at for once."

"I don't wear granny panties!" Jasmine exclaimed.

"Really, your panties aren't cotton and boring?"

Jasmine blushed.

"Come on. I'm sure Blake would be more than happy to pay for these," Lucy said, reaching for some G-strings and throwing them in my bag. "Both you and Blake will thank me later."

She walked away, and we watched as she pulled a salesperson over. Jasmine was just about to reach into my shopping bag when the salesperson and Lucy stopped in front of us.

"Measure her," Lucy said, pointing at Jasmine.

Jasmine was bright red now as the salesperson pulled a tape measure from her shoulders.

"Okay, lift your arms up," she said. Jasmine's eyes were wide as she lifted her arms, and the salesperson wrapped the tape measure around her. "32B."

"Great, thank you," Lucy replied. We then watched as she pulled a lacy push-up bra out of a drawer and brought it over, throwing it into the bag. "And don't even think about taking anything I put into that bag out. Actually, give that bag to me," she said, taking it from me. I was stunned and not sure what to do, handing it over.

"You need some sexier panties too. You never know when the opportunity will present itself." Lucy elbowed me playfully. "We're about the same size," she said as she walked toward a display across the room, reaching for some lacy thongs and throwing them into the bag once she got there.

"I am really regretting this," Jasmine said quietly next to me. "It's probably easier to just buy everything than argue with her." She sighed.

"Don't you need pajamas?" Lucy shouted, making eye contact with me and holding up a silky camisole and shorts set. She threw that in the bag too. "Okay, I think we have everything." She grinned, waving us over to the checkout area. We followed as she began unloading everything at the cash register. After the cashier finished wrapping and bagging everything, Lucy reached her hand out for the credit card. Jasmine blew out a breath and placed it in her waiting palm.

After we walked out, we headed to H&M. On our way, Jasmine's phone pinged. She pulled it out of her purse, looked at it, and groaned. "Oh my Goddess, Lucy!"

"What?" she asked, grabbing the phone out of Jasmine's hand, and laughing, handing it to me to read while she held Jasmine back.

> **Blake Sexy AF**: *I just got a text alert from AMEX that you spent $350 at Victoria's Secret??? I hope it wasn't all for Talia and I get a show tonight.*

Jasmine freed herself from Lucy and grabbed the phone out of my hand. "Lucy, for the love of Artemis, stop reading my texts."

"It looks like Blake is looking forward to tonight." She laughed, rubbing her palms together.

Once we got into H&M, I began picking out some basic clothing such as leggings and T-shirts. Then I checked the sales rack to see what they had. There usually wasn't much good on the sale rack but I found a few things to try on. When I looked up, I spotted Lucy holding a bodycon dress against Jasmine. Jasmine looked very irritated, rolling her eyes dramatically. I chuckled to myself because it was actually pretty entertaining. The two of them had a very interesting dynamic. I couldn't tell if they were best friends or enemies. It could really go either way.

I pulled everything that fit together after going into the fitting room. I was relieved that the prices at H&M were much more reasonable, especially for their basics and sale items. Maybe if I kept a note of how much everything cost, I could eventually pay Blake back. I could also pay Hugo back for the wolfsbane. Once I figured out how to make money of course. I wished I had my cell phone because I desperately wanted to text Hugo to let him know I was okay and had found my mom's old pack. I couldn't even borrow someone else's phone to do that because I didn't have his number memorized. I sighed to myself.

"How's it going?" Jasmine came over to me.

"I think I have everything," I replied, holding up what I picked out.

"Is that it?" she asked. "You should probably get more just in case."

"It's okay. I'm good."

"At least get a couple more T-shirts." She walked over to the basics section, pulling some more T-shirts in different colors off the rack.

"You also need a really sexy dress. Lots of hot warriors in our pack." Lucy winked at me, handing me the bodycon dress. Jasmine shook her head and walked over to the checkout area. I followed, carrying all my things.

We went to Target after, where I found a few more affordable clothing options, some cheap shoes, and toiletries I needed—my legs were not looking so good these days! Jasmine bought herself some workout clothes and picked out an outfit for me, saying I might need one if Blake forced me to start training, since apparently everyone who lived in the pack was supposed to be trained.

"Just say you have your period if you don't feel like training. It always works for me," Lucy chimed in.

After we finished checking out, we went to Applebee's to have lunch before heading home.

"So, where are you from, rog—Talia?" Lucy asked.

"Ontario," I replied.

"Were you just about to call her *rogue*?" Jasmine asked.

"Well, you are a rogue, right?" Lucy looked at me. "Why don't you have a pack?"

"I didn't grow up in a pack," I replied.

"Where did you grow up then?"

After a beat, I said, "Around humans."

"Really?" Lucy asked. "What was that like?"

"I don't know, it seemed normal I guess."

"But like, wasn't it weird once you started shifting into a wolf?"

"I never really shifted much until recently, to be honest."

"And it didn't like, hurt, if you went too long without shifting? I know I get kind of irritated if I don't shift at least once a week."

"I guess I just got used to it after a while."

"What did you think of Blake when you first met him? He's hot, right?"

"Lucy, why are you talking about Talia's brother and my boyfriend like that?" Jasmine glared at Lucy.

Why was she asking that? Did she know? She was Luke's wife, so maybe he told her. My stomach quivered with nausea. God, I'd made such a fool of myself, and I didn't think I'd ever be able to live what I did down.

"Are you okay, Talia?" Jasmine glanced my way.

"Yeah, I'm fine. I just need to go to the washroom. I'll be right back," I replied, getting up, needing to get away. I wanted to leave, but where would I go? Should I just live as a wolf? Plus, how could I leave after I had just spent so much of Blake's money on all those clothes?

I went into the washroom until I calmed down a bit and then I returned to the table. I slid back into the booth. "Did you want dessert?" Jasmine asked.

"No, I'm fine," I replied. After Jasmine paid for lunch, we returned to the car and drove back to the pack.

When we approached the gated entrance, a security guard stopped us. A girl who looked to be about our age with long brown hair in a ponytail approached the car. Jasmine groaned. The girl signaled for her to roll down the window and Jasmine did as asked.

"Can I help you, Alyssa?" Jasmine inquired.

"Just doing randomized inspections today." She poked her head in. "Hmm, why does your car smell like rogue, PJ?"

"Because the alpha's sister is a rogue, and she's visiting the pack," Jasmine replied.

"I don't believe you. That story doesn't even sound realistic." Alyssa narrowed her eyes at Jasmine. "Everyone needs to get out of the car until I find out what's going on."

"Are you fucking serious?" Lucy yelled from the back.

"Yes, I'm dead serious. Now pull over there," Alyssa said.

"What a cunt!" Lucy exclaimed. "This bitch is just pissed because we never invited her to any parties, and now she's going on a power trip. She's got balls pulling over the alpha's girlfriend and the beta's mate. Just wait until Luke hears about this!"

Jasmine blew out a breath, aggressively shifted into drive, and pulled the car over. Once she parked and swung her door open, we all followed and got out.

Alyssa walked over to us. "My superior is getting more information, so wait here until we get the go-ahead."

"You've always been a jealous cunt." Lucy glared at Alyssa. "You're still jealous that Adam gave me a rose on Valentine's Day in third grade! And you're jealous that Jasmine beat you at the spelling bee in fifth grade!"

"Don't talk to me like that or I'll put you in the cells."

"*You're* going to put *me* in the cells?"

"I'll put all three of you in there!"

Lucy burst into laughter. "Goddess, you are dumb as a rock. The alpha will cut you up into pieces if you do that! You're seriously going to put the alpha's girlfriend and his sister into the cells?"

"Do you want to fight?"

"Yes, I do!" Lucy yelled.

"Are you serious? You're always in remediation for training."

"That's why it will be hilarious when I kick your ass. Don't forget, I have warrior blood."

"You also have homo blood."

"What did you just say?" Lucy's skin flushed bright red as she planted her feet into a fighting stance, her hands clenched into fists.

"You heard me."

Before we could process what was happening, Lucy shifted into a wolf, ripping all her clothes, and attacked Alyssa. Jasmine's and my eyes followed as Lucy pounced on Alyssa with her entire huge wolf body, throwing her back. We both flinched at the sound of her skull cracking against pavement. The metallic smell of blood in the air that followed drew our attention to the red stream running from her head. Lucy then ripped her claws across Alyssa's face, peeling her skin in deep gashes.

"I texted Blake when Alyssa asked us to pull over," Jasmine whispered to me. I was about to respond when a group of wolves jumped out from seemingly nowhere and pinned Lucy to the ground. She whimpered loudly as she struggled to free herself from them.

Just as Jasmine took a step toward the commotion, a black Jeep Wrangler pulled up next to us, and Blake and Luke stepped out. "What the fuck is going on?" Blake asked, looking around. He glanced over in our direction and asked, "Jasmine, are you okay?"

Lucy let out a whine.

"Get off my mate!" Luke shouted at the wolves that were currently pinning her down. They all instantly got up, and Lucy walked over to Luke, sitting down next to him in her wolf form.

"Someone better start talking," Blake commanded, cracking his knuckles loudly.

"Alpha, Lucy attacked Alyssa, so we restrained her." A man still in human form approached Blake. Blake turned to face the knocked-out Alyssa, now limp on the ground with a red puddle around her head.

"Someone get her to the clinic," he said in an exasperated tone. The wolves all shifted back into their human forms, and two of them picked her up to carry her away. "Now are you going to tell me the whole story, Derek? You're the one in charge here."

"All I know is that Alyssa stopped the car from entering the pack and had them pull over. I don't know why. Maybe we can ask Alyssa once she's conscious again."

"Jasmine, why did Alyssa have you pull over?" Blake asked in a much gentler tone than the one he was using with Derek.

"She said it was because she was doing a randomized inspection and that she smelled a rogue in my car."

"Randomized inspection? Whose order was that. And why the fuck would anyone do a randomized inspection on the future luna's car?"

"Alpha, I'm sorry. Those were not my orders."

"Derek, you run this patrol station. You should be aware of what your juniors are fucking doing. I'm writing you up for this. And if this continues, you'll lose your senior title. I don't want something like this to ever happen again."

"Yes, Alpha. I'm sorry." Derek flinched as his hands and fingers trembled. I looked up at Blake and noticed that his eyes were murderous.

Lucy sprinted away in her wolf form. Blake turned and Luke said, "Lucy will meet us at home." Blake nodded.

"Jasmine, are you really okay?" Blake went over, pulling her into a hug and kissing her on the head.

"Yeah, I'm fine." She sighed. "I'll meet you at the packhouse." She turned to me, shook her head, and said, "Goddess, what a shit show. Welcome to the Midnight Maple Pack, Talia."

Jasmine

Blake and I both pulled into the packhouse lot at about the same time. Talia and I grabbed all of the shopping bags out of the car and walked into the house. Blake waited for us, holding the door open.

Blake pulled out chairs at the dining room table, signaling for us to sit. "Tell me the whole story of what happened."

Lucy stayed standing and went into a rant, not leaving any detail out. Blake and Luke stared at her as she told the story. I watched their facial expressions as they became angrier and angrier.

"I'm ready to banish her," Blake roared, banging his fist on the table and walking away down the hall toward his office.

"Baby, why don't you go lie down. You've had a hard day," Luke said, taking Lucy's hands. I watched as he rubbed his thumbs against her palms, reminding me of when he used to do the same thing to me. The familiar aching pain in my chest surfaced, and I looked away.

I turned to Talia and said, "We should separate out all of the clothes we bought today. But let's do it upstairs." I glanced at the Victoria's Secret bag. She nodded and the two of us walked up the stairs to her current bedroom. We both sat on the floor and transferred the clothes into two piles.

"Goddess, I can't remember which underwear Lucy picked out for who." I laughed.

"Yours were definitely the G-strings." Talia gave a small laugh, putting them in my pile. She added the lacy push-up bra to my pile as well and asked, "Is Lucy your friend?"

"She was my friend. I'm not sure anymore." I sighed.

"What happened?"

"It's a really long story. I'll tell you more sometime. But the short version is that Lucy used to be my best friend until I found out her boyfriend at the time, Luke, was my mate. As you can imagine, that didn't go over very well. But it worked out for the best because now I'm with Blake."

I reflected on everything that had transpired during the past year, from how much pain I'd gone through while Luke and I tried to make our mate bond work, to the dissolution of Lucy's and my friendship, and the ultimate rejection of Luke's and my mate bond. I realized now that I should never have worked so hard because I already had the person I needed—the person I could be myself around and who loved me for who I was. With Blake, I never had any doubts. I smiled happily, recalling how I'd felt like the situation was completely hopeless at one time, but realizing now that it had all worked out for the best.

"It seems like mates are a big deal." Talia looked at me, furrowing her brows.

"For most people, meeting them is one of the best things that ever happens to them. You finally meet the person that you're meant to be with. I'm the exception." I laughed.

"I guess I must be an exception too." She bit her lip.

I did a double take. While my own mate bond hadn't worked out, almost everyone else's did. Was it really possible I was meeting someone else with a problematic bond?

"What do you mean? Have you met your mate?" I studied her.

"Yes, but I never want to see him again."

"Why?"

"It's also a long story. Maybe I'll tell you sometime," she replied, looking at the ground. My interest was piqued, but I also didn't want to push her.

"Okay, I'm happy to listen whenever you want to tell me," I offered.

She nodded but didn't look up, and I figured maybe she wanted to be left alone. I picked up my pile of clothing and got up. "I'm going to go put these away."

She finally looked up and said, "Thanks for taking me shopping today. I owe you."

"It's no problem at all and you don't owe me anything! I had the day off and it was nice to get out anyway. If you ever need anything else, just let me know. I mean, you're my boyfriend's sister, so I obviously want to get to know you."

"Same," she replied. When she didn't say anything else, I walked out of the room to the master bedroom. Blake had given me a drawer in his dresser, so I figured I could just dump everything in there for now. It's not like I wanted to bring my new G-strings home where my parents might see them. I shuddered at the thought.

Blake was already in his bedroom when I entered. His eyes instantly fell on the pile of clothing I was carrying. "I've been imagining what you bought at Victoria's Secret for hours now," he said in a gravelly voice as I walked over to the dresser.

I opened the drawer he'd reserved for me and dumped it all inside, instantly slamming it shut.

He walked over and reopened the drawer, spotting the G-strings on top, pulling one of them out, smiling mischievously. "Were you trying to hide this from me?"

I groaned. "Lucy made me buy them."

"She does have good taste, I'll give her that."

I groaned again.

He came closer to me, rubbing my arms and leaning forward. He put his mouth to my ear and said in a low voice, "I'd love to see your ass in that sometime."

My whole body heated as his warm breath grazed my skin. I closed my eyes, giving in to the feeling as a shiver traveled up my body. Damn, just hearing his deep, sexy voice turned me on so much.

Stepping closer, he moved his hands up my arms, to my shoulders, and brought them to the nape of my neck. His fingers traveled south, down the length of my spine. I swiftly reached for his torso, tracing the ridges of hard muscles through his T-shirt as his hands slowly made their way farther down my back.

As I stepped closer to him, he grabbed hold of my ass. My pelvis jutted forward in response, and he lifted me up, placing me on top of the dresser. I spread my legs so he could step between them. We inched closer to each other, the bulge straining within his jeans throbbing against my crotch.

He nibbled gently on my ear and whispered, "Your pre-birthday present is overdue."

I quivered as he slowly kissed down the side of my neck and along my collarbone, then lifted my shirt off me and threw it to the ground. I began pulling his shirt off and he grabbed it from me, removing it himself, revealing his strong shoulders, broad, chiseled chest, and deeply cut, well-defined abs. I instantly placed my hands on his body, allowing my fingers to drift along the ridges of his core, memorizing every detail.

My panties were soaked, and my nipples tingled in anticipation. No matter how many times I saw and felt Blake's ripped body, I was still aroused like it was the first time. He kissed down my chest, swiftly unhooking my bra. As soon as it was off, he brushed his thumbs against my breasts, provoking a soft moan from me. I grabbed the back of his head and impulsively pulled his lips against mine, pushing my tongue into his mouth in desperation. He deepened the kiss, continuing to rub his thumbs against my hard nipples. The ensuing sensation traveled down my body straight to the apex of my inner thighs, now aching with need. He pulled his lips from mine and moved them back to my body, kissing me down my stomach. I flexed my core in reaction and he moaned.

"Abs of steel, damn I'm so fucking hard right now."

Hot with need and desiring to speed things along, I reached for his belt, unbuckling it. He quickly undid his jeans and let them drop along with his underwear, his erection springing free. I instinctively grabbed for it and slid my hands gently up and down the length of his shaft. He groaned in response and unbuttoned my jeans, pulling them off along with my underwear. He then slid his hands up the sides of my thighs, and his eyes traced my entire body.

"Goddess, you're so fucking perfect," he moaned. He picked me up and carried me across the room, throwing me onto the bed. Now on my back, I brought my knees up and stared at him through my bare legs. His eyes scanned my entire body, a smirk on his face. The way he looked at me always made me feel so sexy and desired. After a beat, he climbed onto the bed and crawled on top of me. He brought his mouth to mine, kissing me hungrily while I brushed my hands through his thick hair, moving them to the nape of his neck. I squeezed my thighs against his torso, desperate to have his whole body as close to mine as possible. Every element between my legs was swollen, throbbing, craving Blake to rub against it and fill it. I moaned against his lips, wanting him to know how badly I wanted him to be inside me.

He abruptly pulled away and rolled my body over, so I was on my stomach. I heard the bedside drawer open. Damn, I guess Blake was really eager that day—he usually spent much more time, sometimes an exasperating amount of time, on foreplay. I stretched my legs in anticipation as he hovered over me, his body heat warm against my skin. He brushed my hair from my back and kissed down the nape of my neck and across my shoulders. When he pulled his mouth from my body, I felt liquid drop onto my back. Blake straddled my body, his erection brushing against my ass, and leaned forward so his mouth was next to my ear. "Now for your pre-birthday present." He kissed the nape of my neck again and then pulled away, spreading the liquid all over my back.

"What is that?" I asked.

"Massage oil—thought we'd try something new." He began by rubbing my shoulders. I couldn't lie, it did feel very good, especially after training all week. I moaned, encouraging him to keep going, luxuriating in how Blake's strong hands handled my stiff muscles, rubbing my shoulders and upper back, working out all the knots. He slowly moved his hands down my body, adding more oil as necessary. This was very, very nice. I relaxed into the bed, closing my eyes in bliss, mindful only of the feeling of Blake's hands and his dick throbbing against my body. After rubbing the entirety of my back, he moved to my ass, which he spent an inordinate amount of time on, massaging every inch. "I love this ass so much," he gushed.

His hands moved down to the back of my legs and back up to the inside of my thighs, gently massaging the sensitive skin. I moaned more loudly, my legs flexing against his hands, feeling warm, a fluttering within my skin. I gasped in surprise as he pushed two fingers inside me, holding them in place for a moment, and then gently moving them in and out. The pressure and rubbing of his fingers felt so good. He eventually moved his thumb down to my clit, rubbing it with gentle expertise. I moaned loudly as he concentrated all his effort on getting me off. Before long, my whole body was shaking, on the brink of orgasm.

I was about to come when he abruptly pulled his hand away, leaving me extremely frustrated. I turned my head to see where he went and watched as he rolled a condom onto himself, smiling mischievously at me. I gave him a playful glare in return.

He lowered himself back on top of me and moved his mouth back to my ear. "Oh, did you not finish?" He chuckled, giving me a quick kiss on my ear.

He spread my legs with his, making room for himself, and moved one hand underneath me, so that it was back to touching my most sensitive spot. I softly moaned in response. Moments later, he pushed himself inside me, his very large member straining against my inner walls, eliciting a much louder moan from me. He immediately began thrusting, his hips pressing against my ass with every push. I reveled in the feeling of him rubbing against and stretching me, a carnal pleasure within me, wishing we could stay like this forever.

"Goddess, I love you so much," he moaned in my ear, bringing himself closer to me, the warmth of his body surrounding me. I basked in his words, feeling so much affection for him. Our skin was slick with sweat as our bodies rubbed against one another. Blake brought his mouth to my neck, finding all the most sensitive areas, drawing every last bit of pleasure out.

As he sped up his movement, he began rubbing my clit again. His skilled fingers quickly brought me to the edge, and I was practically screaming at this point. My whole body shook against his as I found myself at the point of no return, being pushed to climax. All the tension in my body violently released as Blake kept rubbing me, forcing a second and third orgasm to rapidly follow. He then gave his final few thrusts and let out a guttural growl, falling on top of me and just as quickly rolling off. I felt my canines extending and I quickly bit down onto my fist, so hard that I could taste blood. I knew Blake was doing the same. After a couple of minutes the feeling passed, and I turned to Blake.

"It's getting harder and harder." I whimpered.

He moved closer to me, brushing my hair back, his eyes soft. "I know. It will keep getting worse until we mark each other. I'd mark you now, but I know you want to wait."

"Oh Goddess, I can't show up at home marked. My parents will know."

He laughed. "I'm pretty sure they know anyway."

"Don't say that! I'd rather believe they don't!"

"Don't worry, we'll mark each other soon," he said, winking at me. He kissed my forehead and got out of the bed, moving into the bathroom.

I followed him. "I've got oil all over my back. I need to wash it off," I said as I stepped into the shower.

Moments later, he appeared beside me. "Since you're here, I'm going to take full advantage now before you go back to your innocent double life at home."

Chapter 10

Alexander

Once my sister returned, we finally held a small funeral for my father, burning his body on a pyre, after having stored it in the pack hospital morgue while she was away. In attendance were only our closest family members and the beta family. I couldn't recall the last time I'd seen my sister cry, but I caught her hiding her face as she wept. Between you and me, I believed my father would have preferred her as his heir rather than me. But even if my father had agreed to go against tradition and hand his title over to a female for the first time in the pack's history, I was still older, and so the title rightfully remained mine.

However, my father and sister always had a distinct connection, bonded by their almost identical personalities. When my sister and I were teenagers, my father forced me to witness him torturing prisoners. I'd like to pretend I took to it right away, but the truth is my stomach was weak. The first time, I passed out completely and woke to my father pouring whiskey over my face. He loved his whiskey and always had it on hand. If someone were to give an honest eulogy, it would include a passage describing his favorite afternoon activity—drinking a bottle of whiskey and torturing a prisoner, too drunk to care if the interrogation was even going anywhere. My father was pretty unhinged, if I was being honest.

But my sister adored him. Even though he had never planned to invite her to his tortures, she begged to join us, as if he were excluding her from a father-son trip to Disney World. When he finally agreed for her to tag along, she watched him with glee, a sick smile on her face. Years later, when he finally handed her his knife and let her do the honors, you'd think he'd handed her a brand-new Porsche. Truth be told, neither my father nor my sister was really ever quite all there—they were merciless. I think the proper psychological term is sociopath or antisocial. Clearly never diagnosed, since they weren't the type to go see a therapist and talk about their feelings.

And that was exactly why the relationship between my father and me never worked. Okay, I wasn't exactly a "let's sit around and talk about our feelings" type of person. But I enjoyed things that my father never understood. While my father's favorite afternoon was single malt and mutilation, I much preferred to sit in a quiet corner of the woods with a sketchbook balanced on my lap.

My sister, on the other hand, took to alpha training like a fish to water. She loved to fight and would hang on my father's every word as he'd train her. When he'd criticize her, she'd just work that much harder until she got whatever she had done wrong completely right. And when my father discovered how tough she was in the cold, you'd think someone had given him the best blow job of his life. He spent months training her how to track and be stealthy. That kid could swim *far* in freezing-cold Canadian water—a huge advantage when that was the only way for a werewolf to hide his or her scent from others of the same kind.

All this to say, I was not my dad's favorite by a long shot. By the time I reached twenty, my father was fed up with attempting and failing to mold me into someone like himself, like he'd done with my sister, and shipped me off to Grey Wolf University so they could do the dirty work for him. My mom tearfully said goodbye as I boarded my flight to Siberia. Yes, my sweet and emotional mom was clearly the benefactor of her son's defects.

Even now she bawled heartily for the man who had spent, apparently, decades cheating on her and, for the past many years, was barely ever even sober.

My feelings about the whole situation were complicated. He was my father after all, and there was a part of me that felt something for him. After all, he had raised me and I could understand why he did some of the things he did, even if growing up with him wasn't exactly sunshine and daisies. But I also wasn't exactly weeping like the female portion of my family.

I had planned to set off on my journey to Vermont the next day, but of course, it's never a dull day in my life. The day after my father's body was turned to ashes, my warriors caught a member of the Bois Sombre Pack attempting to sneak onto pack territory. He was foolish to even attempt it because my pack, the Pine Forest Pack, was one of the largest and most notorious packs on the east coast, especially when my father had been alpha. In over two hundred years, we had yet to lose a battle and, until my mate had murdered my father, there had never been such an occurrence previously. People knew not to fuck with us.

To cheer my sister up, I allowed her to do the honors of torturing the idiot who thought he could mess with our pack. I sat back and watched her make slices up and down his body, carving stripes into his skin—perhaps my sister had inherited some enthusiasm for the arts as well. She concentrated on her work as if he were not writhing against his restraints, screaming in agony. After his arms, legs, and torso were completely covered in bloody stripes, she stepped back and said, "*Prêt à parler*, eh?"

I had to hand it to him, he stayed strong—stronger than most. It was only after she'd removed his legs, arms, eyeballs, and nose that he was finally begging for her to just kill him and gave up everything. He had been sent to kidnap a high-ranking person in the pack for ransom. They were pissed we had broken the alliance and their alpha was still desperate to get his mate, Luna Sofia, back. Alpha Édouard had been trying for years to find someone to help him kidnap his mate back for him after her family had brought her home when they'd become privy to the domestic abuse she was experiencing at his hands. Some had attempted and failed, much like this poor sucker here had attempted and failed, to kidnap someone from my pack.

I had one of the juniors I'd forced to observe the interrogation do the honors of packing up a body part of his choice to mail back to Alpha Édouard. The poor kid had vomited his entire lunch earlier and still didn't look quite right. When I was in university, such an act would have resulted in being whipped, but I wasn't quite as punitive as my professors. Lucky for me, my father had already desensitized me enough at that point, so I never had to face the whip. However, there were plenty of others who had.

Because the interrogation had taken until evening, I had to delay my trip by another day. The next morning, I got into my Land Rover Defender and finally began on my journey. There were two packs in Vermont I knew of, both in the same general vicinity, and one was a new ally of ours. I threw my duffel bag into the back seat, my mate's cell phone into my glove box, and shifted my car into drive.

Chapter 11

Jasmine

When I went downstairs the morning of my twenty-first birthday, both of my parents had big smiles on their faces. I sat down to eat breakfast before getting ready for the day.

"Happy birthday, Jazzy. Big one for you today." My dad grinned as he sat across from me. I noticed he was holding my mom's hand under the table, something I didn't often see my parents do.

"We're looking forward to celebrating with you and Alpha Blake at dinner tonight." My mom gave me an uncharacteristically large smile, looking much happier than usual. They then turned to each other and stared into each other's eyes, as if they were having a silent conversation. Something seemed to be off. My parents weren't acting like themselves.

After breakfast, I spent time doing my hair and makeup and then threw on a nice top with jeans. At ten, the doorbell rang, and I went to answer it. My dad followed and stayed behind me as I opened the door.

"Nice to see you, Drew." Blake nodded at my dad.

"See you at dinner tonight." My dad winked and gave Blake some friendly punches in the chest. Why was my dad acting so juvenile and buddy-buddy with Blake? He was being so strange today. I narrowed my eyes at him, hoping he got the hint to stop being so weird.

As soon as I stepped outside and closed the door behind me, Blake tried to pull me in for a kiss, but I didn't let him. "My parents can see us!" I whisper-yelled.

"Some things never change with you." Blake shook his head, leading me to the passenger door to let me into his car.

"So where are we off to?" I asked.

"Where I fell in love with you." He moved closer, brushing my hair behind my ear in a loving gesture, causing my heart to swell. No matter how much he told me he loved me, I never tired of it. I couldn't believe that Blake actually loved me, especially when he could have anyone. He drove us toward our secret place, where we hiked to the top of the mountain.

He pulled out a blanket and set it out on the ground, then he walked over to me. "It's a bit early for lunch, so I think some titty fondling is in order." He chuckled. "Get your timer ready." I slapped him on his shoulder, and he laughed. He then stopped, becoming serious, looked into my eyes, and used his fingers to brush my hair behind my ear. "Happy birthday, Jasmine," he said as he moved his face closer to mine. He slowly and gently kissed my lips, pulling my body toward his.

I wrapped my arms around him, enjoying the tingly, warm feeling that spread from my chest to my limbs, in a place that had become one of my favorite places.

"Thank you," I said after we pulled apart.

He stepped back and looked into my eyes again. He took my hands, held them between us, and said, "I wanted to bring you here today because, until I came here with you, my life was really dark. I didn't think I'd ever feel happy again. But that first time we came here together, I started to feel like the old me again. I didn't know what it was exactly about being with you, but you made me feel safe to finally open up and feel something again." He smiled as his eyes blazed in the sunlight.

After a pause, he continued, "You didn't know me before then, but I was not in a good place, and I did a lot of things I am not proud of. I hurt a lot of people. I was self-destructive and pushed everyone away. But being around you made me realize I didn't want to be that person and I didn't want to be alone anymore. Now that you're in my life, I can't imagine ever living without you in it. Being here with you right now makes me feel like the luckiest man in the world."

My heart was beating forcefully against my chest as Blake got down on one knee and pulled a box out of his pocket. I couldn't believe how distracted I'd been the past couple days that I totally missed all the obvious signs that this was finally happening. I brought my hand to my mouth as he opened the box to reveal a ring with a large blue gemstone in the center and took my other hand in his.

"Miss Alpha, will you marry me?"

Tears fell from my eyes.

"I hope that's a yes." Blake stared up at me. "Although, I can't imagine why you'd ever say no to these abs or this chest or these arms." He gestured at himself, smirking.

I punched him lightly in his shoulder, chuckling. "Yes, it's a yes."

He got up and said, "Good, I wasn't sure whether or not I should have made my huge cock a part of the proposal too." He pulled me back toward his body and kissed me deeply. My body molded into his, and his strong arms wrapped affectionately around me. How amazingly surreal and lucky we were to have found each other.

Am I dreaming? Should I pinch myself? Does that actually work?

After we pulled apart, he grabbed my hand. "Miss Alpha, soon-to-be Mrs. Alpha," he said as he slipped an engagement ring on my finger. "I thought a sapphire would be more meaningful than a diamond."

"I love it!" I exclaimed as I stared at it on my hand. Somehow Blake knew exactly the perfect ring to pick out for me, and I loved that it matched the bracelet he'd gotten for me on my birthday the prior year, which I still wore quite often.

"So, did your birthday wish come true?" he asked, looking at me so proudly and eagerly. I couldn't crush his spirits and tell him what I had actually wished for.

"Yeah, you did." I grinned at him, thinking, in that moment, it was really what I should have wished for. *Goddess, I've been so distracted, missing completely what's already right in front of me.* Never did I ever think I'd meet someone so perfect. Even with how lonely I felt sometimes, I knew I was never truly alone when I had Blake.

He pulled me down on the blanket to sit with him. I turned and inched closer, basking in his beaming face. He reached for his backpack and pulled out some sandwiches. "I obviously couldn't have you making us lunch on your birthday, so I put together some of my home cooking today." He handed me a sandwich. "Ham and cheese special."

"I love your sandwiches." I laughed, feeling nostalgic. We sat down, side by side, staring out over the wilderness, a perfect view of the fall foliage, the leaves now a colorful landscape of yellows, oranges, and reds. There was nothing more magical than Vermont in autumn.

"Obviously the whole marking situation is getting more difficult, so I was hoping we could get married sooner rather than later." He glanced over at me. "I was thinking either the winter solstice or New Year's Eve. Alpha weddings are a big deal, and the whole pack is traditionally invited, so we need time to plan for it. Otherwise, I'd just take you down to the temple today."

At the mention of the temple, a sadness pervaded me, a pain in my chest. "I can't get married in the temple," I said quietly, looking down.

Blake rubbed my back and pulled me close to him. "That's not true."

"It is, though! I spoke to Bernard, and he told me that if I rejected my mate I wouldn't be allowed to marry in the temple. That was why Luke and Lucy couldn't have a temple wedding."

"What if I told you that I also spoke to Bernard?"

I looked up at him in shock. "You did? About what?"

"The morning after we had sex for the first time, I asked him about our canines expanding."

"You didn't!" I gasped. "He knows about that?"

"I mean, I didn't tell him you were the woman I was asking about specifically. But I'm sure it's pretty obvious by now."

"Oh my Goddess." I wrapped my arms around my stomach, thinking I was going to be sick. I couldn't believe Blake had told the priest we'd had sex.

Blake chuckled and said, "You are so funny, Jasmine. He didn't make a big deal out of it. And it was a legitimate question. Anyway, he seemed to believe that you're my second-chance mate. I asked if that meant that we could get married in the temple, and he more or less said that he wouldn't stand in the way if we chose to."

"Second-chance mate?" I asked. I'd never heard of such a thing.

"It would make sense, wouldn't it?" He stared into my eyes and said, "Trust me, I don't deserve a second-chance mate. I did a lot of bad things after Ria died. But you do deserve one. You've always been a good person, Jasmine. Even if you rejected your fated mate, you only did it because he was a complete idiot and you deserved better. And I promise I'll always be good to you. I'll spend my entire life making you happy." He pulled me toward him and snuggled me against his body. I reveled in how perfectly we fit together.

After we finished eating, we hiked back down to the car so Blake could take me to our next destination. As soon as we entered the car and he placed his phone in its holder, the screen lit up with incoming text messages.

"Shit, we must have been outside the service area," he said, grabbing his phone. He read through his phone and said, "Fuck. We have to go back."

He looked at me with a sad look on his face. "I'm really sorry, Jasmine. I wanted today to be perfect, but I can't ignore my pack duties."

"What happened?" I asked as I watched him type back messages.

"Well, it seems Alyssa is awake now, but that's obviously not urgent. However, the alpha of the Pine Forest Pack showed up and refuses to leave until he talks to me in person, and that I have to address. Hopefully, this won't take long." He did a three-point turn and sped back toward the pack.

Chapter 12

Blake

As soon as I reached the pack gate, I pulled over to where a silver Land Rover was parked outside the entrance. I stepped out of my car and Alpha Alexander quickly did the same. I walked over to him, quite annoyed with the interruption to my day.

"Adalwolf, to what do I owe the pleasure?" I asked him.

"Wulfric," he replied, nodding.

"I'm not going to lie. This is not great timing. It's my fiancée's birthday, and I just had to drive back twenty miles because you can't come back later."

"Well, hopefully it won't take long then. I've come to collect my mate."

"Your mate is in my pack?" I asked.

"So rumor has it. I stopped by the Autumn Moon Pack, and they have not welcomed any rogues recently. However, I've been informed by the staff on duty at the entrance that yours has."

Strike two against Derek. His subordinates should know not to give out information. He was definitely not on my favorite warriors list at the moment. "Thanks for letting me know that my warriors need some training in keeping their mouths shut. That aside, what makes you believe this rogue is your mate?"

"The same way you know your fiancée is your mate, of course."

"You would be wrong about that," I replied, not caring that I was being difficult.

"Well, okay then. I take it your fiancée is not your mate then."

"Not my fated mate."

"I'm not sure why you're being so difficult, Wulfric, but the rogue you're housing in your pack is my fated mate, and as she's my mate, I'd like to take her back to my pack. I will not leave until I accomplish what I came here to do. I think you can understand my predicament. And if I have to break the alliance and start a war over this, I will. Not that I want to, as I, until this point, have seen you as a friend."

"First of all, Adalwolf, the rogue is not just property that gets handed over from person to person. So if that's what you fucking think, then I am definitely not bringing her anywhere near you. Second of all, that rogue you are speaking of also happens to be my sister. And you also being someone with a sister, I think you can also understand my predicament. Since you're my friend, I can do you the favor of asking if she'd like to go with you, but I have a feeling the answer will be no as she already expressed she has no desire to be with her mate. Seeing as you apparently think she's a possession, I don't fucking blame her."

"The rogue is your sister?" He looked dumbstruck.

"Yes, she is," I replied, simply.

"What is she doing as a rogue then?"

"We have my shit father to thank for that. Inseminate and eliminate was his MO." I chuckled. "It's actually not funny, but you have to admit that was pretty good."

"Inseminate and eliminate," Alexander echoed and shook his head. "That's pretty fucked-up."

"My father was pretty fucked-up."

"So was my father, until my mate killed him of course," Alexander said. "Which is another reason why I'm not leaving without her. While you may not feel her being my mate warrants handing her over, I'd assume you'd want me to hand over the murderer of one of your pack members, especially if the victim were a family member."

"What—" I said, in disbelief. Talia had killed her mate's father?

"Trust me, I'm in as much shock as you are."

"There has to be a reason she killed him. She doesn't strike me as the type to just go on a killing spree."

"Does it matter? The fact remains she killed him. And therefore, you owe me the courtesy of bringing me my murdering mate."

"And we're just going to ignore the fact that not only was your pack our enemy in the battle that killed my father, but you had also aligned yourself with a pack that killed my fated mate? I don't owe you anything."

"Why don't we just settle this another way." Alexander smiled mischievously with a glint in his eyes. "A fight to the death."

"You're insane," I said, staring at him with my eyes wide.

"I am willing to fight until my death for my mate. So, what do you say? Are you willing to fight to your death for your sister?"

"You're fucking with the wrong alpha," I replied.

He began pulling his clothes off, stripping himself naked. Right before he shifted, he said, "And don't be a pussy and call your men in as backup."

I watched as he turned into a huge white wolf. I rolled my eyes and threw all my clothes off, shifting into my own wolf, a dark-brown wolf that was so dark it was almost black. I mindlinked Derek to hold everyone back and let me fight. I waited for him to approach.

He lunged at me, and I quickly dodged his attack, getting low. As he jumped over me, I grabbed his legs with my claws and brought his back down to the ground. He easily kicked me off him and pounced on top of me, digging his claws into my chest, clearly going for my organs. I pushed him off, watching blood spray out of my chest and feeling the agonizing pain of the cut. He'd gotten his claws in deep. In return, I scratched him across his face and down his neck and chest.

"Blake!" Jasmine screamed. I could see in my peripheral vision that she was starting to remove her clothes. I quickly leaped on Alexander so I could hold him down long enough to use my concentration for mindlinking. Before I could, he grabbed me with his claws and was ready to bite my head off; I struggled to free myself of him.

Jasmine shifted into her wolf and bit into the first thing she could, which happened to be his tail. In shock, he yelped and let me go. She must have bitten really hard. I rolled off him and was about to attack him again when Jasmine scratched him down his back. I watched as he was about to reach for her and I lunged at him, using the force of my body to flatten him against the ground. I opened my mouth and had my teeth at his neck. I knew I could easily kill him at this point, but I didn't. I just held him pinned down, with my mouth around his neck, waiting.

He finally shifted back to his human form and said, "Okay, I surrender." I shifted back at that point. He added, "Of course, you also didn't play fair."

I pulled my pants back on and said, "I forgot to mention my fiancée is a fighter." I grinned with pride and watched with amusement as Jasmine grabbed her clothes with her mouth and ran behind the car to change back into her human form. I turned back to him and said, "Fair or not, I won. I'll take you to see your mate, as soon as I wrap this wound." I looked down at the deep gash just below my rib cage that was slowly healing, then looked back up at him. "But she gets to decide whether she leaves with you or not. And if she says no, you leave alone. If not, you will be escorted out by my warriors, and you are far outnumbered, Adalwolf."

"Fine," he replied, putting his hand out to shake mine, scratches on his face, neck, and chest. I took his hand and gave it a hearty shake.

"Follow me, and I'll take you to her," I said, walking back toward my car where Jasmine was waiting for me, mindlinking Derek to have one of his juniors grab me a bandage.

Chapter 13

Talia

As "payment" for letting me stay at the packhouse, I agreed to help Lucy with her baby. And, to be completely honest, Lucy's baby was a very strong form of birth control. Libby made me never want to spread my legs again. Bring on the cotton panties and grandma bras!

Libby was teething, and so she was spending most of her day crying. Lucy was at work today, so I was stuck trying to soothe her, shedding my own tears out of frustration, and grieving. I missed my mom. She was always so loving to me and always knew the right thing to say or do. I bet she would've known what to do with Libby.

"How's it going?" Luke came by the couch where I was sitting with Libby, taking a seat next to me. I'm sure my face was blotchy. I wiped at my eyes, trying to at least make myself appear normal. I looked over at him and realized he was actually very handsome, with tan skin and light freckles dotting his nose. He and Lucy made a stunning couple, making Libby the winner of a genetic lottery, which I was sure would show in a few years.

"It's fine," I replied.

"She's a handful. May I?" He put his hands out and I handed her to him. He snuggled her against his body and she seemed to calm down.

"Thanks for helping out, by the way. This whole parenting thing is a lot harder than I thought it would be." He cooed at her and then looked back over at me. "Are you okay?"

"Yeah, I'm fine. Just tired."

"You look like you've been crying." Luke studied me.

I shrugged.

"If you want to talk about it, I'm happy to listen. There's no one here today. We gave everyone the day off since they worked on the autumnal equinox."

Just then, the front door burst open, and we looked up to witness Blake walking into the house followed by Jasmine. Behind them, a familiar figure trailed. Luke stood up with Libby, staring at everyone. Blake glanced back and signaled for the figure to stay. That was when his scent drifted into my vicinity—the most sensual and intoxicating scent. I instantly knew exactly who it was that had come.

"There's someone here to see you, Talia," Blake said. After a pause, he continued, "I want you to know that you don't have to go anywhere that you don't want to. He's outnumbered by everyone in this pack, so I'll remove him from here if you want me to."

The man approached, his scent becoming stronger as he came closer. As I stared at him, my heart skipped a beat. He was very handsome—no, he was hot! Now that I wasn't scrambling to run away, I was fully able to appreciate his self-assured composure, looming height, broad shoulders, well-defined jaw obscured by the dirty-blond hairs of his close-cut beard. I mean, Madam Coco had hired many very, very good-looking bouncers, many of whom I had bedded. But this man, holy hell, he was really fucking hot. And his scent was overwhelming. Inhaling it made me wish we were alone and I was already peeling off all his clothes to see what was underneath.

Oh God, what's wrong with me? Look at Libby! Birth control!

"Hey," he said, strutting over. Damn, that strut. I loved a confident man. He came closer, and that's when I looked into his eyes—his black eyes like coals, just like *him*. I instantly felt disgusted with myself for all the thoughts that had run through my mind.

"Go away," I said, getting up, and walking past him to go upstairs to my room.

Alexander

"Well, there's your answer," Blake said to me.

"I'm not leaving until my mate comes with me," I responded. Goddess, she was amazing—no, perfect! I'd never met such a beautiful woman in my life—so tall, lean, and leggy, curves in all the right places, and the face of an angel. I gazed at her as she walked away, her perfect, tight ass teasing me in those leggings. I only had seconds to really appreciate her the last time I saw her. But now that I was seeing her in the daylight, I had more time to really take all of her in, I was really able to grasp what was at stake. She was my perfect match, and I couldn't fathom the idea of going back home without her.

"We had a deal." Blake glared at me.

"Wulfric, please, she's my mate. You had a mate before too, right? You must know what it's like." I tried to reason with him. I was no longer above begging.

He sighed. "She doesn't want to see you."

"Let me stay with you. That way you can make sure I don't do anything you don't approve of. I just want to know my mate."

"Don't you have a pack to go home to?"

"My sister and beta can handle it."

"I won't lie and say you're not being a huge pain in my ass. But I don't have time for this right now, and I can also understand how you feel." Blake shook his head. "You can stay on the beta floor, and I better not catch you up on my floor, specifically the top floor. Luke, keep your eye on him for the rest of today." He looked over at a man who was holding a baby in his arms.

Luke couldn't have looked less pleased with the order, and probably the unexpected guest who had just been thrown on him. I had a hard time feeling bad about it—after all, all's fair in love and war. Blake then turned to his fiancée and grabbed her hand, revealing a sapphire ring that caught the sunlight that was streaming in from a sliding glass door, creating an intense sparkle.

"Fuck," Luke muttered, turning away.

"What was that?" Blake suddenly turned to look at him.

"Congrats," Luke said, turning back around to face Blake. "On the engagement." He was smiling, but his eyes didn't match his mouth.

"Thanks," Blake responded, and turned back around, leading his fiancée away. There was definitely something strange about the situation. I knew all about strange situations.

After they left, I turned to Luke and said, "Luke, is it? You're Wulfric's beta, eh?"

"Yes, I am," he replied, looking me over. "I'll bring you to your room." I followed him as he led me upstairs to the second floor, bouncing the baby in his arms as she fussed.

"How old?" I asked, trying to make conversation.

"Six months."

"Very nice."

Suddenly, Luke turned to me and said, "You're lucky, man. Blake has softened big time in the last year. There's no way he would've ever agreed to this arrangement a year ago."

"He does seem less miserable than when we were in school," I agreed. "It must be his fiancée. What's the deal with that anyway? He said she's not his mate? Whose mate is she?"

"Long story. Here's your room." He opened a door, gesturing for me to go in. "I'll bring you some fresh sheets later. The housekeepers aren't working again until Tuesday, so you'll have to make the bed yourself. The sheets on the bed now were used by my parents who left this morning so you can just throw them in the hamper, and the housekeeper will take care of them on Tuesday."

"Nice hospitality. I'll go grab my bags out of my car."

"I wasn't exactly expecting a guest today."

"It's all good," I said, descending the stairs. I quickly grabbed my duffel bag out of my trunk and the cell phone from the front of my car. I smiled to myself, realizing I could use the cell phone as leverage. I was sure she was dying to have it back. I couldn't imagine going weeks without mine.

Luke let me back into the packhouse. Before I went to drop everything in my room, I turned to him and asked, "Can you let my mate know I have her phone? And I'm happy to give it to her if she'll at least have a conversation with me."

He sighed and nodded, walking up the stairs with me, then continuing up to the third floor. After I threw my stuff into my room for the foreseeable future, I walked out with her phone in hand and waited at the bottom of the stairs leading to the third floor.

Luke came down sans baby. "Sorry, man, she doesn't want to see you. Although, she did seem tempted by the phone."

"Did she say why she doesn't want to see me?" I asked.

"No. She doesn't say much. She's pretty quiet, well, most of the time." He smirked, looking as if he were smiling at some inside joke.

"Most of the time? What does that mean?"

"Nothing. Anyway, I have a bunch of stuff I have to get done today. Just please don't leave the packhouse."

I sat down in front of my room, keeping an eye on the stairs. She'd have to come down at some point. I considered going upstairs and disobeying Blake's orders, but I didn't want to risk getting kicked out. He was right that I was outnumbered here in his pack, and this wasn't something I actually wanted to start a war over.

After what seemed like forever, I heard a baby's crying getting louder and louder, and footsteps coming down the stairs. I instantly shot up and went over. She was about to turn around and I shouted, "Wait!" using my alpha aura. But no such luck, she continued turning around. She wasn't a part of my pack, and likely having alpha blood made her immune to alphas of other packs. "Please, wait," I said more softly.

She stopped midstep and turned back around to look at me.

I straightened up, feeling a renewed energy. "Here, let me help you with the baby." I put my hands out.

She hesitated, but she handed her to me, putting her gently in my arms. The baby started wailing even louder.

"Fuck, what do I do?" I asked.

"I think she's hungry," she replied.

"Hungry, right." I tried bouncing the pup a bit, but it didn't seem to help. "What does she eat?"

"There's breast milk in the fridge."

"Right, breast milk. Obviously not yours," I said, suddenly having dirty thoughts about my mate's breasts. Before I could delve too deep, the baby cried, distracting me. I shook my head and forced myself to stay in the present moment.

My mate led me down the stairs and into the kitchen. She competently prepared the breast milk, following instructions on a piece of paper, while I tried different ways to get the damn pup to stop crying. Once the bottle was ready, she took the pup from me and sat down in a chair, holding the baby while she suckled happily. I watched on appreciatively at what a natural my mate was, unable to tear my eyes away.

Finally, I broke the silence. "You seem to be good at this," I remarked. "You have experience with pups?"

She let a small, cute laugh.

"What's so funny?" I asked.

"It's funny how everyone around here calls kids *pups*. I guess it makes sense. I'd just never heard them called that before." She pulled the bottle from the pup's mouth, now empty.

"You didn't grow up around werewolves I take it?"

"No." She got up, handing me the pup. I snuggled the baby in my arms, who was much cuter now that she wasn't wailing like a banshee. My mate walked across the kitchen and put the empty bottle into the sink, then turned back toward me.

"Why don't you want to talk to me?" I asked, my eyes locking with hers, the most beautiful, mesmerizing blue eyes. I instantly sensed she was simultaneously nervous and angry. The mate bond was definitely something else. I couldn't believe how close to her I felt already, barely having met her. It was taking everything in me not to bring my hands to her body, imagining how nice her skin would feel under my fingertips. I restrained myself, not wanting to scare her off again, now that she finally seemed to warm up a bit.

"Because I hate your father," she spat at me and walked out of the room, leaving me behind with the pup. And I was back to square one. I sighed to myself, shook my head, and took the pup into the living room, sitting with her on the couch. I definitely didn't imagine myself being a pupsitter today at this time yesterday. I sat her on my lap while I Googled what to do with a six-month-old. Peekaboo was a recommended activity, so I laid her down on the couch and began placing my hands over my face, and opening them to say, "Peekaboo!" She laughed, so I repeated the game with her.

I sensed my mate's scent as she approached, clearly realizing she'd forgotten something in the kitchen. I smiled, enjoying the scent as it got stronger as she moved closer to me. "Do you want to play too?" I asked when she was right behind me.

She sat down in a chair adjacent to the couch where I was sitting as I continued the game. I then started doing different things like clapping as the pup mimicked me, and blowing into her belly, setting off more laughter.

"You're really good with her," my mate said.

"Do you want to try?" I nodded toward the pup.

"I've tried all day. I'm useless," she responded, sighing.

"You were great at feeding her," I offered. When she didn't respond, I said, "Please, can we just have a conversation? You're my mate, and I really want to get to know you. I'll trade you your phone for just a conversation. I'm sure you must want it back."

"Fine," she replied, crossing her arms.

"Okay, I'll start. I know your name is Talia Wyatt, and I know you're twenty years old because I found your birth certificate. I also know you were born in Vermont but were raised in Ontario. But I'd like to know more about you."

"There's not much more to know," she replied, not giving any hint that she was interested in this conversation.

"Okay, then why don't I tell you about me?" I paused. When she didn't say anything, I continued, "My name is Alexander Adalwolf, but you can just call me Alex. I'm the alpha of the Pine Forest Pack, which I'm sure you know by now. I'm twenty-six years old. During my free time, I like to sketch, and I'd like to show you my drawings sometime. If you warm up enough, I'd love to sketch you. I don't normally do portraits, but you are honestly the most beautiful woman I've ever seen in my life, and I'd love any excuse just to stare at you for hours on end. You also smell amazing."

She looked up, her mouth agape. She quickly closed it and went back to scowling at me. But I could tell she was warming up. She was definitely a stubborn one. Girls normally threw themselves at me, but this one was really going to make me work for it. And I knew, deep down, that I was willing to work harder for her than I'd ever worked for anything else in my life.

After some thought I said, "Well, Talia, I won't force you to sit here and converse with me if that's clearly not what you want. But I'm a man of my word, and you did tolerate the few things I did say, so here's your phone back, fully charged." I stood up and placed it on the arm of the chair where she was sitting, sneaking a glance into her piercing blue eyes, and then turned to head back to my room. It took everything in me to leave her. My whole body wanted to wrap her in my arms and, well, do lots of very indecent things to her. But I forced myself to give her space. For now.

Chapter 14

Jasmine

Blake and I were seated in his car, heading to dinner at the casino after spending the perfect day together, well, except for the fact that I had stripped myself in front of everyone at the pack entrance gate . . .

"I see you blushing. I can tell you're thinking about it." Blake smirked as he held my hand and glanced over at me.

"I'm not thinking about anything," I replied, wrinkling my nose.

"I know it's bothering you. You're a warrior now. As much as I want to keep your hot body to myself, it's an occupational hazard, having to shift back and forth all the time."

I groaned.

"I loved how you jumped in to defend me today. I had it handled of course, but damn, it's so hot when you fight." Blake had a huge smile on his face. "I miss going to training with you."

I groaned again, reminded of how difficult the transition to warrior had been for me.

Blake's face took on a serious demeanor and he asked, "Was Alyssa one of the mean girls?"

I sighed. "She's always been a mean girl to me. This goes back before being a warrior. She called me PJ in school and made fun of me for everything I did. Lucy was actually a really good friend to me then and would always put Alyssa in her place. I remember Lucy slammed Alyssa against her locker one time. I can't even remember what it was about anymore." I sighed again, feeling nostalgic for my old friendship.

Blake's jaw tensed and his eyes narrowed as he stared into the road ahead. "After what she said to Lucy, and you now telling me this story, I can't fucking wait to banish her from the pack and be rid of her."

As much as I hated Alyssa, I suddenly felt terrible about the idea of her being banished. I wasn't sure the punishment fit the crime. "You can't just banish everyone that's mean to me or has a problem with Jack."

"I fucking want to," Blake replied through gritted teeth.

"You'd lose half the pack if you did that! Alyssa may have acted out more than everyone else so far, but the other female warriors all exclude me too. It's not just Alyssa. And so many people are saying horrible things about Jack and Tyler around the pack. Also, what about the signs on people's lawns? I think the only reason my mom didn't completely freak out is because she went to school with humans, and she's warmed up more now that she got to know Tyler. To be honest, I don't even know why Jack and Tyler stay here. Tyler told me his old pack is a lot more open-minded than ours."

I glanced back over. Blake's eyes had glossed over, seemingly lost in thought. After some time, he said, "I want our pack to be more open-minded. My dad was really old and set in his ways, and he was just a complete dick. But as alpha now, I want to make changes." He paused, then continued, "As for Alyssa, I'll think about it. But I'm not letting her off easy. No one fucks with my fiancée and talks shit about my friend and gets away with it."

"You'll be a great alpha," I said, giving his hand a squeeze.

"You make me a better alpha." He grinned, glancing over at me again. "That's why I need you as my luna."

I smiled at the sentiment, snuggling into his arm.

Soon, we arrived and Blake pulled into valet parking. The valet imme-diately opened the door for me, helping me out of the car. Blake came over and clasped my hand in his, leading me to dinner. We walked close together, the sounds of slot machines echoing through the halls. As we approached a familiar restaurant, my heart dropped into my stomach. "Would you mind if we go somewhere else tonight?" I asked quietly as we approached the Italian restaurant.

"What's wrong with this restaurant?" He looked down at me, his eyes locking with mine. I immediately smiled, his piercing blue eyes so beautiful and familiar.

"I'm not really in the mood for Italian tonight. Maybe we can go to the steakhouse instead," I offered.

His eyes shifted. It wasn't a big deal, right?

"I don't mind waiting if they don't have a table available right away," I added.

"I thought you liked Italian." Blake knitted his eyebrows together.

"I do, but . . ." I groaned, figuring I should just tell him. "Sorry, I didn't want to bring this up, but this is where Luke took me on our first date." I let out a sigh, hating how much he still affected me, clutching my chest at the memory.

"Oh, shit. I didn't know." Blake scrubbed a hand over his face, ex-pelling an audible breath. "Damn, this is where I made the reservation." After a beat he said, "Fuck."

I blinked a few times then he continued.

"Normally, it'd be no big deal, and I'd say, let's get the fuck out of here. But I have both our families meeting us here, and they're probably already seated."

My chest tingled, and I instantly wanted to take back everything I said. "I'm sorry, Blake. It's okay. It's not a big deal. We can go in."

"Fuck, I'm really sorry, Jasmine. I don't know why you're the one apologizing. I really wish I knew."

"It'll be okay." I straightened up. "I'm good." I forced a smile to my face.

"Maybe this is an opportunity to make good memories here." He brushed his hand down my cheek. I forced myself to appear happy, ignoring the aching in my chest—the harrowing reminder of the rejection of my fated mate.

We stepped up to the hostess stand. "Good evening, Mr. Wulfric." The woman behind the stand smiled at Blake. "Your party is all here. Right this way." She led us to a private room where everyone was seated at a large table.

I instantly spotted my parents and paternal grandparents who waved to us as we entered. But then I had to do a double take as my eyes fell on several notable members of my mom's side of the family—three generations of alphas from the Jade Moon Pack. My cousin, the current alpha, gave us a nod as I locked eyes with him. His parents and grandparents, who were seated with him, similarly looked us up and down.

On Blake's side, his mom and maternal grandparents had come and were all smiling at us.

"You invited my mom's side of the family?" I raised my eyebrows at him. I hadn't seen my mom's side of the family in years and wasn't expecting them to show up suddenly at my birthday.

"It's about time we meet, don't you think? Our marriage is making an alpha alliance, which is a big deal. We're no longer aligned just by politics, but by blood."

Before our conversation went any further, my grandmother grabbed my hand. "Very beautiful ring, Jazzy," she said, pulling me in for a hug.

I hugged her back. "Thank you. Blake did a great job." I put my hand out in front of me, displaying the generously sized sapphire that sparkled as the light hit it. I couldn't help but smile as I looked up at Blake, silently thanking him again, for both the ring and for how much he'd been there for me since I'd met him.

"Congratulations, Alpha." My grandfather shook Blake's hand. "You've made a great choice."

"Congrats, Alpha B!" My dad shook Blake's hand next, then gave him a friendly pat on the shoulder. Blake returned the sentiment with a wink and similarly gave him a friendly punch in the arm. The two of them seemed to have gotten close since Blake and I got together. And my dad kept acting like *such a dad*.

"Come meet my family." My mom gestured for Blake to follow her. Blake respectfully went along as she brought him over to my grandfather, an elderly man who had somehow still retained plenty of muscle structure—clearly age hadn't slowed him down—and my grandmother. "This is my father, former Alpha Bruce and my mother, former Luna Catherine."

Blake shook their hands. "Pleasure to meet both of you."

"Likewise, Alpha Blake. We've traveled to your pack before under much worse circumstances. It's nice to be back for a happier occasion. Although, I do understand you're not fated mates?" My grandfather gave Blake a hard stare.

"Yes, that's correct. My fated mate died in battle. But I was lucky enough for the Moon Goddess to send me a second-chance mate, especially one from such a powerful alpha family. The bond will make for a great alpha heir."

"In our pack, we call that a chosen mate. While I am not against the relationship, as it is an honor for anyone to be mated to an alpha, I can't lie and say we are not disappointed about the rejection that occurred prior to this engagement. Our pack takes the scriptures of Artemis very seriously, and we consider insulting our Moon Goddess to be a high offense. But what is done is done."

"I understand, Alpha. However, I'm sure you must have heard the circumstances behind the rejection."

"Yes, and if it were my beta, I would have commanded him to banish the bitch."

I almost gasped, but forced myself to not react. I knew my mom's side of the family was not easy to deal with. I was beginning to understand why we never had a close relationship with them.

I glanced over at Blake who had his jaw clenched and a pinched expression on his face. After a beat, he finally responded. "My father would have done the same. But I'm in love with your granddaughter, and she will make a better alpha's luna than beta's mate." He threw his arm over my shoulder protectively, pulling me toward him.

"I see you are taking destiny into your own hands. Not the way things are done in our pack, but very well."

I looked to my mom to find her glancing down at the floor and fiddling with her hands. She usually seemed so self-assured, so it was odd seeing her appear suddenly so—was she nervous? She finally looked up and gestured to my uncle. "This is my brother, former Alpha Lance, and his mate, former Luna Julia."

"Pleasure to meet both of you." Blake shook both their hands with confidence, as if he were unaffected by his interaction with my grandfather.

My uncle replied, "Pleasure is all ours, Alpha Blake. Like my father said, we're glad to be back under better circumstances. My son recently took the alpha title from me, about two years ago, so I am sure he will be happy to have a new ally on the east coast." He pushed on my cousin's back. "Alpha Tyce."

"Nice to meet you, Alpha Blake." My cousin shook Blake's hand. "Congratulations on the engagement."

"Thank you, Alpha," Blake replied. "I look forward to the new alliance."

Alpha Tyce then turned to me and gave me a friendly smile. "Congrats, Jasmine. I know we never talked much, but we should change that."

"Thank you. Yes, we should." I gave him a big smile. It was a shame I never had much of a relationship with my cousins, and I hoped it would change now that we'd reconnected.

Blake's mom and grandparents came over next. His mom hugged Blake, giving him a kiss on his forehead, and then turned to hug me, saying, "Congratulations to both of you. What a memorable twenty-first birthday for you, Jasmine." Although she was smiling, I could see a hint of sadness behind her eyes. She always seemed sad. I used to ask Blake about it, wondering if his mom was okay, but he never wanted to talk about it, and I eventually gave up asking. Unfortunately, I didn't have the type of relationship with her where I felt comfortable asking directly, not that I'd know what to do if she wasn't okay.

Next, his grandparents gave us hugs and congratulated us, both in a jubilant mood. His mom's family seemed very warm. While I'd never really known Blake's dad personally, and only knew him as the alpha of the pack, Blake never had anything good to say about him. I wondered sometimes how the relationship between his mom and dad worked. It seemed like they were such different people.

Once everyone was done mingling, we all sat down to eat dinner. Blake kept grabbing my hand under the table during dinner conversation and rubbing my knee as we ate.

The dinner seemed to go as normal as it could. My mom's family was very intense, and my grandfather and uncle both made a lot of off-color jokes. I also noticed my mom's parents were very critical of her.

"You've gained weight, Miriam. I guess you haven't been keeping up with your training?" My grandmother Catherine leaned over to my mom.

My eyes almost bugged out of my head. While, okay, maybe my mom wasn't quite as skinny as my Aunt Julia, she was still a very normal weight. And, even if she wasn't, I couldn't help but think how rude of a comment that was to make, especially when reconnecting after so many years.

"Well, you know, it's hard with my full-time job."

"How is the job? Are you at C-level yet?" my grandfather Bruce asked.

"I'm the manager of my department," my mom replied.

"She was employee of the month last month," my dad chimed in. "And she's up for a big raise this year."

"Hopefully a promotion too," my grandfather Bruce interposed.

"Maybe she can afford to hire a personal trainer then," my grandmother Catherine added. "You can never be too careful living in a pack. Everyone should be well trained." She turned to Blake and said, "Maybe my grandson should take a look at your pack's minimal fit standards and make sure that they're up to par. Our pack is very strict about these things. You can never be too careful with so many enemies."

Blake didn't look exactly thrilled about the idea, but he replied, "I'd be happy to speak with Alpha Tyce any time so we can compare notes."

I glanced over at Tyce who seemingly hadn't even noticed we were talking about him, his eyes on his lap. Certain he wouldn't be staring at his crotch, although the thought made me almost snicker out loud, I deduced he was probably on his phone under the table.

"I heard you went to battle just under a year ago?" my uncle Lance asked.

"Yes, we did. And your niece saved my life," Blake boasted. "She's absolutely amazing."

"Yes, well, she does come from a very good alpha family, if I do say so myself," he responded.

"That's why I'm lucky to have her." Blake squeezed my hand, and I squeezed back, my heart swelling from how he always had my back.

About halfway through dinner, Nate, the manager of the Italian restaurant, came by to check in. I groaned internally. He walked over to Blake and suddenly looked at me, confusion on his face. He then looked back at Blake and said, "Alpha Blake, good evening. Thanks for coming in tonight. We're celebrating your fiancée's birthday and your engagement I understand?"

"Yes, that's correct." Blake stood up, pulling me up with him. "Let me introduce you to Jasmine, my soon-to-be luna."

"I believe we've met before, Jasmine." He looked at me, raising his eyebrows. "But congratulations on the engagement, and happy birthday as well."

I smiled at him, trying my best to push aside the pain in my chest from the reminder of when I'd met him previously.

After the dinner was over, Blake shook hands with everyone again and wished everyone a good night. When it was just the two of us, he pulled me close to him and said, "I'd like to buy you your first legal drink. And we'll definitely go somewhere other than this restaurant. I'd rather take you to where you and I had *our* first official date." He led me to the steakhouse where they seated us in the lounge area after we saw the bar was full. When we settled into our seats, Blake leaned over to me and said, "Sorry again about the choice of restaurant. I hope you enjoyed yourself anyway."

"It was a great surprise." I touched his arm. "I just hope my family didn't offend you too much. They're really intense."

"You never really got to know my father, but they were tame compared to him. I'm sure they were holding back since we're still strangers. But, either way, the way they acted tonight was nothing compared to what I went through with my father my whole life. Besides, they're your family, and I want them to be happy with the arrangement. I can tell they have opinions, but it could have gone much worse. Even they can't deny that being with an alpha is an upgrade from a beta." Blake smirked.

I ordered a cranberry mojito and Blake ordered a beer. We sat back in our seats and listened to the live music. After some time, I said, "I have to get up early for training tomorrow."

"Before I take you home, I did have one more surprise for tonight. I know we don't have an excuse to spend the whole night together, but I did book us a hotel room so I could give you your real birthday present, at least until your curfew." He rubbed his hand up and down my inner thigh.

"Suddenly getting a good night's rest doesn't feel that important anymore." I scrunched my nose and pulled his face toward mine.

"Once you move into the packhouse, you're not getting a good night's rest anymore at all, so get used to it."

Chapter 15

Talia

I awoke feeling the most relaxed I had in years. The most amazing sensation was fluttering up and down my skin, almost like sparks that both aroused and calmed me simultaneously, compelling me to practically moan from the pleasure floating through my body. And the scent—oh my, something smelled so delightful. I inhaled more deeply, allowing the fragrance to fill my lungs.

As I became more conscious, I realized I was not alone in my bed. No, there was a warm body, and we were wrapped in each other, with his morning wood pressing against my abdomen.

What the fuck?

I quickly pushed him from me, causing him to roll off the bed and fall to the floor with a loud thump. He groaned and shot up, staring at me from where he was seated on the floor.

"What are you doing in my bed?" I shrieked.

He looked around frantically, confusion on his face. I could sense he was panicked. Then realization played across his face, and he said, "This is my bedroom. You're in my bed!"

"What!" I looked around, realizing he was right. This was not the room I was staying in at all. "How did I get in here?"

"Your wolf must have brought you here."

"My wolf—?"

"Well, we are mates, so our inner wolves naturally want to be together. Since you're fighting the bond, your wolf must have possessed you in your sleep and brought you down here to be with me. It used to happen with my parents all the time. My mom would be pissed at my dad for something and go to sleep in another room, but she'd still end up in his bed by morning."

I glared at him with my brows furrowed at the mention of his dad, staring into his eyes that were just like *his*.

He must have sensed how angry I suddenly was because he continued speaking. "Of course, that was before you killed him. You're angry with me for my father's crimes, but I should really be the one who's angry with you. I wasn't involved in what my father did, but you were actually the person who murdered him. You should consider yourself lucky that I'm not avenging his death."

I turned away from him. "We shouldn't be together," I said quietly, sensing immediately that my words had hurt him. It was amazing that I could innately recognize how he was feeling. It somewhat softened me to him as I, begrudgingly, thought to myself he had a point.

He was quiet. After not hearing a response, I turned around to look at him. He was very handsome, sitting on the floor in only his boxer briefs, revealing how muscular he was, with huge arms, broad shoulders, well-defined pecs. My breath caught in my throat, and an almost electrical feeling flowed through me as I ogled him, regretting pushing him out of the bed. He looked up at me, not saying anything. I suddenly wished I could read his mind so I could know what he was thinking. He eventually got up and went to his duffel bag, threw on a T-shirt and pants, and walked out of the room, his footsteps disappearing down the hall. A part of me almost felt disappointed he had vanished from the room, something deep within drawing me to him.

Realizing I was still in a bed that wasn't mine, I left the room, went back upstairs to what was actually my room, and crawled into my own bed. I reached over to the bedside table where my cell phone was sitting and checked my text message thread with Hugo. My texts to him still showed as unread. That was very strange. It wasn't like him to not read or respond to my text messages. I hoped he'd reply soon because I wasn't sure how much longer my phone would remain in service. I was completely broke and had no way to pay my phone bill.

I sighed to myself and tears built up in my eyes. Lately, it seemed like all I wanted to do was cry. Maybe I was falling into a depression. I missed my mom. For so long, she was the only person I really truly had in my life, and now I no longer had her.

After some time, I finally got up and showered, getting ready for the day. I went downstairs to eat breakfast and was relieved no one was in the kitchen when I got there. I started brewing some coffee and grabbed a couple of slices of bread to make myself toast. Blake came in as I was finishing up and glimpsed over at the coffee machine. "Oh good, you made coffee. Do you mind if I have some?"

"No problem," I replied, having already taken enough for myself.

"I have it rough on Connie's days off. Normally I have to make it myself." Blake grabbed a mug out of the cabinet. "So how did you sleep?"

"Fine," I replied, recalling how rested I felt when I woke up that morning.

"Any plans today?" he asked. I sighed. After filling his mug, he sat down across from me. "I'm not a big talker either, but if you don't mind me asking, why don't you like your mate?"

I eyed him and debated whether to tell him anything. The thing was, I wasn't one to let people in easily, especially having grown up in the environment I had. Finally, I said, "I don't trust him."

"Why?" Blake asked, looking at me curiously.

"Because his father was evil."

"Rumor has it you murdered him?"

My stomach tightened in shock that he knew. I was completely unsure how to reply.

When I didn't respond he said, "I'm going to assume you had a good reason to."

I continued looking at him, not confirming or denying, my skin tingling with discomfort.

After some time, he said, "If that's the only reason you don't like him, maybe you should give him a chance. After all, he's giving you a chance after you killed his father. And I, personally, am not a fan when people compare me to my father. I hated the asshole." He then got up and left the kitchen with his mug.

After I finished my own coffee, I put my mug and plate into the dishwasher and walked out into the living room, taking a seat on the couch and pulling out my cell phone. The text message to Hugo was still unread. Maybe he lost his phone?

I lay back on the couch and turned on the TV, not having anything else to do. It was a very cozy room with the TV mounted over a wood-burning fireplace with very comfortable brown leather couches and soft throw blankets.

Alex walked in and stood over me, a large notebook in hand. "Looks like you have a busy day today."

I ignored him.

"If that's not the case, maybe we could go for a walk in the woods, and you can hang out with me while I sketch, eh? I normally sketch alone, but it might be nice to have some company."

"Why, so you can take me into the middle of the woods where no one will witness you avenging your father's death?" I asked sardonically.

He sat down in the chair I'd sat in yesterday and stared at me. "You know, you'd think you'd, at minimum, feel some empathy for the family you took my father from."

"I don't feel bad about what I did at all. He was evil and he deserved to die. I only wish I'd killed him sooner."

"If you were any colder, I'd mistake you for my sister."

"Must run in the family then."

"Well, yes, my sister does take after my father quite a bit actually. She was certainly the favorite. But I, on the other hand, do not. In case you were wondering."

"I wasn't."

"I really don't understand. Do you not feel the mate bond at all? Because I will be honest with you—I feel it a lot. And if I didn't, you'd already be dead. Because I have no qualms about avenging my father's death, even if he wasn't my favorite person in the world. He was still my father who raised me. He may have had a fucked-up way of showing it, but I know he had my best interest in mind."

"I don't want to feel the mate bond. I don't want to be with you," I said, feeling instantly that he was in pain, even if he didn't show it on his face. I continued anyway, "Blake said that I can formally reject you, so just let me know how to do that." As soon as the words left my mouth, a sharp pain pierced my chest, and I instinctively clutched at it.

"You do feel it, see?" he said. "That pain. It's unnatural to reject your mate, and even thinking about it hurts. It's because we're meant to be together. Also, just so you know, because of the bond, you don't need to worry about me avenging my father's death. Killing you would hurt me more than it would you. Losing a mate completely fucks a person up." I suddenly recalled Hugo's mom who was a shell of a person, alive but not really living.

"I don't want to feel it," I replied. "I don't want a mate. My mom didn't have one. Why do I have to have one?"

He suddenly leaned forward and looked at me more closely. I felt uncomfortable with his eyes staring so deeply into mine. "I know why you killed my father, by the way. It's because he killed your mom, right? You were avenging her death?"

I stared back at him, my chest tightening in discomfort. I was shocked that he knew and wondering how.

"Look, I'm really sorry. I can't say that I don't know what it's like to lose a parent. Goddess, this situation is really fucked-up, eh?"

"I should go," I said, starting to get up as tears gathered at my eyes. He put his hand on my thigh to stop me from standing. And that's when I felt it again—the sparks, a calmness pulsing through my body, making me forget why I had just been so upset. He moved his hand slowly, inching up my thigh, and then back down again. I found myself immobile, giving in to the feeling, my eyes closing from how satisfying it was.

The couch dipped next to me as he moved so he was seated next to me, his scent stronger now that he was closer, arousing my whole body. My inner thighs tingled, a shiver moving up my body. I opened my eyes and stared into his as he continued to rub my thigh, setting off a pulsing between my legs. My breathing shallowed and his face was now centimeters from mine, his rosy lips slightly parted. My heart beat rapidly in my chest as my lips mirrored his, inadvertently parting.

"Waaaa!!!" Lucy's baby screamed as Lucy carried her into the living area of the very open floor plan. I shook my head in realization of what was happening and got up, woken from my trance.

"Talia! Perfect! I need to run out. Here, take Libby." She pushed Libby into my arms, not even waiting for me to reply, and ran straight toward the front door.

I sighed and walked up the stairs, Libby wailing even more loudly now in my arms. A part of me was disappointed—while I was very wary of my mate, I couldn't deny that I was maybe just a little disheartened we hadn't kissed.

Chapter 16

Talia

It had now been about a week and a half since Alex arrived, and he showed no intention of leaving. I'd lock my door at night, waking up some mornings on the floor next to it. He was right. I was sleepwalking, trying to get to him. I tried to mostly stay up on the alpha floor, spending time watching TV in the private living room instead of downstairs where he would try to force me into conversations I had no interest in having. Sometimes he'd catch me during mealtime and invite me to go for a walk with him. One day, he left a bouquet of flowers on the kitchen table for me, with a note asking me to give him a chance.

He was very persistent; I'd give him that. But I couldn't get past his horrible eyes and that his father had killed my mother. The idea of being around anyone who was related to her murderer made my heart and lungs tear, constricting my air and blood flow.

One morning, after breakfast, a knock sounded on my door. I opened it, coming face-to-face with Lucy, surprised she didn't also have Libby in her arms, ready to hand her to me. I was convinced that Libby was the devil reincarnated as a baby, and she really made me reconsider mother-hood big time. I had gotten better at figuring out what Libby wanted at this point, but she was still a handful. "Yes?" I asked.

"My mom is watching Libby for the day. Would you maybe want to go for a run in our wolf forms with me? Luke doesn't want me running alone, so I figured I'd ask you to come with me."

I hesitated, not being a huge fan of Lucy. But it was either that or watch more horrible American television like Judge Judy and Maury. I agreed and went downstairs with her, where she walked me to the back of the packhouse and into the woods. "Just make sure you stay close to me because I can't mindlink you," she said to me as we peeled off our clothes.

"Mindlink?" I asked.

"When you live in a pack, you can communicate telepathically with others in your pack when you're in your wolf form. But since you're not a part of our pack, I can't do it with you."

"Oh," I replied, never knowing werewolves could do something like that. We took off on our run, and I followed Lucy. My mind slowly transitioned from my human brain to my wolf brain. A weight lifted off my shoulders as I began to think more instinctually.

Suddenly, I felt a strong urge to run in a separate direction. Instead of continuing to follow Lucy, I changed routes and headed on a different path through the woods, dodging trees, sprinting. Something deep within me was pulling me in this direction, which brought me to a rocky hill covered in pine cones and moss.

I effortlessly climbed the rocky terrain with my sharp claws, scraping them against the boulders. I reached the top and glanced down below, my mouth dropping in awe. The view was breathtaking—overlooking a river with wildflowers growing along its grassy spots. I took a few moments to take it all in, breathing in the crisp air, mossy earth and rocks, and pine.

I ascended further until I hit a plateau and walked across. Looking down the other side of the hill, I spotted Alex perched on a ledge, a large pad balanced against the thigh of his bent leg, deep in concentration as he moved a pencil across the paper. He looked so peaceful, and I found myself captivated, unable to tear my eyes from him, his dirty-blond hair ruffled by the wind, and his cheeks slightly pink from the cool weather.

A strong breeze blew in his direction and he smiled. Still concentrated on his drawing, he called out, "I'd recognize that scent anywhere." When I didn't reply, he looked up and caught me staring at him, locking his eyes with mine. "Your wolf form is just as beautiful as your human one," he said, continuing to smile.

Instinctively desiring to be near him, I descended the rocky terrain and sat down next to him. He put his sketch pad down on the other side of him and brushed his hands through my fur, the familiar and magical feeling of sparks reverberating through my body. I laid my head in his lap, closed my eyes, and purred. Could wolves purr? My wolf certainly could.

"Your wolf is much more amiable, eh? You must have not bonded much with her in your life, because it seems she has complete control in this form." He put his head down on top of mine, rubbing it into my fur. His chest moved against me as he inhaled deeply, the thumping of his heart so audible now with him so close. I could sense he felt blissful, making me purr again. I'd, likewise, never felt so heavenly before, giving in to the moment, feeling as if there was nowhere else I'd rather be than here with my mate.

After some time, he lifted his head, continuing to brush his hands through my fur and said, "If you want, I can train you to have more control over your wolf. It's something you're taught if you grow up in a pack. But I can't lie, it's nice that you don't. I can finally be close to you."

We stayed lost in each other, my head in his lap, his fingers caressing me. The only sounds were the river moving below and leaves rustling in the wind. He finally broke the silence and said, "Can I sketch you? I'd love to draw a picture of your wolf. Just sit up." Knowing I would do anything he asked, I pulled my head out of his lap and backed up, sitting up straight.

"Perfect. You are so beautiful, majestic!" He smiled, grabbing his pad and pencil from next to him, and turning his body so he was facing me. He bent his knees, and balanced his sketch pad back on his thighs, soon absorbed in his art, his eyes constantly glancing at me over his pad. I sat still, staring at him. He was so handsome with angled cheekbones and a strong jaw, his beard giving him a slightly rugged look. He looked almost angelic as he concentrated on his drawing, his blond eyelashes catching the rays of the sun. Why had I ever wanted to stay away from him?

After he'd been sketching for a while, he said, "Maybe that's why you don't feel the mate bond as strongly as I do—because you never really bonded with your wolf, so your two beings are not communicating properly." He glanced at me for a longer period of time now. As I stared into his eyes, I realized they weren't threatening. While, on the surface, they seemed similar to *his* eyes, Alex's eyes were much softer, kinder, warmer.

As if reading my mind, he said, "You have the most amazing eyes I've ever seen. They are the most distinct shade of blue. And when you look at me, it's like you can see into my soul. I almost wish I were a painter so I could paint them and challenge myself to recreate them on paper. But I don't think I could ever mix enough paint to get the shade quite right. Besides, part of what makes your eyes so beautiful is how expressive they are. Paper wouldn't be the right medium for them." He looked back down at his pad and continued his drawing. We must have sat there for at least an hour, if not longer, mostly in silence, listening to the sounds of nature and Alex's pencil brushing against paper.

After he finished, he turned the pad around so I could see his work. He was very good, professional. I could see how much painstaking effort he'd put into every detail. I purred with delight, wanting him to know how much I liked it, wagging my tail. He smiled widely, as if I had made his entire year. I walked back over to him, and he put his pad down. When I got close enough, he put his arms around my neck, bringing his hands to my head and rubbing me behind the ears, eliciting another purr from me. I licked his cheek, wanting to show him affection in return.

"I'm really sorry about your mom, Talia," he said, keeping his head down as he looked up into my eyes. "Maybe once you're back in your human form again you can tell me why my father did it. As bad as he was, I never knew him to be a straight-up murderer, and I especially can't imagine him killing a beautiful woman like your mom. I saw her picture on your phone lock screen."

I whimpered at the mention of my mom, the wind suddenly chilly against my body and my chest heavy. I didn't want to be around him anymore, so I got up. My feet taking control, I sprinted back to the packhouse with an urgent need to be alone. I found where I'd left my clothing and saw that Lucy's was gone. Oops, I'd completely abandoned her.

I shifted back into my human form and got dressed quickly, finding the glass door to the living room locked. I knocked on it, hoping someone would hear me. When no one came, I walked around to the front and rang the doorbell. Wendy, the housekeeper, let me in, and I ran up to my room, falling into my bed.

I tried to process what had just happened, clutching at my racing heart. I'd been so intimate with Alex without meaning to, and—I blinked a few times—I kind of liked it. No, I really liked it. Well, my wolf really liked it. Whoever that was out there, that wasn't me. Blame it on the Goose—er—wolf.

Pushing everything from my mind, I pulled my phone off the bedside table and checked it again. I'd tried calling Hugo a few times during the past couple weeks, and the calls all went straight to voice mail. I checked his Instagram, which had no updates. He did rarely update it anyway, so that part wasn't so weird. But it was as if he'd dropped off the face of the earth.

Scrolling through his feed, I saw his brother tagged in one of his posts, giving me an idea. I quickly typed up a DM.

Hey Rocco, it's Talia. Haven't heard from Hugo in a while. Is he ok?

I didn't see a response come back by the time dinner rolled around, so I made my way downstairs to see what Connie had left for us. Fortunately, the people who lived in the packhouse didn't eat meals together. Better for me, since I liked to spend as little time socializing with everyone as I could.

"There you are!" Lucy shouted as soon as I got downstairs. She was holding Libby and giving me a death glare. "Where the hell did you go during our run?"

"Sorry," I replied.

"Why did you just run off like that?"

"I don't know."

"What do you mean you don't know? Obviously, there's a reason you would just leave like that, especially after I told you to stay with me."

I shrugged, not sure what to tell her.

"You're very strange." She shook her head. "I should have known better than to trust a rogue."

Well, she certainly trusted me watching her spawn of Satan.

I went into the kitchen where Connie had left a large pot of beef stew on top of the stove. I spooned some into a bowl and heated it in the microwave, then sat down to eat it quickly. After I put the bowl into the dishwasher, I went back upstairs and watched TV, eventually falling asleep on the couch.

However, that wasn't where I woke up early the next morning. No, I woke up in a very familiar position, feeling simultaneously relaxed and aroused, sparks dancing across my skin, a warm body spooning me, his very prominent boner pressed up against my butt.

I gasped, rolling away from him, falling out of the bed, and landing with a loud thud. Ouch, I definitely hit my tailbone.

He shot up, his eyes wide and mouth falling open with a gasp, and then looked down at me. "Are you okay?" he asked, the corners of his mouth lifting upward.

I groaned, standing up.

"Plenty of room if you want to get back into bed," he said, moving over and making more room for me, patting the empty spot next to him.

"No thanks," I said, turning around to leave the room. I couldn't believe that happened again. I could sense he was disappointed as I walked out. I quickly went back upstairs, locking my bedroom door, and falling into my own bed where I went back to sleep.

Chapter 17

Talia

I managed to avoid him for the whole day after waking in his bed again. After my wolf had possessed me during my run the day prior, I didn't want him to get the wrong idea. Although, there was a part of me that longed to be close with him like that again. I tried to shove it from my mind.

After spending the day watching Libby so Lucy could go to work, I was exhausted. I ended the day watching TikTok videos on my phone and eventually drifted into sleep.

The next morning, I awoke, again a feeling of bliss and arousal overtaking my body, the most intoxicating and sensual scent overwhelming my senses. Before I could stop myself, my hands instinctively moved to his body, feeling his abs flex under my fingertips, sparks moving through my hands and arms as I made skin-to-skin contact. I couldn't bring myself to cease what I was doing as I rubbed my hands all over his ripped body, enthralled by the curves of the hard muscles lining his core and chest. He moaned, and I opened my eyes to him staring at me. His eyes no longer felt threatening—no, they felt inviting, sexy.

He moved his mouth toward mine, slowly. When I didn't stop him, his lips gently touched mine. And that's when I lost myself in him, his lips parting as I pressed my entire body against him, giving in completely to the kiss, desperate to have him. I drew his tongue into my mouth. Nothing had ever tasted so right. It was as if I were possessed as our mouths took what they could from each other. His hands grabbed my behind, and I wrapped my leg around him, pressing myself against his erection, and realized that he was really packing.

Damn!

Completely turned on, possessed by his enchanting scent and the sensations triggered by his touch, I began rubbing myself against his shaft. He groaned into my mouth as he rolled onto his back and I likewise rolled on top of him, better positioning myself to continue in the same motion. Sparks, dulled by the minimal clothing we had on, surfaced, heightening the pleasure I felt.

He brought his hand under the silky camisole I was wearing, instantly finding my breast, stimulating my nipple as I continued to rub myself on him. It had never felt so good to have my nipple stroked before, the sparks electrifying my whole body. The accumulation of deep pleasure built within me. I softly moaned, looking down at his face, which could not have looked more blissful. His free hand gripped my hip firmly as his body shook under me, encouraging me to move more aggressively. Before I knew it, the most intense orgasm I'd ever felt exploded within my body, sending a feeling of profound tranquility to my fingertips and toes. A deep and gratifying groan departed his lips in chorus with the eruption within my body, giving voice to the phenomenon that occurred within me.

Oh my God! I can't believe I just dry humped him. And I can't believe how amazing it felt. It was better than any sex I'd ever had in my life. I looked down at his soaked boxer briefs and then up his body to him staring up at me, his breathing heavy.

I took myself out of the straddling position I was in and lay back down next to him, continuing to stare into his eyes.

He smiled at me and said, "Well, good morning to you too." He brushed his hand down my arm, tranquility flowing from his fingers as they caressed my skin.

I closed my eyes and emitted a purr that came from within.

"Did your wolf now completely take over your human form?" he asked.

"I don't know, but that was amazing," I replied.

"It was definitely the best wake-up call I've ever had." He chuckled, kissing me softly. "Can I replace my alarm clock with you?" He kissed me again. I moved closer to him, putting my hands on his shoulders, loving the feeling of how broad and powerful they were. He clearly didn't skip workouts. After more kissing, he pulled away and asked, "Does this mean you're finally willing to give me a chance?"

I nodded into his chest, not wanting to be away from him anymore.

And that was how the best five days of my life, up until that moment, began. After spending the day hiking and sitting with Alex while he sketched, we returned home where I was disappointed to find that my period had started. After the most amazing intimate experience I'd ever had, I was looking forward to the real thing later that evening. But it would have to be put on hold, at least for a few days.

That night, I invited him up to my bedroom. "Sorry, we can't do anything. It's my time of the month," I said.

"That's okay, I just want to be near you." He snuggled up against me. We lay close together, whispering to each other when loud moans echoed from the wall that divided my bedroom from Blake's. We both snickered.

"The walls are thin, eh?" He laughed.

"They're always going at it, like rabbits." I giggled. "You'd never guess with how innocent Jasmine acts, eh?"

He laughed again and said, "I can't lie and say it isn't killing me right now, listening to them when all I want is to do the same thing to you."

I snuggled into him as he rubbed my back, his boner throbbing against me.

"I could always help you with that," I said, rubbing my hand against the bulge in his boxer briefs. He groaned and looked at me. I could sense he had a strong desire for me to make good on my offer. I slipped down his body and pulled off his briefs. Damn, he was huge! I mean, I had gathered as much after that morning, but seeing it now in the flesh, my eyes widened, wondering if my jaw would make it. Trying not to overthink it, I put my hand and mouth on it, and began to gently suck as I bobbed my head up and down.

Through his moans he said, "A blow job from your mate is the most amazing thing I've ever felt."

Encouraged by his pleasure, I continued moving my mouth up and down his shaft in sync with my hand. It was almost like I could feel how good it felt for him as I did it. Before long, he was shaking and let out a loud groan as warm liquid filled my mouth. I quickly swallowed it and moved back up to the pillow to be next to him.

He turned to me and said, "That was amazing. I promise to return the favor as soon as I can. In fact, I'll do it tenfold, a hundredfold." He snuggled me back against him.

That was how we spent the next few days, not being able to get enough of each other. He'd help me with Libby when I had to babysit, and I kept him company while he sketched. We'd go to the gym together, where he began training me in self-defense, desiring me to go back to his pack with him and live as one of them. I was already gearing up to pack my bags and say goodbye to my brother.

Chapter 18

Talia

After the blissful few days we spent together, I woke up alone one morning, his side of the bed cold and his scent already faded. I'd gotten used to waking up wrapped in him and felt disappointed by the loss. I picked up my cell phone and saw that I had a notification from Instagram. I opened the app to see that a reply from Rocco had finally been received.

Hugo got put in jail after you killed Alpha Sr.

I stared at my phone reading and rereading the message that was returned to me, feeling immobile. While I'd been on this trip, my friend had been living in a jail cell. I felt like a complete idiot for never even considering that my actions could have had consequences for my friend. I was suddenly nauseous, wrapping my arms around my stomach. And then I realized who must have put him in there.

I marched downstairs and knocked on his door. When he didn't reply, I threw it open, noticing immediately that his duffel bag was gone. I ran downstairs searching for him and looked out at the lot to see his car was gone. I ran into the office where Blake and Luke were seated together at a desk. "Where's Alex?" I asked.

"He left early this morning, in a hurry to go back to his pack," Blake replied. "Why? Do you suddenly like your mate now that he's playing hard to get?" He smirked.

"Oh no," I cried.

"What's wrong?" Blake asked as he and Luke looked over at me.

"Did he say why he left?"

"No, just said it was urgent."

"I need to talk to him. It's very important," I said.

"Here, you can use my phone," Blake said, unlocking his phone and scrolling through his contacts. He handed it to me. Straight to voice mail. I tried redialing. Same thing.

"Straight to voice mail," I said.

"Maybe he's out of a service area. We are pretty far out in the woods, and his pack is too. You can try again in a bit."

I nodded.

"What's the emergency anyway?"

"I have to go." In a panic, I ran back up to my bedroom, and my eyes fell to a ripped paper on the nightstand next to my bed. With shaky hands, I picked it up.

Sorry, had to return to my pack. I'll be back again very soon. Already miss you. A.

I stared at the note. Why would he have left so suddenly with barely a word? Either way, I had to go back to his pack too and get my friend out of jail. I could possibly run there in one to two days in my wolf form, depending on how long I spent sleeping and hunting for food. Rather than waste time, I descended the stairs and ran out the sliding glass door into the woods, immediately shifting into my wolf and leaping into a sprint. My wolf knew where to go.

After almost two days of running, I finally arrived at his pack on a Wednesday in the early morning, while it was still dark out, having spent the bare minimum amount of time sleeping and hunting. I couldn't lie, I was exhausted, especially after running almost nonstop for all that time. I had never physically exerted myself so much before, and I was shocked I was even able to do so. I hunted once a day, just to make sure I got something into my stomach. I was both desperate to see my friend and full of longing for Alex. My inner wolf was energized by the thought of being near him again, which gave me the stamina I needed to make it all the way.

I entered the pack through the woods, running past the border. As soon as I crossed into the territory, I immediately found myself tackled and pinned down by two wolves, my body hitting the hard ground before I could even understand what was happening.

A third wolf emerged, shifting into his human form. "Shift now, rogue!" he commanded. "Or else."

Not wanting to find out what the *or else* was, I quickly shifted. The man in his human form instantly lifted me up as if I were a rag doll and pulled my arms behind my back aggressively, paining my shoulders. I cried out in response. One of the wolves that was pinning me down sprinted away. The other one looked at me menacingly, baring his teeth. My pulse raced, and my muscles tensed. My hands and fingers were shaking uncontrollably. Where was Alex? Certainly, he wouldn't have allowed his pack members to treat me like this. I recalled how upset Blake had been when Jasmine was mistreated by his pack members.

The wolf that sprinted away returned with something in his mouth. I realized with horror that it was a chain. He dropped it to the ground and shifted into his human form. They aggressively brought my hands in front of my body, and even though I was complying, they still held me far too firmly as they chained them together, the grip of their fingers bruising me. Once I was chained and restricted, they pulled me along like a leashed dog.

"Where are you taking me?" I asked, my voice desperate and shaky.

"You're going straight to the cells. Alpha's orders," one of them replied.

"Why?" I asked, tears threatening to spill from my eyes.

"I'm going to assume for the murder of his father. And trust me, the cells are the least of your worries. Once Alpha gets his hands on you, you'll be begging for death. He doesn't fuck around."

The tears were now running freely down my face. Had he really ordered them to put me into the cells? But why? Was this his plan all along? Get me away from Blake's pack so he could finally do what he really wanted to?

"Do I get a phone call?" I asked. Maybe I could call Blake for help. I didn't know his phone number, but someone could probably look it up. He was an alpha after all, and I'm sure they all communicated with each other.

"What do you think this is? A democracy? You're on pack land now. No phone calls. Once you're in the cells, the alpha decides your fate."

They threw me into the back of an SUV and drove me somewhere on the outskirts of the pack. They then brought me into a cement building with steel bars around every window. As we passed through the jail, I glanced at Hugo who was sitting in his own cell. He got up with his eyes wide and mouth open as he recognized me. I was so ashamed, being dragged through the jail like this, completely naked. They didn't even have the decency to give me some clothes. At least in Blake's pack they had done that.

They opened a door and threw me in. Just a small bed and a toilet with no seat, and no privacy. The floor, walls, and ceiling were all cement, and steel bars for a door.

"Sorry, we can't remove the chains. The alpha can't command you if you're not part of the pack, so we have to keep them on," the man who had led me into the jail said. As soon as they locked the door behind me, I crawled into the bed, getting under the blanket. It smelled stale, like it hadn't been changed in ages. My tears quickly turned into full-on sobs. Why did I come here? Why did I allow myself to trust Alex? After all, he had put my friend in jail, and now I was in jail too. What was he going to do to me? Was this the end of my life? Would I soon be reunited with my mother?

I attempted to shift into my wolf, but it was fruitless. They had locked the heavy chains tightly around my wrists and arms. As soon as I tried, I screamed in pain as my bones tried to stretch against the metal to accommodate the shift, the process immediately halting. I needed room to shift. If clothing were the only obstacle, I would have just torn through it. But my bones couldn't tear through heavy steel.

I lay like that for a long time, crying, not knowing what was going to happen next. And then, finally, someone came to the door and peered in. I looked up to see a very pretty blonde woman with a pixie cut, looking to be in her early twenties, staring in at me. I realized she had a close resemblance to Alex with dirty-blonde hair and eyes like *his*. Hers were much more like *his* than Alex's. Hers were evil, ominous. She looked at me with murder on her face.

"Unfortunately, I promised Alex I'd leave you alive and in one piece for him," she said. "But, fortunately for me, werewolves heal quite nicely. We can't let my brother have all the fun, eh? He was my father too, after all." She pulled out a blade. "Recognize this?" she asked me, an evil smile on her face.

I gasped, realizing right away it was the same one I had shoved into *his* back. I had owned that blade for years, sleeping with it under my pillow just in case.

"John!" she called. "Chain up her legs too. We're going to have some fun today."

A man came over with another chain. They unlocked the door and she instantly sprinted to the bed, pulling my feet so I fell to the cement floor. She held my legs up as I tried to kick them, but she was very strong. She effortlessly kept them in place while the man chained them.

"Safety first." She smiled as soon as he was done chaining me. She had the sickest smile I'd ever seen in my life.

"Now, let's see. Where should we start? We have to keep you alive and in one piece, so no removing of organs or limbs. Luckily werewolves are very difficult to scar, so that leaves plenty of options."

I whimpered, terrified. I could tell that she was completely evil, just like her father had been.

"Hmm, well you do have a nice set of long legs. Let's see how sharp this knife is." Before I could even wonder what she meant, she shoved it into my thigh and dragged it down the length of my left leg.

I screamed in agony. I'd never felt such excruciating pain in my life.

"Nice blade, very sharp." She smiled mockingly. "Let's check the quality and see how many times I can drag it through your skin before it dulls." She then dragged it down my right leg, a sick smile on her face again.

I was surprised I didn't pass out with how terrible the pain was. It was even worse seeing her smile like that, clearly enjoying what she was doing to me.

"Such a pretty face you have," she said, bringing hers closer to mine. "I'd love to mutilate it," she sneered. She made cuts all over my face. I could feel blood seeping from my forehead, cheeks, chin, all gathering at my neck, and mixing with my tears, which burned the cuts on my face. "I'd love to cut that nose and those ears off too, but unfortunately, I made a promise."

She made a shallow cut down my neck and dragged it down each arm, deepening the depth of the knife in my body as she went. I had been screaming so much by the time she finished with my arms that my throat was in pain, my screams hoarse. She cut down the center of my chest, right between my breasts.

"Very nice blade," she said, inspecting it, turning it in her hands so she could check every angle. "I think I might keep it for myself. Very good quality." She looked down at me from her standing position and then crouched back down. "Now, for the grand finale." She smiled menacingly. Why did she have to smile? Just as quickly as she had spoken, she shoved the blade deep into my stomach, where I was certain it must have also punctured my back, and drew it back out, spraying blood violently, dark red liquid staining my torso and pooling underneath and next to me on the floor.

As if this was just another day on the job, she turned her back and walked out, simply telling John to lock me back up. He looked at me with pity as he locked the door and then walked away. I used nearly all my strength to crawl over to the bed, lifting the heavy chains and using what little strength I had left within me to pull myself into the bed.

The cuts in my torso tore as I moved, the sharp pain not allowing me to forget the traumatic experience, not allowing the healing process to begin. Everything hurt. It was so painful that I'd have preferred not to be alive anymore. It was the type of pain where even your gums and bones screamed in agony, your whole body rejecting its existence in this world.

I cried into the pillow, feeling blood flowing out of my stomach and back, soaking the mattress. How much blood did werewolves have? I knew humans could bleed to death. Could werewolves too? When Alex came, would he do worse? I didn't think I could handle it. I was now begging God to let me bleed to death. For Alex to treat me like this crazy bitch just had would destroy me.

Chapter 19

Jasmine

On Monday, I arrived at training after going to temple service that morning. We were on a new rotation, and I'd be part of a different group with a new instructor. I was surprised to see that Lucy was joining our sparring session that morning. All pack members had to spar for two hours every other week, and they signed up anywhere there was space. Lucy had clearly chosen this one.

She instantly spotted me and came over to say, "I love when I can get into a session with Charlie Kemp. All you have to do is flirt with him a little, and he's like putty in your hands."

At the mention of his name, dread filled the pit of my stomach. I knew that Blake's former friend, who had accosted me almost a year ago, was a warrior, but I didn't know he was also a trainer. I hadn't bothered to check which trainer I'd be working with when I got Luke's email with the new schedules. It wasn't like I could have changed who it was anyway. I mean, realistically, I probably could just ask Blake to switch some things around, but I wasn't someone to make waves and be picky like that. And I tried to ask Blake for as little help as possible for two main reasons: one, I liked to prove myself without anyone's help, and two, I already got enough crap for being the alpha's pet. I didn't need my fellow female warriors to have more reasons to tease me for preferential treatment.

At the sound of the bell signaling the beginning of the session, Charlie strutted onto the field looking around, openly leering at a female warrior who was bent over stretching, not even trying to be stealthy. He actually wasn't terrible looking—a tall redhead with lean muscle. But he was a creep.

He walked over to Lucy and me and smiled.

"Ooh, Charlie, have you been working out? Your arms are looking so much bigger than last time I saw you," Lucy exclaimed, touching his bicep.

He then looked at me, clearly expecting something from me. I ignored him and didn't say anything. If Lucy wanted to demean herself to get out of training that was on her. I wasn't one to stoop to her level—I did things the right way.

As he was about to turn to walk away, Lucy stopped him and said, "You know, Charlie, breastfeeding has really strained my body. I think I should take it easy today."

I looked back over to Charlie staring straight down Lucy's shirt, which was quite low-cut, I must add.

"Hmm, yeah, I can see where that could take a lot out of you. I can assign you some less strenuous exercises." Likely some awkwardly sexual yoga positions, deadlifts, and glute thrusts. He turned away from Lucy after spending far too long staring at her chest, clearly recalling he was supposed to be teaching a class. "Okay, everyone, let's start with a warm-up run! One mile!"

"Mind if I walk?" Lucy fluttered her eyelashes at him and touched his chest.

"You're obviously going through a lot right now, Lucy, so do whatever feels comfortable," he replied, smiling at her.

Gag!

I started off on my run, taking the usual one-mile route that we'd all memorized from the time we were in school. We had routes set up for all different lengths, which made it easier for trainers to call out commands without needing to explain anything. I was easily able to keep up with all the other female warriors. Although I'd lost out on two years of official training, I had always taken even my civilian training very seriously. Thank Goddess for that, because I didn't need more things for them to pick on me for.

Tina, one of the girls that was in my group now, paced herself so she was running right next to me. "Who are you gonna get fired next?"

"What?" I asked.

"Don't play dumb, PJ. Alyssa told us everything. She hurt your friend's feelings, so you cried to Daddy to fire her."

I stared at her wide-eyed, in disbelief. The only reason Alyssa hadn't been banished was because of me. In the end, Blake had decided to just discharge Alyssa from her warrior duties and put her in the cells for a week as punishment.

After shaking the shock from my mind, I retorted with, "Wow, Tina, I didn't even realize your mind was capable of that kind of mental aerobics. If only you were that skilled in the field." I sprinted away and mentally gave myself a high five. I wasn't usually great at coming up with comebacks.

When we returned, Charlie had us do twenty-five push-ups, twenty-five sit-ups, twenty-five jump squats, and twenty-five skater jumps. I efficiently performed all the exercises and Charlie came over to me, getting uncomfortably close.

"Bad form. Do it again," he said, walking away.

I *knew* that I had good form. I was always adamant about not getting lazy with using proper form. But what was I supposed to do? I had to do the exercises again as he gathered everyone to explain the sparring exercises. The three female warriors who were in my new group snickered together as they glanced over at me. Everyone began shifting into their wolf forms and being paired off. Once I completed the last skater jump and started to head over to the group, Charlie yelled, "Still bad form, Dale. Try again."

What was his problem? Did he really still have a chip on his shoulder over what had happened almost a year ago?

I went through the cycle of exercises again. After I completed them for the third time, making sure my form couldn't be any more perfect, Charlie yelled, "Three miles, Dale. Watching you try so hard and fail is embarrassing." Holding my head up high, I did as he said, relieved to have an excuse to get away from him anyway. Once I got back, I found that Lucy had finished her mile walk.

"Now get into your wolf forms and start practicing the side knock-over."

Lucy headed toward the changing partitions, and I went to follow her when Charlie stopped me. "Dale, you're a warrior. Partitions are for civilian pack members."

Holy shit! He was really going to make me shift in front of everyone! What a creep! I'd never had any other trainer harp on me for this. Sure, just about everyone else had no problem shifting in front of the group, but I was still a modest person, and there were civilians in our group today. Understandably, sure, if we were in battle, I'd likely have no choice. But for training?!

"No thanks," I said, holding strong and walking away.

"I'm writing you up for this, Dale!" he yelled at me as I walked away, not caring.

Fine, write me up. I'd rather be written up than strip on command for him. Once I was shifted, I went to spar with Lucy. I went easy on her, since she obviously wasn't good at anything that required any type of athleticism.

When it was her turn to attack me, I let her tackle me a few times, even though I knew I could have easily dodged all her attacks.

"Very nice, Hemming!" Charlie nodded at Lucy. "And you call yourself a warrior, Dale?" he tutted at me.

Goddess, what a jerk! I couldn't believe Blake had ever been friends with him. By this point, I'd worked with tons of trainers, and none of them had ever treated me like this.

After the two hours of sparring were up, Lucy left to go home. Unfortunately, I was stuck with Charlie for the rest of the day for our other planned activities. I felt dread, realizing it was going to be a very long two-month rotation.

Chapter 20

Alexander

It was early on a Monday morning when I heard my phone vibrate on the bedside table next to me. I ignored it at first, and ignored it again, assuming whoever it was would just reach out to my beta next. But then it kept vibrating, so I knew it had to be important. I carefully crawled out from the arms of my mate, letting her sleep, already missing her touch as soon as my body was apart from hers.

I snuck into the hallway to take the call, descending the stairs. "Yes," I said, as soon as my feet hit the first few steps.

"Alex, you have to come home," my sister said frantically. "Mom tried to kill herself."

I thought my heart had stopped. While my father's death was upsetting, my mother's death would be devastating. "Fuck," I said, not knowing what else to say. "I'll jump in my car right now. I'm just over four hours away."

I quickly ran into my room and threw my bag together. Before I left, I tore a piece of paper from my sketch pad, and wrote a quick note to my mate so she wouldn't worry. I didn't want to wake her. As soon as I dealt with my mom, I would come back, hopefully, to bring my mate back home with me this time. I wanted to take her now, but I had to deal with this alone. No, it'd be best if I came back later for her.

As I was leaving, I crossed paths with Blake entering the packhouse in his gym clothes. "Going somewhere?" he asked. "Did my sister finally kick you to the curb for good?"

"I have to head back to my pack. It's urgent," I responded.

"No mate?"

"I'll be back for her soon."

I threw my duffel bag into the back seat, my sketch pad on the front one, and jumped into the driver's seat, speeding off the pack land, realizing as I drove that it was also Canadian Thanksgiving. It had completely slipped my mind while I was in the states. And then I realized I should have seen the signs. My mom was normally overly enthusiastic about holidays, and it should have concerned me that she wasn't calling to make plans and to be sure I'd be home that day. Well, I'd certainly be home that day now.

Hopefully we could get some professional help for my mom and get her someone to look after her. Once she was being taken care of, then I'd come back for Talia. I can't lie and say that the past few days I'd spent with her weren't some of the best days I'd ever had in my life. We were absolutely perfect for each other. Now that I had gotten to know her, I understood why the Moon Goddess had gifted her to me. I smiled as I drove, thinking about her, her perfect body, and everything I wanted to do to it once she was finally off her period. It had been killing me to wait. Although I can't lie, she gave the most amazing blow jobs, so it really hadn't been that bad at all. I didn't even dare wonder how she was so good at them, preferring just to enjoy them as she bestowed them on me.

While the ride was off to a smooth start, when you're me, nothing ever really goes as it's supposed to. As if the universe was against me, I got stuck at the border for hours. For some reason, there was a much longer line of cars than usual waiting to cross. Once it was my turn, they forced me to go inside the facility to question me. Okay, part of that may have been a couple of simple assault convictions on my record, due to some bar fights I'd been involved in when I was younger and angrier. But I didn't think they'd treat them as if I'd been charged with aggravated assault. Not that I wasn't guilty of that too, but Canada's justice system wasn't exactly privy to that information.

By the time I'd made it through the line, and they were done questioning me, it was already almost dusk. I was finally on my way when I found myself somewhere between Montreal and Ottawa, speeding along the highway, and a moose came out of nowhere. I must have been too busy daydreaming to notice it in time because my car slammed right into it. It shattered my windshield with its antlers, peeled back the roof of my car with its five-hundred-kilogram body, and ended up in my back seat, dead on impact.

I crawled out of the car with only some minor injuries—nothing that wouldn't heal quickly. Of course, nothing ever goes easy for me. Because most rental car shops in the area were already closed by the time the police arrived on the scene, the animal was removed, and a tow truck took my car, I ended up spending the night at a nearby hotel.

Once my insurance company determined my car was a total loss, I suddenly recalled that I'd left my sketch pad inside of it. While normally this would have only been a slight disappointment, as I mostly just drew as a hobby and didn't do much with the drawings, this time one of the pictures was particularly important to me and I couldn't stand the idea of losing it. If I hadn't cared so much about saving that portrait, I could have just hopped in my rental car and made it back with minimal delay. But, instead, I spent the day scouring the local scrapyards until I finally located my totaled car. Miraculously, the car had not yet been impounded for metal. Using my werewolf strength, I was able to pry open the passenger side door and recover the pad.

I was about to drive home when I exited the scrapyard to find my rental car had been stolen. I mean, crazy things happened to me all the time, but my luck had never been quite so shitty before. Okay, there had been quite a few near-death experiences, one of which Blake had saved me from. But Artemis, what were you doing to me? I just wanted to get home to my mom. I ended up having to spend another night away from home as I considered whether I should just run back in my wolf form. Not wanting to leave my sketch pad behind or possibly damage it while carrying it in my mouth, I booked a hotel room.

By the time I made it back to the pack, it was Wednesday afternoon. I walked into the packhouse where my sister seemed oddly chipper considering the news that had brought me home. "After you go see Mom, I have a surprise for you." She smiled, looking unhinged. Okay, my sister pretty much always looked unhinged, so this was just par for the course.

I spent the next few hours visiting with my mom and sister at the pack hospital. "I'm sorry, Alex. It just hurts so much. Please come back so I can at least be with my son." She sobbed as I hugged her, feeling bad I'd left my mom during a time of so much distress for her. Although my father had never been a good husband to her, she couldn't fight the mate bond during the marriage or now after his departure from the earth.

Once we left, I felt morose, wondering what to do. I didn't want to leave my mother, but I also missed my mate. I was desperate to return to her.

"I have something that will cheer you up. Come, let me bring you to your surprise." My sister pulled at my hand. Not in the mood for a surprise but also not feeling like an argument, I went along with Sara as she drove us to the pack jail. Of course, my sister had found someone to torture. While torture cheered my sister up considerably, it wasn't really something I was in the mood for right then. I sighed as I followed her in. I could always let her do the honors—something she'd never turn down.

She had me walk ahead of her, practically skipping with glee behind me. As soon as I planted myself in front of the correct cell, my blood ran cold, and an overwhelming nausea brought bile to my throat. I didn't know how she got in there, but my poor mate was chained and shaking, completely naked and stained with dried blood, on a bed that was so soaked with blood that it was crimson rather than white. Large blood splotches stained the cement floor. When she made eye contact with me, she yelped, backing herself against the wall, trying to get farther away. I sensed panic, her eyes haunted, lips parted in silent terror, blood draining from her face—chilling fear.

"What the fuck did you do to my mate?" I bellowed at Sara, anger overtaking me. I could feel that fur was sprouting up my arms and legs, my canines growing, my claws extending.

"Your WHAT?" she shouted back at me.

"You fucking bitch!" I yelled at her, using the claws in my half-shifted form to swipe across her face with so much impact she fell over onto the floor. My claws retracted as I gained more control over my shifting. She tried to get up and I balled my hand into a fist, ready to beat her to death for what she had done.

"What the hell is wrong with you! That rogue killed our father!" she spit at me.

"And I fucking told you not to touch her!"

"She's still alive and in one piece!" She rolled her eyes. "And if you don't fucking finish my job, I will, because that rogue bitch deserves to die. Even if you don't give a shit about Dad, you should at least care about Mom and what his death has done to her!"

"Get. The. Fuck. Out. Of. Here." I gritted my teeth as I commanded her using my alpha aura. Unable to overcome it, she bared her neck to me, looking pained, and walked herself out of the building.

I took the keys from the guard and went back to my mate. My stomach contracted as I took in the scene again. Tears fell from her eyes as she trembled, her whole body pressed against the wall next to her bed, trying to get away from me as I came closer. I placed my hand gently on her arm as she flinched, looking as if I was causing her physical pain.

I took her hands in mine and undid the chains from them, letting them fall to the ground. As soon as she was freed, she began hitting me, over and over again. I grabbed her wrists as gently as I could. "Please, Talia, stop. I'm not going to hurt you." I stared into her eyes, her beautiful blue eyes that had a look of horror in them.

She didn't say anything, but I could feel that she was angry, hurt, and scared. Tears threatened to fall from my own eyes, feeling so much disgust at what my pack and sister had done to my mate.

"I'm going to let go of your hands so I can unchain your legs, okay?" I said as gently as I could. I waited until she nodded, and then I moved to unchain them.

She continued to lie there, the look of a deer in headlights on her face.

"Talia, I am so sorry for what happened and whatever my sister did to you. I would never have allowed someone to hurt you like this. Please, I want to help you, Talia." I felt small and desperate. I tried to touch her again and she instantly brought her hands to her face, instinctively hiding herself from me.

I got up and yelled to the guard, "Bring me some clothes, now!" I sat back down on the soiled bed. "Please believe me, Talia, I would never do something like this to you. I would never have allowed any of this to happen to you if I'd known."

The guard returned with clothes in hand. "Just leave them there," I said. He did as I asked and walked away. I retrieved them from the floor and brought them over to my mate. "Here, these are for you," I said. I turned away as she put them on, giving her privacy. Once I felt her stop moving, I turned back around to look at her. "Let me take care of you, Talia, please. I want to help you and take you out of here. I want to help you get cleaned up. Please, Talia, just let me help you," I begged her, desperate to prove I'd always protect her from this day forward and not ever let something like this happen to her again. "How did you end up in here? How did this happen?"

She suddenly looked as if she had an epiphany, and her eyes went dark. "I came to get Hugo out of jail. You put my friend in jail! You're a monster!"

I felt as if I'd been punched in the stomach. I had completely forgotten about Hugo. He completely dropped from my mind as soon as I had reunited with her. "I'll let him out. I'll let him out right now." I got up to do so. I found him sitting on his bed when I arrived, a look of sadness in his eyes.

"I heard everything. I heard your sister torturing her," he said quietly as he looked up at me. "She must have tortured her for at least an hour. All I could hear was her screaming in agony. I've never felt so useless in my life."

I hung my head in shame, not knowing what to say, unlocking his cell door. I finally said, "You're free to go. I'm sorry." He nodded his head in acknowledgment as he walked out. The guard on duty handed him the possessions that were taken from him when he'd initially been put in there.

I walked back over to Talia who hadn't moved from where she was sitting. "Please, Talia. Let me take you to get cleaned up. I promise I won't hurt you. You're my mate and I hate myself for not protecting you when you needed me to. You have to believe me when I tell you that I would never have allowed anything like this to happen to you."

She didn't look at me, but she also didn't stop me when I picked her up and carried her from the cell. I mindlinked one of my warriors from a nearby patrol station to pick us up. He pulled up to the jail and I got into the back seat, holding Talia close to me as he drove us back to the packhouse. She seemed to finally relax from my touch. Boldly, I rubbed my hand up and down her back and was relieved when she didn't pull away, enjoying the feeling of dull sparks on the palm of my hand.

I was further relieved to find that Sara wasn't there when I got home. It was now about time for her to move out and get her own place. I brought Talia to the guest bedroom with an en suite washroom so she could shower and rest, giving her some of my clothes to wear for now. While she was showering, I mindlinked Hugo and asked him to bring all her stuff that was currently at his house to the packhouse. I knew he'd know better than to disobey my orders.

I then called my executive assistant and asked for her to arrange movers to come to the packhouse to pack up all of Sara's stuff today. I was done with her antics, and I wanted to keep her as far away from my mate as I could. She could move into temporary housing in the pack for now until she found a more permanent arrangement. As much as I wanted to banish her for what she'd done, she was still my sister. After the loss of my father, and almost losing my mother, I wasn't ready to throw my sister out too.

Hugo arrived with all of Talia's things. "Is it true that you're her mate?" he asked. "I heard you call her that to your sister."

I nodded. "I won't hurt her." He bowed his head and was about to turn to go when I had a thought. I asked, "Do you know why my father murdered her mother?"

"No," he replied. "Your father was an ass though. He always showed up wasted, and he was into some crazy S and M shit. I know werewolves heal, but it still fucking hurts, man. But she kept him around because he paid well. She needed the money to pay for her painkillers and Talia's housing."

"Painkillers?" I asked.

"That's why her mom had a hard time saving enough money to move out. Because she had an addiction, and anyway, the brothel was the perfect place for her to stay—the steady supply."

"Fuck, man," I said, coming to the realization that there was a lot I didn't know about Talia or her past.

"Talia didn't do any drugs, though, and she did well in school. She'd been helping her mom save up enough money, so they could start their life over."

I felt a whimper within me, a longing to comfort Talia and take all of her pain away. After digesting what Hugo had told me, I said, "Thank you for telling me all of that. You have my word that I will always protect Talia, for the rest of my life, and never allow anything like that to happen to her again. And if you need anything, please let me know. I know you said you're the sole provider for your family. So let me know if you're behind on any bills and the pack will pay them off. After all, it's my fault that you weren't able to work, and I'd like to correct any problems I've caused."

He nodded and turned to go. I watched him leave, feeling like complete shit. Would Talia ever be able to forgive what happened with my sister? Even if it wasn't really my fault, deep down I knew that I was at least partially responsible, since I had created circumstances that allowed something like that to occur, especially allowing Sara to be so involved with pack leadership, knowing how unhinged she was. And then another part of me, a part of me that disgusted myself, recognized that I would not have acted any differently had Talia not been my mate. Even more appalled, I realized I had even admitted as much to Talia.

Chapter 21

Talia

"You can't force me to be with you! I'm not a possession!" I screamed and stomped up the stairs to go back to my room. After I got to the top step, I quickly glanced down to see if he was following me but he had reached for his phone instead. I watched him look at it, opening his phone with Face ID. Suddenly, I had an idea. Of course, the Face ID security feature on his phone was a bit of an obstacle, but I'd just have to be very observant and patient. He was bound to type his password in at some point. And then I'd be able to leave.

I was numb. My visible injuries were fully healed by now, but the invisible wounds within me still had blood pouring from them. After I scrubbed my skin of all the dried blood and filth from that jail cell, I wrapped myself in the very soft T-shirt and cotton gym shorts Alex left me, relieved that they were freshly washed so his scent was not so strong on them. I didn't want to smell his scent. I wanted to forget I'd ever met him and that I had a mate. His family had caused nothing but pain and suffering for me, and I wanted out.

Too weak to leave, I crawled into the bed in the room where he left me, snuggling under the comforter and drifting into sleep. I was exhausted. I'd barely slept while running here, and I definitely didn't sleep in that horrible place where Alex's pack had put me. It was a restless sleep. I could feel myself tossing and turning until I awoke to a soothing feeling on my head, and that enchanting, exasperating scent filling my nostrils. My eyes shot open to him sitting on my bed, his hand patting my head. I gasped and moved away from him, almost falling off the bed again.

"Talia," he said, his eyes pleading. "Please don't be scared of me. Please." I could sense his desperation as the words left his mouth.

I stayed on the edge of the bed, not wanting to move any closer. He needed to be out of my life. The last week had been a mistake, a terrible judgment of mine. But no more. If anyone knew about learning lessons, it was me. I'd learned them over and over again in my life—the harsh reality of how monstrous some people were. There was no limit to how broken and cruel a person could be.

He looked at me sadly, causing a pain in my chest to form. Why did he have to affect me so much? I needed to leave. Once I regained all my strength, I would leave and go back to Blake's pack. I was safe there. I would gather together paperwork so I could get a real job—after all, I was a US citizen, right? Then I could finally move out of the packhouse and become independent and pay Blake and Hugo back for everything they'd done for me.

"Talia, I want you to know that I'm very sorry and I will never allow anything like that to happen to you again. I will make it my life mission to protect you as my mate and the person I've come to care for very much in this last week. I'm also sorry that I jailed your friend, and I plan to make it up to him and his family. Just please, Talia, please believe me. There is nothing I want more in the world than for you to trust me."

I turned my back to him, the pain in my chest not easing. "How can I trust you?" I whispered, my breath shaky.

"You can trust me, Talia. I'm your mate. Some mistakes were made, but I promise I'll make up for them."

"I can't." I was barely able to speak. He continued to sit there. I could feel his eyes burning into my back. After far too much time, he left and closed the door behind him. The rest of the night I felt anxious as I slept, that crazy bitch's smile penetrating my dreams.

I awoke not feeling refreshed at all. But it was what it was. I would run anyway, rested or not. I could not rest until I was out of this house and out of this pack. My eyes scanning the room, I noticed that a paper had been slid under the door. I snuck over to pick it up and see what it was. He had drawn a cartoonish portrait of my wolf form lying on his lap with hearts drawn above our heads. For a second, I felt a tenderness, but I quickly squashed it, crumpling the paper, and throwing it across the room, a guilt within me that I had just destroyed such a beautiful and heartfelt gift. I couldn't think like that. I needed to be rid of him.

I quickly descended the stairs and exited the chalet house, running into the woods behind it. I couldn't strip my body of his clothing fast enough. My stomach grumbled after not eating for over twenty-four hours, but I ignored it, opting to just hunt on the road. As soon as the shorts touched the ground, I shifted into my wolf form. And I tried to run. But I found I couldn't move. My wolf kept her feet firmly planted on the ground, refusing to leave. I concentrated, thinking about my feet moving, but it was useless. I whimpered. Alex was right—I didn't have control over my wolf. She was able to overrule me in this form.

I lay down and began whining, unable to cry as a wolf. I couldn't believe that I was truly stuck, a prisoner in my wolf body. And it's not like I could just leave in my human form. I had nothing. I was defenseless.

After not much time lying there, a rustling sounded behind me. As the rustling got closer, I inhaled that familiar scent. He came around and knelt down in front of me, staring into my eyes. "I saw you leaving from my window. I thought for sure you would run away"—he looked at me sadly—"but you didn't. Why not?"

I put my head down, resting it on the leaves on the ground. He moved closer to me and patted my head. I closed my eyes, enjoying the feeling as his hand brushed through my fur. My wolf wanted to torture me. But I couldn't deny that this felt like exactly the opposite of torture.

"Your friend Hugo brought all of your things yesterday. I have them in the packhouse. I'll put them in your room for you." He got up and walked away, back toward the chalet house. I let out a deep breath. After standing up and trying to run again I finally gave up and shifted back into my human form, putting his clothes back on.

I went back up to my room where I found the few belongings that I owned on the floor. I also found that he had uncrumpled the picture and smoothed it out onto the nightstand. I crawled back under the covers and began to cry. What did I do to deserve this?

I drifted back into sleep where I dreamed that a white wolf was dragging its claws through every part of my body. I screamed in agony, but no one could hear me. It was just me and the wolf in a jail cell.

As the wolf's mouth closed down on my neck, I woke up gasping to find that same exact wolf from my dream had come to life and was in position to pounce at the foot of my bed. I screamed, quickly shifting into my own wolf, tearing the clothes I was wearing, my scream turning into a howl. The wolf pounced on me, pinning back my front paws, and I knew I was going to die. I didn't know how to fight. Alex had only started teaching me, and in my human form since I didn't want to shift into my wolf while on my period, the thought of free bleeding unpleasant.

I knew exactly who this wolf was, recognized her scent. A sickness came over my entire body. I knew there was no way out of this. She tore her claws down the front of me with one paw, and then she pulled back her other paw. Before she had a chance to land her other paw on my body, I rolled away to the floor, knocking her over and crawling under the bed. She quickly regained her composure and dug her claws into my back legs, pulling me out from under the bed as if I weighed nothing. Just then, another wolf entered the bedroom, immediately grabbing her with his claws and throwing her across the room. He threw his entire huge body on top of her, pinning her down, and slashed his claws across her face several times. I saw him stare at her and she whimpered, baring her neck to him. After he got off her, she walked herself out of the room with her tail between her legs.

The very similar but larger wolf came over to me, licking my face. I rolled onto my back, and he began licking my wounds from the scratches, emitting a very wonderful feeling. The soothing feeling of his tongue overrode the pain of my injuries. I purred my appreciation. He did have a very majestic wolf—huge with thick white fur. If he were any bigger, I'd have mistaken him for a polar bear. He snuggled up against me, the feeling so comforting, the warmth of his body mixed with the sparks that radiated throughout me, lulling me into relaxation. I molded my body into his, eyes growing heavy as I fell asleep on the rug on the floor, his wolf body against my wolf body.

When I woke, I felt fully healed and well rested, but he was gone. The sun was high in the sky, indicating it was either late morning or possibly even afternoon. I shifted back into my human form, grabbed some clothes out of my suitcase, dressing myself in a long sleeve T-shirt and sweatpants, and exited my room. I descended the stairs to find Hugo sitting on the living room couch.

Hugo smiled and got up as I entered the room. "What are you doing here?" I asked, going over to hug him, relieved he was out of jail.

"Alpha Alexander hired me to work for him," he replied, holding me tight against his body.

"Doing what?" I asked, already putting two and two together.

"He told me what happened this morning, and I heard what happened in the cells," Hugo said into my ear. "I'm so glad you're okay. He wants someone here to keep an eye on you when he can't do it himself. He offered to pay me more than what Madam Coco was paying me."

I pulled away from him. "He hired me a babysitter?"

"It's not like that, Talia. Obviously, your life is in danger, and I'm worried too. It's for the best that we both keep an eye on you for now."

"I'm not staying," I replied, becoming very annoyed by the situation. I wanted to go somewhere where I didn't need a babysitter. Instead of making me feel safe, it made me feel trapped. Furthermore, if he was that worried about his crazy bitch sister killing me, why didn't he just get rid of her? Why did I have to be the one being monitored 24-7?

"Where are you going?" he asked.

"Well, I'd like to go back to the US. You have a car, right? Why don't you drive me, eh? I'll hide in your trunk so we can cross the border."

He stared at me wide-eyed. "Talia, I am not getting involved in your plans to leave. You're the alpha's mate. If he found out I helped you leave him, being banished would be the least of my worries. As an alpha he has complete control over all his pack members. All he has to do is command me to do something and I'm helpless. He could easily torture and kill me. He could do the same to my family." I suddenly had a flashback of being back in the cell and started to shiver, bile rising to my throat at the memory. "Anyway, he's your mate. Why do you want to leave him?"

"Because I don't want to be his mate. You know what his father and sister both did. I have no desire to be associated with him or his family anymore."

He sighed and said, "I understand. But he really does seem to care about you. I spoke with him, and I don't think he wants to hurt you, Talia. Maybe you should give him a chance."

"I gave him a chance, and I ended up in a cell being cut up with a knife. And now, apparently, I have a minder. Ever since I met him, it's been nothing but trouble." I turned around to head back upstairs when a loud grumble came from my stomach. I was starving. I hadn't eaten for probably two days at this point. I realized I also felt weak and slightly light-headed.

"Wait, Talia," Hugo called to me. I turned my head to glance at him. "Alpha left you some food in the fridge. He told me to let you know once you woke up." Although I didn't want Alex to know that I'd accepted anything from him, the hunger pangs were now overpowering any other desire I had. The only other option was to hunt for food, and my wolf was clearly not cooperating. I sighed and found the kitchen.

The chalet house was smaller, cozier, and much more rustic than the packhouse—objectively, I wouldn't have minded staying here long-term. It had beautiful wide-planked hardwood floors, soft, thick wool rugs in every room, and it was decorated with skull mounts and animal hide rugs, likely hunting trophies. It had the feeling of being snowed in on a mountain, with nothing to do but stay snuggled warm under the covers, our bodies rubbing together, my fingers weaving through his soft blond hair, his beautiful lips and beard skimming every part of my body.

No, no, no! What was I thinking?!

I turned my attention back to the task at hand. The kitchen had a modern farmhouse feel to it, with a huge farmer's sink, light-green cabinets, stone countertops, wood beams, large windows that had a view of the backyard and forest, and an eclectic collection of mugs and plates in a glass cabinet. I was never much of a cook, but being in this kitchen made me want to learn. I opened the fridge to find a large plastic-wrapped plate. I pulled it out to see that someone had made me a well-rounded meal consisting of chicken breast, potatoes, and broccoli. Did Alex cook this himself? I didn't see any indication that staff worked at this house as they had at Blake's packhouse.

I heated it up in the microwave and sat down at the kitchen island to eat it. It was actually really good. The breast wasn't too dry like it normally came out when I tried to make it, even after being microwaved. I wolfed everything down, realizing how starved I was once I started eating. Afterward, I placed everything into the dishwasher.

I exited the kitchen only to come face-to-face with Alex. His eyes lit up at seeing me. "Talia, I'm so glad you're okay. After I left this morning, I realized I forgot something. I can't stop thinking about what would've happened if I hadn't turned around and come back." He then reached his arms out to try to hug me.

I put my arms out and turned my head in reaction, stopping him. I instantly sensed his pain at my response, but I did my best to ignore it. It wouldn't be much longer until I got out of here. I just had to think of a plan.

"Why?" he asked, staring at me.

"We shouldn't be together," I replied. "Please let me know how to reject you." And then I felt it again, the searing pain in my chest from the thought of it.

"Even if I told you how to do it and you tried to reject me, I'd never accept it. You are my mate, and you are perfect for me. After the past week we spent together, I understand now why the Moon Goddess wants us to be together. I could spend the rest of my life searching, and no one will ever even come close to being as wonderful as you are."

Chapter 22

Jasmine

After a horrible week of training, I was so happy to finally have a day off. Because it was the first weekend day off since my birthday, my mom planned for us to look at wedding gowns that day. Blake had his office manager and an event planner taking care of most of the wedding details, due to the importance and size of the event, so I only had a few things I had to do to prepare. Of course, I would have preferred something small, similar to the wedding I had grudgingly attended for Luke and Lucy earlier in the year, but it was out of my hands.

Because Luke and Lucy's mate bond and marriage were considered shameful, they had opted for a small affair, getting married in the local human town hall. On a cold Valentine's Day afternoon, the two of them spoke their vows, Lucy's huge belly squeezed into a wedding gown a month before she gave birth. Afterward, the small group of us (which wasn't actually that small considering the size of both Lucy's and Luke's families) went to a restaurant to enjoy a late lunch together where everyone gave toasts and laughed while Luke and Lucy kept stealing kisses from each other. At the time, it was one of the most painful experiences I'd ever had to sit through. Looking back now, I could reflect on it with less emotion and wished that Blake and I could have a wedding more intimate like theirs—a small temple wedding with just our closest family and friends in attendance. But he was the alpha of the pack, and with that came obligations. Even though it wouldn't be exactly as I would have imagined, I couldn't stop feeling a smile creep to my face at the knowledge that Blake and I would be bound together as mates before the year was over.

After I finished breakfast, while I was cleaning up to head out with my mom, the doorbell rang. I walked over and peered out the window to Tyler waiting outside. I opened the door and exclaimed in delight, "Tyler, what are you doing here?"

He smiled in greeting and said, "Well, I can't exactly leave my sister to pick out a wedding dress without her best and favorite brother's help." He paused for a second and continued. "Of course, Jack has the better taste in fashion of us two, but don't tell him I told you that. He thinks he's straighter than straight men." Tyler rolled his eyes.

"To be fair, I was very surprised when I found out he was gay, and I've known him since I was a kid," I responded.

"How many gay people do you actually know?"

"Okay, good point. I only know the two of you."

"There are others in the pack. They're just in the closet."

"I mean, I figured. But I don't know who they are."

Tyler laughed. "It's not exactly easy to be out and about around here. Jack and I are trailblazers. Hopefully it'll be for the greater good and eventually others won't feel like they have to reject their mates anymore."

I could see some emotion behind Tyler's eyes as he said this. "What do you mean, reject their mates?"

"What, you didn't know?"

"Know what?"

"In your pack, when it was still Blake's dad in charge, people used to reject their mates so they could stay in the closet and not be banished.

That's what Jack had planned to do for a long time, so he wouldn't have to disappoint his family. It's what the temple encourages too."

"The temple encourages people to reject their fated mates from the Moon Goddess?" I looked at him, shocked, not able to believe something like that could be true.

"Obviously it's hypocritical. But religion can be like that. It's people interpreting the words and intentions of a higher power. You must be familiar with the scriptures stating that a mate bond is gifted by Artemis for the purpose of breeding and continuing the race. And that man should not lie with man."

"That's why I always assumed that werewolves couldn't be gay, not like humans at least. I mean, that's what they taught us in school. That being gay is a sin and sinning is a choice. But I had no idea, at the time, that Artemis grants mates of the same sex to people. I had no idea until I found out that Jack was gay."

"It seems your pack shelters you from a lot of things."

"But rejecting your mate is a sin! It's a direct insult to Artemis who chooses your mate for you. Why would the temple encourage it?"

"Because if the temple encouraged accepting gay mates, then the temple would have to admit that being gay isn't a sin, the scriptures are wrong, and mating isn't just for breeding. So, instead, they tell gay people that in order not to live in sin they should deny who they are and reject their mates. The temple sees taking chosen mates as an honorable choice and religious duty in those cases."

"Is that what Bernard told Jack?"

"Jack has never spoken to Bernard, but he's spoken to others who were told that. I was told that at my own temple back home too. My mom took me to see our priest when I came out to her, and that's what he told me. Luckily, our pack is more open-minded, so my mom never made me feel like that's what I should do, but she was definitely upset because she'd always been religious, especially growing up here in your pack. She's accepted me now, and she's obviously really happy that I found Jack. But for a few years it was kind of tense in my family."

"Wow, I had no idea," I replied, hugging Tyler, filled with emotion. "I wish I'd known you then and could have been there for you."

"Oh, hello, Tyler!" my mom said from behind us as we pulled away from each other.

"I'm here and ready to provide some of my fashion expertise." Tyler put on a smile. "Expertise might be a bit of an exaggeration, but I'll do my best to scoff at the bad dresses and cry at the right ones."

My mom returned his greeting with a polite smile of her own. While she hadn't completely flipped out about the whole "secret love child coming back into town, and by the way, he's gay" thing, I could tell it was still something she was struggling with. It did help that Tyler was one of those people you couldn't help but adore, which did aid in my mom warming up to him. But it was a work in progress.

We piled into the Tesla, and my mom hit the road. We had to drive a bit of a way to get there, and I was thankful for Tyler's presence. My mom and I never really had much to talk about besides how I was doing at everything.

"So, Miriam, you must be excited about the wedding. I hear alpha weddings are a huge deal. Your whole family must be very proud of Jasmine for hooking such a great catch," Tyler said from the back.

"Well, my family is a bit difficult to please. But yes, I think things could be worse," my mom replied.

"Could be worse? Jasmine upgraded from a beta to an alpha. You'd think they'd be over the moon."

"It's better we don't think too much about it. Jasmine found herself a great mate, and Drew and I are both very happy. Blake is a very nice man."

"Yes, nice in many ways. I'm sure Jasmine won't mind popping out some alpha heirs with him." Tyler snickered, squeezing my shoulder from the back.

"Tyler!" I gasped.

My mom surprisingly laughed and said, "I do hope the Moon Goddess blesses them with many pups. I was always sad I couldn't have more than one."

I stared at my mom, shocked. She'd never told me this before.

"Well, you got a good one," Tyler said.

"Yes, I did," she agreed, smiling. "So how is work going, Tyler?"

"Work is work. I just sit in front of a computer and write code all day. The internet service isn't great out here, but I can usually just create a hot spot with my phone. Thank Goddess that this pack gets fairly consistent cell phone service. Computer programming isn't super exciting though. I think Jack and Jasmine had the right idea becoming warriors. Unfortunately, I wasn't super athletic in high school, at least compared to others, so they didn't recruit me. But I hear Jasmine was top of her class."

"Top of her class for everything," my mom replied, puffing her chest. "I was the same in high school."

My cheeks heated and a warmth spread through my chest. My mom was normally so critical of me, so it was a pleasant surprise to hear her boast about me.

She continued, "But our pack didn't allow women to become warriors. It was even more conservative than the Midnight Maple Pack, if you can believe it."

"I've heard stories," Tyler replied.

"What was it like growing up in your old pack?" I asked. It wasn't often my mom opened up about her past, and I'd always wanted to know more.

"It wasn't much different than here. But growing up in an alpha family is very demanding. Your whole family has very high expectations of you.

At the time it was challenging, but looking back now, I realize that it helped me become disciplined and successful, and the best version of myself." She quickly glanced at me. "That's why I always kept such high expectations of you, Jasmine. I wanted you to reach your full potential in everything. And now you'll have your own alpha children to raise, who will become leaders in our pack."

As my mom said that a very uncomfortable feeling came over me. I suddenly realized how much responsibility I'd have once Blake and I officially became mated to each other. The whole pack would be depending on me to provide an heir for the pack's entire future. I hadn't thought about it until that exact moment in the car. Previously, it was just about Blake and me, but now, suddenly, it was like a huge weight had been placed on my shoulders—there was an entire pack depending on our relationship.

And that's when I felt it. The tightening in my chest, my heart pounding, gasping for air, the car spinning around me. "Pull over!" I screamed.

"What?" My mom gasped, signaling to turn onto the side of the road. Fur was beginning to sprout up my arms and legs. As soon as my mom's car touched the side of the road, before she even stopped, I threw the door open and ran into the woods at the side of the road, trying to take deep breaths to hold off the inevitable. As soon as I was out of the view of the road, I threw off my clothes and shifted into my wolf. Thank Goddess I made it. I hadn't brought a change of clothes. Would my panic attacks ever stop for good? How could anyone expect me to be a luna when I couldn't even be normal?

I lay down on the ground, letting out a deep breath, and waited for the feeling to fully pass so I could shift back.

"Jasmine!" I heard Tyler's voice. He ran over and squatted down in front of me. "Are you okay, Jasmine? What happened?"

"*Panic attack*," I mindlinked him.

"But, why? We were having a nice conversation. Your mom was opening up to us."

"Because I don't think I can do it. I can't be luna, Tyler."

"What do you mean? Are you planning to break up with Blake?"

"Goddess, no!" I replied, horrified at the idea. *"But don't you think there's a reason I was mated to the beta and not the alpha? I can't lead the pack. I can't raise a future alpha. I can barely even survive as a warrior. I'm getting written up for something every day now. I mean, granted, it's mostly because I refuse to strip myself naked in front of a creep. But still!"*

"Wait, what! What are you talking about Jasmine?"

"Never mind, it's stupid. I can deal with it."

"What creep? Who's trying to make you strip in front of them?"

"One of the trainers, Charlie. You met him at Blake's birthday ski trip last year. Please don't tell Blake. I don't want him to take matters into his own hands. Ever since Alyssa got discharged, the other girls have been worse than usual. It'll only get worse if he starts discharging more people."

"But, Jasmine, that sounds pretty bad if this guy is preying on the people he's supposed to be training. I won't say anything to Blake, but I'm worried."

"Don't worry. I have it handled. He's just writing me up for stupid stuff, so there's nothing to worry about."

"Well, okay. I'll trust you." Although he didn't sound like he would.

"Thanks," I replied. *"Just give me a couple more minutes. I should be able to shift back soon. I'll meet you at the car."*

Tyler gave me a quick pat on the head and then walked back to the car. After some more time had passed, I was finally able to shift back and get dressed. At least I was getting better at controlling the timing of my shifting when these attacks happened. It had been almost a year since the last one, so I had been hopeful they were a thing of the past, but they just loved to creep back when I was least expecting them.

Once I got back in the car, it wasn't much farther to the bridal shop. My mom ran to the bathroom as soon as we walked in, and Tyler squeezed my shoulder. "Jasmine, just relax. Today is a nice day. You shouldn't worry so much about the whole luna thing. You won't be leading and raising your pups alone—you'll have Blake too. Jack told me that Blake's dad trained him hardcore growing up, so he knows what he's doing. He's not going to just let you fail. And, anyway, you've always been good at everything you've done. So, I don't see why being a luna would be any different."

"I guess," I replied, feeling unsure.

"You know I'm right so stop second-guessing yourself. And as for the bitch warriors, you know the saying—they hate you cuz they ain't you. So just let the haters hate."

I sighed and said, "Thanks, Tyler. You always know the right things to say."

"That's what big brothers are for." He winked. "Now let's go find some slutty wedding dresses. Time to show off that warrior body."

"Tyler!" I punched his arm.

"What!" He laughed. "You work so hard. Don't you want to show off what you've got?"

"No, I'm giving my vows under the eyes of Artemis in a sacred ceremony."

"You act like you haven't already sinned several times over. You think anyone's buying that unmarked neck?" He snickered.

"Tyler!"

"Sinner, sinner, Blake's been within her," he sang.

I almost choked at the rhyme and couldn't help but laugh.

"What's so funny?" my mom asked, returning from the bathroom. We both got quiet while she looked at us suspiciously.

Tyler grinned and pulled out his phone. "Have you seen the videos of cats being scared of cucumbers?"

"No, I haven't," my mom replied, looking at him curiously.

He pulled up a video on his phone and handed it to my mom to watch. She burst out laughing. I'd never seen my mom laugh so much before. "Oh my goodness, Tyler, please send that to me! I have to show it to Drew!" Tyler winked at me and text messaged the video to my mom. My mom then approached a saleswoman and said, "We're ready to begin our appointment."

"Wonderful!" the woman replied and led us over to a fitting room with chairs outside for my mom and Tyler to sit.

"So, when's the big day?" the saleslady asked cheerfully, smiling at all of us.

"December twenty-first," my mom replied.

Because it was such short notice, we weren't able to secure the ballroom in the casino for New Year's Eve, so we ended up choosing the winter solstice instead, which fell on a Wednesday that year, making it an easy evening to book.

"Oh, two months away!" The woman jerked her head back in surprise. "I'll make sure I only bring over dresses that can be rush ordered then. Should we take anything else into consideration, such as making sure the tummy is camouflaged or has room for growth?"

"What, no!" I shouted, my face burning at the saleslady's suggestion that I could be pregnant, especially in front of my mom.

"Oh, I'm sorry. I shouldn't have assumed."

"Jasmine is purer than a baby lamb, so assume not." Tyler snickered. I glared at him.

"Please make sure the gowns you bring are modest," my mom said. "This will be a religious wedding."

"Of course." The woman nodded. "Now I understand the rush. It sounds like you're looking forward to the wedding night." She winked at me.

I groaned internally.

Once she left and was out of earshot, Tyler laughed and said, "Well, that lady definitely doesn't have any tact. The day is already off to a great start."

"She is a bit presumptuous, isn't she?" My mom smiled.

After she came back, I began trying on frumpy gown after frumpy gown, feeling very unattractive. While I didn't exactly want to look slutty, as Tyler suggested I should, I also didn't want to walk down the aisle appearing as if I were a dowdy nun. By the tenth gown, I was overheated from the fluorescent lights in the fitting room and having to constantly change in and out of difficult dresses. Tears were threatening to fall from the frustration of putting on ugly gown after ugly gown.

"Did you like any of them, Jasmine?" my mom asked.

"No, I hate all of them," I replied.

"Yes, I agree. They weren't right for you. Let me go help the saleslady. I don't think she understands what we're looking for."

"Don't worry, Miriam. I've got it!" Tyler stood up, winking at me, and gestured for my mom to sit.

"Tyler, it's quite all right. I will just talk to the lady—"

"What we really need is some more fun!" Tyler cut my mom off. "Everyone's taking this way too seriously. Hold up, let me go find some good ones."

"Wha—" I started to say as he quickly disappeared into the racks of dresses.

"What is Tyler up to?" My mom wrinkled her brows.

The saleslady soon returned, another couple dresses in hand. "I had to go way back into the stock room to get these ones!" She hung them up in my fitting room and straightened her shoulders. "Last season—didn't sell. But very modest. Very chaste."

"It's okay, we won't be needing those!" Tyler returned with a huge pile of dresses in arm. "Now, come on, Jasmine, let's get cracking!" He found an empty rack to put all his dresses and then handed me one. He swiftly removed the ones already in my dressing room.

"Tyler, this dress is bright pink!"

"Don't question anything! Just put it on!" Tyler pushed me back into the dressing room. I pulled it on and the saleslady helped me zip it all the way up. I came out and my mom looked like she was about to pass out.

"Well, that dress is certainly something." The saleslady let out a giggle.

"That dress is everything." Tyler laughed jovially. I looked in the mirror at one of the craziest dresses I'd ever seen, with highly reflective sequins and beads all along the bodice, and fluffy, bright pink feathers lining the skirt. If the Flamingo Hotel in Las Vegas were a wedding dress . . . I couldn't help but double over in laughter at how ridiculous it was.

"Come on, Jaz! Strut it! Show off those assets, baby!" Tyler chanted. I let loose and began walking back and forth like a supermodel, exaggerating my gait and giving my best stern model face. Soon my mom joined in on the laughter.

"You're just missing the fascinator!" Tyler put a feathery pink thing on my head.

"Icing on the cake!" My mom laughed. I'd never seen her so giddy before.

"Okay, next!" Tyler commanded. The following gown made me look like a cupcake, the skirt was so thick and fluffy. I couldn't decide if I was wearing the dress or if it was wearing me. I similarly strutted, giving a show while Tyler, the saleslady, and my mom cheered and laughed.

The subsequent dress was so scandalous Tyler had to force me out of the dressing room. "Now that's what I'm talking about! Show off that warrior body!"

Completely out of character for her, my mom whistled. "Ooh la la, Jasmine!"

"Now that will get the groom looking forward to the wedding night," the saleslady remarked.

"Hell yeah!" Tyler laughed and I glared at him and the saleslady. "You just need to add this!" He pulled out the biggest and fluffiest feather boa I'd ever seen, draping it over my shoulders. "And this!" He added a tiara to my head. "Now, work it!"

"Yes, work it!" My mom giggled. I had to do a double take.

I threw my head back and gave in, letting go and strutting my stuff, everyone egging me on. Soon another sales associate came over and joined in on the fun, opening up a bottle of champagne for everyone to share.

"Some for you, ma'am?" she asked my mom.

"Absolutely!" She smiled, taking the flute. This had to be a dream. My mom was laughing and *drinking*? I couldn't remember the last time I'd seen my mom drink. She soon also got into the spirit and began finding funny dresses for me to try on. I was modeling a wedding pantsuit when she shouted, "Try this one on! This is the one! I can feel it!" She smiled at me, looking elated.

I took the dress from her, not sure if she was being serious or joking, especially now that she was two glasses of champagne deep. She'd picked something with long sleeves, and I assumed she'd found another funny, frumpy dress. The saleslady came in to help me zip up the back and then led me out to a mirror.

I was prepared to begin laughing again when I looked at myself and paused. This dress wasn't funny at all—no—it was amazing!

I spun around, looking at myself at every angle, and everyone was similarly silent. This gown looked like it was made for me. It had a mermaid silhouette, with sheer long sleeves that would be perfect for a winter wedding. There were beautiful lace appliqué details that came down the dress and a sweetheart neckline that was just modest enough to still be sexy in a religious setting. The bodice of the dress hugged my body, emphasizing my womanly curves, and the full, tulle skirt made me feel like a princess. Tears trailed my cheeks, from pure joy instead of the frustration I'd felt earlier.

I turned around to face my mom who'd also begun crying, again completely out of character for her. It was as if I was meeting a whole new person.

"I don't know much about dresses, but that is definitely your dress!" Tyler exclaimed, beaming and holding his champagne glass up to me.

"Yes, definitely," my mom agreed, clinking her glass against Tyler's, and they shared a look.

"Is this the one?" the saleslady asked, standing up and fluffing my skirt.

"Yes," I replied, a huge smile on my face. My cheeks were hurting from laughing through all the crazy dresses, but even so, I couldn't stop beaming.

"Wonderful. Now, no hanky-panky before the big night. This dress won't be able to disguise any baby bumps." The saleslady wagged her finger at me.

"There's no need to worry!" I instantly responded, my face burning.

"No, there's definitely no incredibly handsome groom with shoulders and pecs like boulders, and abs so hard they could stop a bullet, that will cause any temptation before the wedding night." Tyler chuckled, practically spilling his flute.

"I'm starting to regret letting you come," I said through gritted teeth, glaring at Tyler.

My mom gave a small smile and followed the saleslady to the cash register to place the order for the dress.

Once she was out of earshot, I said, "Tyler, stop making those kinds of jokes in front of my mom!"

"Come on, lighten up, Jasmine. You're getting married, and it's not like your mom was born yesterday. She did somehow make you after all!"

"We don't talk about sex in my house. You're just making things very awkward."

He rolled his eyes and said, "Fine, I'll stop."

"Thank you," I replied, spinning one last time in front of the mirror before I stepped back into the fitting room.

Chapter 23

Talia

Things were awkward. Very awkward. Alex kept trying to make an effort at conversation with me, ask me on dates, eat meals with me, and I kept having to reject his advances. When he'd leave to do whatever he did all day, relief would flood my body.

There were times that I'd lose control of my thoughts and think back longingly on the five perfect days we'd spent together, softening me to the idea of him. But I'd instantly shove them from my mind when I caught myself slipping. There were many things I forced myself not to think about. It was the only way I could continue to function like a normal person. Things like catching my mom doped up on painkillers and later finding out she'd spent all of her money again. Or being twelve years old and sprouting breasts, suddenly being touched and noticed by different men who worked at the brothel, feeling powerless and defenseless. I'd still sometimes have nightmares about Old Man Joe, who used to fondle my breasts every day. He was one of the dealers who worked at the brothel and felt entitled to my body. Luckily, it never went any further than that, but I was still disgusted by the fact that he thought he had the right to do that, especially to someone so young and helpless. And then there were the clients who frequented the place, who had no problem slapping my ass when they'd walk by me, as if I were just an object for their pleasure.

The bouncers helped, but they couldn't keep watch over me all the time. That wasn't their job anyway. They were there for the employees, not their random children. When I was fourteen, one of them took a liking to me. He worried about me, and he was the one who gifted me the blade. But I didn't realize then why he was being so nice and helpful to me. He was thirty, and I saw him as an older role model and friend. But that was when I learned that men never did anything nice without an expectation. Our relationship turned into an exchange. He would help me with something, listen to me, and I would let him kiss me, take my clothes off, kiss my body. He'd buy me school supplies and food when my mom had spent her money on painkillers again, and I would give him a blow job. Blow jobs eventually turned to fucking, and I realized I'd entered a transactional relationship without even meaning to.

He eventually left after finding a new job, and I was simultaneously relieved and sad—relieved because I no longer had to give out sexual favors, but sad because the one person besides my mother who took the time to listen to me and helped me when I needed it was gone. But he did leave me the greatest gift—the gift of shedding my innocence and learning not to trust people anymore. After that, I knew to stay away from men, to show my blade when necessary. I didn't trust any male again until my first and only boyfriend in high school. And I wouldn't even say I trusted him—more, I allowed him to be intimate with me and began to allow myself to find pleasure in what had previously been torture. I had finally reclaimed something that had formerly been shameful and unpleasant, and I felt powerful from the knowledge.

But, no, I never trusted anyone again until Hugo. Hugo I truly did trust, falling for him not long after we began sleeping together. At the time, it felt freeing, that I could finally be myself with someone else and let them into my horrible world. He knew where I lived, what my mother did, and he never once judged me. He had no true expectations from me, which became clearer the longer our friendship continued. Even after I told him I couldn't sleep with him anymore he stayed my friend, which made our platonic relationship only the more heartbreaking.

But it was strange, thinking about it now. I no longer had those feelings for Hugo. Ever since I met Alex, they seemed to have slipped away, and my new feelings for Alex fought to be acknowledged every day. I fought back. Alex could not be trusted. He was no better than any of those other men who felt entitled to me and my body. Right? Even as I thought that, I wondered if I was punishing him for someone else's transgressions. But I couldn't bring myself to reflect on it too much, preferring to feel angry rather than vulnerable.

It was a Tuesday, and I was on the couch with Hugo watching TV. "How's it going?" Hugo asked, glancing over at me.

"You mean besides being a prisoner in this house, being watched 24-7?" I replied, wrapping my arms around my legs.

"It can't be that bad. Alpha seems like a good guy."

"Why are you on his side?"

"I'm not. But I'm just trying to understand why you don't like him. He seems to care a lot about you. And he's your mate."

"I don't want a mate. Why do I have to have a mate? My mom didn't have one."

"Are you sure about that?" Hugo studied me.

"Why? Do you think she might have had one?" I looked at him curiously.

"I don't know. She seemed really depressed though. Kind of like my mom is now. I just wonder if maybe that's why . . ." He let his voice trail off, not speaking the words, but I knew what he was going to say. He was theorizing why my mom had an addiction.

I didn't respond. It wasn't something I liked to talk about, and Hugo knew that. Anyway, we could all spend days thinking up theories about my mom, but we'd never truly know. The explanation could have been as simple as she fell into a bad situation, the painkillers helped her feel better, and before she knew it, she couldn't stop.

"I miss her," I said.

"I know," he replied, wrapping his arms around me.

"She was a good person. She always loved me and did her best." Tears fell from my eyes again. Would the unbearable, debilitating pain of losing my mom ever go away?

After Hugo and I spent the afternoon together, Alex came home and relieved Hugo of his babysitting responsibilities. He then came to the couch and sat down next to me.

"Talia," he said.

I kept my head turned away from him.

"I wish you'd at least tell me how I can fix whatever made you hate me."

I could sense a deep pain and longing, forcing me to soften toward him.

"I would honestly do anything. At this point, I'm willing to banish my sister for you and turn her into an enemy of the pack. I don't want to because she is my sister, and she's not all bad. I know she did something unforgivable, and I don't want to make excuses. But you have to understand that she loved my father very much. She loved him much more than either my mom or I ever did. She was devastated when she lost him. That was her way of reacting to the loss. I know I can't expect you to understand, but I want to at least give you some perspective."

"You would have done the same." I glared at him, giving him the evilest look I could conjure.

"But so did you, Talia. That's why I can't understand why you're so angry. You did exactly the same thing once your mother was murdered. You took revenge. And I know that if you were capable of torturing my father, you would have done it too."

"Your father was evil. My mother wasn't and neither am I," I replied.

"I'd like to believe I'm not evil either."

"But you torture people."

"As alpha, I have to, Talia. You didn't grow up in a pack, so you don't know what it's like. But werewolves are constantly at war. I don't just torture people for no reason. I do it when I have to in order to protect the pack. That's my job as alpha."

"Why did you tell your pack to put me in the cells?"

He let out a deep breath and said, "I told them to do that long before I found you at the Midnight Maple Pack. The night I found out you were my mate, I wanted my pack to capture you so I could meet you and finally get to know you as my mate. I was afraid you'd run away again otherwise. That's the same reason I went looking for you. Because we're meant to be together."

"You can't just trap someone into being with you."

"I didn't want to trap you. I thought if I explained that I wouldn't hurt you that you wouldn't be scared, and, of course, I just assumed you'd feel the mate bond as strongly as I do. I wish you'd at least give me a chance. I thought those five days we spent together were some of the best days of my life. And I can't think of anything more painful than you not feeling the same way. I mean, I was enchanted by you from the moment I saw you, but now that I've had a chance to get to know you more, I'm really falling for you. You are just everything I ever imagined and more. You spend your whole life wondering what your mate will be like, and now that I finally met you, you've far exceeded every expectation. You're so beautiful, sweet, generous. I even love the parts of you that annoy me, like how you're so stubborn and difficult. It just makes you *you*. I wish you'd let me in so I could learn everything about you."

I looked over at him, feeling him chipping away at me little by little. My stomach fluttered at his words. No one had ever said anything so sincere and thoughtful to me before. I could sense my inner wolf clawing at my insides, begging me to believe him and let him in. But I wasn't ready. It was too much too soon. I had spent my entire life watching my mother suffer at the hands of his father only for her to finally be taken away from me. And before I could fully process what happened, I found out I had a mate. While I'd be lying to myself if I didn't agree with him that those five days had been wonderful—no, perfect—I just couldn't let go. A damaged part of me was having trouble trusting him and allowing myself to be vulnerable.

I knew I should say something, but I was too conflicted and couldn't come up with the right words to explain my feelings to him. I think a part of me acknowledged it was irrational, but I still couldn't help the anger that bubbled within me. When I didn't respond, he eventually sighed and turned his attention to the TV. I did too, considering getting up and leaving the room, feeling so overwhelmed by everything. But then I saw him pick up his phone in my peripheral vision, and I turned toward him as he tried to open it with his Face ID. When it didn't work, he typed his password in and I carefully watched, repeating the code in my head—*007007*. It wasn't even a difficult code to remember!

After some time, he said, "I'm going to make some dinner. Do you like steak? I'm making tenderloin. I'll make you some too." I just nodded and watched as he got up, leaving his cell phone behind.

Yes!

Once he disappeared into the kitchen, I picked it up, quickly typing in the code, and scrolled through his contacts until I found *Wulfric*.

I quickly read his last text message exchange, noticing that my name had been mentioned, glancing over my shoulder to make sure he was still in the kitchen.

> **Wulfric:** *Hey, have you seen Talia? She's been gone for over two days and I'm assuming she went back to your pack? I'm wondering if we should track her*

> **Alex**: *Talia is here. She came to my pack.*
> **Wulfric**: *Ok good. All good?*
> **Alex**: *Yeah*
> **Wulfric**: *Ok let her know I'm here for her if she needs anything*
> **Alex**: *Will do*

I quickly typed the message I'd been wanting to send.

> **Alex**: *It's Talia. Don't reply, I am going to delete this message after sending. I want to go back to your pack. I am trapped in Alex's pack.*

After confirming the message sent, I quickly deleted it. I put Alex's cell phone back where he had left it, my heart racing. I hoped that it worked, and it wouldn't be much longer. But then, another part of me—a part I tried to push away—felt some regret at my actions. Was what I had done really the right thing to do?

Chapter 24

Talia

I woke up much later than usual the next morning, feeling hot, and threw the covers off my body. As I slowly gained consciousness, I started recalling the vivid details of the dream that I'd awoken from. It'd been a nice dream, of Alex's muscular body—his very broad shoulders, strong and protective arms, massive pecs planted above the sculpted ridges of his abdominal muscles. The dream was so realistic—I even recalled the feeling of his body pressed against me, his skin against my nipples as his body slid over mine, his hips between my legs as, oh God, as I finally felt his huge— Damn, I was so horny recalling all of those vivid details. I'd even orgasmed in my dream. I didn't even know that was possible.

I got out of bed and took a shower, falling back into my dream, wanting desperately to feel every single part of Alex's perfect body, wishing he was in that shower with me at that moment. After drying myself off, I threw on just an oversized cotton T-shirt I normally used as a nightgown, ready to remove it as soon as I found Alex. I was eager for him to do anything and everything to me.

I descended the stairs to find Hugo instead, in his usual place, sitting on the living room couch. And then I suddenly recalled graphic details of how it had once been between us, at a time when we couldn't go long without keeping our hands off each other. His eyes were wide as I approached him. He had his hands balled up and shouted, "Fuck!" as he stood up.

He backed away, but I knew he wanted it as much as I did, instantly spotting the bulge that had formed in his pants. I pulled off my oversized T-shirt so I was standing completely naked before him, and that was when I knew he'd give in and give me everything I so desperately wanted at that moment. I closed the space between us, one hand massaging his bulge and the other feeling his arm, gliding my hand up to his shoulder, neck, and pulling his head toward mine, shoving my tongue in his mouth.

He gave in completely, grabbing my ass and pulling me against his body as I wrapped my legs around him. We kissed each other desperately, and he soon threw me on the couch and climbed on top of me, our lips finding it difficult to separate. I quickly pulled his shirt off him, revealing a beautiful tan body that I hadn't touched in so long, finding nostalgia in feeling it all over again as if it were new. His mouth was now all over me, on my neck, kissing down my chest, as I reached for his belt, unhooked it, and pulled it clean out of the belt loops. He hastily unbuttoned his pants and kicked them off with his underwear.

"Fuck," he said as he began kissing me again.

"Fuck me," I said. "Fuck me like you've never fucked me before."

Then we heard a door burst open and both looked up to see we had an audience. Hugo abruptly jumped off me, and I couldn't do anything but stare, a deer in headlights, not able to fully process what had just happened. Standing there staring back at me were Alex, Blake, Jasmine, Jack, and Tyler.

"Damn, now I'm starting to feel bad about myself. I'm literally the only guy in this room that Talia hasn't either gotten with or tried to," Tyler said, and I don't think you could even properly describe how tense the atmosphere suddenly was.

Blake

"The invitations are ordered," my office manager, Mariette, said to me on a rainy Tuesday afternoon in October. "They're putting a rush on them, and they'll be mailed next week."

"Make sure they don't mail the one for the Baker family. I want to hand deliver it," I said.

She looked at me sadly. "Yes, I made sure that that one won't be mailed."

"Good." I left the office and went back to my own, letting out a deep breath. I'd finally have to visit Ria's family and tell them the news. I'm sure they knew by now, it was big news around the pack, but I still knew I should tell them in person. I'd been putting it off—putting everything off. While most of my depression had slowly lifted over the last year, thinking about Ria still seared me. She was a ghost I knew would never truly leave me. This both comforted and scared me. I hated the idea of forgetting her, but it was also difficult to exist some days, her memory now a part of who I was.

I busied myself going through the different work on my laptop, doing my best to take my mind off what I was planning to do.

"Hey, man," Luke greeted me when he entered the office, taking a seat at his own desk.

"Hey," I replied.

After some time, he spoke again. "So, how would you feel about us hiring an actual nanny for the packhouse? Having Talia here for a few weeks was really helpful. And I'm sure a nanny will be useful to you too at some point."

I looked up at him.

"They don't have to live here. But maybe we could find someone to work the same hours as Connie and Wendy." He paused, and when I didn't say anything immediately, he continued, "It's a job, and our dads always said how it's important to make sure our pack members have jobs."

"Do you have someone in mind?" I asked.

"No, but we could put an ad in the next pack newsletter."

"Fine," I replied.

"Thanks." Without me prompting, he continued speaking, clearly not realizing that I was not in the mood for a conversation. "You know, having a pup is really great. Yeah, it's a lot of work and can be super frustrating, but it's also amazing—to know you made a life with the person you love, to know that Lucy and I brought Libby into this world. It's just so cool, watching her grow up every day, witnessing all her firsts—her first smile, eating solid food for the first time, rolling over for the first time, listening to her different babbles, playing with her, watching her get stronger everyday—"

"For the love of Artemis, shut up!" I shouted, slamming my fist onto the desk. Luke instantly shut his mouth and jerked his head back, his eyes bulging. I knew that that was not an appropriate response, and of course, Luke didn't know, but I couldn't take it anymore. I stood up and walked out of the office. As much as I thought I was getting better, it was things like this that always brought me back to reality. There was still something inside me that was permanently broken. I walked into the forest and shifted.

I returned hours later, my chest lighter and breathing easier. I found Luke in the kitchen, grabbing a snack. "Sorry about earlier," I said. "A lot on my mind."

"It's cool," he replied, looking at me, appearing as if he wanted to say something else. But then he walked out. I checked the time and realized that Jasmine would be coming over soon. I'd completely abandoned my work. I'd catch up tomorrow. I sighed, knowing I couldn't keep doing this. I had responsibilities, and disappearing in the middle of the day to run around in my wolf form couldn't keep happening. I shook my head.

When Jasmine came over that evening, she appeared very stressed. She appeared stressed a lot lately. But when I'd ask what was on her mind, she'd act as if nothing was wrong. It wasn't like her. She normally told me everything. I didn't like the idea that there was something she wouldn't tell me. I wanted to fix whatever was bothering her.

I pulled her to me, enjoying the feeling of her against my body. She kissed me with a desperation that had emerged as of late, as if my mouth was the only reason she was breathing. I kissed her back, loving how abandoned she had become over the last year, her hands grabbing for every part of my body.

I smirked, pulling away from her, and asked, "Future Mrs. Alpha, how long do we have to stay downstairs and exchange pleasantries before I can finally do what I actually want to?"

"We can skip the pleasantries." Jasmine smiled, her face softening, some of her stress visibly disappearing.

"Good, because you are looking very fucking sexy tonight, and I've already skipped over the pleasantries in my head." I bent back down to kiss her and grabbed her ass, picking her up to carry her upstairs and quickly climbing the stairs to the third floor. I slammed open the door to my bedroom and threw her on the bed, climbing in after her, throwing off my T-shirt.

She immediately brought her hands to my torso and kissed down the center of my chest, making her way to my belt. She unfastened it and began pulling off my pants. I slid them off and turned my attention to her, pulling her shirt off and unhooking her bra, revealing her beautiful, perky breasts, with the most perfect, erect nipples.

Goddess, I fucking love everything about her.

I quickly kissed my way down her right breast, placing my hand on her left one and gently rubbing the nipple between my fingers, licking the right one, savoring it as I lapped my tongue against it and sucked lightly. Jasmine moaned softly, and I continued what I was doing, reveling in her reaction.

Her hands wove themselves through my hair, moved down to the nape of my neck, and I lifted my head, peering in her eyes. I brought my hand to her hair, gliding my fingers through it and moving my hand softly down her neck, shoulders, and arms. I loved the feeling of her skin on my fingertips as I touched every part of her body. And the way she responded to my touch was heavenly. I basked in her soft moans and shallow breaths, the way her hands grabbed onto me.

I lowered my head down again and kissed her ear before kissing down her neck, chest, and belly, making my way down to her jeans. I slowly unbuttoned them, grazing my lips against the top, where denim met skin. Before long, I had removed everything, and she was completely naked. I let my eyes trail her whole body, taking everything in. Everything about her was perfect. She had such an amazing body from all her training, and I couldn't believe my luck that she was mine and would soon be vowing to spend the rest of her life with me.

I moved down the bed and pushed her legs up so they were bent, kissing both of her knees, then spreading her legs so I could fit between them, kissing slowly down the entirety of her left thigh and then the right one. She moaned and tugged at my hair. I was just as desperate as she was, but I loved it when she begged for it. I knew she'd likely never say it in words, but her actions showed me how badly she wanted it.

I kissed up her pubic bone, up to her hips, rubbing the side of her ass as I did this, then kissed back down, kissing everywhere except where I knew she wanted me to actually kiss her, and then I abruptly stopped. "Hmm, I'm getting tired, I don't think I can finish the job tonight," I teased, glancing at her as she furrowed her brows. I lay down beside her and nibbled her ear a little. "We should just cuddle tonight. I think I'm suddenly feeling very religious and guilty over all my sinning. We should leave this all for the wedding night."

I lay back and watched as Jasmine got up. "I know something that would make you change your mind." She gave me a cute, mischievous smile.

"Really, what's that?" I asked, the corners of my mouth lifting upward.

My eyes followed her as she moved toward my cock, which was now rock-hard, standing straight and at attention, throbbing and desperate to be touched. I licked my lips and watched with anticipation as she brought her hand to it, softly gliding it down the length of it, provoking a soft groan. Soon her mouth was on it, her soft lips surrounding the head. She quickly glanced my way, her beautiful amber eyes locking with mine for a quick moment.

Fuck! I love seeing her naked with her mouth on my cock.

She pushed her head up and down my shaft, and I let out a guttural moan from how good it felt being in her warm, wet mouth as her tongue traced the length of it. I lay back, enjoying the feeling and show, her perfect breasts on display as she bobbed up and down.

When I was close to coming, I stopped her, preferring to watch her climax as I did. "Damn, you're right," I moaned. "My mind is changed." I reached for the bedside table, desperate to be inside Jasmine and listen to her moans. I quickly got up and slid a condom on.

Before Jasmine could lie back down, I positioned her so I could take her from behind, caressing her hips and ass, positioning my cock to enter her. Not able to hold back anymore, I shoved the length of my cock inside her, groaning as I felt the pressure of her inner walls straining against it. I loved having the view of her ass and watching my cock sliding in and out of her, being coated by her wet pussy.

Heaven.

Gripping her hips, I slid in and out, starting slowly and then increasing my speed. As I quickened my thrusting, becoming more aggressive, her moans grew louder as she threw her head back in ecstasy.

Fuck, I'm ready to blow my load.

I held back, moving one of my hands to find her clit and rubbing it between my fingers. Before long, her whole body was shaking against mine, and I rubbed harder, banging myself against her even more forcefully, if that was even possible. She grabbed my headboard as she screamed, her whole body covered in sweat. I kept rubbing her clit, forcing out more orgasms, watching her react. The amazing sight, the feeling of her pussy contracting against my cock, and how wet she was, brought me over the edge. I groaned loudly as I came forcefully, my whole body practically collapsing onto her back.

I pulled out of her, breathing heavily, and then I felt my canines expanding, a strong urge from deep within me to pierce her neck with them and claim her as mine. I quickly balled my hand into a fist and bit into it, falling onto my pillow, my whole body convulsing, burning with need. Every time it got worse. I was starting to doubt my willpower and whether I'd make it to the wedding night.

I knew it was important to Jasmine to appear as if she was pure and chaste, and I would grasp for every last bit of self-discipline I had to make sure it happened. After a couple minutes, I finally felt my canines retreating, and I pulled my teeth from my hand, which was now covered in the blood that had dripped down my wrist and onto my pillow. I turned to face Jasmine, my eyes instantly falling to the trail of blood that had dripped down the length of her arm. I quickly got up and ran into the bathroom to clean myself up and brought out a wet towel for Jasmine, dabbing it gently along the bloodied skin.

"Goddess, what must Wendy think?" Jasmine asked as I kissed her hand.

"She's probably figured it out," I replied, knowing that it likely killed Jasmine inside, chuckling to myself at her deep-rooted desire to always appear pure to everyone. I changed out the pillowcases and lay down next to her, pulling her against my body, loving how perfect she felt against me. I wished I could spend the entire night with her body against mine.

As we lay quietly together, skin to skin, the chime of a text message cut through the silence. I groaned but got up to see what it was, just in case it was important. Hopefully it wasn't another stupid cat video in the group chat I now had with Jack, Tyler, and Jasmine.

I pulled my phone out of my jeans and quickly glanced at it to find a text from Alex.

> **Adalwolf**: It's Talia. Don't reply, I am going to delete this message after sending. I want to go back to your pack. I am trapped in Alex's pack.

"Fuck!" I exclaimed.

"What's wrong?" Jasmine asked, sitting up. I reread the text again, making sure I'd read it right the first time. No, I'd definitely read it right. I crawled back into bed with Jasmine and pulled her back against me.

"I hope you're not busy tomorrow, because you're going on your first warrior mission."

"What happened?" she asked.

"Talia needs our help. We're going to Ontario to rescue her and bring her back here."

"Why? What's going on?"

"Adalwolf has her trapped in his pack. It sounds like he won't let her leave."

"He would do that?"

"He was very possessive of her, especially when he first got here. I mean, I don't really know him that well, but you can't trust most people. She's my sister, and I'm going to help her."

"I hope she's okay." Jasmine turned around so she was facing me and snuggled into my chest.

"She will be. We're going to help her." We were quiet for a bit and then I transitioned to the subject I wanted to broach earlier. "Speaking of helping, what's going on with you lately? You seem stressed. Is it the mean girls?"

"It's nothing. I'm fine," Jasmine replied.

"Is it the wedding? I've heard women get stressed about weddings."

"No, the wedding isn't stressful. I'm barely even involved."

"Do you wish you were?"

"No, it's not the wedding I would have wanted anyway."

I frowned, rubbing her back. "Is that why you've been upset?"

"No," she replied. "I get it. I know why it has to be a huge wedding. Anyway, the wedding isn't what's really important anyway."

"Jasmine, I love you," I said, kissing her on her head. "I'm sorry I can't give you the wedding you really want. But I can at least give you the honeymoon you want. Wherever you want to go, that's where we'll go. Although, to be honest, I don't think it really matters where we go anyway, because I highly doubt we'll ever see outside of the hotel room."

"Yeah, better get started on that alpha heir," Jasmine said sarcastically.

"What?" I said pulling away from her.

"It's what everyone's expecting, right? The whole point of our mate bond and the big wedding. I have to produce the next alpha heir so our pack can continue."

"Fucking Artemis," I replied, staring at her.

"Why are you looking at me like that?" she asked.

"It's just not the way I thought the conversation would go," I replied, lying on my back and feeling myself retreating into my head, shutting her out.

"Shit, I'm sorry, Blake," she said, putting her hand on my shoulder.

"It's fine," I replied, not wanting to make it into a thing now.

She sighed.

We lay there in silence until it was time for Jasmine to go home. I walked her to her car and kissed her good night. Then I realized that maybe what was bothering her was exactly the thing I couldn't talk about. I mean, not the same exact thing, but in the same general subject area.

After I got back inside, I pulled up the group chat I had with Jack, Tyler, and Jasmine, and texted everyone to meet me at the packhouse early the next morning so we could make our way up to Ontario. Hopefully, just the four of us could get her home safely and this wouldn't have to become an official pack matter.

As planned, everyone came to the packhouse early the next day and piled into my Wrangler. I held Jasmine's hand as we drove, hoping to show her that I wasn't mad about the previous night.

"You guys have to see the most hilarious cat video I found this morning," Tyler shouted from the back. I rolled my eyes. I glanced in my rearview mirror to see that he was showing Jack who started laughing and then passed his phone to Jasmine.

"I swear, the only thing he does at work all day is watch cat videos." Jack chuckled.

Jasmine let out a laugh and said, "Oh my Goddess, that is so cute," and then passed the phone back to Tyler.

"I need to do something to give myself a break. There are only so many lines of code I can stare at before I start to go crazy," Tyler responded.

"I get it. Patrol duty can get pretty boring. It's not like we have intruders breaking into the pack every day. I think the last time anything happened was when we found Talia," Jack said. "That was pretty entertaining, though." He smirked.

"Why, what happened?" Jasmine asked.

"Nothing," I cut in. Jasmine eyed me suspiciously and I realized I should say something else. "I mean, it was entertaining in the sense that something happened. But it wasn't any different than any other rogue that we've caught outside the territory."

"Jack, is that true?" Jasmine turned toward the back. I glanced up at my rearview mirror to Jack catching my eye in the reflection and then looking back at Jasmine.

"Yeah, it gets really boring. It's nice when something finally happens," Jack replied. Jasmine pulled her hand out of mine. Unfortunately, she was usually pretty perceptive. When no one said anything, Jack spoke again. "At least my patrol buddy is usually Kyle. He's pretty funny. Makes it not so bad."

"Kyle's hilarious," Tyler agreed. "I think having a kid has made him even funnier. Although, you really have to be into bathroom humor for a lot of his jokes."

"Yeah, that story he told about the flying diarrhea." Jack laughed.

"Classic," Tyler agreed.

"Makes you glad we don't have any." Jack chucked.

I gripped my steering wheel. It had been a while since these types of conversations bothered me. It had really felt like I'd moved on for a while, especially after I'd finally opened up to Jasmine. But with everything happening lately, the topic of pups had started to affect me again.

Jasmine put her hand on my thigh, and I almost instantly calmed down. I don't know what it was, but something about her presence had a soothing effect on me. I covered her hand with mine, feeling better, thankful to have her.

We arrived at the Pine Forest Pack in just under five hours, after having to cross through the border. When we got to the entrance, his warriors called Alex to come to the entrance to greet us. I got out of the car to speak with him when he pulled up.

"Wulfric, this is a surprise." Alex shook my hand in greeting.

"I got a concerning text message," I replied, crossing my arms.

He brought his eyebrows together and touched his mouth in a look of confusion.

I pulled out my phone to show him. He spent a long time reading it, then shook his head and rolled out his neck and shoulders. When he didn't say anything, I asked, "Is it true? Did you trap Talia in your pack?"

"No, it's not true!" he exclaimed with clenched fists. "I never once told her she couldn't leave. Obviously, I hoped she'd stay. She's my mate! But she never once told me she wanted to go back to your pack. In fact, I thought she was going to run away one morning, and she didn't. I assumed she decided to stay."

"Well, the text message I received says otherwise."

He sighed looking at the ground, clearly lost in thought.

When he didn't say anything, I continued, "Bring me to her so we can ask her. If she wants to leave, the right thing to do is to let me take her back to my pack."

"Fine," he replied. "Follow my car. We'll clear everything up. I can't say I'm not disappointed, but I would never trap her if she truly wants to leave."

I noted a deep sadness in his eyes as his whole face took on a down-turned appearance, and I suddenly felt bad about taking her away from him. I couldn't imagine what it must be like for your mate to not want to be with you. I still missed Ria every day. While I loved Jasmine and couldn't imagine my life without her, there was still a pain inside me for the woman I'd lost before I knew her.

We followed Alex's car, now different than the one he had previously. It was still a Land Rover Defender, but a newer model and white instead of silver. After we parked, we all got out and followed Alex inside. He slammed the front door open, the heavy wood thumping loudly against the drywall, and we all stepped in behind him. We followed as he led us to the living room and halted, unable to tear our eyes from the scene that we walked into, our mouths dropping.

Clothes were strewn all over the living room floor, and on the couch was Talia with another man, both completely naked. They looked up and the man jumped to his feet, covering himself with his hands as he stared at us, wide-eyed, his chin trembling.

As if Tyler couldn't pick a worse moment to tell one of his awkward jokes, he broke the silence by saying, "Damn, now I'm starting to feel bad about myself. I'm literally the only guy in this room that Talia hasn't either gotten with or tried to."

No one could help themselves from looking around to see who else was standing in the same room.

Jasmine locked eyes with me and said, "You can't be the only one, Tyler!"

Digging himself into a deeper hole, he looked around and said, "Nope, I'm definitely the only one." And then realization played across his face as he comprehended what he had just revealed. We all turned toward Alex, who was completely red at this point.

Fur had sprouted from beneath the neckline of his shirt and peeked out from his long sleeves, covering his hands and fingers which were now tipped with claws. He turned toward the naked man, gave him an evil glare that would likely put mine to shame, and in a calculated and commanding baritone voice said, "Hugo Bernardi, I hereby banish you from the Pine Forest Pack, and you are fucking lucky that is all I am doing to you."

The naked man nodded, his chin trembling, terror in his eyes. He quickly gathered all of his clothes with shaky hands and bolted out of the packhouse. As he ran past us, the scent of a rogue exuded from his pores.

Talia broke into tears and quickly went to throw on a long T-shirt that had been lying on the ground, turning her back to us as she did.

"Goddess almighty, you're in heat." Alex gasped. "Fuck!"

She looked at him and then at us, clearly confused about what to do, her eyes darting back and forth between our group and Alex.

"Adalwolf, if you don't want me and everyone with me to take you down, I suggest you get out of here right now." I stared him down. "You know she wouldn't normally do what she wants to do right now."

He shook his head and walked out of his packhouse, his shoulders slumped and head hung. I looked back toward my sister and said, "Talia, get whatever you need, and I'll take you back to my pack if that's where you want to go." She gave a half-nod and, without a word, walked upstairs.

"How do I keep ending up around women in heat?" Jack asked, looking around.

"Great way to make this more awkward." I turned to him, rolling my eyes.

"Sorry," he replied, looking down toward the ground.

"Fucking five-hour drive now too," Tyler said. I glared at him. He got the hint, turning his eyes downward as well.

"Does anyone else have some comments?" I asked, my voice seething with anger. When I made eye contact with Jasmine, she was glowering at me, and I did not need the mate bond to sense her wrath.

Talia came downstairs fully dressed, pulling some bags along with her.

"Go help her," I said to Jack and Tyler. They instantly ran over to help her as she went upstairs to bring down more. We all loaded them into the car. Talia sat up front with me and Jasmine sat in back with Jack and Tyler. To say the ride was awkward would be the understatement of the century. No one spoke the entire time. I played music, but it couldn't drown out the tension. And not a single one of us was naive to the fact that Talia was clearly uncomfortable the entire ride, squirming in her seat. Since Talia refused to shift into her wolf and run across for some reason, we had to hide her in the trunk under her bags to cross the border and pray they wouldn't do a search. Luckily, everyone in the car had clean passports, so we made it through with ease.

We all helped Talia bring her bags up to her room and then left her there. I'm sure she must have been relieved to finally have some privacy. When I came downstairs, I spotted Jasmine sitting on the couch and went to go sit next to her.

"Clearly you've been hiding something from me." She looked up at me.

"Look, I'm sorry, Jasmine. I promised Talia I wouldn't tell anyone because she was embarrassed. And to be honest, it didn't seem like an appropriate story to tell you anyway. I knew it would probably upset you and make things awkward with Talia." I looked in her eyes to show I was being sincere.

"Well, what's the story? I know there's a story now, so you might as well tell me."

I sighed and said, "The first time I met Talia, she hit on me. I obviously turned her down because I'd never be unfaithful to you. But then, when I found out she was acting the way she was because she was in heat, I couldn't understand why it didn't affect me. It all started to make sense when Beta Alfred called Talia by her mother's name. The heat didn't affect me because I'm her brother. That's how I knew for sure we were siblings. That's what I didn't tell you. And it's not because I wanted to hide anything from you."

Jasmine kept staring at me, not saying anything.

I continued, "I mean, you'd probably be pretty embarrassed if you tried to get with Tyler and then later found out he was your brother. I'd keep any of your secrets the same as I did for Talia. Obviously, now the cat is out of the bag, and I'm sure Tyler has a video to illustrate that literally." I chuckled.

"How did Tyler know about what happened with you and Talia?" Jasmine crossed her arms and narrowed her eyes at me.

"Jack must have told him. Jack and Luke were both with me when it happened. Otherwise, I never would have told them." I took her hands. "I hope you'll forgive me, Jasmine."

"I forgive too easily," she responded, sighing.

"It's one of the things I love about you. You don't hold grudges and you're so understanding. I could learn a thing or two from you," I said, smiling. "You have such a pure heart."

"That doesn't mean you can keep hiding stuff from me!" She glared at me. "I shouldn't be letting you off so easily!"

"Ask me anything you want. I promise to be honest." I looked at her sincerely.

"It's okay, another time," she said. "I should get home. It's been a long day and it's almost dinner time now."

"You don't want to stay here for dinner?" I asked. "I'm sure Connie is making something good tonight."

"It's okay. My parents have been complaining I'm never home for dinner anymore." She got up. I walked her outside, but something about her seemed cold. I wasn't used to her acting like this. She kissed me before she got into her car, but it was quick and passionless, not how she normally kissed.

I pushed it from my mind. Besides this one situation that had now gotten cleared up, everything else between us was perfect. She probably just needed some time to process everything.

I went inside and decided that it was probably a good time to catch up on work. I took a seat at my desk and picked back up where I had ended the day prior.

Chapter 25

Talia

I woke the next morning feeling like myself again, dread coming over me. And I thought the first time I went into heat had been a disaster. Yesterday had been even worse. I had not only completely embarrassed myself, but I had also caused so much pain to everyone around me. That was not at all how I imagined sending the text message to Blake would go. And, God, that car ride home. If hell was a place on earth—that car ride was only a slight improvement to being tortured by the crazy bitch.

I didn't even want to leave my room to go to the washroom, fearing I might bump into Blake or, worse, Jasmine. I didn't think I'd ever be able to look anyone who was in that living room yesterday in the eye again. And, God, the pain I felt when Alex looked at me. I could sense his emotions so strongly, as if they were my own. His heart had broken right in front of me. I wanted to leave him, but I never imagined he would feel like that when I did. I could still feel the aching in my chest, as if someone had shoved a sword straight through me.

And Hugo. He'd been banished. What had I done? Just the day prior I'd realized I no longer had feelings for him, and suddenly, it was like I couldn't stop myself. The only thing that seemed to matter at that moment was that I was horny and I needed relief—it was like I'd been possessed. And, just like that, I'd pushed Hugo out of his home. He had helped me when I lost mine only for him to lose his own because of me. I fell into my pillow and began sobbing, realizing how much suffering I had caused.

I sobbed until my throat was burning, my head was aching, and my whole body was dehydrated. I used my blanket to wipe all the wetness from my face, neck, and chest and forced myself to get up. I reached for my cell phone so I could text Hugo and hopefully fix things. I was pleased to see my service still hadn't been shut off. I quickly typed him a text message, *Are you ok? I'm so sorry. I will fix this!*

I didn't know what else there was to say. I rolled onto my back and sighed. I had to get my life together. I had to clean up this huge mess. I couldn't just hide in this bedroom forever. Finally motivated in a way I hadn't been since my mother's death, I rolled out of bed and pulled everything together to get ready for the day.

After I showered, I put on makeup for the first time in forever and spent time putting together a cute fall outfit consisting of the bodycon dress that Lucy had forced on me, opaque black tights, and a cropped sweater. I put on some slippers so my tights wouldn't run, now that I finally had access to all of my things, and made my way downstairs.

I entered the kitchen to find Lucy on her way out with Libby in hand. She turned to look at me and said, "Damn, Talia! You look hot! I barely recognized you! What's the occasion?"

"I'm getting my shit together," I replied.

"Looking at you is making me want to party! It's been so fucking long! Luke owes me a night out. We're going out tonight. We can celebrate you getting your shit together!"

"Wha—"

"No excuses. If I say you're going out with me, you're going!" Lucy cut me off. "It's about time we become friends anyway."

I stared at her, baffled. Before I could even say anything in reply, Lucy disappeared through the door. I shook my head and popped a piece of toast into the toaster.

After I finished eating, I walked down the hallway, dreading the fact that I'd have to face Blake. But there was no way around it. I had to speak with him and figure out a way to move forward.

I knocked on his office door, which was open, and both he and Luke looked up at me, gesturing for me to go in.

"Hey, Talia, welcome back." Luke smiled at me. I gave him a small smile and took a deep breath, sitting down in a chair facing Blake's desk. He looked up at me from his laptop, waiting for me to speak.

"First of all, I want to say sorry for everything that happened yesterday. I didn't mean to cause any problems, and I was not expecting any of that to happen when I texted you."

Blake looked up at Luke and said, "Luke, do you mind?" I heard him get up behind me and watched him leave the room, closing the door behind him. Then Blake turned to me and asked, "Who was the guy?"

"I guess I should probably just tell you the whole story," I said.

"I think, at this point, I've basically witnessed all of your most embarrassing moments, and there's not much more you could say or do that would shock me." He chuckled. "But anyway, Talia, I want you to know that you can trust me. I hope I proved myself by dropping everything to get you from Adalwolf's pack. I know we didn't grow up together, but you are my sister and you're the only blood sibling I've ever known, so I'm hoping we can have a relationship."

I sighed and told him everything from the beginning—from the day I discovered my mother murdered. He sat there and listened patiently. When I got to the part about Alex's sister, he balled his hands into fists, but he didn't say anything and let me continue the story until I finished.

"Well, that's a fucking crazy story," Blake responded. "I can see why you wanted to leave Adalwolf's pack." His eyes took on an evil appearance. It seemed like he wanted to say more but he refrained. He finally asked, "What do you plan to do next?"

"I'd like to get a job, become independent, and move out of the pack-house."

"I can help you with that. Our pack has services to help with housing. But if you're planning to stay on pack land, you're going to have to become a member of the pack at some point. You can't live here and stay a rogue forever. So, it's up to you."

I took a deep breath and asked, "What happens if I decide to become a pack member?"

"I become your alpha, which means that you have to follow my rules and the rules of the pack. In return, you'll be protected. We take security very seriously and care about all our pack members. You'll also, of course, be expected to train and to learn how to defend yourself. Obviously, you haven't been training since kindergarten like our other pack members, but we could find you a personal trainer to work with you to learn all the basics. And, of course, the most important benefit is that you get to live with our kind. You won't have to pretend to be a human anymore, and you'll have a place where you'll be accepted. And finally, the best reason to join is you have family here." He gave me a friendly smile that brought a warmth to my chest.

It would be nice to have somewhere where I belonged, and I could finally be myself. Blake was right—after losing my mom, I had gained a brother. My limbs were somehow lighter and less tense at the thought. It felt like the right thing to do. After a couple minutes, I finally replied, "Yes, I think I'd like to join the pack."

"Great, I'm really happy." He beamed. "But, I have to ask, what do you plan to do about your mate?"

"I don't know," I replied, slumping my shoulders, pained and confused by the situation. "He told me he'd never accept it if I rejected him."

"If that's what you truly want to do, then I have no fucking problem making him accept it." Blake cracked his knuckles. "But I have to warn you, it's very painful to reject your mate. So, make sure you're completely sure before you do."

I nodded, recalling how heartbroken Alex had been, suddenly wondering if I really did want to reject him. I'd never known anyone to feel so strongly for me. My feelings about him began to change. Was I making a huge mistake? But I pushed the thoughts from my head and turned my attention back to the current situation, determined to turn my life around for the better.

"So you really want to join the pack?" Blake asked, opening a drawer in his desk and pulling out a blade.

I gasped.

"Don't worry, I'm not going to use it on you! Shit, I probably should have warned you."

"What's it for then?" My heart pounded in my chest.

"You have to bind yourself to me in order to join the pack. We each have to slice down the center of our palms and press them together, and then you need to pledge yourself to me and the pack."

"Oh, okay." I swallowed, my chest tightening with uncertainty about the process.

"Here, I'll go first and you follow my lead." He unsheathed the blade and stood. My neck prickled as, true to his word, he swiftly sliced down the center of his palm, allowing blood to drip down his wrist. He then handed me the blade. "It's best if you don't think about it too much and just do it." He gently touched my shoulder, in an encouraging gesture. "And do it fast, so I don't start healing and have to do it again."

I blinked a couple times and took one look at the blade. He was clearly depending on me to do it quickly, so I forced myself not to think about it and hastily sliced down the center of my palm. I winced from the sharp piercing sensation as the metal tore through the skin of my palm, a tear dripping down the side of my face in reaction. He put his own bloodied palm up, and I put mine against it. "Now, repeat after me," he said. "I, Talia—what's your last name?"

"I, Talia Wyatt," I said.

"Hereby solemnly pledge."

"Hereby solemnly pledge."

"My loyalty and allegiance to the Midnight Maple Pack."

"My loyalty and allegiance to the Midnight Maple Pack."

"And Alpha Blake Wulfric."

"And Alpha Blake Wulfric." After his last name left my mouth, I felt a connection within me snap into place and a tethering to Blake. Once the feeling passed, we separated our hands.

"Welcome to the pack." Blake gave me a friendly squeeze on my shoulder. "Now, about that job. We do have an opening here at the packhouse and you could start immediately if you'd like. This should come as no surprise to you, but Luke is looking for a nanny. The hours would be nine to five, Tuesday to Saturday. You wouldn't have to live here, and we could set you up in housing at the pack apartments. A lot of our young, unmated pack members live there. We'd waive rent for the first couple months until you're more settled."

"Do you mind if I have a few days to think about it?" I asked. While it was convenient to have a job already lined up, I wasn't sure if it was the right fit. I was hoping for something more independent of the packhouse, and Libby wasn't exactly the best baby in the world either.

"Sure, take a few days. We'll be posting the job in the pack newsletter this Sunday, so you have time until then."

"Okay, thanks," I replied, getting up.

After thanking Blake for all his help, I ran up to my room and checked my phone. Hugo had left my text message on read. I sighed, wondering where he was and what he was thinking. I knew I had to fix this. I knew I had to speak with Alex. But I felt dread in the pit of my stomach at the thought. The way he looked at me, the way he had looked at Hugo, and that pain. I thought losing my mom had been painful, but this was surprisingly worse. I didn't even know it was possible. I'd never felt anything like it before. And to know I had caused it—oh God.

I'd just wanted to break away from Alex. I hadn't wanted him to suffer like that. And then I thought back to the time we spent together. Had he really been that bad? No, he hadn't ever been bad at all. All the bad things I thought of him had been in my head. In reality, he'd always been kind and sweet to me. I groaned, forcing myself to stop thinking about it. I'd give it a few days, and then I'd reach out to him. I'd make all of this right. I'd apologize to Alex, and I'd explain everything. I'd ask him to let Hugo back into his pack.

I went through my backpack to find the folder Madam Coco had given me with my birth certificate so I could begin to figure out how to get all my paperwork together, only to find it was missing. I knew I had left it in there. Where was it? I sighed. This was not going to be easy. That birth certificate was the only thing I had to prove who I was.

I went downstairs and sat down on the living room couch with my cell phone and began researching how to piece together my identity. Not long after I'd settled on the couch, Lucy came in bouncing Libby and sat down next to me. "What'cha doing?" she asked. Then she sniffed the air and exclaimed, "You're not a rogue anymore!"

I looked at her.

"Did you join our pack?" she asked.

"Yeah," I replied.

"So, are you moving in here permanently then?"

"No, I'm going to move out." My voice trailed off.

"But?" she asked, staring at me.

"But?" I asked, confused.

"Well, it doesn't sound like you know where you're going. So, what's the deal?"

I sighed and figured I might as well tell her. "I don't have a job or the papers to get one. I was born here in the US, but I have nothing to prove it. I had a birth certificate, but I lost it. So now I need to figure out how to prove my identity."

Lucy smiled and said, "If there's anyone you can count on to get things done, it's me. But under one condition."

"What is it?" I asked, tilting my head at her.

"You're going out with me tonight, and we're going to party until dawn! Then tomorrow, I'll help you with your problem. And when I say 'tequila shot' tonight, you take one!"

I stared at her, wondering what her deal was. But I could use the help, especially not having a car to get from place to place. "Fine," I replied.

"Yes!" She fist pumped and made her way out of the living area. "Luke, baby! Where are you?"

Chapter 26

Talia

After dinner, Luke drove us a half hour outside the pack, to a casino, with Libby in her car seat next to me. She was being uncharacteristically quiet, which was very nice. As Lucy was about to get out, she leaned in to kiss Luke and he said, "I'll have my ringer on, baby, so call me if you need anything."

"We'll take a taxi home, baby," Lucy replied. She then leaned her whole body into the back to kiss Libby on the forehead and got out. Once Luke's car pulled away, Lucy led me inside. "It's thirsty Thursday!" she exclaimed. "The club in here is small, but it's not bad. Unfortunately, it's closed on Thursdays. But that's okay. We can go to the Chinese restaurant. They have a great bar scene."

"Don't you have to be twenty-one to drink in the US?" I asked.

"I have a hookup." Lucy smirked, handing me a card.

"Texas? This doesn't even look like me!" I said looking at the fake ID Lucy had handed me.

"Trust me, they don't care. Just make a bunch of eye contact and flirt a lot. Also, how's your Southern accent?"

I laughed. "You are crazy."

"I have a feeling you're a fun time." Lucy grabbed my arm, and pulled me toward the restaurant. She led me to the bar, and we walked in right in time as a couple was leaving, so we stole their seats. "Nice! The night's off to a great start." Lucy beamed. "Two mai tais!" she shouted at the bartender, holding up two fingers.

"Can I see some ID?" He came over, glancing between the two of us with his arms crossed.

"Sneaky, sneaky, trying to get my name already." Lucy leaned over the bar and put her hand on his forearm, fluttering her eyelashes at him. "One moment, let me get that for you," she said, sliding her fingers into her shirt and pulling out her ID before handing it to the bartender.

He glared at her, but I could tell that he was having a hard time not smiling. "Your ID says you're 5"5"."

"That was before the boob job and new heels," Lucy said with a completely straight face.

He laughed and handed her back her ID. I then handed him mine. "Texas?" he asked. "What brings you up here, Samantha?"

"I've been-a hankerin' to see the north," I said in the world's worst Southern accent. I could tell that Lucy was trying very hard not to laugh, her lips in a straight line and nose scrunched. The man shook his head and handed me back the fake ID.

"See, I told you," Lucy leaned in and loudly whispered to me after he walked away.

Minutes later, the bartender came back and slid two drinks in front of us. "Already paid for," he said. We looked across the bar where two men were waving at us. Lucy smiled suggestively at them and then picked up her drink.

We both got comfortable—the alcohol helped—and I found that Lucy wasn't actually so bad. After we were two drinks and a tequila shot in, with a third drink on the way (thank God for werewolf tolerance),

Lucy leaned over to me and asked, "So, what's the deal with Alex? He's your mate, right?"

"I wish I didn't have a mate," I replied. "And if I have to have one, I wish it wasn't him."

"Mates are overrated anyway."

"Luke's not your mate, right?" I recalled what Jasmine had told me.

"He is now." She thrust her chest out and crossed her arms smugly, giving a slight eye roll. "He's my chosen mate."

"Who's your real mate then?" I asked.

"Who knows. I'll never find out now." She waved her hand dismissively. "But I don't care. Like I said, mates are overrated. It's way better this way."

"Hmm," I said, considering what she was telling me. The bartender put another couple of drinks in front of us, and we picked them up to begin drinking again.

"Maybe we can find you a chosen mate too!" Lucy brightened up. "There are tons of hot warriors in our pack. I mean, they're not alphas like Alex. But they're still hot!"

I took another sip, a fuzzy feeling reverberating through my body and head as I began to feel a buzz come on. At the mention of his name, his image flashed back to me—his broad shoulders, impressive, muscular chest, the deep cuts of his abdominal muscles, and his soft, black eyes. "Alex is really hot though."

"Yeah, he is really fucking hot. But if you don't want to be with him, we can probably find you someone comparable. I have a bunch of cousins that are all warriors, and my older brothers have tons of friends too. So does Luke."

"Well, well, well, if it isn't Hemming." A male's voice sounded from behind us. We both turned around to come face-to-face with a tall redhead.

"Hi, Charlie," Lucy greeted him, a big, flirty smile on her face.

"And who's your friend?" he crossed his arms and gave me a once-over, an appreciative smile spreading to his cheeks.

"This is my friend Samantha from Texas." Lucy smirked. "New joiner to our pack!"

He put out his hand for me to shake. Not wanting to be impolite, I took it but couldn't help but notice that he was staring straight at my boobs as he shook my hand. I'd removed my sweater earlier because it was so warm in the bar, but now I was regretting it. This guy reminded me of some of the disgusting men I'd met throughout the years, back at the brothel. "Texas? I didn't know our kind lived so far down south. Although, I'd love to take a ride down south sometime." His eyes moved toward my crotch.

"Who are your friends?" Lucy asked, glancing over at the two guys behind him.

"This is Mack and Rick," he said, introducing them. "They're both warriors in my patrol group."

"Nice to meet you," she said, shaking both of their hands. "What brings you guys out tonight?"

"We're starting a new group in the pack," Charlie replied. "We're not happy with the changes the new alpha is making, so we're putting some petitions and such together."

"I thought you were friends with Blake." Lucy looked at him curiously.

"Not anymore. Anyway, it's all just political stuff. You wouldn't be interested. Obviously, now that we found out you gorgeous ladies are here, we've decided to put our meeting on hold. Why don't we buy you another round?"

"We can't say no to more drinks." Lucy smiled approvingly, pushing her empty glass to the edge of the bar.

After they ordered another round, Charlie shimmied up next to me and said, "So, Samantha, tell me about yourself." He was giving me really bad vibes.

"Well, the' ain't much tah say," I replied with my horrible Southern accent. I noticed that Lucy had moved her attention to the other two guys that Charlie had come with, letting out an exaggerated laugh. There was no way anything they said could be that funny.

"You've got very sexy eyes," he said, staring so deeply into them that I was uncomfortable. "Bedroom eyes."

I laughed half-heartedly, wondering how I could get out of this situation. He now had his hand on my arm.

He moved closer and said, "You definitely belong on my to-do list."

I reached for my drink, trying to move away from him. He was in my personal space, and Lucy was completely distracted, so I couldn't get her attention to show how uncomfortable I was.

"How's it taste?" he asked, looking at my drink. "I know something that would taste better. Why don't you ditch Lucy and come back to my place so I can show you?"

I was seriously about to throw up.

Suddenly, he turned his attention away from me, and looked across the bar. "Gross!" he sneered.

I turned my head to see a gay couple sitting across the bar minding their own business.

"What's wrong with them?" I asked.

"Blake is making a huge mistake letting them into our pack."

"What! Why would you say that?" I asked, horrified by what he was saying, especially with Lucy, who had a gay brother, sitting right next to me.

"Our group's going to take care of it. It's disgusting," he replied.

"What's disgusting?" Lucy suddenly looked over, clearly not having heard the rest of the conversation.

"Nothing," he said, walking away, his friends following him. I didn't think I had ever been so relieved in my life.

"I don't like him," I said to Lucy after they left.

"He used to be friends with my brother," Lucy said. "But I haven't seen much of him lately. I mostly only see him now when I go to my required training classes. I sign up for his because he goes easy on me if I flirt with him."

"I'm supposed to start training soon," I said. "Blake said he's going to get me a personal trainer."

"Hopefully you get someone good. Some of those trainers are brutal! They think they're drill sergeants or something! It's not like I'm the one going to war!"

"Do werewolves go to war a lot?" I asked, suddenly recalling what Alex had told me, wanting to confirm whether it was true.

"I think our pack goes to war just about every three to five years? My dad's a warrior, so he's been going to battle my whole life. And all my brothers are following in his footsteps."

"Wow, that must be scary," I said, imagining my whole family constantly going away to war. Maybe I had been too harsh on Alex, not giving him the benefit of the doubt.

"I guess I got used to it. People in my family have been warriors going back generations, and my dad is really good. He's one of the best warriors in the pack and has gotten tons of medals for his service. My older brother Jack looks up to him big time and has always wanted to be just like him."

"Beta Alfred told me that my grandfather was a warrior too. That's how he died."

"I bet either my dad or grandpa knew him then."

"Yeah. I guess Alex was telling the truth then," I said, recalling our conversation.

"What did he say?" Lucy asked.

"He said he has to torture people to protect the pack. It's not that I didn't believe him, but it just doesn't sound like something a normal person would do." I started to realize there was a lot I didn't know about werewolves and Alex. The conversation triggered a change of heart and made me regret not asking him more questions, so I could learn more about him and allow him to give me his side of the story. I was so busy making assumptions and being angry, I didn't even give him a chance. Maybe I really was making a huge mistake pushing him away.

Interrupting my thoughts, Lucy replied, "Oh, it's definitely true! Blake tortures people too, and so did his dad—well, your dad too, I guess. I've heard stories. I won't repeat them because they're gruesome."

"Tell me, please," I said, eager to know, begging Lucy with my eyes.

"Okay, I won't go into detail, but I've heard they chop people's arms and legs off and pull out their eyes. Stuff like that. And werewolves don't die. They just heal so they can keep going for hours."

"Why would Blake do something like that?" I asked with a bitter tang in my mouth, my stomach heaving, recalling how Alex's sister had tortured me, suddenly thankful she had at least refrained from removing my limbs.

"The most common reason is to get information, like finding out battle plans and what packs are involved in a dispute. If you torture someone enough, they finally beg for death and that's when they spill everything."

I took another sip of my drink, trying to remove the bitter taste and process what Lucy was telling me. When I didn't respond she said, "I guess, welcome to werewolf pack life, right? Come on, let's do another shot and get on the dance floor!" She waved the bartender over and ordered us two more tequila shots.

While Lucy seemed so flippant about everything, I couldn't help but feel something within me shift with this new knowledge, recognizing there was much more to being a werewolf and part of a pack than I'd ever imagined.

Overhearing Lucy place the order, a man offered to buy the drinks for us, but only if we did body shots off each other. Lucy instantly agreed and begged me to do it with her. Not knowing what I was supposed to do, and feeling pretty tipsy at this point anyway, I agreed to it. Lucy lay down on the bar and pulled up her shirt, so her belly button was exposed. The bartender sprinkled salt on her neck and gave her a lime to hold between her teeth. He then explained to me what to do as he poured tequila into her navel. I followed the instructions, drinking the tequila out of her stomach, licking the salt off her neck, and taking the lime from her mouth, and the whole bar cheered. Lucy gave me a big hug and said, "You're so cool, Talia!"

It was my turn next. Since I was wearing a dress, they agreed to put Lucy's drink into a shot glass. But they still sprinkled the salt on my neck and gave me a lime wedge to hold in my teeth. Lucy took the shot and she definitely took her time licking my neck, clearly putting on a show for her admirers, until she finally took the lime from my mouth. Everyone cheered again.

"Come on, Talia, let's go dance!" Lucy said, pulling me over to where they had opened up a dance floor. We spent the night dancing. Some men would come over, who Lucy would flirt with a little, but she stayed with me the entire night. I found myself really letting loose. I'd never had any female friends before and found that it was actually a lot of fun just hanging out with Lucy, getting drunk, and acting silly.

We stayed until the bar closed and they began turning on the lights.

"Damn, I can't believe the night's already over!" Lucy groaned. "Talia, you are awesome! Me and you are going to be good friends!" She hugged me again.

I could tell she was drunk. I was drunk too, laughing and hugging her back.

We went down to the lobby where the doorman got us a taxi to take us back to the pack. Once we got to the gates, one of the warriors on duty drove us back to the packhouse from the pack entrance. We stumbled into the packhouse, barely able to walk, giggling. Luke was sitting at the dining room table when we entered with Libby in his arms, feeding her. He put his index finger up to his mouth to signal for us to be quiet. Lucy walked over and sat down next to him, falling all over him. "Let's make another one tonight," she said, putting her arms around him and Libby.

"You are sloshed." Luke laughed quietly.

"Talia is awesome," Lucy slurred.

"I'm glad you ladies had a good time," Luke said, smiling.

I made my way upstairs and fell into my bed, snuggling into my pillow. It was nice when Alex was here with me, wasn't it? I suddenly recalled how wonderful those five days we spent together were and fell asleep to nice thoughts of him.

Chapter 27

Talia

True to her word, Lucy began to help me piece my identity back together. She took me down to the town hall that housed my birth certificate on Friday and flirted with the young man behind the front desk. Before long, he had produced a brand-new birth certificate for me. We then spent time emailing all my schools in Canada for records of attendance, so I'd have proof of living long-term outside of the country, and she promised to drive me down to the social security office early the next week.

She then took me down to the bakery café where she worked and basically forced her boss to give me a job. "Do you have any experience working in a bakery or café?" Valerie, a very curvy, red-headed woman, asked me.

"No, but I'm a quick learner," I replied.

"How do you feel about cleaning?"

"I used to help out with housekeeping for my previous job, so I'm good at cleaning."

"Good. I like to keep it clean around here. What about your schedule? When can you work?"

"I have open availability."

"So you don't mind working very early shifts, some that start as early as three in the morning?"

"No, that would be fine."

"Okay, you're flexible. That's good. When can you start?"

"As soon as you need me to."

"Great! Why don't we go easy for your first day? Come in tomorrow at ten, after the breakfast rush, and I'll start training you."

"Thank you so much, Valerie!" I exclaimed, smiling.

Once we stepped outside of the bakery café, Lucy took my hands and jumped up and down in celebration. She then ran back in to work her shift for the day, and I walked back to the packhouse, pleased with my progress. I could finally feel the depression I had been in for just about three months lifting. It seemed like things were finally falling back into place. But then my thoughts drifted back to Hugo, and dread came over me again. I had to speak with Alex. I had to get him to accept Hugo back into the pack. But I was frozen, unable to decide what to say or do. I pulled out my cell phone, knowing I had to do something, only to notice that I no longer had any service. I'd finally been cut off.

I sighed to myself. There were other ways to get in contact with both Hugo and Alex. Once I figured out what to do, I'd do it.

Jasmine

On Saturday, I was surprised to find that Tyler was in my sparring group after lunch. "What are you doing here?" I asked.

"I wanted to see what's going on with Charlie in person," he replied. "After what you told me, I signed up for his sparring class."

"Trust me, it's better that you just don't worry about it," I said, regretting telling Tyler anything.

"I'll judge for myself," he replied, stretching before we started the sparring session. I stretched with him until Charlie arrived, getting in late after lunch as usual. He walked around, leering at all the women, which I'd now come to realize was a part of his normal routine.

Charlie stopped in front of Tyler and me and asked, "Is that the kind of people you associate with, Dale?"

"Excuse me?" I asked in response. He just turned away.

"One-mile warm-up run!" he yelled to the group. Tyler and I kept pace with each other as we ran. I had to admit, it was nice having someone I was friendly with in my training group for once. Tyler mostly joked with me while we jogged, which made it fun.

When we got back, Charlie started assigning warm-up exercises. "Twenty-five burpees and twenty-five push-ups!" he shouted. Then he walked over to me and said, "Dale, fifty of each for you. Don't think I forgot last time."

I sighed as he walked away. "What happened last time?" Tyler asked before we started the warm-ups.

"Don't ask," I replied and began the first of fifty burpees.

When I was about halfway through, Charlie came back over and shouted, "Chest to the ground. No slacking on those burpee push-ups. Not like you have the chest to get away with it, Dale!"

Haha, my boobs are small. So funny and original!

I finally finished my last push-up and got up to see that Charlie had already put people in sparring groups. And, surprise, surprise, we were sparring in our wolf forms once again today.

"You're already behind. Hurry up and get in your wolf form, Dale!" Charlie shouted at me. As usual, I walked over to the changing partition. "You're wasting time. Why can't you be like everyone else and just shift on the field?"

"Because she doesn't want to!" Tyler shouted.

"And who the fuck are you?" Charlie walked over to Tyler.

"You know who I am!"

"I'm the fucking trainer in this class. You have no right to question me."

"That's my sister you're trying to make strip in front of you, you pervert!" Tyler yelled at him. Everyone was quiet now, staring at the interaction.

"I'm the pervert? Are you for real?" Charlie stared at him. "I don't do perverted shit like you do."

"And what kind of perverted shit is that? Please enlighten me."

"I don't take it up the ass. I'm not a fucking donut muncher. I can't believe the pack even allows disgusting creatures like you to live here!"

"At least what I do is consensual. You are a creep that gets off on staring at women you're supposed to be training. You're a predator is what you are. None of these women consented to being your personal sex objects. You make even me uncomfortable with how you openly gawk at them while they bend over and shift."

"Get the fuck out of this sparring class now!" he yelled, then stared at Tyler when he didn't move and said more quietly, "You will pay for ever questioning my authority."

"Oh, I'm so scared! Some creep that can't get women the normal way, so he has to intimidate and force himself onto them instead, is going to come after me. What are you going to do? Force yourself onto me now?"

"You fucking wish!"

"No, that you're wrong about. I'd rather force myself straight than ever touch you. You repulse me. Just like I'm sure you repulse every woman in and outside of this training class."

"Fucking faggot!"

"How dare you speak to him that way?" I yelled, seeing red and incensed by Charlie using that horrible word to insult my brother. As much as I'd taken everything Charlie had dealt me up until this point, seeing someone I cared about being harassed triggered something within me. I was at the point where I wasn't going to be able to bite my tongue anymore.

"Jaz, it's okay. I got this." Tyler stepped in front of me, giving my arm a quick squeeze as he did.

"Cocksucker," Charlie said in a deep, menacing voice, completely red, his fists clenched.

After a beat, Tyler scoffed and responded, "Is that all you have? Repulsive and uncreative. See you later!" Tyler turned and walked away, shaking his head.

It seemed as if Charlie was holding himself back from chasing after him, his body stiff and jaw clenched. He then turned to me and said, "Dale, one hundred burpees now!"

I hesitated for a moment, not wanting to put up with his shit anymore, but resigned myself to doing as he asked, somewhat glad to have the physical work to burn off all the anger I felt.

Later that evening, I was relieved to finally be going home after having to deal with Charlie's wrath for the rest of the day. I appreciated that Tyler had stuck up for me, but all the verbal abuse he'd had to endure to do that had been devastating. Things had gone from bad to worse. I sighed and sat down on a bench, quickly shooting Tyler a text to make sure he was okay.

Again, I appreciated him and that he had come into my life, but was our pack really the best place for him? It couldn't have been more painfully clear how unwelcome he was today when, not only did Charlie attack him with a horrible slur, but no one even seemed bothered by it. Their silence was loud and clear. Granted, we were all taught not to question our trainers or those senior to us in the hierarchy, but it was still devastating.

While I had been doubting the whole "becoming a warrior" thing for a long time at this point, I was finally at my breaking point where I didn't think I could take it anymore. As I was pulling all my things together in the locker room to head home, I sent a text to Blake to see what his plans were for that night, wanting desperately to see him. But he replied to say he had to oversee all the patrol stations.

Feeling tears pool in my eyes, I blinked them back and turned to go, surprised to see one of the girls in my new group approach me. Her name was Paige, and I knew she was one of the newer recruits. She was a pretty, strawberry blonde girl.

"Hey," she said, getting my attention. "I'm really glad your brother said something to Charlie. He was really creeping me out. He kept trying to get me to have drinks with him after training every day. I had to keep making excuses. I've been wanting to report him, but I'm so new, so I didn't want to cause trouble. When I told some of the others, they told me that I just need to get used to it as a warrior, especially as a female. They said we need to fight for our right to even be warriors, so we shouldn't make waves. But I don't think it's right."

"I know what you mean," I replied. "I've been afraid of making waves too. Especially since I don't fit in with the others."

"I don't know why the others don't like you, to be honest. You seem nice to me."

"Thanks," I replied.

"Also, what Charlie said to your brother was horrible. I couldn't believe it. I know that the religion is against being gay, but we're also taught to be loving, kind, and respectful to others. And, anyway, the new alpha took away the ban on gay people, so Tyler has as much right to be here as everyone else."

"Thank you, I appreciate that so much! You have no idea!" I said to Paige, her words getting to me.

"I know you're religious too. So maybe I'll see you at temple tomorrow?"

"Yes, I'll be there." I smiled at her.

Chapter 28

Blake

After the trip to the Pine Forest Pack, things seemed to be back to normal with Jasmine and me. Between our work and training schedules, we didn't have much time to meet up, but Jasmine seemed to have forgiven me. After almost a week of mostly text conversations and quick meetups just to bring her coffee before training, I was looking forward to seeing her later that night when she'd be over for dinner.

It was a Tuesday, and Luke and I were, once again, seated across from each other in the office, catching up on our paperwork. After my father passed, my work had practically doubled, now that I was also in charge of the casino. Fortunately, the casino had a whole management team, so my job was mostly just oversight. But there were still constantly decisions to be made, and I had to keep tabs on what was going on to make sure things weren't getting mismanaged, especially since the pack relied on the casino's income to stay afloat.

"Hey, Blake," Luke called out to me.

"Yeah?" I replied.

"I'm going through the write-ups from the past couple of weeks, and there's probably something I should bring to your attention."

"What is it?"

"Jasmine's been written up regularly for two weeks now."

He had my attention now. I looked up. "For what?"

"Random stuff. Things like disobeying orders, causing conflict, disrespecting superiors, not meeting training standards, taking breaks that are too long."

"That doesn't sound like Jasmine at all." I narrowed my eyes.

"I know."

"She's a rule-following perfectionist. There is no fucking way that she would have done any of those things. Who the fuck wrote her up?"

"Charlie Kemp."

I balled my hands up into fists at the mention of his name.

Clearly noticing my reaction, Luke asked, "Are you okay?"

"Yeah, fine," I replied.

"You just made your evil face," Luke said. When I didn't say anything in return, he asked, "Isn't Charlie one of your buddies?"

"He was my buddy, until he cornered Jasmine during my birthday trip last year and tried to force himself on her. I haven't spoken to him since."

"I'm taking it that you don't want these write-ups transferred to her record?"

"Obviously I don't want some petty fucking bullshit part of her record. Not that it matters, because she's going to be the luna anyway. But I'm going to find out what the fuck is going on."

I then looked down at my desk and noticed the envelope. I took a deep breath and picked it up, getting up from my desk. I couldn't avoid it anymore. "I'll be back," I said to Luke. "I have something I have to take care of."

He must have noticed the envelope in my hand because he got up and walked over to me. "Look, man, I know things have been weird with us for a while now. But I just want you to know that I still consider you my brother. And I'm here for you if you ever need anything." He put his hand out for me to shake. I took it and he pulled me in for a hug, patting me on the back.

"Thanks, man," I replied, feeling comforted by Luke's gesture, nostalgic for our old camaraderie. I had fucked it up six years ago when I was too deep in my own misery to be able to accept Luke's friendship, anyone's friendship. And, out of all my buddies, I probably lashed out at Luke the most, an unfortunate consequence of living in the same home as him. The fact that he was mated to the woman I'd inadvertently fallen for a year ago didn't help the matter, driving a larger wedge between us. Deep inside, I wanted to be brothers again, but I was still figuring out how to accept friendship into my life, still affected by the ghosts of my past.

I took a deep breath and, giving Luke a small, painful smile, said, "I'll be back."

"Good luck." He returned it with a small sympathetic smile of his own.

I exited the packhouse and decided to walk. It was a little chilly but sunny. I didn't feel like rushing to get to where I was going. A deep pain stabbed me violently in my chest as I approached the familiar house—a house I used to spend hours inside, a family I used to be close with.

I walked up the familiar steps and rang the familiar doorbell that made the familiar chiming sound. The whole experience was both nostalgic and horrifying simultaneously. I forced myself to push through it. I could do it. I was alpha now, and I couldn't let something like this destroy me. Goddess, if others only knew how easy it was to obliterate the big bad alpha wolf.

"Blake!" Ria's mom opened the door. She wrapped her arms around me and started sobbing. Her tears soaked my chest, and her body trembled against me. It shattered me. Everything in me was breaking down, compelling me to do the same, but I stayed strong, clenching my fingers into fists to steady my shaking hands. If I didn't talk too much, I could get through this.

"Come in, come in." She sniffed and wiped at her nose, her whole face splotchy. When my feet didn't move, she pulled my arm, leading me over the threshold and into the living room. "Please sit, Blake. Let me go make some tea. What a wonderful surprise."

Her mom was a beautiful older woman with curly hair that had now fully grayed. When Ria died, I had noticed from afar that her mom had aged ten years practically overnight. Now, six years later, she looked even older. Logically, I knew I wasn't the only person Ria's loss affected, but I found it difficult to see past my own pain.

After several minutes of sitting alone, Ria's mom returned to the living room, bringing two mugs that she dropped onto the coffee table. She then left again and returned with cookies, milk, and sugar and took a seat on the love seat adjacent to the couch where I was sitting.

"We've heard the news, of course." She gave me a small smile.

"That's why I came. I thought I should tell you in person." I handed her the envelope.

She took the envelope and put it onto the coffee table, then she moved forward in the love seat and clasped my hands in hers. "Thank you for coming, Blake. There's not a day that goes by that I don't miss my Ria. I know you also loved her very much. You were such a good mate to her. I'd never seen her so happy as when she had you in her life. And I wish the two of you could have had a long life together. But we can't control what happens in life." Her voice broke as she looked down at our hands. After a few moments, she looked back up, staring intently into my eyes. "But you're still alive, Blake. You need to live."

She removed her hands from mine and took a sip of her tea. I knew I should say something, but I couldn't bring myself to speak. After all this time, it was still difficult. My chest was so tight I could barely breathe. I sighed, taking a sip of my own tea, trying to soothe the scratchiness.

"Your mom comes to visit sometimes. I don't know if she told you."

I looked up at Ria's mom, my breath catching. My mom had never told me.

"She's going through her own loss now, of course. The poor woman. I've always liked your mom. She's a good one."

I nodded in agreement.

"It's okay if you don't say anything, Blake. I understand. I have something to return to you." She stood up and walked out of the room and then returned with her hand balled up. I opened my hand to catch whatever she'd brought over. And into my palm dropped a small engagement ring.

"I can't accept this," I said, trying to hand it back. "It was a gift for Ria."

"Ria has no use for it now. I'm not taking it back. Sell it and use the money to buy something nice for your new mate. Just please don't be a stranger. It's nice to see someone who was once a part of Ria still alive. It makes me feel like a part of her is still here."

"To be honest, Mrs. Baker, I believe there's a part of Ria that's still alive inside me and never left."

"I always said her spirit was too big for her body. She was probably relieved to find another body to deposit some of the extra."

After I returned from my visit and finished up with work for the day, Jasmine came over at six. I had the table set for two and had asked Connie to make Jasmine's favorite—Connie's chicken cordon bleu and potatoes au gratin. I set everything out on the table along with two small salads in preparation for the evening.

She came into the packhouse, looking stressed as usual. "How was training?" I asked, pulling her in for a kiss as soon as she walked in.

"It was fine," she replied, pulling away. "I'm glad I finally have the day off tomorrow."

"Connie made your favorite." I smiled at her, taking her hand to bring her over to the dining table. "I hope you came hungry. Although, if you aren't, I'd be happy to skip straight to dessert." I smirked, trying to cheer her up.

She walked over to the table and took a seat. We each put food on our plates and began eating quietly. "Is there something on your mind?" I asked, noticing she was being much quieter than usual.

"No, everything's fine," she replied.

"Really? You're not getting written up for anything in training?"

She looked at me wide-eyed. "What did it say I was written up for?"

"I knew it was bullshit. But why didn't you tell me?"

"Because I didn't want you to get involved. Ever since you discharged Alyssa everyone's been worse than usual. And then Tyler came to my sparring class on Saturday, and now something that I didn't think could get worse has. So please, just stay out of it!" She glared at me.

"What did Tyler do? Jasmine, please, can you tell me what's going on?"

"Why should I? It's not like you tell me what's going on with you, ever. You just retreat into your own world whenever you don't feel like talking about something, and I'm supposed to just accept that that's who you are. And then I was the last person to find out about what happened between you and Talia."

"Nothing happened between me and Talia!"

"You know what I mean!"

I sighed. "Jasmine, I don't want to fight with you. I explained why I didn't tell you about Talia, and I thought you understood. And I know I have a really hard time talking about certain things, but I'm trying. I don't do it on purpose. I've told you more than I've ever told anyone else. But I still have limits to how far I can go."

"Why is that?" Her features softened, and she reached out to touch my hand.

"I don't know. My dad and Ria both fucked me up. Sometimes it feels like I'm getting better, but then I realize I'm not."

She came around the table and sat in the chair next to me, taking my hand. I put my arm around her and pulled her close to me, kissing her head. Still feeling a sharp pain from earlier that day, I pushed through it and said, "There's something I should tell you, Jasmine. I went to see Ria's mom today to tell her about our engagement. It was really hard. I haven't been able to face her family since she passed."

Jasmine looked up at me and squeezed my hand. We sat like that for some time and then I said, "We better finish eating before our food gets cold. Then we can continue this upstairs."

She nodded and went back to her seat. We spent the rest of the meal eating quietly, reflecting.

Talia, Lucy, Libby, and Luke came into the dining room as we were finishing up. I'd noticed that Talia and Lucy seemed to be really close now.

"I'll go reheat this," Luke said, grabbing the ceramic dishes with the chicken and potatoes. Jasmine and I put our dishes into the dishwasher as Luke threw the food into the oven. He then turned to Jasmine, gave her a small nod, and said, "Nice to see you, Jasmine."

"Hi, Luke," she said, walking out of the kitchen as I followed. We walked upstairs to my bedroom, and Jasmine stopped after closing the door, looking at me as I came closer to her, stopping me. "Do you mind if we just cuddle tonight?" she asked. She then walked toward the bed and lay down with her clothes on.

"I mean, I'd prefer to do something else before the cuddling, but I can put up with skipping it for one night," I said, crawling into the bed and pulling Jasmine close to me. "It is kind of nice though. It reminds me of the first time we ever lay in bed together."

"I just think we should finish the conversation we started downstairs."

"Are you going to tell me what's been bothering you then?"

"No, I think you should tell me more about what's going on with you. What you said about your dad and Ria fucking you up and how you're not getting better. What does that mean?"

I sighed, now regretting I'd ever said anything, realizing how much I didn't want to have the conversation Jasmine was asking me to have with her. It was just easier to live with the damage inside me. It wasn't something I thought I could release into the world. I turned onto my back, trying to decide what I could possibly say.

"You're doing it again," she said.

"Doing what?"

"You're retreating into your world. You're pushing me out."

"Jasmine, I'm sorry. I just can't talk about it," I replied.

"Why? Does it hurt?"

"Yes."

"I guess I can understand that. It still hurts when I think about Luke, and I don't like talking about him either."

"Do you still have feelings for him?" I asked, turning toward her again.

"No. I've thought about it, and I don't."

"Thank Artemis."

"But it still hurts in my chest when I see him and think about him. And it hurts even worse when I see him with Lucy. I hate that he has to live in the same place where I'll be moving soon."

"Jasmine," I said, pulling her closer toward me. "Goddess, I hate that you feel that pain. I really hope once I mark you that it will finally go away for good. Just two more months and hopefully you'll get better."

"What about you?" Her eyebrows drew together, and she reached out to touch my cheek.

"What about me?"

"You're not going to get better, are you?"

"Jasmine, it's okay. I've accepted my fate in life. It could be worse. I have you. I know I'm not 100 percent better, but I have healed since I met you, a lot! I'm barely even the same person I was before. I think what I was able to do earlier today proves it."

"I love you, Blake." She moved closer to me and ran her fingers along my jaw and neck.

"I love you too, Miss Alpha," I said before kissing her deeply.

Chapter 29

Talia

It had been two weeks since I'd joined Blake's pack, and the dread in the pit of my stomach was getting worse. I'd been completely avoiding the situation with Hugo and Alex. We were in early November, and it was now cold enough to require a coat when I went outside. I'd finally be moving out of the packhouse and into my new apartment in less than a week. For now, I was saving money so that I could afford some furniture once I moved, even if it was just some random old furniture people posted for sale in the pack Facebook group. I at least wanted to buy myself a new mattress. I was grossed out by the idea of sleeping on a used one.

I was still able to use the Wi-Fi on my phone, so it wasn't a complete brick. Not that it was easy to find places with Wi-Fi around here, but both the packhouse and the café had it. It wasn't always super reliable, but it got the job done. I could easily try to reach out to Hugo again through an Instagram DM, but then I was ashamed that I had promised to fix things and I had never made good on my promise. God, I was such a horrible friend. What was wrong with me? I just couldn't do it—thinking about reaching out to Alex left me frozen. I knew I had to take responsibility. I promised myself I would stop dragging my feet and finally do something about the situation.

I worked the early shift at the café that day and got out at one thirty. I then had a personal training session scheduled at two. Luckily, the person who Blake had paired me up with wasn't bad. His name was, ironically, also Alexander, but he went by Xander, and he was also shorter than my mate and had curly black hair.

"I think we should start training in your wolf form today," he said after we got warmed up.

"I don't know if that's a good idea," I replied.

"Why not?"

"I don't have a lot of control over my wolf. Lately, she's just been doing her own thing whenever I shift."

"I see. In that case, maybe we should work on meditation instead until you get more comfortable with the idea of shifting."

"Meditation?" I asked.

"Yes, meditation will help strengthen your mind and help you have greater control over both parts of your brain. Werewolves have used meditation going back thousands of years to strengthen their focus, especially when in their werewolf forms. It is also used in our religion to have a deeper spiritual connection with the Moon Goddess.

"We can start with a focused meditation. To begin, just close your eyes and focus on your breathing. Keep your mind on just the sensation of what happens within your body when you breathe in and out, and try not to let it wander. Do your best not to think about anything."

He helped me get into a proper position for the meditation and guided me as I followed his instructions. We spent around fifteen minutes working on focused meditation, and then we switched to doing different general strengthening exercises with weights. Before I left, he assigned more meditation as homework.

I got home to Blake and Luke in the middle of the house in a heated discussion. Rather than go upstairs, I sat down at the dining room table pretending to go on my phone while I listened in, curious to know what was going on.

"When was the last time anyone saw Jimmy?" Blake questioned in a raised voice.

"It seems he must have never gone home after his shift. They sent the juniors in the northeast patrol station out one hundred yards at the beginning of the afternoon shift, and it was actually Jasmine who smelled the scent of the Bois Sombre Pack and noticed Jimmy's blood on the ground," Luke replied.

"Fuck."

"You know, I don't really like that Jasmine is going outside the pack territory for duty. That could've easily been her that got kidnapped, Blake!" Luke's voice was tense and his arms were crossed.

"Jasmine is going to be luna! She should be involved in the same things everyone else is."

"Blake, that's really fucking reckless!"

"Why are you so fucking concerned about Jasmine?"

"Because I care about her, Blake! I mean, how can I not after having spent so much time with her? Plus, if other packs find out she's your new mate, that'll make her a high-value target. Now that you've mailed out the wedding invitations, it'll only be a matter of time before the news spreads."

I recalled learning that Luke had been mated to Jasmine in the past. I began to seriously question what the consequences of rejection were and suddenly came to a realization that maybe Lucy wasn't the best person to speak to about it as she had never personally gone through it herself.

"Fuck," Blake said. "I guess I never thought about that."

"I'm taking her off patrol duty immediately. She can start helping in the packhouse with your work instead."

"Good idea," he replied. "But what are we going to do about Jimmy?"

"I can send some trackers out to find him. But my guess is they took him for either interrogation or intimidation. I can't see any other reason they would take such a low-ranking pack member."

"Well, I can't exactly face his family unless we at least make an effort to find him. He's still alive. I haven't felt his death yet."

"Okay, I'll send some trackers out," Luke replied.

"Thanks."

"And I'm taking Jasmine off patrol duty," Luke walked away toward the hall that led to the offices.

Blake pulled out his phone. He put it to his ear and then said, "Adalwolf, we've had an incident at our pack. I wanted to see if you've had any news on your end. One of our juniors has been kidnapped by the Bois Sombre Pack"

. . .

"Why didn't you tell me about that incident in your pack?!"

. . .

"I'm going to call our other allies and let them know. That fucking Alpha Édouard is completely unhinged"

. . .

"Yeah, she's fine." Blake glanced my way, then brought his attention back to the phone, not saying anything for a while. Finally, he spoke again. "She told me what your sister did, and I can't fucking blame her."

After he hung up, he was about to walk away down the hall toward his office when I got up and stopped him. "That was Alex?"

"Yeah."

"I need to speak to him," I said, knowing this was my opportunity to finally clean up the huge mess I'd caused.

"Is that what you want?"

"The thing is, he banished my friend from his pack. And I need to help him. He supports his family, and I don't know where he went or how he's living now. He's always been a good friend to me, and I need to at least try to help him."

"Okay, here." Blake handed me his phone. "I'll go use the landline to call the other packs."

I scrolled through his phone and found Alex's number, dialing it, my heart beating loudly in my chest as the phone rang and I paced the room, unsure of what I'd say to him.

"Wulfric?" he answered the phone.

"It's Talia," I replied.

"Oh."

"Hi."

"Hi," he replied. This was feeling very awkward.

"How are you?" I asked, knowing that I was doing a very bad job of getting to the point.

"I mean, I'm completely shitty to be honest. But how are you?"

"Alex," I started, trying to decide how to continue. "The thing is, I'm worried about my friend, Hugo."

"Hugo!?" he shouted.

"You banished him from his home. He's the sole provider to his family. His father died, and his mom and brother both depend on him. I'm really worried."

"That's who you're worried about? Are you serious?" He sounded very irritated.

"Is there someone else I should be worried about?" I asked.

He sighed. "Talia, I feel like I'm on some bad trip. I've waited for weeks for you to call. And when you do, it's to speak to me about the man I caught you screwing in front of me, your fucking mate! And, oh yeah, apparently you've been getting around with half of Blake's pack, including your own fucking brother!"

"What! That's not true!" I shouted.

"Really, well, that's certainly how it sounded. I guess I shouldn't have expected more from someone that grew up in a brothel. For all I know it wasn't just your mom that was a whore. I always thought your blow jobs were suspiciously good."

"Alex!" I shouted. "How can you say that to me? That's so cruel!" Tears fells from my eyes, turning into full-on sobs.

"Shit! Talia, I'm sorry!" he yelled, and I hung up before he could say anything else. I was about to throw the phone across the room when I remembered it wasn't mine, and I brought it back to Blake, wiping the tears from my eyes as I walked down the hall. Blake was on the phone at his desk when I placed his cell phone onto it. He looked up at me with furrowed brows and a tilted head. I didn't bother to stick around and explain and headed up to my room.

What a mess. And how horrible. Now I really knew what Alex thought of me and my mom. A debilitating pain pierced my chest at the thought. I fell into my bed and found myself not able to get back up. Was this how I would always feel now? I was so pathetic. I thought I was getting better and finally getting my life together, and then this happened. I clutched at my chest, wishing it would go away and I could just forget about him. I hadn't asked for a mate—it had just been forced on me. And to hear him say those awful things to me, I couldn't help but wish I'd never met him.

A couple hours later, I heard a knock on my door. "Come in!" I said and Lucy walked in, bouncing Libby.

"Are you okay?" she asked, sitting down on my bed.

"It hurts so much," I replied.

"What does?" She reached out to touch my shoulder and drew her eyebrows together.

"Alex," I said. "It's so painful."

She stared at me for a while and then finally said, "They did teach us in school that being away from your mate for long periods of time will make you weak. Maybe that's what's happening. When was the last time you saw him?"

"Two weeks ago."

"I don't know how long it takes for the weakness to kick in, but you should probably do something about it."

"What should I do?"

"Well, you're going to have to either decide to be with him or reject him."

"What happens if I reject him? Blake said it's really painful." As the words exited my mouth, the same piercing sensation jabbed at my chest. I clutched at it in reaction, as if I'd been stabbed.

"Blake's right. It is really painful. When Luke rejected Jasmine, I'd never seen him in so much pain before. He could barely get out of bed."

I felt helpless at her reply. How much more pain could I take? But then another thought came to me that cut through the sorrow. Should I maybe speak to Jasmine to get a better perspective?

"There's a way to get rid of the pain," Lucy added, giving me some hope.

"How?" I looked up at her, desperate for all her knowledge about how to fix the situation I was in.

"You need to find a new mate—a chosen one—to mark you."

"To mark me? What does that mean?"

She pulled down the sweater she was wearing to reveal a mark where her neck met her collarbone. "They have to bite you after having sex with you. And you do the same. Then you will officially be mates. But since you currently have an unconsummated mate bond in effect, you'll have to reject him first in order to be able to be marked by someone else. It won't work otherwise."

"But that means I have to find someone else to be my mate. And what happens once we become mates anyway?"

"It means you're bound for life. You will feel each other's emotions and have a deep connection that you'll never have with anyone else."

"That seems like a really big commitment." I sighed.

"Then just find someone that you want to commit to, silly!" Lucy smiled.

How did everything seem so simple in her mind?

"I know! My brother Mark is turning eighteen next week, and we're going to have a birthday party at our house for him. You can come over and meet my cousins. I have some hot, unmated warrior cousins. You've seen Jack—they're like him—all tall, blond, and muscular! Come on, cheer up. We'll figure this out!"

I groaned and Lucy held Libby on her hip as she pulled me out of bed using her free hand. She was surprisingly strong for someone who hated the gym so much.

Chapter 30

Talia

Just under a week later, I'd finally moved into my new apartment on my day off from work. Lucy had borrowed her uncle's truck, so we could go buy and bring back a new mattress. At the moment, I didn't have much. It was just the mattress on the floor with no bed frame and a kitchen table and chairs that I bought for cheap from the pack Facebook group. Jasmine had gifted me a brand-new set of pans as a housewarming gift, which was very nice of her. And Blake had brought over a fancy coffee maker and a couple mugs. Lucy and Luke gifted me really nice towels and linens and a bunch of toiletries. Jack and Tyler came with them and gifted me a blender.

I was completely in awe of everyone's generosity and gave everyone big hugs in gratitude. Everyone was so welcoming. It was nice to have friends. It felt like I finally belonged somewhere.

It was now Saturday, and Lucy had invited me to her brother's birthday party that day. I wasn't sure that I was up for socializing, especially with the pain in my chest that continued to linger. But Lucy had been so kind to me, and so helpful. I wanted to go to the party that she'd invited me to.

Not sure what to buy for her brother, I ended up settling for an Amazon gift card that I was able to purchase from the pack grocery store. I put it in an envelope with a birthday card and made my way over to Lucy's parent's house, which wasn't far from the grocery store.

The door was open when I arrived, with a house full of people inside. I entered, looking around.

"Talia!" Lucy shrieked when she spotted me, throwing her arms around me. She pulled me over to another blonde girl, much shorter than her. "This is my sister-in-law, Emma. We've been friends forever, and now we're family, after she found out her mate is my brother, Kyle."

"Nice to meet you, Talia." Emma pulled me into a hug.

"Talia is awesome. You have to come out with us one night when Kyle finally lets you out of the house." Lucy playfully punched Emma's arm.

"Yeah, I won't be leaving the house for a while now," Emma said with a sly smile.

"Why not?" Lucy asked.

"Well, your brother knocked me up again. I'm almost two months along with our second. That's why I've been acting so busy lately."

"What!" Lucy exclaimed. "Aren't you breastfeeding, and don't you use protection?"

"I told you, I didn't produce enough milk, so we had to formula feed. And, I mean, we always have good intentions to use protection, but sometimes we just get so horny, and things happen. Actually, I think this one was conceived on the kitchen table."

"Okay, that's enough visuals for the day. I don't need to imagine my brother fucking you over the kitchen table!" Lucy lightly shoved Emma.

"What about you? Any plans for a baby sister or brother for little Libby? You still have to make the beta heir, right?"

"Libby's a handful. I think we're going to wait until she's a little older and better behaved before we go for another. Anyway, there's no alpha heir yet, so there's no rush."

"We got the invitation in the mail. I've been meaning to congratulate Jasmine. But I feel like things are weird with her now. Ever since what happened with, well, Luke, I haven't really heard from her. Neither has Madison. We all used to be so close. I feel bad about what happened. But it all worked out in the end, right? Can you imagine, someone from our class is going to be our luna now?"

"Hey, baby." A blond man with a strong resemblance to Jack came up behind Emma, wrapping his arms around her.

"Where's Ethan?" Emma asked.

"He's with his great-grandma right now. She can deal with his spit-up for a change. Maybe she can change his diapers too, and someone else can get a golden shower from him for once. Last time it ended up in my mouth."

"Oh my Goddess, stop, Kyle." Emma elbowed him. "You're making me nauseous."

"Nothing like pregnancy and babies so you can enjoy the full range of fluids the body has to offer," Kyle deadpanned. "I'm Kyle, by the way." Kyle reached out his hand to shake mine. "Don't worry, my hands are clean."

I took his hand and shook it. "Nice to meet you. I'm Talia."

"You're Alpha Blake's sister?"

"Yes, I am."

"Welcome to the pack, Talia."

"Thank you," I replied.

"Hey! There they are!" Kyle glanced up suddenly. I looked behind me to see Jack and Tyler approaching. He went to give them both hugs and they both came over to greet me.

After chatting with everyone for a while, Lucy led me away and brought me into another room, pointing out a really handsome tall blond man. "That's my cousin, Tom. No mate yet. He's twenty-eight.

Come on, I'll introduce you." She pulled me over and tapped him on the shoulder.

"Hi, Lucy. Nice to see you." He hugged her in greeting.

"Tom, I want you to meet my friend, Talia." She pushed me forward.

"Nice to meet you, Talia." He gave me a wide smile, shaking my hand.

"Talia is Alpha Blake's sister, and she's single. She's really hot, isn't she?"

He looked at Lucy curiously and said, "Yes, Talia is very pretty."

"I think you have a lot in common with her. I have to go help my mom with the food, but you should get to know her." Lucy walked away leaving me with her stranger cousin, feeling very awkward.

"Well, that's Lucy for you." He gave a small chuckle, shaking his head. "Always up to something." He then turned to me and asked, "So, what brings you to our pack, Talia? I didn't know that Alpha Blake had a sister."

"Half sister," I clarified. "We just met each other a couple months ago. I found him when I found out this was my mother's old pack."

"Very interesting. I guess the rumors must be true then."

"The rumors?"

"About the late Alpha James, your father I assume?"

"What are the rumors?"

"I probably shouldn't be the one to tell you, but there have been rumors for many years around the pack that he has many illegitimate children that he's banished throughout the years. I'd imagine you have more siblings out there somewhere."

"Blake mentioned something along those lines. What else do you know about my father?" I asked, suddenly curious.

"I don't know too much. He always seemed like a pretty friendly guy to me. Very charming. He was good at working a crowd. Everyone in the pack respected him."

"Oh," I replied, thinking how different Tom's view of my father was from Blake's. It seemed everyone had a different opinion of him. Who was my father really?

"Anyway, why don't you tell me about you, Talia? How old are you?"

"I'm twenty," I replied. "Lucy tells me you're twenty-eight. And you're a warrior?"

"That's correct. What do you do for work? Or are you a student?"

"I work at the bakery café with Lucy."

"Oh, I should come by and visit you sometime! I try not to eat too many pastries, but damn, the ones they have there are really good. Anyway, if it means the opportunity to see you again, I have no problem having a small cheat pastry." He smiled at me.

He was quite handsome. Not as handsome as Alex, but handsome enough, I supposed. It's not like looks were everything. But, damn, Alex really was hot. But Tom seemed nice, and, plus, his father hadn't murdered my mother and his sister had never tortured me. He'd also never called my mom a whore and accused me of being one too. Tom for the win!

We spent most of the remainder of the party chatting, and he was actually super sweet and polite. He refilled my drinks for me and pulled out my chair for me when we went to eat. Lucy kept winking at me from across the room. When the party was over, she walked with me back to the packhouse so she could give me a ride home, Libby in her stroller in front of us. "So, what did you think of Tom? He was great, right?" she asked.

"Yeah, he was really nice," I agreed.

"What do you think? Do you think you could see him as a mate?"

"I don't know. I just met him. We did agree to go on a date soon. But he seemed weird about it and told me to keep it on the down low."

"Oh, that's just our pack. Everyone thinks it's the 1950s around here, so people don't like to openly talk about dating. Anyway, Tom's the best.

You're going to fall in love with him in no time and then you'll be saying, 'Alex who?'" She laughed.

The next day, I had to work the early shift. Around eight thirty in the morning, true to his word, Tom stopped by with a big smile on his face.

"Good morning, Talia," he said as he stepped toward my register. "It's worth waking up a little earlier to see you at the start of my day. You are quite a sight for sore eyes."

"Hi, Tom. What can I get you?" I asked.

"How about a large coffee with cream and sugar, and I can't say no to those delicious cinnamon rolls they have here." I slowly typed in his order, still in the process of learning the register system.

"That will be six eighty-eight," I said. "Would you like me to warm the roll up for you?"

"Yes, that would be great." He smiled.

He was very smiley; he had a really nice smile, with bright white teeth. And really nice blue eyes. Yes, everything about him was nice, very nice. I pulled out a cinnamon roll from the case and put it into the small oven to warm it up. I then turned around and watched as he slid his card into the reader.

Valerie handed him his coffee and stood next to me, looking him up and down. "Lucy's cousin, right?" she asked.

"That's correct. I'm Tom."

"You Owens all look alike," she said.

"So I've been told."

"I don't see you in here much."

"I came in to see a special person," he said, winking at me. I turned around to pull his bun out of the oven and put it into a to-go bag. "Thank you, Talia! See you again tomorrow!" he sang out. Since it was a Sunday, it wasn't too busy yet. We normally got busier closer to ten on Sundays, so I decided to go clean the tables to get ahead of things getting too messy.

I was about to reach for the cleaning spray when Valerie stopped me. "Is there something going on between you and Lucy's cousin?" she asked.

"I don't know, maybe," I replied.

"Did Lucy tell you much about him?" she asked.

"No, not really. She just introduced me at her brother's birthday party yesterday and thought we should go on a few dates."

"So you're not mates then, I take it."

"No, we're not."

"Not that I'm against it, but werewolves don't normally date unless it's with their mates. And I'm wondering what Lucy is up to trying to get you to date her cousin."

"Oh, I'm sure it's nothing crazy," I said, but began to question it a bit. Lucy never told me werewolves didn't date others who weren't their mates. Clearly mates were a lot more meaningful than I had understood.

Valerie looked at me curiously and said, "I know you didn't grow up around werewolves, so I'm going to explain some things to you that you might not know. Lucy's cousin more than likely isn't looking for anything more than a fun time. There's nothing wrong with that, if that's what you want too. I had plenty of fun myself before I met my mate. But I want to make it clear to you that he is not going to want to settle down with anyone who's not his mate. I know that Lucy and Luke ended up together even though they weren't mates, but in my close to fifty years of life, that was one of the very few times I ever saw something like that happen. So I want you to be aware of what's going on before you get hurt."

"What about Blake and Jasmine?" I asked.

"Blake had a mate before Jasmine that he was going to settle down with, but she died. And Jasmine's mate rejected her to be with Lucy. So their circumstances are completely different. However, Lucy's cousin has a mate somewhere out there, and he is certainly going to hold out for her. Anyway, that's my lecture for the day. Now, go clean those tables."

I grabbed the spray bottle and a clean rag and did as asked, walking the whole café, making sure all the tables and chairs were spotless. Then I started to wonder—was that why Hugo never wanted anything more? Was it because he was also holding out for his mate? And if I rejected Alex, would that mean I'd be alone forever if no one ever settled down with anyone who wasn't their mate? Why did all of this seem so simple in Lucy's mind? Clearly it wasn't as simple as she made it out to be.

Chapter 31

Talia

Tom came in again the next day, and then again on Tuesday, when he convinced me to go on a date with him that night. After what Valerie had told me, I began to feel suspicious of his intentions. But I figured that one date wouldn't kill me. We agreed for him to pick me up that night at six in front of my apartment.

After work, I had my personal training session after two days off on Sunday and Monday. I began to understand that most of the pack shut down those two days. We started the session off with stretches and some warm-up exercises. Then we practiced some more meditation. After that, Xander had me do some weighted exercises.

"You know, I've been keeping track, and you don't seem to be progressing on the weights at all. I'm becoming concerned because werewolves normally progress fairly quickly, and it isn't normal that you'd still be at the same level as you started almost a month ago, especially with us training together five days a week."

"What could cause that?" I asked.

"The most common cause is being away from your mate. But seeing as how you don't have a mate, I'll have to look into it more. I'm thinking maybe you should go by the clinic and get checked out."

"Thank you, I will," I replied. Blake and Lucy had both told me I'd grow weak without my mate, but I hadn't taken it as seriously as I probably should have. Now it was clear as day that the effects of being away from Alex were beginning to transpire, and it scared me.

I headed home after my training session to shower and get ready for my date, what Xander told me still on my mind. I was growing weak. Or, at least, I wasn't growing stronger. I took my time doing my hair and makeup and threw on a sweater dress and leggings with booties. Feeling desperate about the situation, I began to hope things would work out with Tom, just like Lucy had suggested. He seemed like a nice guy. It wasn't far-fetched to believe our feelings would grow for each other. Then everything could be fixed and set right. I'd just reject Alex, and Tom and I would become mates, and I wouldn't become weak.

Right on time, Tom rang my buzzer at six. I ran downstairs to meet him, and he escorted me to his car.

"You look very nice tonight, Talia," he said, smiling as he hooked his arm in mine. "I think it's best if we go somewhere outside the pack territory. There's a restaurant that's not too bad nearby."

"Okay, sounds good," I said as he opened the car door for me. We quickly sped out of the pack territory, and he brought me to a barbecue restaurant nearby. "I figured you can't go wrong with barbecue," he said. "Especially with a werewolf."

"Do you ever go out with anyone who isn't a werewolf?" I asked, curious.

"Werewolves aren't usually interested in going out, at least not in our pack. Most of the women are so prude and uptight. So, I mostly hang out with humans. They tend to be much more open-minded."

With his reply, I started to realize that Valerie might be right. I was beginning to doubt that this was going to work the way I'd imagined.

After we ordered and were sipping some lemonade, I asked, "So have you never had a serious relationship?"

"What's the point, right?" he replied nonchalantly.

"Why do you say that?" I asked, taken aback.

"Well, we're going to meet our mates at some point, and then things just get really messy. It's easier just to keep things casual and have fun and then amicably move on."

"I see," I replied. "So you're not planning to ever become serious with anyone that's not your mate, eh?"

He looked at me and frowned. "Talia, I hope you weren't expecting more than just hanging out for a bit. I just assumed with you being a werewolf that you'd want to be with your mate once you met him."

"Of course, why wouldn't I want to be with my mate?" I muttered.

"Plus, with how Alpha Blake was, I just assumed that maybe you were the same, being his sister and all."

"What does that mean?" I asked.

"Well, you know, how he used to be."

"I only just met Blake, so I don't know how he used to be."

"I mean, he's not like that anymore now that he found a new mate. But back in the day, he used to sleep with any woman with a pulse. I'm pretty sure he's been with half the women in the pack."

Suddenly I was nauseous, realizing exactly what he thought of me, wishing I'd never agreed to this date.

The waitress came around and placed our orders in front of us and refilled our water. When she walked away and was out of earshot, I asked, "So you think I'm a whore, eh?"

He looked at me wide-eyed and said, "No, I don't think that! Goddess, I really put my foot in my mouth, didn't I? No, I just thought maybe you were more open-minded. I mean, I'm no saint either. And we all have needs. I'm very discrete. I'd never tell anyone what we did together, and I'd also never judge."

God, I felt sick. Was that all men ever wanted from a woman? I mean, I knew that, but it was still devastating to hear it said to me so directly. I had no idea why I'd listened to Lucy and gotten my hopes up that there was an easy way out of my mate situation with Alex.

"I'm sorry if I gave you the wrong idea. I'm still learning about how werewolves do things. I didn't grow up in a pack," I said, shoulders slumping as I picked up my fork. I figured I may as well just get through the meal, and then we could go our separate ways.

"No, Talia, I'm sorry! I shouldn't have assumed anything. But I'm glad we cleared everything up. Let's just enjoy each other's company tonight. I mean, there are worse dining companions I could have ended up with." He smiled. He did at least seem like a nice, decent guy.

After the date, I asked him to drop me at the packhouse. I rang the doorbell and Blake answered, standing next to Jasmine. "Talia, what are you doing here?" he asked.

"I came to see Lucy," I replied.

"Okay, I'll go get her, one second," he said, climbing the stairs.

I then turned to Jasmine. "Jasmine, I have a question, and can you be honest?"

"Sure," she replied, raising her eyebrows, and came closer to me.

"Do you know of anyone that ever settled down with someone who wasn't their mate, except obviously Lucy and Luke and you and Blake?"

She crossed her arms and looked upward, appearing lost in thought. After a moment, she finally said, "The only other person I know is Tyler's mom."

"Why did Tyler's mom settle down with someone who wasn't her mate?"

"Her mate rejected her because she had Tyler. But it ended up being for the best because he was a really bad person."

"My mate might be a bad person too," I said. "But what if I can't find another mate to mark me after I reject him?" A sharp pain sliced through my chest as the words escaped my mouth, compelling me to clutch at it, wincing.

She touched my arm in a comforting gesture and asked, "Goddess, Talia. Is he really that bad?"

"I think he might be. I'm not sure. But what happens if I reject him?"

Luke stepped into the room, interrupting us, and Jasmine's whole demeanor changed. She stepped backward, her eyes taking on an almost pained look as she glanced between Luke and me. "Maybe we should talk about this somewhere else."

"Talk about what?" Luke asked.

"Rejecting your mate," I said, immediately regretting it as the sharp sensation stabbed at my chest.

"Oh." He looked down with a slight flush across his cheeks, not making eye contact with either Jasmine or me. I had made things very awkward. Blake came down the stairs, and Lucy followed with Libby in her arms.

"Talia!" she called out. "How was your date?"

"You went on a date?" Blake asked, looking between the two of us.

"Of course she went on a date! Look how hot Talia is! The whole pack's going to be all over her in no time! She's going to have tons of hot men to pick from. She doesn't need her dumb mate." Lucy smiled, bouncing Libby up and down.

"Lucy, what are you doing?" Luke looked up at her with furrowed brows and crossed arms.

"I'm helping my friend! Duh!" she replied.

"How are you helping?" he asked.

"Talia wants to reject her mate. So I'm helping her find a replacement mate. You have tons of friends, Luke! Maybe you can introduce Talia to one of them. Of course, maybe the date went really well with Tom tonight and then we don't need your help anyway. So how'd it go, Talia?"

"Tom? Your cousin Tom? The one with the reputation?" Luke gave her a pointed look.

"What are you talking about? He doesn't have a reputation!"

"Really, Lucy?"

"Okay, so things have been said about him. But everyone gets gossiped about in our pack. It's not like Blake didn't have a reputation either. And he's been great to Jasmine. Right?"

Everyone turned to Blake, and he didn't look happy at all. He actually looked pretty pissed looking back at Lucy.

"Anyway, Talia, how'd the date go?" Lucy asked, clearly ignoring the look Blake was giving her.

I looked around at everyone feeling overwhelmed. Finally, I blurted out, "He just wanted to fuck me. That's all anyone wants, right? I'm just like Blake—sleeping with half the pack! It's in my blood! I'm a fucking whore!"

Jasmine gasped. Everyone was silent, staring at me.

"Fucking Artemis." Blake broke the silence. "Lucy, what the fuck are you doing?"

"I was just trying to help!" she whined.

"Well, maybe it would help to at least fucking explain some things to Talia before you just start setting her up with every unmated man in our pack. Like the fact that they're probably not going to want anything serious with her if she's not their damn mate!"

"But Luke and I worked out great!" She grinned. "See, we have a beautiful daughter and everything."

"Lucy, you fucking stole Luke from his mate!" he bellowed.

"You know what, fuck you, Blake! Don't act like it didn't work out perfect for you. You were all over Jasmine the entire time! You were just waiting to pounce once Jasmine rejected Luke! You guys were a couple not even a month after everything went down!"

"Lucy, that's enough!" Luke shouted at her. "Just stop, okay! We don't need to dig everything up that happened."

"Maybe we should dig it up! Everyone pretends like none of that happened, and we're all going to be living together soon. What, are we just going to spend the rest of our lives pretending that you didn't fuck my best friend?"

"I should go," Jasmine said, pulling open the front door and stepping outside before closing the door behind her.

"Holy fucking Artemis," Blake said under his breath and stomped outside, following Jasmine.

Luke was completely red staring at Lucy, his jaw tense. "Lucy, that was really insensitive."

"Insensitive to who?" she snapped back.

"I just can't right now!" He threw his hands up. "I'm going for a run. I'll be back later," he said, stomping toward the living room, opening the glass sliding door to step outside.

"I should probably go too," I said, baffled by what had just happened.

"Don't worry, Talia. We'll find someone for you," Lucy said. "So, Tom didn't work out. There are plenty of other fish in the sea!"

"Thanks," I said. "Are you going to be okay?"

"Oh, yeah! I'm fine! Luke's just going through a thing. He'll be fine when he gets back." She smiled and then snuggled her face into Libby's belly.

I tried to figure out if she was just saying that or if she actually thought that. I wasn't sure but decided to just accept what she said and stepped outside.

"Going home?" Blake asked as soon as I closed the door behind me.

"Where's Jasmine?" I asked.

"She wasn't feeling well so she left." His frowned and blew out a breath.

"Is she okay?"

"Yeah, she'll be fine. Why don't I walk you home? It's pretty dark out."

"Sure, thanks." We began our stroll toward my apartment. After a beat, I said, "Sorry for what I said earlier. About you sleeping with half the pack. It just came out, and I didn't mean to say it like that. And if you did, there's really nothing wrong with it. I was just…" My voice trailed off as I realized I was rambling.

He gave my arm a squeeze. "Don't worry about it."

"I guess I was just hoping to meet someone who saw me as something more."

"Are you really trying to find a replacement mate?"

"It was Lucy's idea," I replied.

"Lucy, always full of ideas." He rolled his eyes and shook his head.

"She told me that it's the only way to get rid of the pain after you reject your mate." I flinched at the sting in my chest.

"So you've decided to reject Adalwolf then?"

"I think I should. We're just not right for each other."

"I see." We walked in silence for a while and then he asked, "When do you plan to reject him?"

"I should probably do it soon, right? The trainer told me that I'm not progressing, so I'm clearly not able to get stronger now. And—" I paused.

"And?"

"I just remembered. I'm going to go into heat again, right?"

"How long has it been since your last one?"

"When you brought me back from Alex's pack. That was about a month ago."

Blake stopped me and looked at me very seriously. "Talia, this is very important. Do not leave your apartment when you go into heat again. Promise me."

"Okay, I promise." I looked into his eyes.

"Good. It's one thing if you want it, but there are men out there you won't want to be with, even while you're in heat, and some of them won't resist and will force themselves on you. It hasn't happened for many years in our pack, but you can just never be too careful. And if it does happen for some reason, you better fucking let me know. Because

I will take care of them." Blake's whole face took on an evil appearance, his eyes almost demonic.

"When you say there are men I won't want to be with, does that mean I don't want to just be with everyone when I'm in heat?"

He chuckled, his face softening again. "No, heat is different for men and women. Women want to be with men they are attracted to and would probably want to be with anyway even when they're not in heat. They just get really horny, but they're still selective. However, unmated men can smell the heat in women, and the scent makes it really hard to resist, no matter who the woman is or what she looks like."

"God, that just makes me feel even more disgusted with myself, Blake!"

"What can I say, I'm so hot even my sister wants a piece." He snickered.

"Gross! Stop!" I laughed, pushing on his arm.

Chapter 32

Alexander

My mom finally seemed to be feeling slightly better. The hospital prescribed her some strong antidepressants and tranquilizers, so strong that she was no longer able to shift into her wolf.

"I don't care. I have no reason to shift into my wolf anymore." My mom sighed as I finally drove her home after being away for over a month. I'd hired nurses to keep watch over her when I couldn't, and one of them would be starting the next day.

I helped my mom to her bedroom and helped her lie down in her bed. It was so strange having our roles reversed after she'd always been the one taking care of me my whole life. But everything was strange in my life. This was normal compared to everything else. Yes, how sad, my mom barely able to function as an adult was "normal" to me. Fuck my life.

I sat down on a chair next to her bed while she got settled. "Will you be okay, Mom, if I go work on some things?" I asked.

"Alex"—she stared at me—"you seem unhappy."

"Of course I'm unhappy, Mom. Dad is dead and you're in bad shape. Why would I be happy?"

She let out a deep breath and said, "Yes, but it seems to be more than that. You're not yourself."

"I'm fine, Mom. Just get some rest. I'll be downstairs. I'll bring you some lunch up in a bit."

"Where's Sara?"

"Sara doesn't live in the packhouse anymore."

"She moved out? Why? Did she meet her mate?"

"No, it's because it was time for her to move out. I need to be alpha on my own, and she needs to find her own path in life."

"But she's your sister, Alex. And it's always good to have help, eh?"

"No, she meddles too much, and she's too impulsive. I don't like how she does things. Now that Dad is gone, it's time for her to leave too."

"Alex, I don't like this at all." She looked at me sadly.

I kissed her on her forehead and said, "It's for the best. It's time for me to do things on my own. Now get some rest, and I'll be back with lunch later."

I stationed myself at the kitchen island downstairs, deciding to work from home that day. Normally I worked from the dairy processing plant, or I was out and about either training or overseeing the patrol stations. But I didn't feel comfortable leaving my mom home alone. I sighed. If we were on better terms, Sara probably could've stayed and kept watch over my mom while I worked, but I just couldn't stand to face her anymore. Anyway, it's not like we couldn't afford to pay nurses to keep watch over my mom.

My chest burned. It never ceased. Ever since that day I came home and caught Talia and Hugo together—my heart had been shattered. I'd never felt anything like it before. Goddess, I loved her so much, I realized. Why did she hate me? Why had the Moon Goddess sent me someone so perfect who refused to be with me? It was a cruel joke.

She'd finally called me two weeks ago, after I'd felt miserable for two weeks, barely able to force myself out of bed to attend to my pack duties. And it was to speak about Hugo—the man I'd foolishly trusted, who'd thrust himself at her at the first opportunity he got.

Okay, okay, she *was* in heat. And I don't know exactly what happened and how they ended up in that position together. After all, heat was one of the most difficult impulses for a male werewolf to resist. I'm sure it must be similar for a female. And they did happen to be in the same house at the same time that day. If I put emotions aside, it may have not been as deceptive as it felt. But Goddess, it fucking killed me. It tortured me. I'd rather Sara run her blade through my whole body than feel how much my heart ached after witnessing what had happened.

So, could you blame me for what I said to her? Could you blame me for the low blow I'd dealt her, calling her dead mother a whore? Goddess, what was wrong with me? I'd never insulted someone's mother in my life, only to do it now to my mate.

Fuck my life.

Later that evening, my mom begged to see Sara. I had no choice. I'd have to face her and bring her back into the packhouse. I couldn't deny my mother seeing her daughter. So I texted her. When I didn't see a confirmation of the text being received, I called. Her phone was off. That's okay, I could just do things the old-fashioned way. I drove down to the townhouses where Sara was living now. I rang her doorbell, no answer.

"Oh, hello, Alpha!" an elder lady who lived next door greeted me as she was walking into her own townhouse.

"Hello there. Have you seen my sister today?"

"You know, I haven't seen her for a few days. She's normally in and out. I think last I saw her she had been walking out back into the woods."

"I see," I replied. "Thanks, have a good day."

"You too, Alpha!" She smiled, entering her home.

I shook my head, wondering what Sara might be up to. If she'd gone into the woods, it was likely to shift into her wolf form. Something didn't feel right. No, she never hesitated to act on her impulses. And her warning still echoed in my head.

If you don't fucking finish my job, I will, because that rogue bitch deserves to die.

I returned home to find my mom where I'd left her and sat down in the chair next to her bed again. "I went to go find Sara, but it seems she's out. I'll bring her over as soon as she returns."

"Okay, honey," she replied, her eyes drooping closed.

As soon as I stepped out of her bedroom, my phone rang. *Wulfric.* My pulse quickened, hoping it was Talia again, desperate to hear her voice.

"Hello?" I said, eagerly answering the phone.

"Hey." Blake's voice sounded on the other end. I slumped my shoulders in disappointment. "As my ally, I'm giving you the courtesy to tell you that we have your sister in confinement, and we don't plan to kill her. However, don't think I've forgotten what she did to my own sister." He paused. When I didn't say anything, he continued, "Torture happens to be one of my favorite activities, and the opportunity doesn't present itself often enough. I plan to bring Talia with me to the cells tonight, and it's up to her to decide your sister's fate. You can collect her whenever you feel like making your way down here."

"Fuck," I said, not knowing how to reply to something like that.

"That's all," Blake said, hanging up. I made my way downstairs and paced the floor. I'd have to leave the next day. I called the hospital to line up nurses to attend to my mom for twenty-four hours a day. And then I called my beta, making sure he was okay to handle the pack in my absence. I wasn't sure how long I'd be gone. But a part of me was ecstatic. I finally had an excuse to see Talia again. As much as what she'd done had hurt me, I still couldn't stop missing her and desperately wanting to be with her. A gravitational force constantly pulled me in her direction. Tomorrow we'd be reunited.

Chapter 33

Talia

The day after my date, I woke up to my alarm, feeling overheated, and threw the covers off me. God, I was horny. And then I knew—I'd gone into heat again. What a pity that I hadn't invited Tom over after dinner. He could have been lying in bed next to me right now, relieving the desperate, swollen ache between my legs. I'd made a huge mistake acting so virtuous when that didn't serve me at all.

I began recalling my dream. Just like last time, it'd been so vivid. I recollected all the details of Alex's amazing body. God, why had I ever wanted to reject him? He was so ripped, and the way he kissed me, so passionately, so lovingly—I knew he had to be good in bed. I wished so badly I could confirm my suspicions at that moment.

Then I remembered, I had to work that day. I turned to look at the time on my practically-a-brick cell phone. Hey, the alarm still worked, so that was something! I could also use most of the features on it when I was connected to Wi-Fi, which I wasn't while in my apartment. That was a luxury I didn't want to splurge on until I felt more secure.

And then I recalled what I'd promised Blake. I couldn't leave my apartment today. So how would I tell Valerie I couldn't make it to work? Maybe I could run to the café real quick. It was very early in the morning.

No one was bound to be out this early. I'd just sneak over, let Valerie know, and sprint back. If she wasn't there, I could always leave a note.

I hastily dressed, muscling through the incessant pulsing between my legs. It's okay. I'd take care of it soon. I just had to make it over there and back. I threw my hair into a messy bun and snuck out of the apartment before jogging toward the café. When I got there, my coworker Liz was inside loading pastries into the oven. She was a short, quiet girl who mostly kept to herself.

When I walked in, the chime of the door announcing my presence, she came out front to see who it was and gasped, staring at me wide-eyed.

"You're in heat!" she choked out and instantly covered her mouth with her hands.

"You can tell?" I asked, squinting at her.

A flush spread from her cheeks down to her neck. "Please don't tell anyone." She brought her hands to the sides of her head, her chin trembling. "Please," she pleaded.

"But I thought only unmated men could—" And then realization came over me.

"Please, Talia, don't tell anyone." She had tears in her eyes now.

"I promise I won't say anything. I just came in to tell Valerie why I can't come in."

"You shouldn't be out. You need to go home. It's really dangerous."

"Okay, I'm going home. Just let Valerie know, okay?"

"I will. Now leave! It's really hard for me!" she shouted.

I quickly stepped out of the café, ready to run home when I stopped in my tracks at a bunch of warriors heading to their cars. Shit, I hadn't considered that warriors might be out this early in the morning. Of course, they worked shifts at all hours of the day.

"Samantha!" A familiar voice sounded, and I felt dread at the pit of my stomach.

"Don't fucking do it, man!" another man yelled at him. "Leave her alone!"

"But she smells so fucking good," he replied.

"I will take you down, Kemp!" the man said back to him.

"I will take you down too," another man chimed in. "Leave her alone."

"You're all a bunch of buzzkills!" he yelled back to them.

Terrified, I fell into a sprint, running back to my apartment as fast as I could, wondering what would've happened if he'd been alone. Would he really have tried to force himself onto me? And then I realized, he was a warrior, and I was weak. He would've easily been able to overpower me. I couldn't get inside my apartment fast enough, locking the deadbolt behind me.

The next day, I returned to work feeling much better. I was working the late shift that day. When I came in, Valerie pulled me aside. "You were in heat yesterday?" she asked. "Does that mean you have a mate?"

"Yes, I do," I admitted, realizing there was no way around it now.

"Then what was that whole thing with Tom? Why were you going on dates with Lucy's cousin when you have a mate?"

I sighed and said, "Because I want to reject my mate. I don't want to be with him. Lucy was just trying to help by finding me a replacement mate."

She raised her eyebrows and said, "Well, there's a story I'd like to hear."

"Maybe another time."

Lucy came in not too long after me, late as usual. Punctuality was clearly not one of her positive qualities. I mostly worked the front of the house while she helped Valerie put together pastries in the back. After we closed for the evening, I walked with Lucy toward the packhouse since I had to walk in that direction to get to my apartment anyway.

"Why don't you come into the packhouse for a little bit, and we can hang out? Luke is going to be working late, so we can have a girls' night." She looked at me eagerly.

"Sure," I agreed.

After having dinner and giving Libby a bath, we were just about to get settled down to put on a fire and movie in the living room when Blake walked in.

"Talia, good, you're here. You need to come with me."

"What happened?" I asked.

"Just come with me. I'll explain in the car."

Lucy and I looked at each other, and I got up to follow him.

Once we were in the car, he said, "We have your mate's sister in custody."

I looked over at him and, again, his eyes took on that demonic appearance. His blue eyes were so cold, hard, and dead that it was as if he'd lost his soul and instead become a ruthless predator.

"We caught her trying to sneak into the pack. She's tough, but our warriors were able to take her down. Anyway, we've got her chained up in the cells now. I've already informed Adalwolf about the situation. I let him know that it's up to you how we handle her. Don't think I forgot what she did to you."

I stared at him. When I didn't say anything, he shifted into reverse and pulled out of the packhouse lot. Then I asked, "What are you planning to do to her?"

"Like I said, it's up to you. But happy to give you some of my ideas if you need any. Torture is one of my specialties." He had a very sick smile on his face, one that reminded me a lot of the one Alex's sister had as she tortured me. Holy shit, Blake was just as fucked-up as she was!

When we got to the jail, Blake led me inside and brought me down into the basement, into a room that was clearly set up specifically for torture, with no windows to the outside world. I felt nauseous entering, smelling the strong scent of blood and bleach mixed together, possibly old considering the lack of ventilation. One of the walls was lined with various swords and knives, and there was a table with heavy straps and chains as well as more straps on the walls. In one of the sets of straps, Alex's sister hung by her wrists and feet, her mouth gagged with a ball, completely naked.

"Since she didn't remove any limbs or do any permanent physical damage, I think we can keep it pretty tame today." Blake's eyes glistened, as he pulled a knife off the wall. "Got this one freshly sharpened recently."

God, his smile was sick. I looked over at Alex's sister and her eyes look terrified. Much different than the woman I'd witnessed before when she'd been the one torturing me.

"So, what do you prefer? Gagged or not gagged? I personally like to hear their screams, but I'm taking it this is your first torture." Blake patted my shoulder. "Our dad didn't go easy on me for my first one, but happy to ease you in if that's what you'd like."

Jesus fucking Christ. He was actually planning to torture her. And he looked elated to get started. I wanted to vomit. As much as she'd hurt me and traumatized me, I didn't think I could do the same to someone else, even if that person was the one who'd done it to me. No, even though Alex thought I'd be more than eager to torture his father, that was not true. I wouldn't have ever tortured his father, and I wouldn't torture his sister either.

"Do we have to torture her?" I asked.

Blake rubbed his chin and furrowed his brows. "Well, no, we don't have to. But I just assumed after what she did to you, and now after she was caught sneaking onto our territory, clearly coming after you, that you'd like nothing more than to do that. I know I'd like nothing more than to run this knife through her skin." He taunted her with the knife, touching it to her neck.

"It's not that I don't think she deserves it. But I'm not like her. I don't get a sick pleasure from torturing. Anyway, at what point does it end? Do I torture her now, and then she comes back and tortures me again? Or worse, does she find one of my friends to torture next? No, I don't want any part of this."

Blake looked really let down. "Damn, well, that's really anticlimactic. I guess I'll just have to find someone else to use this knife on." He hung it back up on the wall.

"Sorry to disappoint."

"Well, there'll be others," he said, giving me a reassuring smile. "I'll have my warriors escort her back into a cell, and Alex can pick her up whenever he makes it over here." He began toward the stairs and I followed.

"Alex is coming here?" I asked, practically tripping over the first step, grabbing onto the railing.

"I'm assuming he's going to want to bring his sister back to his pack. Although, I don't know that I'd ever collect my sister if she tortured my mate the way she tortured his. If anyone ever hurt Jasmine like that, I can tell you for a fact that they wouldn't still be alive. I don't care if they're blood related or not."

Chapter 34

Talia

The next day, I was on the early shift and was more than ready to leave when I punched out at one thirty. I had my regular personal training at two that day where Xander and I worked on meditation, and he taught me different fighting moves in my human form.

"Tomorrow, I want us to start training in your wolf form. I'll be here supervising, so you shouldn't worry about your wolf doing anything crazy. I've been trained in de-escalation and containing savage wolves. But usually, wolves only become savage when you live mostly in that form, so you really shouldn't worry. Plus, I'm sure the meditation has been helping."

"Okay," I agreed, not wanting to tell him the real reason, preferring he believe his own explanation.

"Great. I'm starting to think that might be part of the reason you're not improving. It might be because you're suppressing your wolf form, and that's where us werewolves get our strength. It's not natural to live only in your human form."

I nodded.

"Have you gone to the clinic to get checked out?"

"No, I've been busy," I replied, looking at the ground.

"Well, I think I may have figured out what's going on. But, anyway, you should still go by the clinic to get checked over. The doctors have thousands of years of records of werewolf ailments, and they may catch something. It's better safe than sorry."

"Okay, I will."

After training, I quickly took a shower at the gym and headed home. I just had to walk a bit outside the downtown area, about a half kilometer past the packhouse.

It was a cold day, the wind blowing harshly. I snuggled my thrifted parka and pulled down on my tuque, making sure it fully covered my ears. I was staring down at the ground when the wind blew a familiar scent in my direction as I approached the packhouse, compelling me to look up.

And that's when I saw him.

He stood next to his car, deep in conversation with Blake. God, he was so handsome. My breath quickened and heart pattered. My skin tingled with need for him to wrap his warm body around me.

Had I been overly harsh on him? Was I making a huge mistake keeping my distance? He looked up, locking eyes with mine. "Talia!" he yelled, waving his hand.

I stopped. Seeing him in front of me now, I realized how much I desperately missed him. My whole body was aching for him.

God, why does he affect me like this?

Blake glared at him. And then I remembered—Hugo. Fuck, I still hadn't gotten Hugo back into Alex's pack. God, I was such a terrible friend. Here I was, getting my life together, and I had completely abandoned my homeless friend.

Fuck fuck fuck. I had to talk to Alex.

So, I turned to the packhouse and walked up the drive. I could sense relief as I approached. Relief and desire. Yes, very strong desire. God, it was so hard to hate him when I could sense everything he felt. Behind those feelings, I sensed pain, reminding me of how hurt he was on that day. A whimper within me vibrated against my vocal chords.

"Talia," Alex's features softened as he made eye contact with me, his hands in his pockets. "I'm sorry about what I said last time we spoke. I didn't mean it. Please, I'd like to talk to you."

"You don't have to talk to him if you don't want to," Blake cut in. "We can escort him out of the pack, and we'll bring his sister to him there."

Alex hung his head, looking at me through his lashes, and I sensed fear, likely fear that I'd ask Blake to do exactly what he'd offered to do. I felt flattered by Blake's loyalty to me, but I also knew that speaking with Alex was the right thing to do. Plus, I still had to help Hugo, and I couldn't do that if they kicked Alex out.

"Okay," I agreed, breathing out a sigh.

"Great, thank you, Talia." His eyes lit up, and he reached out to touch my arm gently, giving it a light squeeze. Dulled sparks traveled up my arms, and my lips parted in reaction, a warmth spreading throughout my chest. "Maybe we should go inside. It's very cold out here. Do you mind, Wulfric?" He looked at Blake meaningfully.

"Fine." Blake turned on his heel, leading the way into the packhouse as we followed.

Alex and I walked into the living room. I took a seat in the chair and he sat down on the couch, reminding me of the first time we'd conversed or, more accurately, Alex had talked to me and I'd grudgingly listened. He gave me a sweet, closed-mouth smile, the corners of his eyes crinkling, and I realized suddenly how much I loved his eyes now. They were so soft and emotional. His scent wafted through the air, and I softened toward him, aroused. God, he affected me so much. And I could feel that he felt the same as he looked at me. I couldn't hate him. No, I couldn't hate him at all. How could I suddenly feel so sympathetic to him?

Why does he affect me so much? I kept asking that question to myself over and over.

"Talia, I'm so glad you agreed to speak with me, and I hate how we left things between us last time we spoke."

I could sense remorse. I knew he was being sincere. We all said things we didn't mean sometimes, right? And, I knew deep down, that he'd only said those things to me out of his own pain.

I inhaled his scent more. God, it was so intoxicating—the most amazing fragrance I'd ever smelled. Almost like a musky leather or tobacco. A scent I couldn't quite put my finger on. It beckoned me toward him, and it took all my willpower not to succumb to him, wanting desperately to feel his arms wrapped around me—to feel his huge hands tracing every inch of my body. I could already imagine how they'd feel tracing their way up my legs and grabbing my hips. A shiver made its way up my body. I was very warm and aroused, my inner thighs tense with need.

Fuck! What is wrong with me? How could I just forgive him for calling my mom a whore?

I glared at him, overcome with emotion. Not meaning to, I blurted out everything that I had been holding deep within me. "I know my mom wasn't perfect, but she was my mom and I loved her. I miss her every day. She was the only person in this world I loved, and your father took her from me." Tears tumbled down my cheeks. I wasn't able to hold back. Once I started, I couldn't stop, continuing to verbally vomit everything from within me that I wanted Alex to know. "For years, he tortured her. He used to cut her, bruise her, and do all kinds of horrible things to her, and she kept him around because she had an addiction and he paid for it. And then, when we finally saved up enough for her to leave and not need him anymore, he killed her. We were going to start our lives over without him, without the brothel, and my mom never got the chance." I began sobbing.

Alex pulled me out of the chair and to him, holding me tight against his body. I cried on his shoulder, feeling as if I were being healed, the calming sparks drifting through my whole body, his intoxicating scent in my lungs. I cried against him for a long time until I had no more tears to cry, and I was just dry sobbing, feeling light-headed.

"Goddess, Talia, I'm so sorry," he said, rubbing my back. "I wish so much I could bring your mom back to life for you. I hate that my father did that."

"But you still take his side. You take his side, and you take your sister's side. My mom never did anything to harm either of them, but you think it's okay!" I shouted at him.

"That's not true, Talia," he responded firmly.

I pulled away and looked into his eyes. "And I want you to know something. Blake took me to see your sister yesterday. He took me to torture her so I could pay her back for what she did to me. And you know what? I didn't torture her. So, you're wrong about me. I wouldn't torture someone as revenge. I would never do that. Yes, I killed your father, but it was quick and painless. I didn't drag it out for hours, listening to him scream, watching him suffer, completely helpless. But that's what your sister did to me. And that's what you would've done to me too if I weren't your mate.

"And I'm sorry about what happened with Hugo and what you witnessed. If you want to know the truth, I'd actually gone looking for you that morning. I woke up, wanting to be with you. But when I saw my babysitter that you hired, against my will, by the way, I went after him. And I wouldn't have normally done that. But I couldn't help myself. The heat just completely possessed me. It was like the only thing that mattered was relieving how horny I was. That was the same thing that happened with Blake. And when I found out he was my brother, I was disgusted with myself. I still feel disgusted with myself. But Blake and I never hooked up. Never!"

Alex was staring at me, not saying anything, so I continued, "And you've banished my friend now. I feel like such a terrible friend. Hugo helped me so much. He gave me money when he didn't have any to spare.

And he put me up in his house and helped provide for me when he was already providing for both his mom and brother. And because of me, he ended up in jail and now he's banished. I've been dragging my feet as to how to help him all this time, feeling horrible. My friend doesn't deserve to be banished. He's a good person, and his family needs him. So please, at least let him back into your pack."

After I said everything that needed to be said, I felt relief. Relief that I had finally told Alex everything and let everything out from inside me. The heaviness in my chest lightened. All the anxiety and heartbreak was finally outside of me, and I didn't have to bear it alone anymore.

Alex stared at me for a long time. It was completely silent as we looked into each other's eyes. Finally, Alex responded, "Okay, Talia, I will let him back. I'm sorry I banished your friend." He paused and took a deep breath. His eyes filled with emotion, and he continued, "But I hope you understand why I did it. When I saw the two of you together, it was the most painful thing I'd ever experienced in my life. Goddess, Talia, I'm in love with you. I know we haven't known each other long, but I would do anything for you. To me, you are perfect. And seeing you with someone else—I can't think of anything that could hurt more except maybe you dying. That's the only thing I can think of that would hurt me more."

I sensed his pain, the same pain I felt the day that it happened. It wasn't as sharp this time, clearly having dulled with time, but it was still there. He was still hurt by the incident.

"Thank you for letting my friend back into your pack." I took his hand in mine, feeling the soft sparks as they calmed both of us, slowly healing the pain within us.

"I just want to make you happy, Talia. I can't control what my family does. But Goddess as my witness, I will do my best to always protect you from them. I can't lie and say it isn't going to kill me to let the man that completely broke my trust back into my pack. But if that's what you want, I'm going to do it."

"Thank you, Alex," I said, the tension instantly releasing from my muscles with the knowledge that my friend would finally be let back into his pack to be with his family.

"If that's what it takes for you to stop hating me, I will do it. But please, Talia, tell me something. Do you have feelings for him?"

I looked into his eyes and saw how pained they were. A realization came over me that I'd been so caught up in my own problems that I'd just completely overlooked Alex's. Although I hadn't asked for this mate bond, neither had Alex, and he was clearly also suffering from it. I could sense a whimpering deep in my chest at the recognition. Finally, I replied, "No, I don't. I did before, but I don't anymore. I just want to be a friend to him like he has to me. That's all."

Alex nodded, and I could sense relief.

I felt like I should say more. "I'm really sorry about what I did. I really am. I didn't mean to hurt you like that."

He let out a deep breath and said, "I'd like to start over, Talia. Obviously, a lot has happened, but I know we can move past all this."

"Okay," I replied. I still felt a bit wary about the whole thing, but being in front of him like this, the two of us finally having this open conversation, I knew it was the right thing to do.

"Does that mean you'll come back with me?" he asked, looking at me eagerly.

"No, I can't go back with you. I have a life here now."

"What do you mean?" He searched my face.

"I have a job, an apartment, and friends here now in Blake's pack. I'm finally getting my life together and becoming independent," I replied. After feeling trapped in that brothel with my mom for so many years, my life was finally on the right track. I wasn't ready to just give that up yet.

"You can have all those things in my pack too."

"But it wouldn't be the same. You're going to bring your sister back, you're going to expect me to live with you, and you're going to hire a babysitter for me again. I'm an adult. I don't want a babysitter."

He shook his head. "But, Talia, you're my mate. If you don't come back with me, we'll both become weak over time. Mates aren't meant to live apart."

"Why don't you just stay here in Blake's pack for a while then like you did before? Then we can date and see how things go."

He looked down at the ground sadly. "I wish I could. I'd even consider letting my beta run the pack for a while and letting my sister sit in a cell for now." He looked up, locking his eyes with mine. "But there's something you should know, Talia. My mother, who I love very much, tried to commit suicide. That's why I left so suddenly that day. I rushed back to get to her. When a werewolf's mate dies, the widowed mate usually goes crazy and becomes severely depressed. My father never treated my mother well, but even she isn't immune to the mate bond. And I had to leave my mother to come here. I've left her under twenty-four-hour care, but I'm worried, Talia. I think you can understand that."

"Oh, I didn't know," I replied, looking in his eyes, seeing how anxious and sad he was. Shit—I'd been so selfish. I vowed silently to become more considerate of his feelings moving forward. Why hadn't I even let him explain what he was going through? I was so ashamed of my actions. "I'm really sorry, Alex. I had no idea," I said again, knowing it wasn't adequate for my behavior and what Alex was going through.

He gave me a small smile and patted my knee. The sparks danced up my leg, calming the anxiety I was feeling. After a beat, he said, "I obviously can't force you to come back with me, but you need to think seriously about this. I'll go back today so you can have some time."

I nodded.

"But, Talia," he said, raising his voice, "we can't continue to live apart long-term. At some point, you'll either have to move to be with me or we'll need to reject each other." At his words, the sharp pain I'd now become accustomed to pierced my chest, signaling how grave the situation was. "I have an entire pack that's dependent on me, and if I become weak so does my pack."

"What do you mean?" I asked, not understanding what he meant about his pack.

He shook his head and replied, "That's how it works for werewolf packs. A pack draws its strength from its alpha. And if a pack has a weak alpha then the whole pack will be weak. That's why it's so important for us to be together."

I looked at him in surprise, suddenly realizing exactly what was at stake for him.

He continued, "I don't want to reject you. So I really hope it won't come to that."

"Because rejection is really painful?" I asked.

"Yes, but that's not the only reason. I actually want to be with you. You are my mate. We all get one mate and that's it. If we reject each other, we don't get someone else. We could probably find chosen mates, but it won't be the person that the Moon Goddess chose for us—our perfect match. Just really think about it, Talia. That's all I ask. I won't force you to be with me, but at least consider what it will mean if we reject each other."

"Okay, I will. I promise," I replied sincerely. While I couldn't make a decision at that moment, I vowed I would take his words to heart.

"Maybe we can talk on the phone for the time being and get to know each other more," he offered, giving me a sweet, shy look. My heart thumped in my chest at how endearing he was at that moment as he gazed at me through his eyelashes.

"My phone doesn't have service anymore, and I don't have internet in my apartment. I ran out of money to pay my phone bill. But maybe I can borrow Blake's phone."

"Send me your phone bill and I'll pay it. You're my mate, and I'd like to keep in touch with you. Please."

"I can't ask you to do that," I said, realizing how much more debt to everyone I was accumulating.

His eyes softened, and he said, "It's for me, so I can reach you. I don't care about the money. Okay?"

"Okay," I replied. I'd still add it to my tab. I'd already put aside enough money to pay back Hugo plus some for the trouble I'd caused him.

"Thank you, Talia. I appreciate it." He leaned forward, took my head in his hands, and kissed me on my forehead. "And I promise when I go back today, I'll track Hugo down and bring him back into my pack. You have my word."

"Thank you, Alex."

"So I take it you don't hate me anymore then?"

"No, I don't hate you anymore. But I hope you understand why I'm not ready to be mates yet."

"As long as you don't hate me, I can live with that. And you said 'yet,' so that means there's hope you will be ready to be mates eventually."

Chapter 35

Jasmine

Being a warrior was becoming harder, and I really began to question whether it was worth it anymore. Blake was always so encouraging, and the way he believed in me was infectious. But after spending the day with Charlie harassing me during physical training, strategy, and planning class, and cleaning the gym as part of our warrior duty (where Charlie made me clean the toilets, as usual), we had sparring as the last part of the day. I couldn't wait to finally be done in two hours.

He started the session off as normal, telling us to go for a mile run, and then he had us do a round of burpees, jumping jacks, and push-ups before he paired us off. I was surprised when he didn't have me do extra of anything, thinking that maybe the rest of the day would go smoothly. He paired me with a guy named Rob who I mostly got along with. We went through all of the different moves as he barked them out, and he didn't even make a single negative comment to me! The session couldn't have been going better.

"You know, I don't know why Charlie's always on your case," Rob said to me quietly at one point. "You're actually really good at this."

"Thanks," I replied, giving him a big smile in appreciation.

"Seriously. Like you're better than some of the guys. I can totally see you as luna of our pack."

"You're good too," I replied sincerely. Rob did have good technique, and it was challenging when I sparred with him. I hoped we'd get paired up again in the future.

"Okay, kids!" Charlie clapped his hands together. "Let's get into our wolf forms!" I instantly turned to run to the partition.

"Dale!" Charlie yelled. "No partition!"

I groaned, thinking the session was going too well.

"What was that?" He stepped in front of me.

"Nothing."

"Good, now shift here." He stared me down.

"No!" I replied angrily. I was completely fed up and didn't want to take his shit anymore.

"Did you just say no to me?" He had his arms crossed, glaring at me.

"Yes, I did!" I challenged him. "I'm not stripping for you. Now if you'll excuse me." I tried to push past him.

He grabbed my shoulder pulling me back. "You will fucking do whatever I tell you to. Shift into your wolf form now!"

"Fuck you!" I shouted and everyone gasped.

"That's it. I've had enough of you, you prissy bitch!" He got into a fighting position. "You think you and your brother can question my authority. Let's go, Dale!" He was completely red, his brows furrowed in anger.

At that moment I knew I'd be the one to beat him or die trying.

Before I had time to really think, he ran toward me, swinging his fist, ready to punch me using his full force. But I was quick and instantly ducked out of the way as he stumbled, completely missing me. In return, I jumped, getting a good kick into his stomach. I knew if I wanted a chance at winning I'd have to use my legs, which were much more powerful than my arms.

He gave a loud, "Oof!" in response, but he was right back at it, trying to punch me. I, again, dodged his fist but didn't anticipate that he would then grab my ponytail.

He yanked it so hard that I shrieked in pain, and he used it to throw me to the ground with the force of all his strength. My whole head was throbbing. He was about to stomp on me with his foot when I rolled and tripped him, and he fell back into a muddy puddle on the field. The whole group laughed at the sight of mud splashed all over him, and I couldn't help but beam in satisfaction.

Of course, this only angered him more, and he transformed into his wolf form, tearing his clothes. I quickly did the same, knowing I'd be useless against him as a human. Before I knew what was happening, he slashed his sharp claws across my face, getting a good swipe in. I gave a whimper in response. He was about to take a second swipe at me when I jumped as high as I could, my back legs landing on his head, and used the weight of my body to push him down.

He quickly threw me off, but I rolled in the grass and got up instantly as I'd practiced hundreds of times. He had his teeth bared in a menacing way, and I knew if I didn't stay on top of my game, he could kill me. We were now circling each other, both considering our next moves. I could feel the whole group's eyes on us.

"*You're dead, prissy bitch,*" Charlie mindlinked me as he charged.

I pulled a move that I'd witnessed Blake pull with Alex. As he jumped, ready to attack me, I got low and grabbed his hind legs with my claws, throwing him backward onto the ground. He fell onto the grass with a loud thump. Before he could get up, I jumped on him, energized by all my anger from how he'd been treating me and still upset about how he'd insulted Tyler. I violently shoved my claws under his chin, pushing his head back so I could get my teeth onto his neck, in position to bite his head off. If I'd been looking to kill, I could have at that moment, and he knew it.

I suddenly felt several pairs of arms wrap around me and pull me off. "Enough!" someone shouted from the crowd. "You guys are going to kill each other!" Rob put himself between me and Charlie, and said, "She's our future luna."

Charlie looked between us in anger, and for a moment, I thought he might attack. But instead, he ran away in his wolf form, clearly ashamed of what happened. I breathed a sigh of relief.

Rob jogged over to where we kept extra clothes on hand and brought me a T-shirt and shorts so I could change back into my human form. When I came back out from behind the partition, everyone was already walking away, back toward the gym, but Rob waited for me.

"Damn, Dale. You were really good," he said. "And did you see the look Charlie gave you at the end? He was pissed! He's totally going to let you have it next time!"

"Ugh!" I groaned in response.

"But hey, you finally stuck up for yourself! It was getting kind of awkward constantly watching you just take it from him. I think everyone was impressed."

I gave a small laugh in response. "Yeah, I guess I did, didn't I?"

"It was pretty fucking awesome."

"Thanks."

"You're always sitting alone at lunch. Maybe you should sit with some of us guys next time."

"I'll think about it."

"Cool. I've gotta go, but see ya next time," he replied and then ran off toward the men's locker room.

I smiled to myself as I headed into the women's locker room to gather up all my things to go home for the day. Paige was in there when I entered.

"Oh my Goddess, Jasmine! I can't believe that just happened!" she exclaimed.

"I just couldn't take it anymore," I replied.

"Good for you for finally letting him have it! Although I can't lie, I'm a little scared for you."

"I know," I groaned. As satisfying as it was to finally fight Charlie, I knew he'd only be that much worse moving forward. But I decided not to worry about it, enjoy the victory for the time being, and head home. I pulled my cell phone out of my bag to see I had a text message from an unknown number.

> **Unknown**: Hey, Jasmine. It's Talia. Blake gave me your number. I have some questions. Can we meet to talk?

I was surprised, since I hadn't ever really spoken much with Talia. I wondered what she wanted. But I was also glad that she was reaching out since she was my fiancé's sister, and I did want to get to know her. I quickly responded.

> **Me**: Sure, I'm just heading home now to shower and have dinner. Do you want to meet after?
> **Talia**: That would be perfect. Want to come to my apartment?
> **Me**: Sure
> **Talia**: Ok see you soon!

When I got home, I quickly showered, playing music and singing along, the high from my win against Charlie still on my mind.

When we all sat down to dinner, my dad commented, "You're in a good mood tonight, Jaz."

"Excited about the wedding?" my mom asked. "My parents called earlier today, and they're both looking forward to it."

"See, I told you they'd come around." My dad gave my mom a meaningful look.

"You know how they are," she said, rolling her eyes.

After dinner, I drove over to Talia's apartment, wondering what she wanted to talk about. She met me outside, brought me upstairs to her floor, and let me in. "Sorry, I don't have much furniture yet," she apologized. "Why don't you take a seat at the kitchen table, and I can make some tea."

"Sure, tea sounds good," I replied, looking around the apartment as I entered. It was very bare, with close to no furniture and no decorations, giving it a cold and lonely feeling. As she put the kettle on, I asked, "So what did you want to talk about?"

She let out a deep breath. "You rejected your mate, right?"

"Yes, I did," I replied, my high suddenly squashed, flinching at the reminder, the lingering pain making itself present.

"Oh, sorry." She bit her lip and furrowed her brows, clearly noticing my reaction.

"It's okay. You didn't know."

"Does that mean it still hurts?"

"Yeah." I sighed at the dull ache within me.

"How long has it been?"

"About a year now."

"Oh," she said. After a beat, she continued, "It's just that, as you know, I have a mate. And I have to decide whether to be with him or reject him. And since you had experience with rejection, I thought you could help me figure out what to do."

"Why do you want to reject him?" I asked, studying her.

She seemed to hesitate, but then she said, "I'm not sure I want to anymore. But it's just such a big decision. I'm finally becoming independent now. I have a job and apartment, and I started making friends. I'm still learning all this werewolf stuff, but shouldn't we get to know each other more before I just give all that up and move to be with him?"

"Did you talk to him about that?"

"I did, but we're both going to become weak if we stay apart, and it'll make his whole pack weak too. He basically gave me an ultimatum."

I sucked in some air, the situation hitting close to home.

"Are you okay?" Talia asked.

"Sorry, it's just bringing back bad memories," I replied, recalling the day of the rejection, tears brimming my eyes. Even though so much time had passed, and I was with Blake now, it still stung me. The hot water boiled, and Talia poured it into two mugs before sitting down across from me and passing me one.

"I probably shouldn't reject him, right?" she asked, her eyes pleading with me as if her whole future hinged on my response.

I took a deep breath, wanting to help her. "Here's the thing, rejection is really painful. It was so bad, I couldn't even get out of bed for a long time. I basically lost my will to live. But don't stay with him because of that. Being mates is permanent. There's no divorce. Once the two of you mark each other, that's it. You'll both be bound for life, and there's no way to remove a mark as far as I know."

She nodded, appearing lost in thought.

"You said he was bad before. What did you mean by that? Is he mean?" I asked her, curious to learn more about her mate. He seemed okay when he was staying at the packhouse, but I never really got to know him that well.

"I thought he was bad, but the more I get to know him, I realize that maybe I misjudged him," Talia said, looking down at her mug. "I just don't trust people that easily."

"Why did you misjudge him? Did he do something that was a red flag?"

She continued looking down at her mug, clearly hesitating in telling me more.

"You don't have to tell me, but I promise not to judge if you do."

She looked up at me, locking eyes with mine. "It's a long story, but the short version is his father killed my mother. Then I took revenge and killed his father. And that's how we met. He literally caught me killing his father." She gave a small, dry laugh. "I know, really messed up, right?"

"Wait, seriously?" I asked, my mouth falling open.

"Yeah, seriously," she replied, chuckling again. "It's such a crazy situation—you can't make it up. Anyway, it's just been so hard for me to get past the fact that he's the son of my mother's murderer. My mom is the only family I had until I met Blake. And he took her away from me. How can I just move past that?" she asked, blinking back tears.

"But, Talia, he's not the one that killed your mom. Blake's father also did a lot of really bad things. He used to cheat on Blake's mom all the time, and he banished all his mistresses. But Blake would never do any of those things. He's always been so sweet and he's always there for me. You can't decide your mate is a bad person just based on what his father's crimes were."

She nodded.

"What is your mate like? Has he ever given you any reason to believe he would hurt you?"

She appeared to space out for a moment, lost in thought. Then she finally replied, "No, he's actually almost always been really nice to me."

"Maybe you should give him a chance then. The Moon Goddess sent him to you for some reason. Maybe you should find out why."

"Why do you think the Moon Goddess sent you Luke?" Talia asked.

I took a deep breath and replied, "I think if he'd never started dating Lucy, we actually would've worked really well together. We have a lot in common. But, to be honest with you, I think it was really for the best. I was already in love with Blake before I figured out Luke was my mate.

I was just in denial because I was so hung up on the idea of being with my mate. But now I can't imagine not being with Blake. We just get each other—being with him is so comfortable and easy." As I said it, though, my feelings about being luna rushed back to me, my stomach churning and my limbs tingling.

"I want what you and Blake have. I see the way he looks at you," Talia said wistfully. "Maybe you're right. Maybe I should give Alex a chance."

"I mean, you don't have to mark him and decide to be with him tomorrow, but maybe you could take a couple weeks to stay with him at his pack and see how things go?"

"Yeah, maybe I'll do that." She nodded. "Jasmine, thank you so much for coming here. You've really helped me sort out my thoughts. You've been really nice to me since I got here and I really appreciate it. I can definitely see what Blake sees in you and why he thinks you'd be a good alpha mate."

My heart swelled at the very nice compliment she gave me. Talia was quite sweet.

"Friends?" I said to her.

"Friends." She smiled back at me, and I realized that I'd never seen her smile before that moment. Much like Blake, smiling was not her natural state. But when she did smile, she had a really nice one. The more I got to know her, the more I was seeing similarities between the two of them.

Chapter 36

Blake

The weather was frigid, and it was the week leading up to Thanksgiving—the whole pack was in a festive mood, with the winter holiday season kicking off. While we didn't celebrate Christmas, we were still influenced by human culture, watching their TV shows and movies. Many pack members had adapted the Christmas customs by setting up decorated trees in their homes and putting lights up outside for the winter solstice and New Year's. It was a joyful time of year, and this winter would be more special than usual for me.

I was with Jack one evening, doing a loop outside the border in our wolf forms during my patrol run, when we took a break to chat.

"You know, I don't like how they just kidnapped and killed Jimmy, and we haven't seen or heard anything since. It's making me very suspicious," I mindlinked Jack.

"It is pretty sus," he agreed.

"I've reached out to the other packs, but there haven't been any other incidents since."

When he didn't respond, I glanced over to find Jack clawing at the partially frozen earth, letting out pained cries. Before I could react, his cries turned to agonizing howls.

"*Jack, are you okay?*" I got closer to him.

He howled more loudly, falling to the ground and rolling onto his side, his eyes shut tightly, extending and retracting his claws.

"*Jack! What's happening?*" I demanded.

"*It's Tyler,*" Jack finally mindlinked me back. "*Tyler's hurt.*"

"*Where is he?*" I asked. Jack whimpered loudly, rolling on the ground. "*Where is he, Jack!?*"

His whole body shook. Jack continued to let out pained cries and whimpers.

"*Jack, where is he? Tell me where he is so I can help him,*" I begged. But it was useless. He was clearly in so much pain he couldn't reply. I mindlinked all the seniors on duty to see if they had seen Tyler, but all their mindlinks came back one after another to say they hadn't.

After what seemed like forever watching him convulse in agony, Jack began to get up. "*They stopped hurting him,*" he mindlinked me, his blue eyes dull, and his jaw trembling.

"*Where is he?*"

Jack galloped forward and I followed, sprinting after him because he was able to sense the direction of Tyler. We finally found him, in the woods, not far from the warrior gym. He was completely naked, beat up, bloodied, and bruised.

My eyes traced his body, shocked at how evil whoever committed this crime was. They hadn't simply roughed him up a little. No, his injuries were extensive. Whoever had done this had really wanted to hurt Tyler, possibly even kill him. His face had survived several blows, both eyes swollen shut, his whole face purple from bruising. They'd snapped his neck, and it looked like his body had been dealt several blows with a heavy object. His skull was cracked, clumps of blood clinging to his hair, and a red puddle spread on the ground next to him. And that was only the beginning of the list of what had been done to my future brother-in-law.

Jack shifted back into his human form. "Tyler!" he cried, as he wrapped his arms around his mangled body, holding him close to his chest.

"Fucking Artemis!" I yelled. "Jack, I will find out whoever the fuck did this and they will pay. I promise you, they will fucking pay!"

"Help me get him to the clinic." Jack looked up at me, devastation in his eyes.

"Wait here, and I'll bring my car over," I said, shifting back into my wolf form. I sprinted as fast as I could back to the packhouse, and ran inside to grab my keys, quickly throwing some clothes on myself and grabbing extra for Jack and Tyler. I drove as quickly as I could to the gym, then parked haphazardly. We quickly dressed Tyler and carried him to my car. Jack sat with him in the back seat while I drove us to the clinic.

As soon as I parked, we both jumped out of the car and brought Tyler inside where I ran directly into the back, looking for my mom. I found her in her office. "Mom, please, you have to help!" I yelled.

"Blake, what happened?" She got up.

"Tyler's hurt. Where can we bring him?"

She stepped out of her office, where Jack was waiting with Tyler, and we followed her as she found an empty room. We carefully lowered him onto the bed, and Jack quickly removed Tyler's shirt so she could see his injuries. She gasped loudly, her hand over her mouth, tears coming to her eyes.

"Blake, Jack, I will take care of this," she said, taking Tyler's hand and looking down at him.

"Thank you, Mom," I said, hugging her.

"Just wait out in the waiting area, and I'll call you back in when he's stable."

Jack looked like he was hesitating to leave, but I finally pulled him out. We walked out to the waiting room and sat down. He put his elbows on his thighs and his head in his hands, sighing loudly. "Blake, maybe this is a sign we should move to Tyler's pack."

*** *Five and a half years ago* ***

It was mid-March, and my father had finally agreed to put off transitioning the alpha title to me until I completed college. I'd be leaving for Siberia in less than six months. While I should've been relieved, I couldn't see past the pain that'd taken over my entire mind and body. I was completely possessed, with no relief in sight. It was just dark, always dark.

It hurt so much most days that I was sure my chest would cave in. When I'd breathe in deeply to stop the caving, it was as if my ribs were puncturing my lungs. What was the point of living anymore? The woman who'd finally brought light and relief to me after I'd tolerated years of my father's abuse was gone from this earth. The woman who'd been carrying my pup, whom I'd promised to protect and foolishly allowed to go to battle with me. I deserved this anguish. I hadn't protected my mate. I hadn't protected my offspring. And now I was supposed to protect an entire pack? I was completely worthless. My father was right. All those years of training and I amounted to absolutely zero when it finally mattered.

A knock sounded on my bedroom door. Goddess, I wish they'd all just leave me alone and let me suffer by myself. I didn't need their sympathy. I just needed to be alone.

"It's Jack. Can I come in?" My friend spoke from the other side of the door.

"Come in," I replied.

He slowly opened the door, peeking his head in first, and eventually stepping over the threshold and taking a seat at the foot of my bed. "Hey, man, how's it going?"

"Fucking terrible."

"Let's go out and do something. You should get out."

I was about to decline and tell him to leave when I had a change of heart. "You know what, you're right," I agreed. "It's been a while since I've gone out and gotten some pussy. We should go out tonight. I know someone that can get us some molly. I'll book us rooms at the casino."

"Are you sure that's a good idea?" he asked.

"Of course I'm sure! It'll be great! Leave it up to me. Just meet me back here at nine tonight, and we'll head over."

"Okay." Jack looked as if he didn't think this was a good idea at all, but I didn't care. I was already on the path of self-destruction—a little drinking, molly, and human pussy wasn't even that bad compared to everything else I'd done. At least I wouldn't be shitting where I ate tonight.

Jack met me back at the packhouse later that night as planned, and we headed over to the casino. I valet parked and checked us into the hotel as soon as we got there, booking rooms next to each other. Jack came into my room so we could both drop some molly before heading downstairs to the nightclub. I made sure to get enough for six people, knowing that werewolves had high tolerances to everything compared to humans. That seemed to be the right amount from my past experiences.

I'd booked us a table at the club, clearly free since my family essentially owned it. "Everything's comped, so drink whatever you want," I said to Jack. Before long, a group of girls for a bachelorette party came over, all very attractive. Nice! We invited them to sit at our table and drink with us, while I tried to decide which one I liked the most. I also wondered if I could convince two to have a threesome with me.

At one point, a song the girls liked came on and they all jumped up to dance together. I leaned over to Jack and said, "Thanks for coming out with me tonight, man. Which one do you like? I'll give you first pick. I was leaning toward the redhead, but if you like her, the brunette's cute too."

"You know what, Blake, it's your night! I'm just glad you're getting out and finally showered. The redhead's all yours!"

"Thanks, man," I said, sensing that the molly was finally starting to kick in, bringing bliss into my body. I hadn't felt that kind of happiness in a long time. Suddenly my problems didn't seem so bad anymore. Maybe I should do molly more often.

A man walked by and winked at us. I scrunched my face in confusion. "Goddess, does he think we're gay or something?" I said to Jack. Jack didn't say anything in return. The girls all returned, and I grabbed the redhead, planting her on my lap.

"Oh, hello there!" She smiled at me, turning around so she was straddling me.

Under the influence of molly, I began rubbing my hands up and down her arms, relishing the feeling of her soft, smooth skin under my fingertips. "You're cute," I said. I saw from my peripheral vision that Jack had taken one of the blondes by the hand and was leading her to the dance floor. Not a bad choice.

"You're really fucking hot," the redhead said to me, and before I knew it, we were making out on the couch in front of all her friends. We both took a shot and then headed out to the dance floor where she ground up against me as we danced. We returned to the table a few more times to take shots in between dancing, and then she led me outside toward the end of the night to have a smoke. I was surprised to find Jack out there when I got outside. I'd never known him to smoke, since he was determined to make something of himself as a warrior. As soon as he saw me, he nodded at me, put out his cigarette, and walked inside. I must've been hallucinating, but I could've sworn the guy who'd winked at us followed him. No, it was just a coincidence.

The redhead pulled out a pack of cigarettes, and I took one from her. As we smoked, she said, "I have a room upstairs, if you'd like to come see it."

This night could not have been going any better. I wouldn't have to find a nice way to kick her out of my room. I could simply just sneak out once I got what I came for. And it had been a minute, so I was really looking forward to what I came for.

I followed her upstairs, instantly pulling her toward me as soon as we entered the room. Our clothes were off in no time. "Damn, you're fucking huge!" She looked at my cock, her eyes wide. "What are you, part horse?"

"Part wolf actually." I smirked.

"I hope you fuck like a wolf," she said.

"I fuck better, like an alpha wolf." I pushed her against the bed.

When we finished, I got up to dress.

"What, you're not going to stay and cuddle?" she asked.

"I'm not much of a cuddler," I replied. "Actually, I have to get home. I have to get up early for work tomorrow," I lied.

She looked disappointed. I didn't care. Thankfully, I was in a different wing of the hotel, so the likelihood that we'd bump into each other again was low.

I took the elevator back downstairs so I could get to my wing, then rode a different elevator upstairs. I walked down the hallway until I found my room. I was about to touch the key card to my door when Jack's door swung open, and the man who had winked at us snuck out. What? I was dumbstruck. Maybe I had misremembered which room was Jack's. Maybe it was the one on the other side of me. I was drunk and high. I couldn't be expected to remember which room was which. No, I was probably tripping and imagined that that had happened at all. I slipped into my room and passed out in my bed.

The next morning, I awoke to a hangover, the physical pain practically unbearable and all of the emotional pain that had disappeared from the molly now returning twice as bad as it was the previous day. I was a wreck, and I suddenly remembered why I didn't do molly more often. Fuck. I didn't even know if I'd be able to drive home in this state.

I practically crawled my way over to Jack's room—or what I had remembered was Jack's room and knocked on the door. "Coming," I heard Jack's groggy voice on the other side of the door. Okay, so I had remembered his room correctly. He opened the door for me, and I went in, falling over on his couch.

"Fuck, man, I thought werewolves weren't supposed to get hangovers!" I moaned.

"Yeah, it's pretty fucking bad," he agreed.

"Man, I was so tripped out last night I thought I saw a man sneaking out of your room!" I laughed. "Goddess, I was so fucking trashed!" But I soon realized I was the only one laughing and looked up to find Jack sitting still on his bed, staring at the ground. Oh. I must have not imagined it at all. Was Jack—? "I didn't imagine it, did I?" I blinked, trying to wrap my head around this new information.

"Fuck, man, I don't know what to do." He dug his hands into his bedsheets, clenching his jaw. "I've tried so hard not to feel the way that I do, but I can't help it! It's fucking killing me!"

"But you had that thing with Vanessa for all those years."

"We were just friends. I only pretended it was more as a cover. I thought about hooking up with her—but I couldn't do it. She's not what I really wanted." When he finally looked up at me, I saw a deep sadness in his eyes.

"Do your parents know?"

"No. I can't devastate them like that, Blake. There are only two options for someone like me. Either I get banished from the pack, or I have to reject my mate and live the rest of my life pretending to be someone I'm not."

"That's not true!" I exclaimed.

"Really? Because I can't see any other future for me."

"Jack, I'm going to be the alpha! Not right away, obviously. But eventually I will be. And you're my friend. I wouldn't banish you!"

"Really? You'd go against our religion and pack tradition just for one person? You know there are many people who wouldn't be happy with you. Something like that could start a coup."

"No one is going to start a coup over this! It's the twenty-first century, and everyone watches human TV shows and movies. Being gay is normal everywhere else outside of our pack. We live in fucking Vermont, probably the bluest state in the entire country."

"I don't know, Blake. I feel like you're underestimating how stuck in their ways everyone is in our pack."

"Trust me, Jack! It'll all be good! Just hold on until I'm alpha, and it'll be fine. I'm going away for four years, but I'll be back, and my dad won't be running the show anymore."

"It's just such a relief to finally tell someone." He sighed.

"Hey, man, it's cool," I said. "I mean, I'm definitely shook. But you're still my friend."

"Thanks, I appreciate it," he said. "Goddess, I hope this doesn't freak you out, but I seriously used to have the biggest crush on you." He glanced over at me, a small smile on his face.

"I mean, doesn't everyone?" I laughed, trying to lighten the mood.

"Thanks for being so cool about this, seriously," he said, lying back in his bed. "Goddess, this hangover sucks though."

I lay back on the couch I was on and said, "This hangover is bullshit. My life is fucking bullshit right now."

"You know, you're acting a lot more normal today than you have for months."

"It's nice finally thinking about someone else's problem for once."

"You're welcome."

After a long time, my mom finally came out to call us in. We followed her back into the room where she'd wrapped Tyler up in bandages and put him on an IV.

"There's no permanent damage. He just needs to heal. Whoever did this cracked his skull and may have given him a very severe concussion, so it might be a while until he wakes up. But he's going to be fine." My mom hugged Jack.

"Thank you, Dr. Luna," he replied.

"I have some other patients to attend to, but I'll be back." She stepped out of the room.

"Jack, I will seriously fucking kill whoever did this. This will be a lesson that I make the fucking rules around here. And if anyone has a problem with you or Tyler, they will know the consequence."

"I think I know who did this, Blake."

"Who?" I asked.

He sighed, sitting down in a chair. "Tyler asked me not to say anything to you, but I think it was Charlie."

"What the fuck!"

"I know."

"That kid used to be our friend. How could he do something like this?"

"Well, you heard him at your party last year. I think he made his feelings about who I am pretty fucking clear. I don't know. He's just not who I thought he was. Tyler told me some crazy shit."

"Like what?"

"Apparently, he's been harassing Jasmine during training, trying to get her to strip in front of him and shit, going really hard on her during training when she won't do it. And he also just acts like a predator around all the other females. Anyway, you know Tyler. He confronted Charlie, and Charlie threatened him, telling him he'd pay. And then Tyler went back several more times and observed what was going on, taking notes, threatening to formally report him if he didn't stop what he was doing."

"Fucking Artemis. That kid is as good as dead at this point. And I can promise you that it's not going to be quick and painless. He's harassing our future luna, which is a high disrespect in our pack. And what he fucking did to Tyler! That kid is dead, and no one can talk me out of it. You're welcome to watch of course." I turned to Jack.

"Seeing Tyler like this, there is nothing I'd love more than to watch you torture him," Jack replied.

"Thank Goddess. I had to put my favorite knife away the other night, but I'm glad it will finally get a chance to come out and play." I smiled.

Chapter 37

Jasmine

Just as predicted, Charlie was even worse now after what'd happened. He spent the entire morning constantly forcing me to do burpees randomly. Blake came by to bring me coffee during our morning break. As soon as he left, Charlie pushed the coffee cup out of my hand, acted like it was an accident, and then forced me to clean it up. I thought about confronting him again, but I didn't want to end up in another fight. During the afternoon, he made me run several miles while everyone else sparred.

I'd never felt so relieved to go home, practically in tears from the day. I jumped in the shower, finally relaxing with the hot water hitting my muscles. I just had to get through it a little longer, and I'd be in a new rotation, not having to deal with Charlie anymore.

Of course, that didn't address all the other problems I was having. Luke and Blake had decided that they no longer wanted me to go to patrol duty anymore, so once again, I was getting preferential treatment and, like a good alpha pet, helping the alpha with his paperwork. It's not that I minded. It was actually nice to spend the extra time with Blake, and he set me up in an office in one of his spare bedrooms, so I wouldn't have to sit with him and Luke, which would have been awkward, for me at least.

It also meant less time I had to spend with the other female warriors who still didn't accept me into their group. Paige had warmed up to me a bit, and we said "hi" to each other now, but she still hung out with the other girls instead of me. I mean, I got it—I was the dorky kid at the uncool table, and she got to hang out with the cool kids. I thought about taking Rob up on his offer to sit with his friends, but he was quite a bit older than me, probably in his thirties, and I felt weird about it. So I continued to sit alone.

After drying off from my shower and throwing on my sweatshirt and leggings, I started on dinner, and my mom helped with the finishing touches once she got home. After dinner, I headed up to my room to wind down and crack open a book. Not long after getting settled, the doorbell unexpectedly rang.

My dad's footsteps sounded downstairs as he went to answer, and I stepped out of my room, moving to peek down from the stair railing.

"Good evening, Alpha. Are you here to see Jasmine?" my dad asked. I bounced down the stairs, warmth spreading through my chest at the surprise visit by my fiancé.

"Actually, I'm here to see both you and Jasmine," he replied, stepping inside. I stood next to my dad as Blake looked between the two of us. His facial features were downturned and his eyes emotional. I moved closer, tempted to reach out to touch him. "There's been a situation, and Tyler's been hurt."

"What happened to Tyler?" My dad's eyes widened as he crossed his arms, taking a step back. "Is he okay?"

"Maybe we should all sit down," Blake replied, and my dad led him into the living room. After we were all seated, he told us the whole story. Nausea overtook my body as Blake described what happened in graphic detail. By the time he finished, I felt light-headed, on the edge of passing out, feeling so much hurt and fury about what had happened to my brother—someone so kind, loving, and generous. I couldn't believe someone could have so much hate inside them to do something like that.

"Dear Artemis," my dad said, his gaze unfocused, rapidly blinking. My mom grabbed his hand. "When can I see him?"

"He's healing now, but my mom thinks he should be awake by tomorrow morning," Blake replied.

"I'd like to see him tomorrow before I leave for work, please. He's my son, Alpha."

Blake nodded and said, "I'll speak with my mom and call you tomorrow morning once I know how he's doing and if he can accept visitors."

"Thank you. Please keep me updated." My dad then got up and stepped toward the kitchen. "I'm making myself a drink. Can I get you anything, Alpha?"

"I'm all right, thank you," Blake replied. "I'll be heading out now. I wanted to make sure I let you know what happened."

Blake got up, and I walked him to the door. As soon as we stepped outside, my dad followed. We both turned to look at my dad as he shut the door. "What do you plan to do to the person or people involved?" he asked.

Blake's eyes were cold, taking on an evil appearance, as he replied, "More or less what was done to Tyler, but I don't intend to let him live."

"I see," my father replied. "Well, have a good night, Alpha. Please let me know if I can see my son tomorrow." He then stepped back into the house.

"Do you know who did it?" I asked.

"While I'm not positive yet, I have an idea."

"Who?" I asked.

"Charlie Kemp."

I gasped, my skin bubbling with wrath. I already disliked him, but now my feelings toward him were pure, feral hatred. Just hearing his name made me see red.

"I can't wait to cut him up until he's begging for death," Blake said in a low, menacing voice, his eyes devilish.

"You're going to kill him?" I asked, confirming I'd heard what Blake said earlier correctly.

"Do you have a single reason why I shouldn't? Because from what I understand, Tyler isn't the only person he's been harassing."

"But death?" While Charlie deserved every bit of torture that Blake had planned, something suddenly didn't feel right.

"My pack, my rules. It's about time that everyone learns a lesson about what happens when they don't obey their alpha."

"But death seems so—I mean, he's horrible. But I don't know, death is so permanent." I was in shock over what Blake planned to do.

"Jasmine, you have a good heart." He took my hands in his. "I'm sure you feel like maybe Charlie just needs to be roughed up a little and rehabilitated. But that's not how werewolves do things. If I don't show the pack that I'm a strong leader and that my word is law, you're going to see more incidents like what happened with Tyler. I can't just make empty threats and not act on them. While I have the alpha aura, it is still possible for an entire pack to overthrow me. Always remember that."

I looked at him and didn't say anything. I knew he was right, and I was completely disgusted with Charlie. If I never saw him again, it would be too soon. He was possibly one of the worst people I'd ever met in my life. But still, I couldn't help but think capital punishment didn't fit the crime. Torture, sure—and I knew Blake would make him suffer far more than I could likely even imagine. Banishment, definitely. But death just seemed one step too far.

I mean, Charlie could have so easily killed Tyler. All he had to do was shove his sharp claws into Tyler's body while he was unconscious and pull out one of his essential organs. But he didn't. Although what Charlie had done was heinous, Tyler would fully heal at some point. It just didn't seem right to take his life when he hadn't taken Tyler's. And, I wondered, why hadn't he? I was relieved, of course, but it seemed strange that he had come so close, but then stopped before finishing the job.

"It's also time everyone learns what happens when they disrespect their luna." Blake clenched his jaw and furrowed his brows.

"Disrespect their luna? This is only going to make things worse at training for me, Blake! Now everyone's going to think that you killed Charlie because he went so hard on me."

"First of all, I'm going to make it very clear why Charlie was punished—for both his crime against Tyler and for disrespecting the future luna of our pack. And second of all, so fucking what? You keep trying to fit in with all these people when you should be standing out! You trying to fit in is just as stupid as me trying to fit in with everyone when I'm their fucking alpha! They should be respecting and obeying you, not being your drinking buddies! In one month, you are going to be the female equivalent of an alpha, so stop being so insecure and down on yourself. You have me, you have your family, and you have my family too, or what's left of it. That's more than many people have!"

"I just miss having female friends," I practically whispered.

He wrapped his arms around me and said, "Jasmine, those girls you train with aren't friends. Consider it a blessing that they treat you the way they do. That's who they are and now you know, and you know not to trust them only to have them blindside you later on."

I nodded into his chest. He was right, but it still hurt. How could Blake understand what it was like to be left out? I didn't think Blake had ever been left out of anything.

Blake

The next day, I met Jasmine and her dad at the clinic to visit Tyler. When we arrived, Jack was already there in a wrinkled T-shirt with dark circles under his eyes. Tyler stirred and gave us a bright smile as we entered, flinching as he tried to sit up. Jack instantly moved to help him, affectionately running his hands through Tyler's hair.

As we all took seats at Tyler's bedside, Jack gave me a friendly pat on the shoulder and went to exit the room to give us some space, but abruptly stopped at the door, fidgeting with his fingers and letting out a deep breath, giving Tyler one final glance. I gave Jack a nod as we communicated silently, and he finally closed the door.

"Tyler, how are you?" Drew moved closer to his son and patted his shoulder.

"My bones are still healing, but the cuts and bruises are gone now. Mostly just a bruised ego at this point." Tyler gave a self-deprecating laugh. "Kind of hard to even have a chance at winning a fight when it's three against one."

"Fucking Artemis." Drew covered his nose and mouth with his hands, letting out a choking noise.

"I honestly thought they were going to kill me. I'm surprised they didn't."

"Goddess, Tyler. Thank Artemis you are still alive," Jasmine burst out, then moved closer.

Drew's chin trembled as he looked down at Tyler. "I know I didn't raise you, but you mean just as much to me as Jasmine does. And to know that this happened when you came to live in my pack . . . Fucking Artemis." Drew closed his eyes and slowly shook his head.

"Thanks for coming by, guys." Tyler looked around at all of us. "I know who my people are at the end of the day, and that's what really matters."

"I'm so glad you're going to be okay." Jasmine flung herself at Tyler to give him a hug, and he let out a loud groan. "Oh, sorry." She quickly jumped back into her chair.

"The ribs are still sore," he choked out. "Jack probably felt that one." And just as predicted, Jack opened the door and instantly ran to Tyler's bedside.

"Tyler, are you okay?" Jack demanded.

"Just getting boned, and not in the good way." Tyler chuckled.

"There's the Tyler we all know and love." I laughed.

When Jasmine's dad had to leave for work, I walked with him to see him out. Once we made it to the front of the clinic, and I was about to open the door for him, he pulled on my elbow. I instantly turned to face him. His nostrils were flared and he cracked his knuckles. "Do you still plan to do what you told me you would yesterday?"

"Yes," I replied, the corners of my mouth lifting upward.

"I'd like to join if possible. I'd like to see the assholes that hurt my son suffer."

I nodded and replied, "We can consider it father- and son-in-law bonding time."

Chapter 38

Blake

The next day, I checked Charlie's schedule and saw he had patrol duty. He'd be doing a twelve-hour overnight, from four at night to four in the morning. For these assignments, warriors normally went out in groups and rotated throughout the night in two-to-three-hour shifts, taking turns keeping watch while the others slept. I snuck out of the packhouse a little after four while Jasmine was working upstairs in the office we'd set up for her.

I made my way to the eastern border, where Charlie was stationed that evening, pulling up to the patrol station in my car. When I exited, I asked the senior on duty, an elderly warrior close to retirement named Fred, where Charlie was.

"He took one of the new recruits out for some training. Told me she needed some one-on-one attention. Nice girl. Comes from a good family. I see them at temple every week," Fred replied.

"Any idea where Charlie took her?" I asked.

"I saw them head over in that direction." Fred pointed toward the forest.

"Thanks, Fred." I nodded at him.

"We got the invitation, Alpha." Fred smiled at me, before I could turn to go. "Your new mate is a good girl and great at being a warrior. She's worked this patrol station a few times, and she's very hardworking with great instincts. She'll make a good luna."

I smiled back at him. "Yes, she will."

I turned on my heel and headed in the direction Fred pointed, eventually catching Charlie's scent and following it into the woods. I found I had to walk quite a bit in until I began to hear voices. Luckily, due to the season, the ground was mostly covered in snow, allowing me to stay quiet as I crept toward the sound. I found a pine tree to hide behind, watching them through the pine needles.

"You're always such a tease during training." Charlie had a pretty strawberry blonde girl pinned up against a tree, his arms on either side of her.

She looked young, like someone fresh out of high school, and didn't seem to be happy with the position she'd ended up in. She was looking around frantically.

"You always turn away when you shift, acting all innocent, giving me a nice view of the freckles on your tight little ass." He moved his hand to her backside. "Feels just as firm as I imagined."

"Don't do that." She whimpered, trying to move away from him as he tightened his grip on her.

"Such a tease. Always acting all innocent." I noticed a tear slide down her cheek. "I know deep down you're a dirty girl."

"No, I'm not." She tried to push him off her and he grabbed her wrists, holding them up between them.

"You like it rough, huh? I can be really rough with my cock."

"Let me go!" she yelled, struggling to get herself free while Charlie smirked at her.

"Let her go!" I bellowed, coming out from behind the tree, having witnessed enough of this exchange.

He instantly dropped her wrists, turning to stare at me. "Blake? What the fuck are you doing here?" he yelled at me. The girl looked relieved, letting out a deep breath and rubbing her wrists.

"I should be asking you the same," I replied angrily, glaring at him.

"We were just having a little fun," Charlie replied. "Don't act like you never hooked up with anyone during your patrol duty. Everyone does it."

"Fun?" I asked, walking closer to him.

"Yes, fun! What you used to do before you became pussy-whipped by some prissy bitch."

"You watch how you talk about my fiancée!" I pushed Charlie against the tree.

"You're not even half the alpha your dad was." He looked directly in my eyes. "You're just some loser who couldn't become alpha when you were supposed to because you couldn't stop crying like a little baby. Waa! Waa!"

I punched him in the face, instantly breaking his nose.

"You probably like it up the ass too!" he spat at me, blood pouring out of his nose, covering his mouth and chin.

"And if I did? So what? At least I'm not a worthless piece of shit like you!" I punched him again, throwing him to the ground.

He got up ready to fight as if he even thought he had a fucking chance against the alpha. "*Na kaleni, suka!*" I bellowed, using my alpha aura and he instantly bowed his neck in submission and sank to his knees in the snow, frozen in place.

"What the fuck did you just say to me?" he shouted, his face red and brows furrowed in anger.

"'On your knees, bitch.'" I chuckled. "Just a little phrase I learned in Siberia while being trained in how to deal with dickheads like you." I turned to the girl who had witnessed the whole exchange and said, "You can go."

She nodded and sprinted away.

"And you." I looked at Charlie. "I'm fucking done with you and your antics. I'm taking you to the fucking cells. Now walk with me and keep your mouth shut." I used my alpha aura and pulled him up by his jacket, dragging him behind me.

Once I had Charlie hung in restraints down in the torture chamber, the thick metal shackles tight against his wrists and ankles so he wouldn't be able to shift into his wolf form, I went out to locate his minions after questioning him helped me identify who they were.

That night, after Jasmine went home to make curfew, Luke and I went to the pack jail. We were met there by Jack, Kyle, and Drew.

"Kyle, you're coming too?" I asked looking around at everyone who had arrived.

"If someone has a problem with my brother and his mate, then they have a problem with me too," Kyle replied.

The group of us headed down into the basement where Charlie was still hung against the wall where I'd left him, dried blood clinging to his skin and staining his shirt. He was now joined by his two lackeys, the group of them all gagged.

I grabbed my favorite knife off the wall, the one that I had to neglect the other night. But not tonight. I smiled to myself. I approached Charlie and looked him in the eyes, pulling off his gag. He looked terrified, practically whimpering, his chin trembling. I smiled at the thought of how he'd had to wait in dread and anticipation for several hours at that point. Not so tough now.

"You brought a whole group with you? What is this, your bachelor party?" he asked mockingly.

I looked around, smiling, and said, "I suppose it is my bachelor party. Yes, I brought my friends, something you used to be, if I recall. What the fuck happened, Charlie?" I glared at him.

"No, Blake, what the fuck happened to you? You've gone soft. You used to slay pussy like no one's business. And now you're losing it over one stuck-up bitch."

"You watch your mouth, Charlie." I put the knife to his throat. "That's my fiancée and our future luna you're talking about."

"The pack isn't happy with you, Blake. You're going against the temple and making changes people don't like. I'm not the only person."

"It's one thing to be unhappy and another thing to assault a pack member. I want to make one thing perfectly clear, Charlie. You're going to die tonight as a lesson to the rest of the pack. You've broken pack rules, you've disrespected my authority, and you've harassed our future luna and other women. You are not the person I thought you were."

He looked at me wide-eyed, horror on his face. I continued, "You know, I honestly thought you would've been different, Charlie. Especially after your father died in the same exact way. I watched my father torture him after he raped another pack member. I thought you would have taken a better path than him." I continued looking in his eyes and watched as emotion played across them. "But I guess the apple doesn't fall far from the tree."

The whole room was silent as we stared at him. Finally, I broke the silence. "Did you try to make Jasmine strip for you?" I yelled at Charlie, using my alpha aura.

"Yes," he replied, not able to defy my control. I stabbed him in the stomach, and he screamed in agony. His screams resounded for several minutes as blood spilled out of his stomach and down his legs, onto the floor, creating a puddle. I could see he was struggling against his restraints, his arms flexing against them.

After several minutes, his screams turned into whimpers, and I approached him again, using my alpha aura. "Whose idea was it to attack Tyler?"

"It was mine," he squeaked out.

"Why'd you do it?" I asked him menacingly, ready to tear him to shreds, the graphic images of Tyler still fresh in my mind.

"He was asking for it, thinking he could just show up in our pack, question our ways and my authority!" he spat at me.

"Jack, want to take a stab at him for Tyler?" I asked, handing Jack the knife.

Jack took it from me and walked over to Charlie. Once Charlie looked up at him, Jack spoke. "I spent years being disgusted with who I was, wishing I could change myself. But now I realize that there's nothing wrong with me. It's shitty people like you that hurt people. You didn't even give Tyler a fair fight. You ganged up on him when he was alone and didn't even have a chance to defend himself." Jack shoved the knife deep into Charlie's chest and pulled it out violently, spraying blood. He then handed my knife back to me. Charlie's piercing screams echoed in the room. Kyle patted Jack on the shoulder.

"Drew"—I looked at Jasmine's dad—"I'm sure you'd love to teach this piece of shit a lesson for how he's treated both your pups."

He took the knife from me and stabbed him in each thigh, leaving deep gashes. "One for each pup!" he yelled as Charlie's agonizing screams sounded. Most of his body was red now, and a large puddle was forming underneath him.

"Now, you two." I looked at Charlie's minions. "You're not getting out of this either. We're going to have a lot of fun with both of you tonight."

They both had the look of deer in headlights, the sounds coming from their mouths muffled by the gags.

"But I'll let you both live this time, and you can spread the word that nobody disobeys the alpha. And if you ever harm a pack member again, well, you'll see what happens to Charlie tonight." I gave an evil chuckle. "I can't lie. Having real people is much better than the fake blow-up dolls that are normally at bachelor parties." I pulled the gags off them. What fun is torture if you can't enjoy the screams of suffering? My sadistic side was fully awakened now.

I turned away from the three of them, walking straight to the wall that held all the weapons that had been collected over the decades for occasions such as this one. I smiled, pulling a couple axes off the walls. "I've heard that axe-throwing bars are the latest human trend. Seems like a fitting activity for a bachelor party." I handed an axe each to Jack and Drew. "Let's see what you've got."

Drew stepped into position, winding his arm back, and we all watched as the axe left his hand, a loud crack echoing as it hit the shoulder blade of one of Charlie's friends, his scream following.

"Not bad at all!" I nodded my head in approval. "Especially for someone without warrior training."

Jack followed, hitting him directly in the center of his rib cage.

"Nice, Jack!" Kyle slapped his brother in the back.

"Let's see if you can do better, little bro." Jack smiled back at his brother, pulling the axes out of the body and handing one to him.

Kyle got into position, and we all watched as he flung the axe through the air, hitting him in the left side of the rib cage. The loud sound of bones breaking and screaming followed.

"Not bad, not bad." Jack nodded in approval. "Maybe with a little practice you'll be as good as me." He winked.

"I'm just tired. Not much sleep when you're a parent," Kyle replied.

"Excuses, excuses. Just admit it—I've got the better shot." Jack wound his arm back and hit Charlie's other friend perfectly in the center.

"Damn, good to know I've got a great warrior on my team." I put my hands on Jack's shoulders. "I hope you don't have plans to fight for a different pack." I collected the axes, aggressively pulling them out of their bodies and leaving a stream of blood in their wake. "Luke?" I turned to my beta.

"I'm good," he replied, wrinkling his nose, appearing a bit nauseous.

"It's cool." I put the axes down on one of the tables and patted him on the back. "Let's get some beers from the mini-fridge for everyone. Since it's a bachelor party we need to celebrate accordingly."

Luke nodded and walked with me into the corner, where I kept drinks on hand. We grabbed beers for everyone. Although I'd come to embrace torture, I could empathize with those who hadn't been broken in quite like I had, and alcohol was a great way to loosen up.

When everyone had a beer in hand, I picked one of the axes back up off the table and said, "My turn," and threw it, getting a perfect shot in the center of Charlie's chest, where he'd already started healing from Jack's stabbing.

"Nice, man." Jack patted me on the back.

"Lots of practice." I smiled. I took a sip from my beer and we continued the axe throwing. Once everyone was a little buzzed, I pulled a bat off the wall and handed it to Luke. "Maybe axe throwing isn't your thing, but you've always been good at baseball. There are some kneecaps begging to be broken."

Luke looked a bit unsure, and then I wondered if I should be pushing him so much. He'd been raised very differently than me and had never been the violent type.

"If you get the kneecaps, I'll do the skulls after," Kyle encouraged Luke.

And then I saw something flash in Luke's eyes, and holy shit, he did it. He swung the bat against each kneecap, one by one, crushing them. Everyone cheered, and then Kyle took the bat from him.

"Motherfuckers, you don't fuck with our brother-in-law!" Kyle yelled, subsequently cracking the bat against each victim's forehead. We all cheered again and grabbed more beers, everyone in good spirits, feeling a sense of catharsis in avenging the brutal assault on Tyler. We continued for hours, finding new and creative ways to torture the three assholes, getting drunker and drunker off the beers. At one point, Luke ran out to grab more beer from the packhouse after we ran out.

Around four in the morning, we were all finally feeling exhausted, ready to retire to our beds. I pulled a sword off the wall. "And now for the grand finale." I looked Charlie in his eyes, touching the blade of the sword to his neck, preparing to finally behead the piece of shit. "Any last words?" I asked him. He stayed silent, closing his eyes, seeming to accept his fate.

I pulled back, getting the heavy sword in position for the perfect slice. And maybe it was the buzz or the exhaustion, but I began hearing voices. The first one was my father's, repeating a phrase he'd said to me all my life, "*Never show weakness, son.*"

But then, another voice came in even more loudly. Jasmine spoke clearly in my head. "*But death seems so—I mean, he's horrible. But I don't know, death is so permanent.*" And that's when I hesitated. Straightening my shoulders, I tried to push her voice out of my head, getting back into position, ready for the kill . . .

Chapter 39

Jasmine

It was the Wednesday before Thanksgiving, and I had training scheduled once again. Tomorrow I'd have the day off. Not all warriors got Thanksgiving off, but I'm pretty sure Blake had a hand in my schedule. I went to visit Tyler at the clinic before I had to start my workday.

"How are you feeling?" I asked, taking a seat next to his bed.

"They're saying I'm fully healed now, and they're planning to discharge me after one of the doctors looks me over today. Thank Goddess. My mom is getting in tonight, and she would flip if she saw me like this."

"Does that mean I can give you a hug now?"

"Yeah, my ribs are feeling much better now." He smiled. I leaned forward to hug him.

"I'm so glad they didn't do any permanent damage," I said.

"Yeah, me too. It could have been worse." He looked at me sadly. "Maybe it was a dumb idea to try to live here and be out of the closet. I really wanted to do something good and make a difference. But if they had killed me, Jack would've had to live with that the rest of his life. I keep thinking about him having to live with a lost mate, and it's killing me."

"Tyler." I squeezed his hand. "Goddess, that thought is so horrible. I'm so glad you're going to be okay." He nodded, and I continued, "I'll understand if you leave. What happened to you is so awful. I'll be really sad though. You are practically my only friend here now."

"What happened to all your friends from high school?"

"They were really more Lucy's friends than mine." I frowned.

"But that doesn't mean they don't still want to hang out with you. Maybe you should reach out to them."

"Maybe." I sighed.

"What about Blake's sister, Talia? She seems nice."

"That's true. I did recently hang out with her. But I think she might be leaving the pack soon, to be with her mate." I shrugged.

"What about Lucy? Are things over with you and Lucy for good?"

"I think so. For a little while, it seemed like maybe Lucy was moving past everything that happened. But she's not. Just the other night she brought it up all over again. Anyway, it's so hard for me. When I see her with Luke, it's so painful. It's like a stabbing pain in my chest."

"It will go away, Jaz. Once Blake marks you."

"I hope so," I replied.

After my visit with Tyler, I made my way over to training. We were now mostly training indoors due to the weather, but sparring was still done outdoors. I made my way onto the field and jogged in place to keep warm. I was surprised to see Lucy arrive a few minutes after me.

She came over, which surprised me considering her comments the other night. "Goddess, it's fucking freezing! I think my nipples are about to fall off!" she exclaimed. I looked over at her, unsure about her presence. "Maybe I can convince Charlie to move things indoors."

And then I remembered what Blake had told me two nights ago. When had he planned to do the deed? Had he already done it? I mean, Charlie was always late, so it *was* possible he was still alive.

"You look like you've just seen a ghost." Lucy was looking at me curiously.

"Did Blake go out after I left last night?" I asked her.

"Yeah, he went out with Luke. They were probably just doing their patrol duty run thing. Although now that I think about it, Luke got in really early this morning. They were definitely out much later than usual." She looked like she was lost in thought. "Why? Where do you think they went?"

"Luke didn't tell you?"

"No. We don't normally talk about his work. Anyway, he was sleeping when I got out of bed this morning. Thank Goddess for the nanny!"

Just then, a new trainer came out onto the field. "Sorry I'm late! I was put in as a sub last minute!"

"Where's Charlie?" Lucy demanded.

"Not here today," he replied. "Now, let's start with a one-mile run."

"Excuse me, sir, what's your name?" Lucy approached him.

"Sam," he replied.

"Sam, you're quite handsome actually and with a handsome name to match. You clearly work out." She touched his bicep. "I bet you could lift me clean over your head like I weigh nothing!"

"Where is this going?" he asked.

"Well, Sam, it's just that my butt is a bit sore from the workout I did yesterday." She turned around him to give him a view. "I was hoping I could take it easy today."

"You're just sore, not dead. Now one mile, no walking!" he yelled. I cringed at his phrasing.

"Come on, Lucy, I'll keep pace with you," I said, waving her over to me.

"What a waste of my biweekly sparring. What terrible luck that I signed up the day he has a sub!"

"Lucy, Charlie's not coming back," I said.

"What does that mean?" She squinted at me, tilting her head.

"I'm pretty sure Charlie's dead."

"What!" she screamed. "How did he die?"

"Blake killed him."

"What the fuck! Why would he do that?"

I was thankful that everyone had already run far ahead of us with how loudly Lucy was reacting.

"I guess you didn't hear what happened to Tyler."

"Of course I heard! He's my brother-in-law. Was Charlie involved?" Her eyes widened.

"Yeah."

"Holy fuck! I mean, Charlie's kind of awkward. But I didn't think he was evil!"

"Well, he was the one who did it," I replied, thinking how *awkward* was not the word I would have used to describe Charlie at all.

"Damn, Blake doesn't fuck around. Sounds like he's just like Alpha James."

"What do you mean?"

"I've heard stories from my dad and brothers. Alpha James was brutal. He never hesitated to kill someone—in fact, he enjoyed it! My dad said he's been to several tortures, and Blake's dad would smile while he did it. Fucked-up, right?" I suddenly recalled how Blake smiled evilly when he'd talk about torture. I had no doubt Blake smiled while he did it too. I felt a shiver travel up my back at the thought.

Chapter 40

Talia

I had to get up early on American Thanksgiving since it was apparently one of the busiest days of the year for the bakery café. I made my way in at five to clean and open. Valerie, Lucy, Reena, and Liz were already all there when I arrived, clearly having gotten in much earlier than me to set out all the pastries, cakes, and pies for the big day.

Right before we opened, Lucy pulled me aside and said, "You should come by my family's house today. Thanksgiving is always huge at our house, and I can introduce you to another one of my cousins."

"It's okay," I replied. "Blake is taking me to Jasmine's family's Thanksgiving today."

"You can always come by before. I think they do their Thanksgiving at night. Ours is early, at two."

"Okay, I'll think about it," I replied, not wanting to be set up with another one of Lucy's cousins.

It was a very busy morning as it seemed the whole pack descended onto the café, picking up their pastries for that evening. Valerie, Lucy, and Reena all helped me run the register and package all the sweets as people came in. I was ready for a nap when we finally closed at eleven.

Once we locked up, I walked home with Lucy. On our way, she turned to me and said, "Oh! I almost forgot to tell you! A package came in for you yesterday. I have it at the packhouse!" She pulled me inside as she went to go find it. "Wendy's always moving stuff around!" she yelled while looking in the hallway closet. I waited at the front entrance while she ran around. The packhouse was quiet today, well, besides Lucy banging around. She finally located it and came running. "Here it is!" She smiled as she handed it to me. It was thin and rectangular. I saw that it had been sent from Canada. "Looks like it might be from your mate. So, are you guys back on then?"

"Not exactly," I replied, not wanting to elaborate to Lucy.

"In that case, I better see you at two today! Tom was just a practice date. The next one will go much better!"

"I'll think about it," I responded, trying to appease Lucy while knowing there was no way I was going to show up.

When I got home, I opened the box to pull out a framed picture. It was a sketch of my mom and me—the one that was on my lock screen. Tears brimmed my eyes as I studied every detail his pencil had made. It was so beautifully done. I went to place the packaging in recycling when I noticed an envelope had dropped to the floor. I quickly picked it up and opened it to see a note.

A belated housewarming gift. Miss you, A.

Yes, he was definitely chipping away at me. I was finding it harder and harder each day to think of reasons to reject him. True to his word, he'd gone to Hugo's family for help locating him and brought him back into the pack. He then paid off all my past-due phone bills and reactivated my phone.

I had also started shifting into my wolf more often during training, and I realized that each time I did, my feelings for him grew. But I still wasn't getting stronger. Xander was becoming concerned and kept trying to push me to go to the clinic. I knew I should just tell him that I knew why, but I still felt weird admitting to people that I had a mate, especially since I hadn't decided what to do about him.

I sat down on the floor of my apartment, balancing the beautiful portrait against the wall. When had anyone ever given me such a personal and thoughtful gift in my life? And then I began to remember that day when he had sketched me in my wolf form. I could feel a pang in my chest, recalling how intimate and special that moment was between us.

I picked up my phone to see there was a text message from him.

Alex: *Good morning, my beautiful mate. Will you have time for a facetime today?*

I dialed his number through FaceTime, and he answered almost immediately.

"Hello, Talia. You look beautiful as always." He smiled. He looked quite handsome himself.

Butterflies filled my stomach as I looked at his face staring back at me. I could see that he was in his office at the dairy processing plant. That's normally where he made his FaceTime calls from.

"Thank you for the portrait. It's beautiful," I said.

"Oh, good, you got it!" He smiled even more widely. "I assumed you don't have much artwork for your new place yet, so I'm sure there's plenty of wall space to hang it."

"How'd you get the picture?" I asked.

"I may have taken a photo of your lock screen with my phone a while back," he said coyly.

"How long did it take you to draw?"

"A few hours. I enjoyed my time working on it very much. I want to say again how sorry I am for what I said to you before. I didn't mean any of those things. You and your mom are both beautiful angels. And I feel honored to be your mate." His eyes were downcast as he spoke, appearing remorseful.

"But you must have thought those things," I responded, feeling suspicious. "Why else would you say them?"

He looked uncomfortable as he shifted in his chair. "I only said them out of anger, Talia. I never would have otherwise."

"But you wonder if I was like my mom, right?"

"Were you?"

"Maybe I was. Would you still want me as a mate then?"

He sighed and didn't say anything for a few moments. After some time, he finally spoke. "I mean, it would definitely be hard for me to digest. It wouldn't be my favorite thing to learn about you and your past. But you're my mate, and I will accept anything about you that you tell me. I know you hated my father, but he was still my father no matter how you feel about him. And I'm even able to look past the fact that you killed him. I think that should show you how I feel. I really wish you'd give me a chance, Talia."

"Well, I was never a sex worker, so you don't have to worry about that," I replied bitterly. "And there's nothing wrong with it anyway. It's a job some people do for a living."

"I didn't mean to offend you, Talia. I still have a lot to learn. I'd like to learn—more about you and your past and your upbringing. I'd like to know you. Both the good and the bad things. You don't need to hide who you are from me. I want you to know that."

I stared at him, not knowing what to say, trying to decide if I could trust what he was telling me. We sat like that for some time, just looking at each other through our phones. Finally, he broke the silence. "Talia, will you have some time off from work? I'd like to bring you up to my pack for a little while. Just as a vacation. Then we could get to know each other better. And maybe this is wishful thinking, but I'm hoping that you could one day start to feel at home at my pack like you do at Blake's."

"I'll speak to my boss," I replied, thinking about how Jasmine had suggested the same thing. Perhaps they were both right and that was the best way for us to move forward.

"Thank you, Talia." The corners of his lips lifted and the sides of his eyes crinkled. "So, what are you up to today?"

"It's Thanksgiving here in the states, so I'm going to my first American Thanksgiving dinner."

"I hope you enjoy yourself. Call me again later if you can." He smiled. He did have a very nice smile.

When I hung up, I noticed several texts from Lucy telling me to come by her family's Thanksgiving. I lay down in my bed and ignored her texts, deciding to take a nap instead. It'd been a busy morning and I was tired. It seemed like I had much less energy lately. Every day it was harder to become motivated to do anything. I set my alarm so that I'd wake in time to get ready to go before Blake picked me up.

Chapter 41

Jasmine

I spent the entire morning and afternoon with my grandmother in her kitchen, the two of us working side by side to put dinner together for that evening. This was something I'd done for most of the past many years, except last year. I cringed, remembering what a sad state I'd been in at that time, embarrassed by how useless I'd become.

My parents came over early to help set the table and assist with any last-minute things. Just as we were putting out all the side dishes, the doorbell rang. I went to go answer it to find Blake with his mom, grandparents, and Talia at the front door. Blake pulled me in for a hug and kissed me on the cheek as soon as he walked in. I then gave hugs to all of Blake's family members, including Talia. "Thanks for coming, Talia." I smiled at her.

"Thanks for having me," she replied. I wanted to ask her if she'd made any decisions about her mate, but I didn't want to do it in front of everyone. I'd try to text her later.

"Blake!" my dad exclaimed, coming into the entranceway. "You made it!"

"Wouldn't miss it." Blake smiled, shaking my dad's hand. "It's always nice to spend time with Jasmine's family."

"You're part of the family now too." My dad patted Blake's shoulder, and they both gave each other a look as if they were suddenly best friends.

"I definitely feel like family after all the bonding we did the other night," Blake replied, confusing me. And then I remembered—hadn't my dad gone out the same night that Blake had? Did that mean? I was sick at the thought. Had they really bonded over killing someone?!

My dad went over to Blake's mom and gave her a hearty handshake. "Dr. Luna, I want to thank you for taking care of my son."

"It was my pleasure, Drew." She gave him a smile, but her whole face was downturned in a look of sadness. "In all my years of being a doctor at this pack, I'd never seen another pack member attack one of ours so brutally. I just thank the Goddess that Tyler was able to survive such an awful attack in one piece. I pray this doesn't set a new precedent."

"It's hard for conservative packs to change their ways," my mom chimed in. "I would know. The one I come from is even more conservative than this one. I'm proud of your son for being a brave leader and making positive changes." My mom gave Blake's mom a genuine smile.

"Thank you, Miriam. Blake's a good boy." Blake's mom patted his back. "I'm lucky to have such a good son."

"I'll be honest," my grandmother cut in, "I wasn't keen on the idea of homosexuals being allowed in our pack. It seemed like a slippery slope to me. But then after I met my grandson and saw how happy he was with his mate, I realized that I was the one in the wrong. Artemis doesn't make mistakes, and if she sends male mates to men then we should accept it. But it's not going to be easy convincing everyone else."

"Why don't we go sit down?" My dad began taking people's coats and cajoling them into the dining room. We were all soon seated at the Thanksgiving table. Blake sat next to me and reached for my hand, but I pulled it away, putting both my hands on the table. I was still peeved at the interaction he had with my father earlier.

"Time to cut the turkey," my dad said, bringing the huge bird out to the table. "Blake, maybe you should do the honors this year. After all, you really know how to handle a knife." He gave a dry chuckle.

Blake chuckled back and replied, "Drew, I saw how you are with a knife, and you're a natural. This is all you!"

As my dad began carving the turkey, everyone fell into loud chatter. I leaned over to Blake and whispered in his ear, irritated, "Do you have to joke about it?"

He looked over at me but didn't say anything. He could at least mindlink me something. I suddenly wished I could mindlink in my human form because there were a lot of things I could say to him right now.

We all said a quick prayer to Artemis and then passed around the different dishes. We almost immediately began eating, and the whole table fell into chatter again. It wasn't quite as loud and rambunctious as dinners at the packhouse were, but everyone seemed to be enjoying themselves.

"Mrs. Dale, did you make all this?" Blake looked over at my grandma. "It's all very good! This stuffing is to die for!"

"Oh please, you can call me Mary," she replied. "Jazzy and I both worked hard today."

"You both did a great job." He gave her a thumbs up. "I knew I was making the right decision marrying into this family." He looked over at me with a smile on his face, giving me a quick squeeze on my shoulder. I didn't return the smile.

"Mary is the best cook in the pack, and our Jasmine learned from her," my grandfather boasted.

"It's one of the many things I love about her," Blake responded.

"Yes, this is all very good," Blake's grandma agreed. "I hope we'll be invited back next year."

"We'd be honored to have your family return next year," my grand-mother replied.

I looked over at Talia, who was sitting on the other side of Blake, but she was very quiet, similar to the first night I'd met her. Blake's mom was quiet as well, not saying too much. Had she always been like that, or had she changed after losing her mate?

After dinner, Blake pulled me aside and asked if I'd go with him to drive Talia home so we could hang out a bit, just the two of us. I agreed, wanting to talk to him privately.

"Thanks for inviting me. The food was really good," Talia said as we got close to her apartment.

"Thanks for coming," I responded, looking into the back seat, giving her a smile. "It was nice to see you."

She nodded and got out of the car.

Once Talia disappeared into her building, Blake glanced over at me and said, "I know it's bothering you." He pulled away from the curb and headed in the direction of the packhouse.

"Why wouldn't it bother me?" I replied. "I mean, it's one thing to punish someone for a crime. But then you bond over it and joke with my dad like you didn't just take away someone's life."

He sighed and didn't say anything at first. After some time, he finally responded and said, "Yeah, I can see how that's in bad taste. We probably got a little carried away. Sorry, Jasmine."

"I just can't understand how you could do it. And my dad?! I didn't know my dad was like that."

"We need to talk. Let's go for a walk." As soon as he parked, we got out of the car, and he came over, trying to take my hand. I pulled it away again. We walked down the driveway of the packhouse and turned onto the main road, walking next to each other. He didn't say anything for a while, leading me toward the center of town and into the park. The night was chilly. The winter weather had arrived, bringing crisp air. Our breathing appeared as smoke in front of us. If I weren't so upset with Blake, I'd be tempted to snuggle into his warm body.

Once we were standing in the dark, empty park, Blake turned to face me and gently grabbed my wrists, holding them between us. "Jasmine." He stared into my eyes. "I didn't kill him."

"What?" I looked back at him, surprised by what he was telling me. Blake wasn't the type to say he was going to do something and then not do it.

"Trust me, I had every intention of finishing that piece of shit off. When a pack member assaults another pack member, they become an enemy of a pack. As far as I'm concerned, Charlie is no better than someone who broke into our territory and attacked someone. Obviously, since it was Tyler, it was personal. But, either way, I can't just allow this kind of thing to go on in my pack."

"So why didn't you go through with it?" I asked.

"Honestly"—he paused, shifting a little—"because of you. I was seconds away from slicing a sword through his neck, ready to behead him. But I heard your voice in my head, and I couldn't do it. I ended up banishing him instead. But I let him know that if he ever goes near this pack again, I won't hesitate next time."

"Wow, Blake," I said, my eyes wide, staring at him, speechless.

"And, well, I thought back to my friendship with him. He wasn't always bad. He definitely ended up on the wrong path, and I will never forgive him for what he did to Tyler. But maybe there's still a chance he'll learn from his mistakes and make positive changes. I can only hope that I didn't make the biggest mistake of my life letting him leave, letting a monster out into the world."

I threw my arms around Blake. "I'm really proud of you," I said, sensing that Blake was changing for the better. While I didn't know the extent of what Blake was capable of, or what he had gone through, I could feel deep within me that there was an old Blake who would never have shown mercy.

"I told you—you make me a better alpha," he said, kissing me. "Although, while I didn't kill him, I may have taken some liberties." He smiled sheepishly.

"What does that mean?"

"I may have cut off a ball or two before I let him loose."

"Seriously?" I took a step back.

"Hey, act like a dog, get treated like a dog." He smirked and continued, "Anyway, it's not like we want him out there procreating."

I can't lie, the visual did make me a little nauseous even though I did think Charlie deserved it. I looked up at Blake smiling menacingly, clearly recalling the moment when he must have done it. Suddenly, so many thoughts began rushing through my head, all my insecurities coming forward, everything I'd been feeling for the past couple months becoming overwhelming.

"What's wrong?" Blake asked, searching my face.

I sighed, looking at the ground, and said, "I just feel like I'm not cut out for this alpha stuff."

"What do you mean?" he asked, forcing me to make eye contact with him again by pulling my chin up with his hand.

"For a while, I've been thinking that maybe that's why I was mated to the beta and not the alpha. This alpha stuff is just too much for me." I started walking forward and Blake followed.

"But you are mated to the alpha." He took my hand in his, the warmth of his calloused palm feeling nice in this weather. "You're my second-chance mate. Anyway, why would you sell yourself short like that? You yourself come from an alpha family. To me, it seems like a perfect match. You're intelligent, strong, great at fighting, and you have an amazing ass." He smirked.

"What does my ass have to do with being an alpha mate?"

"It has everything to do with it. I'm the alpha and I love that ass. I want to tap it nonstop, all the time. Perfect trait for this alpha's mate." He had a glint in his eyes.

Annoyed, I replied sardonically, "I see, perfect for making alpha heirs. What am I now? An incubator?"

"Why are you saying that?" Blake stopped me again and looked me in the eyes.

"That's the whole point of an alpha having a mate, right? To make alpha heirs?"

"That's not the whole point!" he exclaimed. "I mean, yes, it is expected and necessary that the lineage continues so that the pack can continue. But you are more than that." He brushed his hand through my hair and softened his voice. "Why do you think I've encouraged you to become a warrior? And now you're helping me run the business side on the days you work in the packhouse. You're my luna—that means you're the other half of the alpha pair. You strengthen and help the pack as much as I do." We began walking again, doing a lap along the perimeter of the park.

"I just feel like . . ." I paused, not sure if wanted to continue.

"You feel like what? Please tell me, Jasmine, so I can fix whatever is bothering you."

After hesitating, not sure if I was ready to share my innermost struggles with Blake, I finally took a deep breath and let it out. "I feel like everything I do is just to be your luna. I don't feel like I'm my own person anymore."

Blake gave my hand a gentle squeeze and moved closer to me. "Well, that's easy to fix. What do you want to do? I honestly thought you enjoyed being a part of my world. I know you struggled with the mean girls. And I also now know that Charlie was harassing you, which I wish you'd told me about sooner so I could have nipped it in the bud much earlier. But you're so fucking good at fighting. I figured that if you could see past all that stuff, you'd realize how great you are at what you do. But if you really hate it, I would never expect you to keep doing it. I want you to be happy, Jasmine. And if doing your own thing makes you happy, then I'll support it."

"Let me think about it," I replied. Blake wasn't wrong. I had recently beaten Charlie during training. Although I was constantly doubting myself, I was damn good at being a warrior. In fact, I was probably better at it than I had been at school, even when I was getting all As.

Blake led us to a bench and had me sit down next to him. "To be honest, I really hate all of the paperwork that being an alpha requires. It's been bogging me down. And if you wanted to take ownership of managing the casino and pack funds, I'd be more than happy to hand over the keys. That way you could lead the business side, and I could continue to handle the politics and warrior stuff. Then you wouldn't have to feel like you're in my shadow anymore and can lead in your own right. I already know you're really intelligent and capable."

I looked down at the ground. "But you have a business degree. I'm a college dropout."

"Do you want to go back to school then?"

"I can't," I choked out.

"Why not?"

"I'm just so ashamed of how bad I did during the fall semester last year," I cried out.

He wrapped his arms around me, and I snuggled into his warm chest. "Jasmine, you're so hung up on being perfect all the time that it's holding you back. I know your parents were really hard on you growing up. My dad was hard on me too. But the thing is, we all fuck up sometimes. Trust me, no one knows more about fucking up than me. And my dad never let me live any of my mistakes down, ever. But nobody is perfect. I mean, you're pretty damn close, but still. Even you're going to screw up sometimes. But you can't let it take over your life. I let it take over mine for a long time. I blamed myself for years for what happened to Ria. I still do. But I'm finally starting to learn to move forward, and you've helped a lot with that."

I rubbed his back in empathy. "I didn't know you blamed yourself for Ria." My throat and lungs tightened with the awareness of the burden Blake was carrying.

He let out a deep sigh and blinked a couple times. After a beat, he said, "Let's not talk about it." I nodded, and we sat side by side in silence, both reflecting, wrapped in each other.

After a while, I broke the silence but kept my head down, not able to look up, ashamed about the confession I was about to make. "I didn't tell you, but I had another panic attack," I said into his chest.

"What set this one off?" he asked as he rubbed my back.

"It's so embarrassing."

"Jasmine, you don't need to be embarrassed with me. For Goddess's sake, I bought you a fucking vibrator, twice actually, if you don't remember. To be honest, I'm still waiting for the day when you'll let me watch you use it on yourself, but I digress. Please tell me. Whatever it is, I can promise you I won't judge you for it."

I chuckled a little, feeling calmed by his humor that was so Blake. I still hesitated in responding to his question but eventually did. "My mom was talking about raising the next alpha and I panicked. How is someone like me going to raise someone to lead the pack?"

"Goddess, Jasmine. Is that what's been bothering you? Is that why you keep talking about alpha heirs?"

I nodded into his chest.

His hands tightened on my jacket, and his whole body went stiff. "This obviously isn't the easiest topic for me to talk about."

"It's okay. I'm sorry I brought it up."

"No, Jasmine, we need to talk about it. We can't just ignore it forever." I sighed, and he continued. "First of all, we can wait to have pups until we're both ready. My dad was forty when I was born. We probably shouldn't wait that long, but you get what I'm saying. Second of all, there is no way you will ever fuck up more than my father did raising me. I just thank the Goddess I had my mom because otherwise, I would have just run away long ago, and my dad would have had to track down one of his illegitimate sons to take over the pack. The point being, even with what a terrible father I had, I still became the alpha, and the pack hasn't been destroyed yet. So don't be so hard on yourself."

Blake lifted my chin so he could look into my eyes and continued, "Anyway, it's not like you'll be raising the next alpha alone. That will mostly be my job anyway, especially once he starts shifting. I'm going to have to train him to do what I do. You just have to give him a lot of love, and I know you have a lot of love to give. There is no way you could ever fuck that up."

He brushed his hand through my hair, his fingertips comforting as they skimmed my scalp. I let out a heavy breath, trying to release all the tension within me. When I didn't say anything, he spoke again. "Do you at least feel better now that we talked about it?"

"Yeah, I'm glad we talked about it," I replied, snuggling into him. I still didn't feel convinced, but I was happy that Blake made the effort to finally have the conversation with me. Deep down, I still felt insecure and terrified about the whole thing, a feeling of impending doom within me, of *What am I getting myself into*? No matter how hard I tried, I just couldn't seem to shake it off, like a heavy coat I just couldn't seem to get off.

"Does that mean we can go back to the packhouse now and practice making the next alpha heir?" He chuckled, taking me out of my thoughts.

"You have such a one-track mind." I pushed on his chest.

"Makes it simple on you. I'm easy to please." He smirked.

Chapter 42

Alexander

On Friday afternoon, I went to meet with the head trainer of the pack to get my monthly status update, as I did on the last Friday of every month. We sat down in his office at the pack gym. I was planning to do my own workout after. I'd become concerned as I wasn't making quite the same gains I used to. In fact, I'd found my progress had stalled. If anything, I was lifting ten pounds less than I had been before.

"Alpha, I have concerns," he started, and I instantly knew what he was about to tell me. "I've been tracking our warriors' workouts for the last month, and their progress has been very slow. That's fine for some of our more advanced warriors as they're bound to plateau at some point, and progress slows down. But for the newer ones, they should be gaining strength and endurance quite rapidly. It's not normal for werewolves to plateau when they're just starting out. I've gone by the high school, and the trainers there have observed the same thing."

"I see," I said, knowing exactly what was happening. As alpha, my strength and weakness affected the pack. And if I was being weakened by my mate so was my whole pack. I was light-headed at the news. I knew I had to do something about it, but I was afraid if I pressured Talia too much it would just push her away. It was a very delicate situation, and I knew my two options—convince Talia to move to my pack so we could be together or—I clutched my chest, wincing . . .

"Alpha, are you okay?" The trainer raised his eyebrows at me.

"Yeah, fine. Just not the greatest news, eh?" I replied.

"Look, Alpha, I like you. You've been a good alpha to this pack—much better than your father, who was drunk, angry, and erratic most of the time. Which is why I'm going to tell you that there have been rumors going around."

"What kind of rumors?" I asked.

"People are saying you've met your mate. Is it true?"

I didn't say anything. I supposed it was only a matter of time before word got around, especially after I had shouted it in the cells.

When I didn't say anything, he continued speaking. "It won't be long before pack members put two and two together and realize that you being away from your mate is causing the whole pack to grow weak. Like I said, I like you, and I won't say anything. But people talk. They're not going to be happy if their leader is putting the whole pack in danger."

"Noted," I said. I had no desire to have any sort of heart-to-heart. But he was right. I had to do something about the situation.

I pushed myself harder than I normally did during my workout that day, grunting as I shoved a sled filled to the brim with heavy weights across the gym floor, all my muscles contracting, sweat soaking my T-shirt. After downing a bottle of water and resting for a few minutes, I grabbed a heavy kettlebell and began performing Turkish get-ups, one after another. To complete my workout, I went outside and ran five kilometers.

Were things really that bad? I could still do all these exercises. But I knew, deep down, I didn't have the same stamina I had previously. Everything was becoming more and more difficult, and I had to work harder and harder.

I was just about to hop in my car to drive home when a call came in. Alpha Édouard. I rolled my eyes and answered the phone. "Yes?"

"Bonjour, traitor," he said.

"Just get to the point," I snapped at him, not in the mood for his bullshit.

"My pack's watching yours."

"And that's supposed to scare me?"

"Your warriors are good, but everyone makes mistakes."

"Your pack is weak. It's been years since you've been near your mate. You're crazy if you think you have a chance against my pack. No one wants to align themselves with you anymore because everyone knows."

"I don't need to take down your whole pack. All I need is to find your one weakness. And everyone has a weakness." He laughed like a maniac.

"You better stop threatening my pack because we have far more allies than you, and we will attack if we have to. My father may have had a soft spot for your pack, but my father is no longer around. So whatever history you had with him is now over."

Alpha Édouard hung up without replying.

Was this a look at my future? Would I become this desperate and obsessive? Fuck. No, if it came down to it, I'd have to just reject her. I couldn't risk my pack like that. I slumped my shoulders as I got behind the wheel of my car. Was that really where my fate was headed? The rejection of my mate? Every part of me hated the idea of it—it felt as if I may as well commit suicide because there was nothing left for me without her.

I entered the house to my mom and sister sitting together on the living room couch.

"Alex, come sit with us," my mom called out to me.

I hesitated—angry at the sight of Sara—at this point I'd prefer her to be dead. Only two things kept me from banishing her after I picked her up from Blake's pack: my mom, and the fact that I had more control over her as her alpha. If I banished her, my aura would no longer work on her, and that suddenly seemed much more dangerous.

I sat down next to my mom, refusing to make eye contact with Sara. My mom took my hand in hers. "Isn't this nice, eh? The family together."

"Yeah, isn't this nice?" Sara taunted. "Too bad Alex hates his family."

My mom narrowed her eyes at my sister. "Sara, why would you say something like that?"

"Why else would Alex care more about some rogue bitch than his own sister and father?"

"Alex, is that true? Who is this rogue?"

"*This rogue* is the bitch that killed Dad!" Sara spat out.

"What!" My mom put her hand to her heart. "Alex, what is Sara talking about?"

"You fucking cunt!" I shouted at Sara, incensed she was bringing our mom into this, especially in her fragile condition.

"Alex! How dare you talk to your sister that way!" My mom slapped me across the face.

Fuck! That actually kind of hurt. I rubbed my jaw.

"Yeah, Alex, why are you taking Dad's murderer's side?" Sara sneered at me. "Why were you having her live here while I was kicked out of the packhouse? Why did you hire her a bodyguard? Care to explain to Mom?"

"Alex, tell me what Sara is talking about right now!" My mom grabbed my arms and stared up at me, trying to shake me.

I hesitated, not wanting to spring this on my mom. It wasn't going to go over well that my mate had killed hers. But I was now cornered with no way out. "She's my mate, okay?" I shouted.

"Your mate!?" My mom gasped. "You've found your mate?"

"Yes," I replied.

"Why didn't you tell me? Why have you been hiding such big news from me?"

"Because his mate is a rogue bitch murderer. She killed Dad, and Alex would rather keep her alive than me, his own flesh and blood!" Sara replied on my behalf.

"Alex, tell me what's going on! Why did your mate murder your father?" My mom sniffed, pulling a handkerchief out of her pocket and rubbing at her eyes.

"Because my wonderful dad had been fucking and abusing a sex worker for two decades at a brothel not far from here. So those nights when he didn't come home, that's where he was."

My mom's face paled, but I continued anyway.

"That sex worker was my mate's mother. And I don't know why he did it, but he killed her. He murdered my mate's mother. So she came here to avenge her mother's death. We didn't know we were mates at the time, but now that I do, I want to be with her. Yes, I'm upset about Dad's death. But, let's be honest, he was never a good person. He was actually a huge asshole." I looked between my mom and Sara. Sara was glaring at me, and my mom looked as if she was about to vomit.

"You're so fucking ungrateful!" Sara snapped at me. "Even though you weren't worthy, Dad still trained you for years to be the alpha of this pack. Even when you sucked at everything, he still never gave up on you! I should have been the alpha of this pack! I was always better at everything than you. And I care way more about this family and pack than you ever will!"

"Well, too fucking bad. I'm older and I'm stronger, so you can die trying to take my title from me." I glared at her, anger pulsing through my entire body. I was about to start sprouting fur and claws. "And if you ever try to hurt my mate again, I will kill you. She is my mate, and I plan to be with her. If you don't like it, you can find another fucking pack to live with." I got up and stomped out of the packhouse and into the woods, throwing all my clothes off, giving in to my anger, and allowing myself to shift fully into my wolf.

Chapter 43

Jasmine

I'd never really had a normal relationship with my father, at least not the kind that other daughters seemed to have with theirs in sitcoms. My dad was just never really the goofy, understanding, "his princess has him wrapped around his finger" type. He was always strict growing up. My mom was worse, but he definitely wasn't the type where I could go ask Dad after Mom said no. It was only in recent years that he'd begun to lighten up some, especially after the whole "secret love child" thing came to light a year earlier. Suffice to say, we'd never been close.

However, now I felt even more distant from him, like I didn't know him at all. While you couldn't really describe my family as warm, I'd never thought my father was the type to be a cold-hearted torturer. Granted, Tyler was his son, and what had happened to him was horrible and sickening. I still felt nauseous when I thought about it. Blake didn't spare any details when he told the story, graphically explaining the bruises all over his body, the deep, bloody cuts drawn deep into his chest, the cracked skull, how his fingers appeared mangled as if someone had snapped them each one by one. With how injured he was, I was surprised he'd survived.

My dad walked around the house humming on the Sunday after Thanksgiving. He and I would be leaving shortly to meet up with Tyler and his mom and stepdad before they headed back home after visiting for the long weekend. My mom had decided not to go, saying it would be too awkward.

When it was time to head over, we got into the Tesla, and my dad drove us to a barbecue restaurant not too far from the pack. We didn't say much to each other during the ride. When we parked, we pulled up right next to Tyler's car.

As soon as we walked into the restaurant, I spotted the group. Tyler got up and rushed over to greet us. He leaned close to my ear as he hugged me and whispered, "Don't tell my mom what happened, okay?" I nodded as I pulled away, familiar with hiding stuff from parents. As soon as we got closer to the table, Tyler's mom got up to hug my dad. "Drew! It's been ages!"

"Katie, you look great!" My dad gave her a big, friendly smile, looking her up and down.

"You do too," she replied. "Come meet my new mate, Brian!" A man with a beard stood up and shook my dad's hand.

"Nice to meet you. Katie's told me a lot about you," Brian said.

"Pleasure's all mine," my dad replied.

"And this is Drew's daughter, Jasmine." Katie pushed me toward Brian, and I shook his hand. He had very friendly gray eyes surrounded by fine lines, wrinkling now as he smiled at me.

"Very nice to meet you, Jasmine. Tyler has told me great things."

"Nice to meet you too," I replied politely, smiling back at him.

After we all sat down to lunch, Katie started off the conversation. "So, Drew, how have you been? Do you still go hiking all the time like back in the day?"

My dad chuckled. "No, I don't do much of that anymore. Too many responsibilities now. Not like back then when we could just disappear for a few hours after school every day."

"It was nice," Katie agreed, shutting her eyes as if she were remembering something from her past. "But yes, I suppose we all have to grow up."

"I definitely had to grow up fast after Tyler was born. But he turned out to be a great kid." My dad squeezed Tyler's shoulder. "You did a great job raising him. I only wish I could take some of the credit."

"You helped too." Katie smiled at my dad. "It's expensive to raise a pup. I really appreciate all those summer jobs you took on and even putting your life at risk for him. You really stepped it up, Dale Dog." They both snickered.

"Dale Dog. I haven't been called that in years!"

"Dale Dog?" Tyler asked, laughing. "I love it! I'm calling you that from now on, Dale Dog." He lightly punched my dad in the arm. "And what's this whole putting your life at risk thing all about?"

"It was a long time ago." My dad appeared lost in thought, looking out at the restaurant.

"Are you going to tell us the story or what?" Tyler pressed him.

"Yeah, you never told me anything about putting your life at risk," I chimed in. Had he really done something exciting at some point in his life? My dad just always seemed like, well, such a *dad*.

He let out a breath and said, "This goes back over twenty years ago. I was home from college during the summer between my junior and senior year, and we all threw a huge lake party one night when a bunch of people had just gotten back from school. It was actually a great party, and this was before they patrolled that area so heavily. Anyway, we were all under the influence, and not paying attention to our surroundings, when an attack came in from the woods. A group of hunters had figured out what we were."

"Hunters?" I asked. "I didn't think hunters existed anymore."

"They're not common anymore since we know to hide what we are from humans now, and fortunately for us, humans who believe in werewolves are thought to be mentally ill. But they do pop up occasionally," my dad explained.

"We had an issue with hunters at our pack too," Brian said. "This is going back before I was even born. My parents dealt with them. Haven't had any issues since."

"So what happened with the hunters?" I asked, at the edge of my seat.

"Did you bite their necks and tails off Dale Dog style?" Tyler asked.

My dad chuckled and continued, "They decided to attack us the night of the party. They clearly must have done their research because they created wolfsbane grenades that they threw into the crowd. Before we realized what was happening, a bunch of people were killed, including my best friend, Eric." My dad blinked a few times.

"Eric was a good kid," Katie added. "I still think about him sometimes."

"Yeah, it was hard losing him." My dad slumped his shoulders, looked down at the table, and shook his head. After a beat, he looked back up and continued, "As soon as we figured out what was going on, we shifted to attack them. Luckily, we were a lot faster than them and were able to get most of them. We kept a couple alive and dragged them into the cells for interrogation.

"Of course, it's a lot harder to interrogate humans since they die much more easily. You have to be really careful. Alpha James got some information out of them but not everything. Afterward, he asked for people familiar with living with humans to volunteer for a mission to find this group and go undercover, so we could eliminate them from existence, especially before the group grew too big and too many humans figured out that werewolves exist."

"And you volunteered?" I asked, my chest swelling with admiration.

"After what happened to Eric, I was first in line to volunteer. Plus the pay was good compared to what I would have made working a minimum wage job, which was important because I wanted to help support my son." He beamed at Tyler. "I spent the summer pretending I was interested in joining the group until we were able to track down every last member and eradicate them."

"Damn, Dale Dog, you're badass!" Tyler exclaimed.

I just stared at my father, a bit light-headed from this revelation. He had always seemed so straitlaced and, well, boring! This story wasn't lining up with my image of my dad at all. Who was he really?

The next day was Blake's birthday. After not even realizing it was Blake's birthday the previous year, I really wanted to find something special and meaningful to give him this year. It took me weeks of deliberating, bouncing ideas off Tyler. And then I finally figured something out that I thought would work.

We decided to meet at noon to hike to our secret spot. Ahead of our meeting, I put together a lunch for the two of us. I decided to be ambitious and made pepperoni and sausage calzones, which I wrapped in tinfoil to keep them warm and put into an insulated lunch bag. I also made a tortellini salad and baked some cupcakes. For a final touch, I packed two thermoses—one with black coffee for Blake and the other with hot chocolate for me. I had much more of a sweet tooth than he did.

I placed everything into a tote bag and headed over to the packhouse. When I arrived, Blake came out to meet me, climbing into my car. As soon as he got in, he leaned over to kiss me and said, "As long as today ends with you naked and on your knees, it'll be a perfect birthday."

I smiled and shook my head as I backed out of the driveway to head out of the pack territory.

It was now almost December, and the ground was covered in snow, the Vermont landscape was a winter wonderland, trees and mountains layered in white. Throughout my time growing up in this area, I never tired of the changing seasons and all the unique sceneries they brought. I couldn't decide if I enjoyed autumn or winter best. Both had a magical feeling to them.

When I arrived at our usual parking spot, Blake and I exited the car, both in our snow boots. Blake took the large tote bag from me, and we held hands as we hiked to the top of the mountain. While I still felt wary about everything that had happened recently, I wanted to put my worries aside to enjoy Blake's birthday.

When we reached the top, I pulled out a thick, waterproof picnic blanket, and placed it on top of the snow at the summit. Blake took a seat next to me and pulled me against him, kissing my head. I reached for the tote bag and pulled out the thermoses and food, handing him his. We began eating while looking over the magical landscape below.

"As usual, you hit it out of the park with your cooking, Miss Alpha." Blake smiled at me.

I tried so hard to just stay in the moment and not let my hesitations about our future—my future as his luna—get in the way of enjoying his birthday. The dark thoughts of how inadequate I was kept choking me.

"Are you okay?" he asked.

"Happy birthday." I smiled at him.

His eyes softened and he put his calzone down, using his now-free hand to push my hair behind my ear. He traced his fingers softly down my earlobe and onto my neck and collarbone as I closed my eyes, giving in to the feeling, nostalgic for how he'd done the same when we'd first met. His lips touched my forehead, and then he moved away again to finish his food.

Once we were both done eating, I packed everything up and pulled out his gift. "It's nothing big, but, well, you'll see," I said, handing him the small, wrapped box. He took it from me and carefully unwrapped it, pulling the top off the box. I watched as he lifted the necklace out. The cord was made of leather and there was a single charm. It was a jade stone covered in silver that looked like claws wrapping themselves around the stone on one side and fully covering the stone on the other with a cutout in the shape of a maple leaf in the center.

Blake held it up and turned it, keeping his eyes trained on it, not saying anything at first.

"It's a necklace of the Jade Moon Pack and Midnight Maple Pack coming together." I blushed, wondering if I had gotten him a really dumb gift.

"I love it." He smiled widely. "Put it on me. I want to wear it now."

I got up on my knees and put the necklace on him. After it was on securely, he swiveled his whole body and grabbed me, pulling me on his lap, lowering his head down to kiss me deeply.

"Miss Alpha, after being just a shell of a person for the past six years, you are making me whole again, and that's what I'm going to think of every time I look at this necklace."

"There's a second gift for you too." My face burned. "But it's for later."

"What is it?" he asked.

"I may possibly be wearing the thong and push-up bra I bought when I was out with Lucy."

"Well, now I'm really fucking hard. Is it too cold outside for me to just open that present now?"

"Yes, it is, so you're going to have to wait."

"You just love to torture me." He shook his head, kissing me again.

Chapter 44

Talia

The week after Thanksgiving, in early December, Lucy convinced me to go over to her house after we finished up with work for the day. "Luke is so busy lately. It's nice to have someone to hang out with." She smiled at me as she unlocked the door to the packhouse. After we walked in, she took Libby from the nanny, dismissing her for the day. The nanny looked relieved as she pulled on her coat and practically sprinted out the door.

Libby was in terrible spirits, howling. Lucy looked overwhelmed trying to calm her. She walked the entire first floor of the packhouse rocking her. When she got close to me, Lucy moaned, "I forgot colds even exist! I haven't had one since I was probably twelve years old! Poor Libby." She looked devastated looking at her daughter. "It will be so nice once she gets her wolf and doesn't get sick anymore. Of course, then I'm going to have to deal with a teenager in the house. Ugh!"

"How did she get sick?" I asked.

"It's been going around the pack, with all the pups. She probably got it from one of Luke's nieces or nephews. The older ones are in school, so they're constantly exposed to different things." Lucy did a few more loops and Libby finally seemed to calm down. "Do you mind holding her for a minute? I'll go grab us some snacks."

"Sure," I replied, holding out my arms and cradling Libby as she was handed to me. I looked down at her. Her face was red and blotchy and her nose running. She gave a small, cute cough. I too had forgotten what it was like to be sick, not having experienced it in years.

Lucy returned with a bag of popcorn and a couple of cans of hard seltzer. "I need a drink to deal with this," she said, walking over to the living room. I followed. Once she put down the refreshments, Lucy took Libby from me, deposited her in her Pack 'n' Play, and took a seat next to me, grabbing a can from the coffee table and opening it. I followed her lead and did the same.

She flipped through different channels until she settled on one playing *Love Actually*. "You missed out on a great party last week. I told my other cousin Ben about you, and he's interested!" Lucy exclaimed. "He's also blond and a warrior, but so is every guy in my family. I told him I'd give you his number." She grabbed for my phone. "What's your password? Let me enter it for you!"

"I'll enter it," I replied, not trusting Lucy to go through my phone and know my password. I took my phone from her. "What's his number?" She told me what it was, and I typed it in, not having any desire to reach out to him. Besides the fact that I didn't think dating more unmated werewolves was a good idea, and I had decided to get to know my mate better now, I also felt so lethargic lately. I had no desire to do much besides lie around scrolling through my phone. Just going to work was a huge effort for me.

I stayed with Lucy for the evening until Luke got done with work. They had me stay for dinner, and then Lucy gave me a ride home. As soon as I changed and fell into my bed, I passed out, exhausted with the day once again.

After a fairly normal week, I woke up two days after my visit with Lucy, on Sunday morning, feeling more exhausted than usual. My throat was dry and painful. I coughed, feeling as if there was liquid in my lungs. I clutched at my chest at the unfamiliar feeling, coughing again. I forced myself out of bed and into the shower. The hot water was nice, especially since I felt colder than usual. Normally I felt pretty warm, even hot, especially indoors. But, no, I felt cold today. As soon as I exited the shower, more coughs sounded in my small washroom.

Was I sick? Did Libby infect me? Was that possible? While I wasn't confident in all my knowledge of werewolves, it had seemed I'd previously been immune to sickness and illness. Even Lucy had said as much two days earlier. But coughing now, my lungs heavy, and snot beginning to run from my nose, I couldn't imagine what else it could be.

I dressed and walked to work in the dark, the trek feeling a lot more difficult than normal. I wanted nothing more than to pass out in my bed, but I pushed through it, arriving at work on time. I smiled at Liz when I entered, beginning my opening duties. I couldn't stop myself as I started coughing again and grabbed at a napkin to blow my nose.

"Are you sick?" Liz widened her eyes. "How is that even possible?"

"I don't know," I replied, blowing my nose again.

"You need to go to the clinic right away!" she shouted, coming over to me.

"I'll be fine. It's just a cold," I replied, not wanting to go to the clinic.

"Don't be stupid!" she lectured me. "This is really bad. There's no such thing as 'just a cold,' don't you know that?"

"I'm fine." I waved her off.

She shook her head at me. "I'm not going to force you to do anything against your will, but this is not good. You could be dying!"

"I'm not dying!" I exclaimed.

When Valerie got in twenty minutes later, it was a repeat of the same conversation. But Valerie was much pushier. "If you don't go to the clinic right this second, I'm going to have someone drag you there!" She gave me a stern look and finally forced me out of the café. For a moment I considered just going home, but then she made Liz escort me.

After I was seated in the exam room, I was surprised when Blake's mom walked in. "Oh, Talia!" She blinked. I gave a cough in response. "Are you sick?" She gave me a very motherly and concerned look.

"I think so," I replied, blowing my nose on a napkin I'd taken with me from the café. "I forgot you were a doctor."

"Oh my goodness. Let's get you checked over." She did a full physical exam, taking my temperature and blood pressure, looking in my ears and down my throat, feeling my neck. She used her stethoscope to listen to my back. Then she had a nurse come in and take my blood. Once everything was done, she said, "So far, it seems like a common cold. To be honest, I'm quite baffled. I've never seen a young, full-grown werewolf with a cold before. We're going to test your blood for some other things too, and I'll have more information on Tuesday once the lab at the neighboring pack's hospital is able to test it when they open again. I want to make sure we check you over thoroughly because you can never be too careful with these things."

"Okay," I replied, coughing.

She began jotting down notes in the computer as I sat there. Suddenly, she turned to look at me, appearing as if she'd just solved a very difficult problem. "Blake told me you have a mate. Is that true?"

"Yes." I sighed, knowing I should probably be honest.

"And your mate is far away if I'm not mistaken?"

"Yes." I looked down at my feet.

"Talia, that's why you're sick. You're becoming weak. Your wolf is losing its ability to heal you, and you're becoming more and more like a human as time goes on now that you're away from your mate. This is very bad." She shook her head. "Not just for you, but also the Pine Forest Pack. If the alpha is becoming weak, so is the pack. If another pack attacks them, it could be devastating. Our pack grew weak for a different reason six years ago." She sniffed and a tear escaped her eye. She quickly dabbed at it with a tissue and continued, "Far too many pack members were lost in a battle we fought. I fear it could be the same for the Pine Forest Pack and your mate."

I clutched at my chest, the thought of losing Alex deeply stinging me. "What should I do?" I asked, processing all the information being thrown at me.

"I highly recommend you go back to your mate and either stay with him or"—she looked down, clearly hesitating to continue what she was going to say. After a moment, she looked deep into my eyes—"or reject him. But I don't recommend the second option."

"Right, because it's painful, I know." I flapped my hands.

"Yes, but it's not just that. The Moon Goddess gives every werewolf one mate. It is considered a direct insult to Artemis to reject your mate, and it is believed she curses those who do. While I can't say for sure if that's true or not, it's not something I'd want to gamble on. Yes, you should be with your mate. Artemis gave you your mate for a reason. Go to him."

I nodded, not knowing how to respond. I felt so trapped in my predicament. So many thoughts were going through my head, and I felt paralyzed at having to decide the best course of action.

"For now, I'm going to give you a few different things to take to help with your symptoms. But, please, Talia, you should go to your mate. You need him." She looked at me meaningfully.

I walked home, clutching a bag filled with different medications and a paper that explained how and when to take them. The cold air blew against my hot face. I felt light-headed and woozy as I walked home. I didn't recall ever feeling this unwell in my life before. Once I got back inside my apartment, I fell into my mattress, only to hear my phone ringing loudly. I picked it up to see that a FaceTime call was coming in from Alex.

"Hello, beautiful," he sang out as soon as I answered the call.

"Hi, Alex," I said. A coughing fit followed.

He stared into his screen, looking as if he was concentrating. "Was that your cough? You sound terrible! You look terrible!" He drew his eyebrows together.

"Thanks," I replied, sarcastically.

"Talia, you're always beautiful. But, are you—" He stared at me. "Are you sick?" he shouted.

"Yes," I replied. "I'm sick."

"Fucking Artemis! Did you go to the doctor? Fuck. Talia, we need to get you checked up right away. I'm leaving right now to come see you. This is very serious."

"It's just a cold. I'll be fine." I tried to downplay it.

"No, you are not fine. Werewolves don't get sick. This is very concerning. It could mean you're dying, that's how serious it is. I am calling Blake and I am leaving now. Fuck, I'm so worried." He shook his head.

"Alex, it's fine!" I shouted back at him. "You don't need to come here! I'll be fine!" I let out a cough.

"It is not fine, Talia. I need to take care of you. You are my mate, and I won't let anything to happen to you. I'm coming as fast as I can. Now get some rest, and I'm going to ask Blake to check on you to make sure you're okay." He hung up the call.

As soon as I put my phone down on the bed next to me, I drifted into sleep, only to be woken by a banging on my door.

"Talia, it's Blake. Open the door." I heard my brother's voice. Why was everyone overreacting about this?

I rolled off my frameless mattress onto the floor and got up onto my legs, moaning as I did. I dragged myself to the front door and opened it for him, and he immediately stormed in.

"We need to go to the clinic right now," he commanded, staring at me as I walked back to my room and fell back onto my mattress.

"I already went," I replied, exhausted and exasperated.

"Who did you see while you were there?" He came over, squatting down next to me.

"Your mom."

"What did she say? Did she check you over? I'm sure she did, but Goddess, Talia. This is very serious."

"She said I have a cold," I replied, sniffing, annoyed with this invasion into my apartment.

"Is that all? That's all she said?" he demanded, his stare piercing me.

"I'm fine," I replied, rolling onto my back, a fit of coughing ensuing. "I'm just tired."

"Talia, this is really serious. You're not supposed to be able to get a cold."

I sighed and said, "I'm just becoming weak like you said I would. That's all it is. It's nothing serious."

"That is serious, Talia!" he exclaimed. "You need to see your mate. He told me he's on his way here. I normally wouldn't allow him onto the pack territory without your permission, but you need him right now."

I groaned. "Why do I have to have a mate?"

"Everyone has a mate," he replied, sitting down next to my bed.

"My mom didn't."

"Maybe she just hadn't met him yet. Our dad didn't meet his mate until he was almost forty."

I turned to face Blake. "It seems like mates are more trouble than they're worth. Our dad cheated on your mom throughout their entire marriage, right? And Alex's dad did the same thing. And now that their mates are finally gone for good, they're both depressed. Alex told me his mom tried to kill herself."

Blake blinked a few times. "What?"

I continued, "My friend Hugo's dad died too. And his mom was also really depressed. She could barely get off the couch. I mean, is that going to be me one day?"

Blake leaned back against the wall. "Shit, I didn't know Adalwolf's mom tried to commit suicide."

"He told me that's why he left that day to go back home without saying anything to me."

Blake turned toward me. "Talia, I don't know if Adalwolf will be a good mate to you or not. To be honest, I don't really know him that well. I saved his life when we were in school, and then he saved mine about a year ago when we fought in the same battle, which is why we started our alliance. But other than that, I don't really know much about him. The thing is, for most people, meeting their mate is incredible. When I met my fated mate, it was the best thing that ever happened to me. She was so amazing. I just wanted to be with her all the time." He paused and sighed deeply. "I'm sorry, it's hard for me to talk about her. Losing her still hurts."

"I'm sorry, Blake. You don't have to talk about it."

"Anyway, that wasn't the point I was trying to make. Where I was going with that is sometimes people end up with bad mates, as unfair as it is. Being mated to someone doesn't change who the person is. It just makes you very attracted to each other. Unfortunately, our father was a shit person. My mom is the most wonderful, caring person you'll ever meet, and he just walked all over her the entire marriage and never kept his dick in his pants. I will never forgive him for how he treated my mom." Blake's jaw tensed, and he had his fists clenched. He clearly harbored a lot of anger at our father'.

"How will I know if Alex is like that?" I asked. "How do I know if I can trust him?"

"You don't. You just have to get to know him. Just don't let him mark you until you're 100 percent sure you want to be with him. Because once he marks you, that's it. You're stuck with him forever until one of you dies."

A shiver crept up my back.

Chapter 45

Alexander

Fuck, fuck, fuck.

I was worried. This was really bad. I'd never seen a full-grown werewolf get sick before. Adult werewolves didn't get sick. At least not until they got past a certain age. I'd, of course, known of elderly werewolves who got sick, growing weak from the aging process. But not twenty-year-old ones!

My legs were restless and my stomach churned. My heart incessantly beat in my chest, as if my inner wolf was clawing at me, needing to get to my mate. When I'd hit traffic during the ride, I'd grow impatient, throwing my palm against my car horn. I needed to be with Talia.

As I drove, I also worried about my mom. She'd aged ten years since my father died and was a shell of who she'd been previously. Even when things were bad in her relationship with my father, she still always managed to have a smile on her face, humming different songs as she cooked and cleaned, always presenting herself immaculately. I'd never known my mother to have a hair out of place. Now she didn't even bother with her hair anymore, allowing her gray roots to grow out, simply throwing her hair in a bun. She always begged for my sister and me to sit by her bedside, crying to us that she needed us. My mom had grown desperate and needy, as if there was something within her that had been left empty and couldn't be filled again.

Then that whole conversation between Sara and me had occurred, and my mom became even worse as if she was slipping away. I hired more nurses, making sure there would always be two at the house when I wasn't there. My mom could be sneaky, and I didn't want a slip up because a nurse had to use the washroom for five minutes.

I gripped the steering wheel and pushed down on the gas pedal, keeping my Waze app on to be on the lookout for police. I couldn't get to my mate fast enough and prayed to Artemis it would be an uneventful drive today. I didn't think I could handle more drama and stress. Previously I'd found it semiamusing, but now it was wearing me down.

I was relieved when I passed through the border with no issue. I was ready to just abandon my car and run the rest of the way in my wolf form if I had to. It would only be about a fifteen-minute run from the Quebec–Vermont border in my wolf form. It almost felt too good to be true when I crossed into the United States without issue. When I reached Blake's pack, I exhaled a sigh of relief. I'd be reunited with my mate soon.

Blake met me at his pack's entrance, and I followed his car as he drove it to an apartment building. I couldn't get out of my car fast enough after I parked.

"How is she?" I asked as soon as he exited his car.

"Well, she's not dying."

"Thank Goddess." I breathed a sigh of relief. "Has she seen a doctor yet?"

"She told me she has."

I nodded.

"Adalwolf, I know she's your mate, but I want you to know that I don't trust you." Blake glared at me. "I'm not letting you see her unless I go in with you."

"As long as I can see her, that's all I care about." I was desperate, needing to confirm she was okay, needing to be close to her. Blake led me up the stairs into the building, and we walked up to the second floor once we were inside. I followed him down the hall until we came to her apartment, and he knocked on the door. I looked around to see where my mate lived, interested to know what she experienced every day. I inhaled all the different scents of people's cooking. I felt my stomach grumble. I hadn't eaten in hours, but that wasn't important right now.

After Blake knocked a second time, she finally opened the door and let us in. Her scent instantly hit me, bringing calm and arousal to my body. I'd almost forgotten how intoxicating the scent was. I couldn't inhale enough of it. Her apartment was bare, with only a kitchen table for furniture and nothing else. I suddenly considered ordering furniture for her, but I didn't want this to be a permanent living situation. I needed my mate to come home with me, and the less settled she was in this life the better. Blake and I followed her into a small bedroom where she had a mattress on the floor.

She fell into the mattress and sniffled and coughed, unraveling a roll of toilet paper to blow her nose. I went over, squatting down next to her. "Talia."

Her exquisite, emotional blue eyes glanced up at me, and I could sense sadness and arousal from her. Goddess, she was so beautiful, even in this state.

"I'll be in the kitchen," Blake said, exiting the bedroom and closing the door. I was thankful that we could be alone.

"Please, Talia, let me hold you," I said, feeling deep within me that this was the right thing to do—that she needed my touch, and it would help her. She nodded. I wondered if she could feel the same thing. I sat down on her mattress and wrapped my arms around her body, holding her close to me. She was tense at first but soon relaxed into me. I could instantly feel an energy coming back to me, the fatigue I'd been feeling lifting, her body strengthening mine. "I missed you so much," I whispered.

She didn't say anything in response. I looked around her room as I held her and saw the drawing I'd done propped up against the wall. I'd offer to hang it for her later.

It felt so good having her in my arms, sparks dancing across my whole body where hers met mine. I couldn't stop the thoughts that entered my mind, of how much I wanted to glide my hands all over her, kiss between her thighs, and see her beautiful naked body. She moaned into my chest. My pants felt uncomfortably tight, the whole moment was so intimate, her scent and the feeling of her body against mine so arousing. She looked up at me, and I couldn't help myself as I leaned in to kiss her, pecking her lips gently at first, soon deepening the kiss. When she kissed me back, I pushed my tongue into her mouth, which she willingly accepted. We fell into the bed together, her fingernails digging into my back as we kissed. She pushed her whole body against mine, and my erection pulsed against her, desperate to be inside her. I wanted her so badly. I resisted doing anything more than kissing her but, oh Goddess, how badly I wanted to.

After we stopped kissing, we lay next to each other, looking into each other's eyes. I loved her eyes. They were such a unique shade of blue, and so mesmerizing. I could spend all day just looking into them. She snuggled into me, and I held her close as she eventually drifted into sleep. She looked so angelic as she slept. I wondered if I could get rid of Blake somehow, aware that he was still just on the other side of the wall and feeling awkward at the fact. It was as if there were a parent here in her apartment with us.

Eventually, I forced myself to get up. She instinctively moved her hand to me as I moved off the mattress, clearly needing me as much as I needed her. I sighed, wishing we didn't have to be apart anymore. She was my mate—my missing other half. It wasn't natural for us to live like this. But how could I convince her?

I walked into the kitchen area where Blake was sitting at the kitchen table on his phone. "Do you have to stay here and babysit me?" I asked.

"She's my mate. I would never hurt her. You know what it's like to have a mate, eh?"

"It's not about you. It's about my sister. She doesn't have anyone in the world except me to protect her anymore."

"She has me now."

"And you didn't protect her from your sister."

I clenched my hands into fists. "Low blow. I didn't know she had left your pack to go to mine. If I'd known, I'd never have allowed something like that to happen to her."

"Where the fuck were you then? It doesn't take two days to get to your pack from here."

"I totaled my car hitting a moose. And it was just a bunch of bad timing and circumstances. You should know by now I have shit luck. You're the one who dug me out of an avalanche."

"I guess that explains the new ride."

"Yes, and I'm lucky this one's still in one piece."

"It's up to Talia. I'm not leaving unless she says it's okay."

"She's sleeping now. When she wakes up, we can ask her. But it might be a while. I hope you didn't have plans for today." I rolled my eyes as I turned my back to him, heading back into the room. My mate needed me, and I intended to stay as close to her as I could.

Chapter 46

Talia

I awoke feeling well and relaxed—better than I'd felt in weeks, possibly months. My whole body was energized. Calming sparks flooded up and down my skin. I was lying against a warm body, my nipples hard against the thin fabric of my shirt, pressing into his torso. My thighs were warm and tingling. I instinctively threw one leg over his body, pushing myself further against him, his erection throbbing against me. Mmm. I was so aroused and so relaxed. It reminded me of how I often felt during midsummer afternoons, the sun's rays warming my skin, a feeling of ease overtaking me.

He moaned next to me, and my eyes darted open as I suddenly became conscious of where I was and what I was doing. I quickly separated from him, unsure about the situation. It had felt so good but . . .

"How are you feeling?" he asked.

Then I remembered. I'd been sick. I could barely get out of bed. It seemed so long ago, now that I was feeling so awake and energized, my cough completely gone. "I feel good," I replied, looking into his dark eyes.

He stared back at me, a smile on his face. He really had come down just to cure me.

"Now that you're awake, maybe you can ask Wulfric to leave." He smirked.

"Where is he?" I asked.

"He's acting like a dad, sitting in the kitchen, protecting your virtue."

"Blake's in the apartment?" I asked, a little embarrassed by the thought. I was seconds from throwing myself at Alex.

"Yep, seems he has nothing better to do than be your overprotective brother." He chuckled. "You've been out for a couple hours, and he hasn't left."

"Oh, I should tell him to leave," I said, a bit baffled by what Alex was telling me.

"Yes, you definitely should."

I got up, running my hands through my hair, sure it had probably gotten ruffled up while sleeping, and opened the bedroom door. As Alex claimed, Blake was sitting in a kitchen chair, staring out the window. He turned toward me as I approached.

"You don't have to babysit me," I said.

"I wasn't about to just leave you alone in your apartment with someone who feels entitled to you while you were in a vulnerable position, especially after I was the one who brought him in here. If anything happened to you, I would've only had myself to blame." He paused and looked me over, then asked, "So, do you want your mate to stay then?"

"Yeah, he can stay," I replied. "He's okay."

Blake nodded and got out of the chair. He touched my shoulder and said, "If he does anything against your will, you better fucking let me know." I watched as Blake walked out my front door, and then I was left alone in the apartment with my mate.

I went back into my bedroom where he was sitting up on my mattress. "Can I make you some coffee or tea?" I asked. "Sorry, I don't have much to offer. I'm still sort of getting set up. I'm sure you noticed I don't have much furniture yet."

"Why don't I take you out for dinner?" Alex looked at me eagerly. "We've been mates all this time, and we still haven't gone on a proper date."

"I am pretty hungry," I replied.

"I'm starving." He smiled. "I'll text Wulfric for a recommendation around here. He can't be against me taking you out for an innocent little dinner."

Before long, I'd gotten dressed and we were on our way out of the pack. "Wulfric said there isn't much nice around here except what's in the casino. Do you like Italian?"

"Sure," I replied. At this point, I was so hungry, I probably would've eaten anything. Spaghetti and meatballs sounded like an extravagant delicacy to my hungry mind. I'd honestly be happy with a can of SpaghettiOs.

Alex led me inside and we found the restaurant easily. After we were seated, a waiter came by and said, "On Sundays, we have a Sunday Gravy special, where we cook a large pot of different meats, including our house-made sausages, country-style ribs, and meatballs, served family-style with our fresh spaghetti." I was practically drooling at the description, and I could tell Alex was too.

"How can you say no to that, eh?" Alex asked.

"It sounds so good," I agreed.

After we ordered and were waiting for our food, I turned to Alex and asked, "How's your mom doing?"

"Not good." He looked down at his lap, and I could sense a deep sadness and anxiety. "But thank you for asking." Last time he came here, he'd told me he didn't want to stay away from his pack because of how worried he was about his mom. And yet, he still rushed back to make sure I was okay, and now he was taking me to dinner, spending time with me instead of his mom.

Again, I was reminded of how I had been so concentrated on my own problems that I had completely overlooked the fact that Alex also had his own emotions and worries. I'd been so selfish. Same as I was with Hugo. It'd taken me weeks to finally do something about the fact he'd been banished from his pack. I was a horrible person. I felt sick with myself.

"Talia, are you okay?" Alex squeezed my shoulder. He could clearly sense all the anxiety I was feeling at that moment.

"Alex, I'm sorry," I said.

"Sorry for what?" He drew up his eyebrows, studying me.

"I've been so selfish to everyone. I've taken advantage of everyone who's helped me. I'm a terrible person."

"Talia," he said softly, putting his arms around me, relaxing my whole body. I inhaled his scent. It was so delicious, better than anything I'd ever smelled before. "You've gone through a lot. And I'm sorry my family has caused most of your problems. But I want to help you. I want to be a good mate to you. I won't ever let them or anyone else hurt you again. I spoke to my mom and sister, and I told them I want to be with you, and if they have anything against it, they'll have to deal with me."

It was at that moment that something within me shifted, and I realized that maybe I could trust him. Like Jasmine said, I had to stop punishing him for his father's and sister's crimes. Hadn't he proven how much he cared by coming here to heal me, especially while he was worried about his mother? I owed him a chance.

After we finished dinner and dessert, we got back into Alex's car to head back to the pack. We exited the parking garage to a snowstorm that was well underway. But we were from Canada, so it wasn't anything we weren't used to, and Alex seemed to have a pretty good car for the weather. We drove carefully while Christmas music played on the radio.

"I don't know what it is, but I just love Christmas even though we don't celebrate it." Alex laughed. "I just love all the lights, the Christmas tree, the idea of everyone opening presents together on Christmas morning. I wish werewolves celebrated something similar. I guess we have winter solstice, but it's not really the same, eh?"

He looked so sweet as I peered over at him, a small smile on his face as we drove. He was so handsome, his face so perfect like a master sculptor had carved it. I looked back at the road only to spot a flying deer heading toward the windshield.

A flying deer???

It all happened in slow motion. Alex slammed on the breaks as the deer in the sky shattered the glass in front of us. Our car spun out, sending us in sporadic circles until we abruptly stopped with an earth-shaking thud. My whole body crashed against the seatbelt and my neck ached from whiplash. I instantly undid my seatbelt to turn in my seat to see what happened. We'd hit a tree, denting the whole car inward—luckily toward the back of the car rather than the front. I probably wouldn't have died, but it would have been painful had the car landed against the tree a meter forward.

Alex instantly jumped from the car, tearing his clothing as he shifted into his wolf form. And then I saw them—a group of three wolves dashing toward us. Was Alex going to fight them by himself? I watched in horror as they attacked him, swiping their sharp claws at him and biting into his fur. But he was good, really good. While the wolves got some good swipes and bites in, overall, Alex was skilled at blocking and dodging them and avoiding serious injury.

Because I was so captivated by the scene going on—

Fuck! That hurt!

I was caught by complete surprise as a heavy object collided with my shoulder, shattering the passenger window during its flight, small pieces of glass forming shallow cuts on my face. I cried out in agony as sharp pain pulsed up and down my arm. On impulse, my left hand shot to my right shoulder as tears flooded my eyes. I wasn't sure that whatever hit me hadn't fractured a bone. I barely even got a chance to look at the large, heavy rock that landed between my thigh and door when claws reached in through the now open window, instantly clasping me on the sides of my arms, puncturing my parka, and digging into my flesh.

I screamed in terror, trying to shake the wolf off. But it was useless. He was clearly much stronger than me as he pulled me out of the car as if I weighed nothing, feathers flying from my parka as it got dragged against the jagged edges of broken glass that eventually cut through my pants and into my legs. He slammed me onto the ground, and I instantly shifted into my wolf form, tearing through everything I was wearing. If I even wanted a half chance at survival, I knew I couldn't stay human.

Before I had a chance to get used to being in this new form, the wolf swiped his thick, sharp claws across my body. I tried my best to block him, bringing my front paws up, the movement irritating my shoulder and provoking me to howl in agony as my injured front leg throbbed. His claws ripped into the flesh, scraping against my bones and tearing into nerves and veins. My front legs were soaked with blood. I wondered how long I'd be able to keep taking the blows to my body before he finished me off. I was surprised he didn't just get it over with and kill me, especially since I was such an easy, untrained target. All I could do was lie there and hold my injured front legs up, completely hopeless against the enemy, howling and whining into the cold air.

He swiped down my underside, tearing into the sensitive nipples on my front, and a string of yelps followed. His goal was clearly not to kill me but to torture me, just like Alex's sister. The whole situation brought me right back to being in that cell again, completely hopeless as someone tore into my body, doing whatever they wanted to it, taking away all my control and dignity. My howls turned more agonizing as I went into a bad place.

And then, miraculously, the wolf stopped as his entire body came crashing down on top of me. I yelped from the impact of a grown man's full weight hitting my body. Once I recovered, I opened my eyes to see

Alex holding an entire bloodied vertebral column with his claws, clearly ripped from the wolf's body. I instantly pushed the dead man off me and sprinted away as Alex threw the vertebrae away and held off the other three wolves, one of whom looked like he wouldn't get too far as a bloody puddle formed under him and he eventually turned human, dropping to the ground.

Alex continued fighting the other two wolves, but I could tell that they'd gotten him pretty bad. Patches of his white fur were crimson and matted. Something from within gave me a renewed energy, seeing my mate like that. My blood boiled at what these assholes had done to him. I knew I was either insane or dumb as a rock, with close to no training, but I couldn't stand to the side and allow them to continue hurting him.

I limped toward the group, opened my mouth, and bit the tail clean off one of the wolves, my sharp teeth easily slicing through bone. The wolf yelped loudly, which turned into pained howling, and gave me the opportunity to jump onto him, getting my claws into his back. I had no idea what the fuck I was doing, but I didn't care. He'd chosen to mess with my mate, and I was going to figure it out. But I wasn't expecting him to then fall back and slam my entire back into the gravel.

Fuck, that hurt!

That wolf was not light, and I was completely crushed under him. Now I was totally and completely useless. Alex glanced my way, and I sensed a deep grief and worry from him, only making my situation that much worse. He looked as if he was going to move toward me, but the other wolf plunged his claws into Alex's back, and Alex turned his attention away from me instantly, trying to keep himself alive.

Fighting through the pain, I figured out how to plunge my claws into the front of the wolf I'd tried to fight as he hovered over me. What did Hugo say? I had to remove an essential organ to kill him. I dug around all his guts, trying to figure out what everything was. This is when some medical training could have come in handy. I had absolutely no idea what

I was doing and didn't have enough time to educate myself in the art of dissection. The wolf was easily able to pull my front paws from him. And as I looked in his face, I saw primal rage with his teeth bared, murder in his eyes. And I knew it was over.

He easily got his teeth around my neck. I could do nothing but whimper as his razor-sharp incisors tore through fur and skin, hitting the bone. As a last-ditch effort, I used the claws on my hind legs to tear into his man parts. I kicked until I got a good swipe, ripping into one of his balls. He yelped, pulling his teeth from my neck. Just in time as I transformed back into my human form, clearly now too injured to sustain my wolf one. I was left completely naked in the cold, not able to move now that my head had been mostly severed from my body. I couldn't even believe I was still alive.

I clearly must have at least left a good opening for Alex, as he was able to finish the job I couldn't, beheading the wolf while he was distracted by his torn ball. As his head plummeted to the ground, he transformed into a human corpse—dead.

I watched in horror as the last-standing enemy wolf used the weight of his body to cannonball himself into Alex. The two of them fell into a brawl on the ground. I couldn't move my head to watch, my neck barely hanging on, my vision blurry and fading anyway. But I continued to listen as their growls rang into the frozen air, and Alex's emotions gave me an idea of what was happening. I could sense his fear, adrenaline, and worry. I was fading, but I forced myself to hold on, desperate to know my mate would be okay, as if staying conscious would help keep him the same.

After what seemed like far too long, a final loud whimper echoed through the air, and then silence.

"Talia!" Alex's voice rang out, and tears flowed freely from my eyes with relief that he was still alive. "Talia, what did they do to you?" He was now bloodied and naked above me, his face gashed and disfigured, his dark eyes peering into mine.

"Alex," I choked out, my words coming out as simply a puff of air. I couldn't speak.

"Fuck, your neck!" he shouted. "Don't worry, I think I know what to do." I wondered what he meant as I felt a puff of air and he was back in his wolf form, his fur now completely red and matted as if he were a demon wolf. I cried even more at the sight. He used his paw to push my head back toward the rest of my body, and I screamed silently in agony at the movement. What was Alex doing? Was he trying to hurt me more?

He then brought his muzzle down to my neck and began licking. The ensuing feeling soothed me as he traced his tongue along the ripped seams of my neck. Once he finished with the front, he licked the sides, and shoved his tongue underneath me, trying to get everything.

He then moved his tongue along the entirety of my body, not leaving any gash or scratch untouched. The sparks of his touch mixed with the calming of his wolf tongue made my whole body instantly relaxed. I breathed in and out. While I could sense my organs still weren't fully healed, I was finally able to move my neck again, and my skin no longer pulsated with the pain of it tearing every time I moved.

Alex shifted into his human form and helped me up to a sitting position, then kissed me all along my forehead and cheeks, holding my head in both his hands. "You're okay, Talia."

"How did you do that?" I asked, now finally regaining my ability to speak.

"It's the mate bond. It allows us to seal each other's wounds with our saliva when we're in our wolf form. That's something only mates can do. Even a parent can't do that for their children. See, it's something really special, and I don't want to lose it with you, Talia."

"I'm sorry, Alex. I'm so sorry I ever doubted our bond," I cried out, overcome with emotion. "I didn't know anything about werewolves and mates, and I want to know. I want to learn."

"Shh, it's okay, Talia. I'll teach you. Let's just go home for tonight and get some rest."

I nodded in response, my neck still a little sore but clearly healing.

"But first, I have to get rid of these bodies before a human finds them."

He sprinted toward his car and stopped at the side of the road, pulling some snow from the ground to clean himself. He then grabbed some more snow and came over to me. "Sorry, this is going to be cold."

"It's okay," I replied. I was shivering, but I also knew that my entire body was covered in blood. I allowed Alex to move the snow along my face, neck, and arms, and a new feeling came over my body as my skin heated even with how icy cold the snow and air felt. A different type of shiver ran down the length of my back. I couldn't help but feel a warmth from the look on his face as he diligently worked to clean me, reminding me of how sweet he looked when he was in his own world, working on his passion, sketching in the woods.

The warmth of his body and his scent wafted toward me, his large muscular arms, torso, and legs revealed to me. He must have sensed what I was feeling because his eyes darted up to mine. I moved my face toward his, touching my lips to his. Before we could stop ourselves, he had his arms wrapped around me, keeping me warm, and I pushed my tongue into his mouth. He deepened the kiss and we found ourselves lost in each other, forgetting the frosty night. Before we could get too carried away, an owl's call woke us from what we were doing, and Alex moved his face from mine.

"I have to get rid of these bodies," he whispered.

I pulled him in for one more kiss, brushing my hands through his bloody beard. "Okay."

He got up and sprinted back toward his car, opening his trunk, which surprisingly still worked. I was unsteady on my legs, but found I was able to get up, relying on my left arm as my right shoulder was still sore. I limped over to him, and he helped me put on some sweatpants and a sweatshirt that he pulled out of a duffel bag. Once he was also dressed, he started hauling the bodies into the woods. I did my best to help, following him as he brought them down, one by one, piling them up in a clearing next to a brook.

"Thank Goddess I always carry extra gasoline in my trunk," he said. "Go find some sticks or branches and throw them on top of the bodies."

I did as he said, pulling low-hanging branches off trees, shaking them so the snow would fall off them, and throwing them on top of the bodies. When he returned, he poured the can of gasoline over the wood and bodies and then lit a match that he threw on top. We watched as flames engulfed the corpses, instantly warming us.

"Who were they?" I asked.

"One of our enemies, the Bois Sombre Pack. But they've grown really weak. I know it didn't seem it, but four of them should've been able to easily overpower us." He shook his head. "I probably should've kept one alive for interrogation, but fuck them." He turned and threw his arms around me. "I'm just glad you're okay."

"Why are they weak?" I asked.

"Their alpha's been away from his mate for years—over six years now. He's desperate to get her back, but his whole pack is too weak now. It's only a matter of time before he pisses someone off enough and they eradicate it. After what they did tonight, I'd be lying if I said I wasn't tempted to myself."

"Why didn't the wolf kill me?" I asked, suddenly curious.

"What do you mean?"

"The first wolf that pulled me out of the car—he just kept hurting me. He could have easily killed me but he didn't. He just wanted to hurt me."

Alex wrapped his arms around me. "He probably just wanted to weaken you so you'd shift back into your human form. He was likely trying to kidnap you. But don't worry, Talia"—he rubbed his palm up and down my back—"I won't let anyone kidnap you."

We walked back to his car with his arm around me. He pulled his phone out of the car. "Damn, no signal here," he said, spinning around with his phone. "We're just going to have to run back to Wulfric's pack. It's not far from here. Can you shift into your wolf?"

I peeled off my clothes and tried. It wasn't as easy as usual but, with enough concentration, I shifted. My shoulder was still bothering me, but I could tell that the inner injuries were already starting to heal, and the pain was slowly fading.

After Alex turned into his wolf, we sprinted back to Blake's pack. It was a short run from where we were. We got to the packhouse where Alex shifted into his human form and rang the doorbell.

Luke answered the door and looked between us. "What's going on?" he asked.

"Can you or Wulfric give me a lift? We were attacked by the Bois Sombre Pack, and my car's a bit banged up at the moment."

"Fuck!" Luke said loudly. "Let me get Blake." I watched as he lifted his eyes toward the ceiling and moments later, Blake came sprinting down the stairs.

"The Bois Sombre Pack is in the area?" Blake shouted.

"Well, they were, until I killed what there was of them."

"No one left for interrogation?" he asked.

"My bad," Alex replied.

"Fuck, this is bad," Blake said, shaking his head.

"They're weak, Wulfric. There were four of them that attacked us. And even with four of their warriors fighting me and my untrained mate, they couldn't take us down. At this point, Alpha Édouard is a joke."

"It looks like they got a few good swipes in though," Blake said, taking a look at Alex's face and chest.

"Meh, nothing an alpha can't handle. May as well have been kitten claws." He laughed.

I wish I could say the same. While I was healing, my body still radiated with a dull ache, and I still couldn't put my weight on my front right paw.

"Anyway, I'm pretty sure my brand-new car is now totaled. So do you mind at least driving over so I can grab my stuff? And then I can just call a tow truck tomorrow morning. Never a dull day." He shook his head.

Once we got to the mangled car, I put the clothes Alex had let me borrow back on, taking a seat in Blake's car where he'd left the heat running. Meanwhile, Blake, Luke, and Alex sniffed the area, tracking for more enemy pack members. When they were satisfied that there were no others, they returned to Blake's car and we all went back to the pack.

Chapter 47

Talia

Blake dropped me off in front of my apartment building, and I opened the car door to exit. "Let me walk you to your door," Alex offered, opening his door as well. "Be right back," he said to Blake, then climbed out, following me to the front of the apartment building.

"Do you want to come in for a cup of tea?" I asked.

"I thought you'd never ask." Alex smiled. "Let me send Blake home then." He turned to walk over to Blake's car, and I watched as he spoke to him through the opened window. Blake looked over at me, and I gave him a thumbs up. He nodded and drove away.

As soon as we got into the apartment, I noticed that Alex's shirt was wet with red stains. "You're bleeding!" I exclaimed, walking over to him.

He pulled the bloody shirt off and said, "It'll heal quickly. But I should probably wash all the blood off. Do you mind if I take a shower?"

"Sure, let me get you a clean towel," I said, pulling one out of the linen closet and handing it to him. I couldn't help but notice how amazing he looked standing in front of me. My eyes trailed his massive shoulders and chest, muscular, powerful arms, and abs so perfect it was as if they were carved in stone. My thighs were burning, and I was weak on my feet. I wanted him so badly. Every part of me desired to feel his body on top of mine. I didn't want to fight the feeling anymore. I was ready to give in completely to him.

I followed him into the washroom. "Let me turn the water on for you," I said, reaching into the shower. I then turned around and pulled off the sweatshirt I was wearing. I'd barely gotten it off when he pushed me up against the wall and pressed his mouth onto mine. My hands went straight to his torso, tracing the ridges of his muscles as I moved my hands down, finding the elastic of his sweatpants, pushing my thumbs inside and pulling them until they fell to the ground. He subsequently had both his hands on my breasts, kissing down my chest. The sparks from his hands on my nipples practically made me orgasm from how good it felt. I was pulsing so hard between my legs that I could barely stand, needing desperately to feel him inside me.

I loosened the ties of the sweatpants I was wearing and let them fall to the ground, kicking them off my legs. He kissed down my body, past my belly button, and down my pubic bone. I arched my back against the wall as his lips continued to travel south, kissing between my legs, putting his hands on my ass and pulling my lower body forward, giving him the perfect angle to lick his tongue the whole length between my legs, from back to front before finding my clit.

I let out a guttural moan, the feeling was so overwhelming—the brushing of his beard against my sensitive skin, his tongue and lips licking and sucking on me, the sparks being emitted against my clit as he continued to flick his tongue back and forth. I'd never felt anything so amazing in my life. Suffice to say, I didn't last long. Just seconds after he started, I found myself at the point of no return, wishing I could hold on to that feeling forever, the pleasure spreading to every limb. It ignited within me, and my whole body was shaking violently as I let out a loud moan, practically collapsing as he held me up by the hips. The most intense and gratifying orgasm I'd ever felt spread from the center of my body outward.

The whole washroom was steamy and hot as I tried to catch my breath, panting heavily, supporting myself against the wall. Holy hell, no one had ever gone down on me like that before. All this time, I could have been enjoying *that* and I had been avoiding it!

He stepped into the shower, his huge erection prominent. Fuck, he was huge. I'd almost forgotten. I followed him in, ready for another round. I felt insatiable in his presence. The water fell down around us as I pulled his head toward mine, bit his bottom lip, kissed down his chin. He lifted me up, and I wrapped my legs around him. He held me as if I weighed nothing. Damn, he was so jacked. He positioned me so his cock was right at my opening, and I'd never wanted anything so badly in my life.

His eyes were half-closed, his hands gripping me tightly, but he was hesitating.

"Fuck me," I whispered into his ear, coaxing him, desperate to have him.

"Talia, before I do, there's something I have to tell you," he said, practically moaning from desperation.

"What?" I asked, not understanding what he could possibly need to tell me that was important enough to interrupt what we were about to do.

"You're going to want to mark me when we finish. If you don't want to go through with it yet, then resist, okay?"

"Okay," I replied.

He let out a deep breath and plunged his huge cock inside me, and goddamn, I felt like a virgin all over again with how big it was. It completely filled me, straining against my inside walls. He pushed me up against the shower tiles and began to thrust, repositioning himself until he was hitting what I realized was my G-spot. No one had ever found my G-spot before and holy hell. I'd always enjoyed sex before, but I'd never known it could feel like this. With every thrust, I saw stars. The lower half of my body was practically numb with how amazing it felt.

I moaned loudly, losing myself in the feeling of his entire body pressed up against mine and the friction of his cock as it slid in and out of me. His mouth found mine, and our tongues pushed up against each other. We were completely in sync, lost in ourselves. And I knew it was just as good for him as it was for me—I could sense how absorbed he was in the feeling overtaking both of us. Again, I didn't last long. Before I knew it, I was trembling, my nails digging into Alex's shoulders, my thighs shaking, giving way to another intense orgasm. Alex's deep groan instantly followed as he gripped me even harder, bliss on his face as he came.

And then a trance come over me. My eyes darted to Alex's neck, finding the perfect place, and I was overtaken by a strong desire to sink my teeth into his skin. As I was about to do it, I stopped, blinking a few times, recalling Alex's warning. I peered at him to find his eyes were closed tightly with his canines enlarged. His eyelids unexpectedly shot open, and his warm dark eyes locked with mine as he gently lowered me to the floor of the shower.

"Talia, I promise I won't mark you until you're ready," he said, kissing my forehead. "And that was amazing." I couldn't disagree with him.

After we got out of the shower and dried off, we snuggled up against each other in my bed. Alex took my chin in his hand and lifted it so we were looking into each other's eyes. At that instant, I knew—he was mine—my perfect match, and I finally understood why the Moon Goddess had sent him to me.

"Come back to my pack with me," he said.

"Okay," I replied, knowing it was right and that I no longer wanted to be apart from Alex.

Chapter 48

Talia

The next morning, after Alex called a tow truck and secured a car rental, we loaded my few possessions into the back of the temporary vehicle. After he shut the trunk, he pulled me against him, staring into my eyes. "It feels too good to be true." He smiled widely, his whole face glowing. He kissed me deeply and we got into the car, stopping at the packhouse to say goodbye to Blake and Jasmine.

"If you need someone to walk you down the aisle at your wedding, just give me a buzz." Blake hugged me. "And I hope you're still planning to come to mine!"

"I'll be there," I replied, hugging him back. Even though we hadn't known each other long, I could feel that we had developed a close, familial relationship, and I hoped we'd be able to sustain it from a distance.

"I'm so glad things worked out with your mate," Jasmine said. "Stay in touch."

"I will. We're friends, right?"

"Right." She gave me a huge smile, and I felt a warmth in the knowledge that I was finally making friends and a little disappointment that I was leaving so soon after meeting them.

I then went by the café where Lucy and Valerie were working. "But you were so fun! I can't believe you're leaving me!" Lucy whined. "You better come back and visit so we can go out again."

Valerie pulled me in for a hug next and remarked, "I'm so glad things worked out with your mate."

To get through the border, I shifted into my wolf form and ran across, meeting Alex on the other side where he pulled over near a wooded area. After we left Montreal, we couldn't help ourselves, so we pulled over in another wooded area and climbed into the back seat, our bodies becoming entangled, desperation to be together overtaking us. I may have also given Alex road head as we got closer to our destination.

When we arrived back at Alex's pack, we were both ready for another round, not able to pull our hands from each other's bodies. As soon as we parked and exited the car, Alex ran over to me, swiftly picking me up as if I weighed nothing. "You can unpack later," he said, carrying me toward the chalet. "Considering what I have planned for the rest of the day, you don't need your clothes anyway."

He flung the door open, carrying me inside, and was about to bring me upstairs when he stopped and let me down gently.

"I see you brought the rogue bitch back." His sister glared at us. "How does Mom feel about the murderer of her mate being under the same roof as her?"

"Sara, you need to leave now!" Alex puffed up his chest, facing his sister.

"You can't keep me away forever."

"Yes, I can. I'm alpha and I can banish you if I want to."

"Really? You'd hurt Mom like that? You'd banish her daughter so she could never see her again?"

"Leave the packhouse now!" he bellowed. I watched as his sister bowed her neck, a pained look on her face, and walked out of the house.

"How did you do that?" I asked after she closed the door.

"Do what?" he asked.

"Force your sister to leave like that."

"It's my alpha aura. I can command anyone in the pack. I can also temporarily halt someone outside the pack. But it only works for a few seconds. I tried to do it to you actually, but it didn't work. I'm guessing because you have alpha blood."

"Oh, I see," I replied, and then I recalled how Hugo had expressed that I'd done the same to him.

"Come on, why don't you come meet my mom?" Alex grabbed my hand. "I'd like to introduce you."

"Maybe this was a bad idea." I winced. Looking around, familiar feelings began flooding back—depression, pain, fear, confusion. I became light-headed, my legs weak, recalling everything that had happened since my mother was murdered. I thought I was going to pass out, feeling overwhelmed by the fact that I had made such a hasty decision and now was going to be stuck with the consequences, trapped in Alex's pack.

"Talia," Alex said softly as he pulled me against his body, patting my hair. "Goddess, I can feel your emotions." He moved his hand lower and rubbed my back in circles. I began to relax under his touch, but a part of me still felt tense and uneasy. "Come on, let's go lie down. It's been a long drive." He took my hand and led me upstairs, bringing me into his bedroom. The whole room smelled like him, his enchanting scent clinging to all the furniture and fabrics. I inhaled deeply as I lowered my body into the bed, breathing in the fabric of the pillows as I laid my head against them.

He pulled me against him, wrapping his arms tightly around me, and whispered, "It's going to be okay. It will work out. We're mates."

"But why does being mates mean anything?" I asked, staring into his eyes, not understanding how he could feel so confident about the situation.

"Because Artemis blessed our match. Every werewolf gets one mate—you're mine and I'm yours. She's our goddess and all knowing. If she believes in us, then we should believe in us too."

"But to me, that just sounds crazy." I bit my lip. "I never even heard about a goddess called Artemis before, besides in Greek mythology. I definitely never heard of werewolves having a Moon Goddess. How can you be so sure that she even exists? How can you believe that any higher power exists?"

"Because, Talia, don't you feel the bond when I touch you?" He brushed the back of his hand gently on my cheek, and I closed my eyes in reaction, calming sparks flowing through my skin. "I know I've never felt anything so magical before. And how I can sense how you feel. You must sense how I feel too. When you look at me, what do you feel?"

I looked into his eyes, and I felt affection, arousal, and anxiety flowing from him to me. I snuggled in closer to him as I concentrated on every emotion I sensed, finding myself unable to argue. He was right, the bond we shared was more powerful than my conscious mind. Logic was no longer applicable. "But your sister won't rest until I'm dead," I cried out, unable to push away the feeling of unease, bile rising to my throat as the memories of being in the cell rushed back to me.

"Shh, Talia." He rubbed my back. "Don't worry about it. I will take care of you. What happened will never happen again. I swear on my life."

I wanted to believe him. Everything within me wanted to believe him. "Just lie down for now. I need to check on my mom." He pecked me on my lips, then went in for another, longer kiss before finally pulling himself from me and exiting the room. I lay back and sighed, wondering what I had done.

Chapter 49

Alexander

It constantly felt like one step forward and two steps back. Okay, maybe it had improved. Previously it was about one step forward, ten steps back. Now it was just a shuffle, back and forth, back and forth. Talia and I had made progress as a couple; we seemed to be back on track. Until, of course, my sister had rained on our parade.

And I was stumped.

As much as I wanted Sara gone now, and I didn't care if I ever looked at her face again, I also knew she was right. My mother was very fragile at the moment. One step in the wrong direction and I wasn't sure she'd survive. Finding out about my mate had already edged her in that direction.

"Alex!" my mom called out as soon as I entered her bedroom. I mindlinked the nurses to ask for privacy and closed the door as soon as they walked out.

"Mom, how are you?" I sat down at her bedside, taking her hand and kissing her on the forehead.

"Where have you been, honey?" she asked, searching my face. "I've been asking Sara and the nurses, but no one could tell me."

"Mom," I started, suddenly nervous about what I was going to reveal, my muscles twitchy. After taking a deep breath, I finally blurted it out. "I've brought my mate back to our pack."

My mom blinked at me a few times. "Is this the mate Sara's been talking about?"

"Yes."

"The one that murdered your father?"

"Mom . . ."

"Alex, I don't know. This is a lot for me." She looked up at the ceiling, not making eye contact.

"But she's my mate, Mom. You always told me how important mates are, and how Artemis sends all of us the perfect match for us. Obviously, there are a few obstacles, but I love her." Okay, maybe *obstacles* wasn't quite the right word, but I wasn't entirely sure what the correct term was for the fact that one's mate had murdered one's mother's mate.

"Alex, I've been doing a lot of thinking." My mom looked up at me. "I just don't know if I believe in mates anymore."

"What do you mean?" I leaned forward.

"What you said about your father was not wrong. He was horrible. Except for maybe the first year or so of our relationship, he was a dreadful and disrespectful man. But because of the mate bond, I was tied to him all those years, stuck with a bully. And how could I leave him, Alex? He was the alpha of the pack. If I left him, the whole pack would become weak, including my whole family. And now that he's gone—" She broke down into sobs, reaching for tissues on her bedside table, blowing her nose.

"But you're free from him now, Mom." I tried to console her.

"Am I though? I can't even be bothered to put on proper clothes anymore. I'd rather be dead, Alex. This is not a way to live. The only thing I have left are my children, and now you're both going to leave me for your mates." Tears were freely falling down her cheeks. I couldn't believe that my mother, who had always been so poised and put together, had fallen apart like this.

"Mom, I'm not going to leave you. My mate is going to come live here with us. You're going to live with us. We'll be a family together." I was desperate to find words that would comfort her.

"I don't know, Alex."

"Mom, please don't worry. It will all be fine. Just give it some time. You'll start to feel better eventually."

"Alex, there's no more future for me." She turned away from me signaling the end of the discussion.

I kissed her head and said, "Mom, I love you." Sighing deeply to myself, I exited the room to return to Talia.

When I entered, I saw her sitting up in the bed. I went back over to her, wrapping my arms around her, relishing the feeling of sparks as they embraced my body, inhaling her beautiful scent. "Let's go out for a walk," I whispered into her ear. "We can get some fresh air and stretch our legs after being in a car for so many hours."

She nodded, not saying anything.

After we bundled up for the cold weather, I took her hand in mine, leading her toward the downtown area of the pack. It wasn't much, but we had an ice cream shop that was open year-round and a small pub where pack members often met up for meals or drinks. I took her inside, where we were immediately seated—being alpha had its perks.

"Want to share a poutine?" I asked her as we browsed the menu. "The cheese curds come from the pack's processing plant. Hopefully you like them, otherwise we're going to have to make some changes." I smiled at her. "Maybe I can make you our official taste tester."

"Poutine sounds good," she replied.

I could sense that she still had an uneasiness to her. This was something I feared, bringing her back here. But I knew it would work out. I couldn't bring myself to believe otherwise. And I would never treat Talia the way my father had treated my mother. No, I would always do everything in my power to make her happy. With how strong the mate bond was, I was surprised my father didn't feel the same way when looking at my mother. What had gone so wrong for him to hurt his mate the way he had?

"Good evening, Alpha." An older woman approached our table, who I knew was named Carol. She'd worked at the pub for years as a waitress, probably longer than I'd been alive. There'd been many times she'd waited on tables I occupied. "May I start you and your friend off with a round of drinks?" She looked at me and then turned to look at Talia, her eyes suddenly widening. She gasped audibly. "Bianca?"

"Bianca?" I asked in confusion, suddenly recalling the name of my mate's mother from the passport I'd found.

Talia turned to the woman, blinking rapidly, confusion on her face. "You knew my mother?" she asked.

The woman burst into tears and wrapped her arms around Talia. "Your mother was my son's mate."

"What?" I shouted. "Your son? You have a son?" She pulled away from Talia, gave me a pointed stare, and then walked away. I looked back at Talia, and she was sitting back in her seat, a blank look on her face, not saying anything. "Your mom had a mate?" I asked her, but she didn't respond. I could sense she was anxious. "Did you know?" I asked gently. She silently looked down at the table and shook her head.

I got up, put my hands on her shoulders, and softly said, "Stay here. I'll find out more, okay?" I went to follow where Carol had gone. How could she drop a bomb like that and just walk away? I got to the door that led to the kitchen when another woman stepped in front of me.

"Where do you think you're going?" she demanded, glaring at me.

"To speak with one of my pack members," I retorted.

"She doesn't want to speak with you." She had her arms crossed, blocking the door.

"Well, my mate needs some answers. Carol approached us and gave some shocking information, then just walked away as if she had simply commented on the weather. Now, please move." I was becoming irritated, preparing to use my alpha aura. I tried to avoid it as I'd been told it was painful, but I'd do it if this woman didn't get out of my way.

"Alpha, please." She reached out for my arm. "Don't speak to Carol about this. It's very hard for her."

"What is? Do you know about her son?"

She nodded her head but didn't say anything.

"Well, spit it out. Tell me what you and Carol seem to be hiding from me!"

She shook her head, her eyes closed, almost a pained look on her face.

"Tell me about Carol's son!" I bellowed, using my alpha aura. I no longer had any patience.

"Your father killed him," she blurted out, instantly covering her mouth.

"What!" I shouted. "But why?"

"Please, Alpha. I wasn't supposed to say anything. Don't make me reveal more." A tear fell, leaving a wet line down her face.

"My mate has a right to know about her mother's past. Both her mother and my father are now dead. So if Carol knows something, it's only right that she tells us."

"Please don't do this to Carol. She's still in pain from losing her son. It's been a long time now. So just let sleeping wolves lie."

"I am not going to just let sleeping wolves lie. Clearly a lot has been kept from me and kept from my mate, and I want some answers. So either you tell us, or I will make Carol talk. It's up to you who you'd like it to be."

"Alpha." Her eyes were emotional, glancing down at the ground.

"My mate has a right to know about her mother's past and to get closure."

She shook her head. "Fine, I'll tell you. Just please, leave Carol alone. She's suffered enough. Let's go somewhere else." She led me to the back of the pub through the back door.

We stood in the freezing weather as she took a deep breath and began the story. "Carol's son met his mate one day when he was visiting a human town not far from here. They met at a small shop, locking eyes from across the store. She tried to hide what she did from him, but he eventually found out she worked at a brothel. But he didn't care because he fell in love with her and made plans to move her to the pack and support her and her young daughter, so she wouldn't have to do that kind of work anymore.

"When he went to speak to your father about moving Bianca to the pack, your father became furious and refused, banishing Carol's son. Your father threatened that if he ever even looked at Bianca again, he would kill him. Apparently, your father had already been seeing Bianca for a few years at that point and didn't like the idea of her being mated to anyone.

"However, Carol's son and Bianca were in love and made plans to run away together. When your father found out, he became enraged and made good on his threat. From what I understand, he was obsessed with Bianca and did everything he could to keep her dependent on him, so he could continue to have her whenever he wanted."

"My Goddess," I replied, feeling ill about what Carol's friend told me but refraining from using the more offensive language I would have preferred.

"I'm sorry I had to tell you. It's not a story that was ever supposed to be repeated." She patted my shoulder.

"Thank you for telling me," I replied, not knowing what else I could say. "Please let Carol know I'm sorry about her son, and that if she ever needs anything, to not hesitate to ask. I know I can't bring her son back, but I would like to be a good alpha to my pack and begin to make up for my father's misdeeds."

"Don't be so hard on yourself. You're not to be blamed for your father's transgressions. I believe I speak for most of the pack when I say that we are all watching you and hoping for a brighter future." She gave me a small smile and turned to walk back inside. I grabbed the door before she could get to it, holding it for her while she walked in.

"Holy fuck," I whispered to myself before I walked inside. I returned to the table where Talia was sitting, moved into the booth so I was touching her, and hugged her close to me. She looked up at me, her eyes large, searching my face. "I know what happened to your mother's mate," I whispered.

"What?" she asked.

"Let's enjoy our meal, and I'll tell you later."

Chapter 50

Jasmine

It wasn't long before word got around about what happened to Charlie. Additionally, his two friends that were involved were discharged from being warriors and given jail sentences, now stuck in the cells for the foreseeable future. Sam went from being a sub to a permanent trainer for our group.

For strength training that day, Sam set up a circuit for us inside the gym. He went around and paired us off in partners for the different stations. I was, unfortunately, paired with Tina, who was not my favorite person. She'd been a year above me in high school, friends with Alyssa, and was never particularly nice to me.

Fortunately, she wasn't in a talking mood that day. I got through deadlifts, overhead presses, and walking lunges just fine. Then when we got to the plank station where we had to hold a plank for five minutes straight, Sam came by.

"Nice form, Dale." He nodded at me. Then he looked over at Tina and said, "Butt down, Mitchell."

"Are you sucking his cock too, PJ?" Tina taunted me.

"What?" I asked, shocked by the accusation.

"Or did Daddy threaten to banish him if he isn't nice to you?"

"Why do you keep calling Blake *Daddy*?" I snapped back at her.

She laughed. "Because he treats you like he's your daddy. Like, you know, the daddy with the shotgun. 'Be nice to my daughter or else!'"

"That's not true!"

"It seems to be. Everyone that's mean to you keeps getting discharged or banished. Clearly you're going to Daddy and whining to him about how we're all not worshipping the ground you walk on."

"So do you think Charlie should have been allowed to stay in the pack after he assaulted someone else?" I yelled at her. "Because first of all, I don't tell Blake anything that happens during training. And second of all, Charlie was a horrible person. And if you're defending him attacking other pack members, then I'm not sure why you're even a warrior!"

Everyone was staring at us now. I felt my cheeks burn at the attention I'd brought on myself. I hadn't meant to argue back. But I had finally hit my boiling point with how my fellow warriors spoke about and to me.

"She's right!" Paige chimed in. I turned my head toward her, shocked at her jumping in to defend me. "Charlie was horrible. And if you're defending him, then I'm ashamed to call you a friend. Jasmine has never done anything to any of you, but you're just nasty to her for no reason, to the point where you're defending someone who's practically a rapist! That is not how Artemis tells us to behave!"

Everyone was now staring at Tina. For a moment, I thought maybe she'd back down, perhaps realize how terrible she was being. But my hope was short-lived.

After a beat she snapped back at Paige. "What, is Jasmine licking your pussy now too? Must run in the family!" She cackled loudly. All of the guys in our group started smirking and whispering among themselves, looking between Paige and me. I could feel that my body was completely red at the attention being focused on me, certain that they were now imagining exactly what Tina had accused us of doing.

"Mitchell! One hundred push-ups!" Sam yelled. "Inappropriate conversation for training!"

I breathed a sigh of relief that at least Sam wasn't going to accept that kind of behavior. Tina glared at me and began doing her push-ups.

After strength training was over, the bell signaled for lunch. I sighed as I walked over to my locker to grab what I had packed for myself so that I could, once again, sit by myself on the bleachers. As soon as I sat down, I turned to open my lunch box when I noticed that Paige was taking a seat next to me.

"Do you mind if I join you today?" she asked.

"Not at all," I replied. "Don't you want to sit with the others though?"

"No, I'm good." She smiled back at me and opened her own lunch box. "How's Tyler doing? I heard what happened to him."

"He's fully healed now. Thanks for asking."

"Good, I'm glad. I can't even believe that Tina would blame you for Charlie getting banished when everyone now knows what he did. It really shows what kind of person she is, right?"

"Thanks for sticking up for me," I responded. "It really means a lot."

"Of course!" she exclaimed. "Those who stand by instead of helping are just as bad as the ones who commit the crime. You know, I didn't tell anyone, but I honestly thought Charlie was going to rape me."

"What!" I gasped.

"He basically put me in a position where I couldn't say no to going into the woods with him during patrol duty, and he backed me up against a tree. I knew he was a lot stronger than me, so I wasn't sure what to do. I was so scared." Her lips trembled as she spoke. "You were so good at fighting him, but I don't think I'm at that level yet."

"Goddess, so what happened? Did he—?" I began, recalling how Charlie had put me in a similar position a year earlier. Thankfully we weren't alone, so he probably wouldn't have been able to get too far, but the thought still terrified me. While I was well trained, he was still far stronger than me. All he had to do was punch me hard enough or hold me down, and I wouldn't be able to overpower him.

"Alpha Blake showed up out of nowhere. He was looking for Charlie and happened to arrive while he had me in that position. And he stopped him. I'm just so grateful he showed up. I don't know what would have happened if he didn't. Especially now, knowing what he's capable of. So please tell him 'thank you' for me."

"Oh my Goddess, Paige," I said, throwing my arms around her. "I'm so glad you're okay."

"Anyway, it made me realize something." She looked eagerly into my eyes. "As women, we have to stick together and help each other instead of tearing each other down. If I hadn't been so scared of rocking the boat and had reported Charlie, and everyone backed me up, we could have gotten him discharged weeks ago. But instead, I listened to them to keep my head down, not wanting to be ostracized, and look what almost happened."

"You're right," I said. "We can't just go along with how things have always been. We have to work together and make positive changes."

"And you know what?" She straightened up.

"What?" I asked.

"You're going to be luna! That means you'll have the power to make those changes."

And then I realized that Blake was right. I was so in my head, trying to fit in with everyone, when this whole time I could've been leading. I could've offered to help Paige report Charlie when she'd first told me what he was doing. In fact, I could have gone straight to Blake to ask for help. But I shied away from it, wanting so badly to fit in, when I shouldn't have even let that be a factor. If Blake hadn't shown up at the right place at the right time, who knows what would have happened to Paige? What kind of luna was I? I felt sick with myself.

Paige, who was younger than me, and without a relationship with the alpha of the pack as her crutch, had done far more to help me. She had completely turned her back on her good social standing with the other female warriors and chosen to eat lunch with me, the outcast. She would've made a better luna than me. My chest felt tight at the thought, an uneasiness coming over me. I was completely worthless as a luna. Although I never met her, I was certain Ria would have made a much better luna than me too. That's why she had been mated to Blake. I, on the other hand, would be a fraud as luna.

The wedding was only weeks away. Before I could stop myself, thoughts began spiraling in my head. Maybe, for the good of the pack, I should break things off. Then maybe Blake could find someone more worthy. I wanted to throw up at the thought. I hated the idea of Blake being with someone else. But he deserved better—the pack deserved better. I could feel myself falling back into my old depression from when Luke first rejected me. Every negative adjective flowed through me—worthless, inferior, weak, useless, inadequate . . .

"Hey, Jasmine, are you okay?" Paige's voice interrupted my thoughts.

"Oh yeah, I'm fine. Just spacing out." I gave a small, nervous laugh.

"You just looked really pale, like you were about to pass out or something."

"Oh, did I? That's weird." I shook my head and stopped thinking about it.

After training ended for the day, while exiting the locker room, I spotted Blake with some other guys doing dumbbell exercises. As soon as our eyes locked, he put his weights down and ran over to me. He wrapped his arms around me and kissed me on my cheek. It felt so good to be in his arms.

"I've missed you, Miss Alpha," he whispered into my ear.

"It's only been a couple days," I replied.

"A couple days too long. How long until you finally move into the packhouse?"

"Blake, I've been thinking," I started.

"What about?" He stared into my eyes with his piercing blue ones.

"Maybe we should talk about it later," I said, looking around at how many people were in the gym now.

"You've got office duty tomorrow, right?" He smiled at me. "We can talk then. Although I hope you're planning to do more than talk." He gave me a mischievous smile. "Let me walk you to your car now. And I won't stop you if you try to seduce me into the back seat. Although, it might be a bit cramped in your car. But we can make it work." He leaned close to my ear and whispered, "Could be fun seeing how we can contort our bodies."

I couldn't lie, I began to feel very aroused, my stomach fluttering and my skin heating, imagining the positions we'd get into.

When we approached the car, he rubbed the side of my arm and kissed me. He did always make me feel better when I was feeling down. "So, back seat?" He chuckled.

"My windows aren't tinted enough for that." I lightly punched his arm.

"It's more comfortable in a bed anyway." Blake kissed me again.

"Have you done it in a car before?" I asked.

"I mean, that was basically my teenage years." He laughed. "A lot of sneaking around."

"How many girls have you been with?" I asked, feeling insecure about the thought of it. I'd known he'd gotten around, but I never gave it much thought before. Now it suddenly felt like a sticking point.

"It doesn't matter," he replied. "That was the past. I'm not like that anymore. Now there's only one woman for me." He smiled meaningfully at me.

"But there are probably women I pass by and talk to in the pack all the time that have been with you. And I have no idea! But they've been with you!"

"It's not a big deal, Jasmine. They've all moved on now. It was all just hookups."

"But maybe it wasn't for them! You told me that one of them chased you with a bat. There are probably other stories you haven't told me."

"Where is this coming from?" He searched my face. "Why is this coming up now? I've always been honest with you, Jasmine. I made a lot of bad choices in my past. I took my pain out on other people. Trust me, I feel bad about it now. But I'm not like that anymore. I grew up. And I love you. I will never treat you the way my father treated my mom."

"Why do you love me though? You could have someone who would make a way better luna than me." I looked down at the ground in shame, shame that I felt that way and that I admitted it to Blake.

"There's no one better than you." He wrapped his arms around me again. "I wish you could see what I see when I look at you, so then you'd stop being so down on yourself." I sighed into his chest, and he continued, "To be honest, I think the rejection is clouding your perception. You've changed since you and Luke rejected each other. You're always unhappy and stressed now. I'm so anxious to finally mark you so you'll get better."

"Maybe it's better if you don't," I replied, a tear falling at the thought.

"What! Jasmine, why would you say that?" He lifted my chin so I was looking at him.

"Because if you mark me, you and the pack will be stuck with an inadequate luna."

"Jasmine, stop. There is no better luna for me or the pack. I can't imagine my life without you. I love you. I'm ready to mark you right here, right now. I will take you into the back seat of your car and show you with my body how much you mean to me and then sink my teeth into your neck without hesitation."

I put my head against his chest, feeling insecure. Was it really the rejection making me feel this way, even to this day?

"Jasmine." Blake interrupted my thoughts, speaking quietly. "Are you saying all this because you want to break up with me?"

I jolted my head up, looking into his eyes, a deep sadness in them. "What? No. But I just thought . . ." My voice trailed off.

"Thought what?"

"That it would be better for you and the pack if you found someone who's more luna material. I'm not a leader, Blake." My throat prickled as I said that. "I've been a follower my whole life. I did what my parents told me, and now I'm doing what you tell me. I don't even know how to lead."

"You have it in you, Jasmine. I know you do. You're a tough and brave woman. I've witnessed it many times during the little time I've known you. And didn't you recently kick a certain douchebag trainer's ass?" I looked up at him and his eyes were sparkling, a smirk on his face.

"You found out about that?" I asked in surprise.

He laughed and said, "It's all anyone's been talking about. I was waiting for you to finally tell me so I could celebrate your victory with you."

"It's no big deal." I shrugged.

"It *is* a big deal, Jasmine! You kicked someone's ass who was a warrior longer than you—someone who was good enough to be a trainer. If that's not luna material then I don't know what is. Trust me when I tell you that I would not be better off with anyone else and neither would the pack. Because without you, I . . ." Now his voice trailed off, and it sounded shaky. He shook his head and looked back at me. "Jasmine, I love you. Just know that."

"I love you too," I replied. He kissed me and smiled as he pulled away. Knowing I had been keeping him from, likely, more important things than listening to my angst, I said, "I should get home, and you probably have to get back to your workout."

"I miss working out with you, Miss Alpha. But I'll see you tomorrow." He kissed me again, and then I got in my car to drive away. I knew that right now should've been the happiest time in my life, but I couldn't help all the feelings that kept invading my insides, taking away all my confidence. All I ever felt anymore was an impending doom—that nothing would ever get better.

Chapter 51

Talia

Alex was quiet throughout our meal, giving me sad glances as we ate. I could sense his anxiety—it overwhelmed me. I knew whatever he discovered was not good. I almost wondered if I even wanted to know. It was difficult to learn so much about my mother that she'd hidden from me all these years. I not only had to accept that there was so much I never knew about her but also address my grief at the same time. I couldn't even enjoy the food that came out. I was just eating for the sake of eating.

When we stepped out into the cold air after our meal, Alex took my hand and looked down at me, giving me a heartbreaking look, only made more intense by the emotion being emitted from him. "Talia, I want to say I'm very sorry again for all of the pain and suffering my family has caused you and your mom. I honestly had no idea how evil my father was. I mean, he'd always been tough on me growing up, but there were a lot of things he did that I never knew about. And learning about them now, I feel sick and disgusted to be related to someone like that."

My heart beat forcefully against my chest, my anxiety mixing with his. "What did you find out about my mother's mate?" I asked.

He told me the story as the cold, harsh wind blew around us, painful against my exposed cheeks. When he finished, a whimper escaped my chest, my knees felt weak. Alex held me up and held me tight against him. "Talia, I'm sorry. I'm so sorry," he said into my ear.

"How can someone be so evil?" I asked, barely able to get the words out.

"I don't know. I honestly don't know. Talia, I'm learning so much about my father now that I hadn't known my whole life."

"All that time, my mom was suffering because she'd lost her mate." I looked up at him. "You told me yourself that losing your mate fucks someone up." As I said it, I felt my voice shake, vividly recalling how depressed my mom had been my whole life, depending on painkillers to survive, continuing to see *him* so that she could afford them. The same person who was the root of most of her suffering. How could she stand to see him after he killed her mate? And then, I realized, maybe it hadn't been a choice. Maybe he had threatened her in the same way he'd threatened her mate, finally making good on it when we had planned to leave that life behind.

I couldn't help it as tears tumbled out of my eyes, cold piercing my cheeks as the wind froze them. Alex pulled me tightly against him, shielding me from the elements. I sobbed against him, unable to hold back my grief and sadness for my mother. He rubbed my back and held me, supporting me, comforting me.

"Let's go home, Talia. It's cold out here," he said softly. I nodded, he put his arm around me, and we walked back to the chalet slowly, side by side. When we entered, he took me into the living room and pulled me next to him on the couch, kissing my head. "Let me put on a fire," he took my head in his hands and looked into my eyes. "My mom has a good mulled wine recipe. I think some warm wine would be appropriate right now. Would you like some?"

I nodded but didn't say anything, feeling numb. Maybe alcohol would help.

He moved to start a fire, piling a couple logs in the fireplace. Then he pulled out a warm blanket and placed it on top of me, kissing me on my head again. I couldn't help but feel so cozy in this room, with the warm fire, soft blanket, and bearskin rug covering the floor. I looked around and noticed that there were new drawings hung on the wall that weren't there previously, and I recognized that they were likely his. One was a sketch of the downtown area of the pack, with the chalet in the background. Others were of forest landscapes. He did have quite a gift with his hand.

After some time, he returned and handed me a mug, sat down on the couch close to me, and pulled me against him. I snuggled into him, the feeling of his body against mine helping me relax. We both sat silently, sipping from our mugs. Once we finished them, he got up to refill them before returning to the couch again.

"Your drawings are beautiful," I said as the buzz began to come over me. I realized that he had definitely added something stronger than wine into the drink.

"Thank you. That means so much coming from you," he said. "My father never appreciated them, to be honest. He actually hated that I drew. One time, when I was probably around fourteen or fifteen, he burned all of my sketch pads. Years of work all gone in a flash, right in this very fireplace."

"Why would he do that?" My mouth fell open at the story.

"He didn't think it was a manly activity. He was always insulting me for doing things he thought were girly. And one day he just got fed up I guess. He went into my closet and pulled out all my sketch pads. I tried to stop him, but he forced me to submit with his alpha aura and all I could do was watch in horror as he threw them into the fire one by one. I never cry, and I started crying. That obviously didn't go over well." He shook his head and I could feel all of his pain, especially now touching his body.

"What did he do?" I asked.

"I'll spare you the details, but he basically beat me half to death. If I were human, I'd be dead. I still feel helpless to this day when I think about how he was able to just overpower me like that and do whatever he wanted to me. After that day, I trained so hard to make sure no one would ever be able to do that to me again."

I put my hand on his cheek and he turned to me, holding my gaze. I felt such compassion for him. I couldn't believe that I ever thought he was evil. He was clearly just as affected by his father's crimes as I was. We sat unblinking for a few moments, as if in a staring competition, but it wasn't long before we were pulled toward each other as if by a magnetic force. Our mouths connected, and Alex fell on top of me. We couldn't help ourselves as we once again pulled off all our clothes, rolling onto the floor, our bodies rubbing against each other, unable to get close enough. We ended up on the bearskin rug, the sweat coating our skin glistening from the flames. As Alex thrust in and out of me, the skin of his body gliding over mine, our tongues intertwined. The only sounds were us breathing and the crackling of the fire. And I realized at that moment that I had never made love before. Everything before that moment was just sex. This was true, passionate, all-encompassing love—our bodies coming together as one.

I'd never felt so in tune with another person before. Alex lifted his head slightly so he could stare into my eyes as I wrapped my legs around him, desperate to be as close to him as possible, never wanting to forget this moment. In response, he thrust harder, positioning himself again so he was hitting exactly the right spot. Both our bodies began to tremble as sparks danced inside and outside our bodies. I moaned loudly as all of the built-up pleasure became overwhelming, my entire body tensing. As Alex let out a groan I felt the intense release flow throughout my entire body, spreading to my fingers and toes, my whole body like jelly under Alex as he collapsed on top of me.

Almost immediately, I felt my canines expand and a strong desire to sink them into Alex's neck. I resisted, turning my head sideways while I kept my eyes shut. Once the feeling passed, I opened them to a brunette woman standing over us. I gasped and Alex got up off me.

"Fuck! Goddess! Mom!" he yelled, grabbing the blanket and throwing it over me, keeping a piece to cover himself with.

"I'm safe to assume that's your mate?" the woman asked.

"Fucking Artemis. Of course this would be how my mate gets introduced to my mom." He chuckled to himself. Then he looked up at the woman and asked, "How long have you been standing there?"

"What, you think I just stood here and watched?"

"Dear Goddess, I hope not. Do you mind turning around so we can get dressed at least?"

"I'll be in my room." She walked out, and we listened to her footsteps as she ascended the stairs.

"Okay, that was maybe slightly less embarrassing than the time my mom walked in on me rubbing one out when I was a teenager." Alex laughed. "Anyway, as awkward as that was, I should probably properly introduce you, with your clothes on." He shook his head and got up, reaching for his clothes. I quickly gathered my own clothing and fumbled pulling it on. I grimaced, my face impossibly hot and my chest tight with mortification. It seemed as if I had a knack for getting caught with my pants down, literally!

Once we were dressed, he pulled me against his body and said, "Don't worry. My mom is really sweet. She's nothing like my dad or sister. She's just a bit depressed right now after losing her mate."

"Are you sure you should be introducing us?" I asked, feeling a bit sick about the idea. Besides the fact that she had just walked in on me in the act with her son, I was also her husband's murderer. I wasn't sure how Alex expected this to work out.

"Well, you have to meet at some point. We're all going to be living together in this house. And I'd like for her to know you as more than some girl I was banging on the living room floor." He smirked. "I know it's a little uncomfortable, but she knows you're my mate. And I know with time she'll come to love you as much as I do." His eyes sparkled as he said that. It almost made me want to believe him. But it seemed naive to think we could just be one happy family living together under one roof. There was just too much damage done.

He took my hand and pulled me upstairs. I felt faint, a pressure at the pit of my stomach. Everything about this seemed terrible. He knocked on a door upstairs. "Come in," a woman's voice said.

He pulled me into the room. After we were inside, two other women walked out. He brought me over to her bed and had me sit down on a chair next to it. His mom was sitting up in a sweatshirt and sweatpants. She was actually quite pretty, with a sweet face and light-brown hair, with long gray roots that were in need of coloring, pulled up into a bun. She was much shorter than Alex. He had clearly gotten his height from his dad.

"Mom, this is my mate Talia," he said as he squatted down next to her bed.

She stared at me, not saying anything. I felt like throwing up from how nervous I was. This was too much. Alex and I had only just established ourselves as an official couple, and I was already being expected to move in with him and his mom. Maybe it wouldn't have been so bad normally, but his mom had a legitimate reason to hate me, and his sister, his mother's daughter, was out for my blood. I couldn't expect his mom to take my side over her own flesh and blood.

After sitting in silence for about a minute, his mom finally spoke. "Well, I can tell why you like her. She's very pretty. But looks can be deceiving."

"Talia is beautiful both on the inside and outside, Mom."

"How long have you known her. Because I thought the same about your father. And your father never murdered any of my family members."

I clutched my stomach. The world spun around me. How could Alex have put me in such an awkward position?

"Mom." Alex glared at her.

"What, Alex? Your judgment is being clouded by the mate bond. Listen to me. I was once in your shoes. I thought your father was the greatest thing since sliced bread. Don't make the same mistake I did."

"Mom, I'm going to forgive how rude you're being by speaking about my mate as if she's not here because of what you're going through." Alex's jaw tensed. "I intend to be with my mate. I know there are some hurdles to jump with what's happened in the past, but Dad wasn't some innocent angel who didn't deserve what he got. I'm sorry you had to be mated to him, and I feel worse about it now that I've learned more about what he's done. But Talia's life has been just as badly affected by him as all of ours were. I think the only person in this world who doesn't have something bad to say about him is Sara, and that's only because she's an exact clone of him, just female."

"Sara is not as bad as your father." His mom narrowed her eyes at him.

"Are you sure about that, Mom? Maybe your judgment is clouded by being her mother. I know my judgment was by being her brother."

"Can't you see what's happening? Our whole family is being torn apart." Tears tumbled out of his mom's eyes. I didn't want to sit there anymore. I was very uncomfortable.

He took his mom's hand in his and leaned closer to the bed. "It's not being torn apart. It's just changing. The Moon Goddess wants Talia and me to be mated to each other for a reason. We have to trust her judgment. Please just give her a chance, Mom. I love her."

"You love her?"

"Yes, I do. So please, Mom. It would mean a lot to me if you could at least try to get to know her."

After a beat she finally said, "Alex, this is a lot for me right now. Do you mind just giving me some space?"

"Okay," he said quietly and got up to kiss her on the cheek. He helped me up and walked me out of the room with his arm slung around my shoulder. It took everything in me to put one foot in front of the other, dizzy from the conversation. It was too much, and Alex was clearly much more equipped to deal with these tough conversations than I was. I felt light-headed and like I could pass out at any moment. He brought me into his room and had me sit on the bed with him. "Talia, I really appreciate you meeting my mom." He took my hand and stared into my eyes. "It didn't go how I was hoping. But I know my mom will come around. I don't want you to worry. It'll all be okay. Just give it some time."

"Alex, maybe I shouldn't have come here yet. This is too much too soon," I managed to choke out.

"Please don't say that. We're meant to be together." He sighed and said, "I'd set you up in your own home, but it's too dangerous. I need to protect you."

"Because your sister wants to kill me."

He shook his head. "I know it seems like everything is keeping us apart right now. But have faith, Talia, please."

I looked into his eyes that were filled with emotion and felt the affection he held emitting from him. I nodded. I knew it was a terrible idea to stay, but I couldn't imagine being without him anymore. While a path forward with him seemed daunting, one without him was dark and terrifying.

Chapter 52

Talia

A few days after Alex moved me into his house, the two of us went for a walk in the forest. The day was marginally warmer than it had been, now slightly above freezing. We bundled up so that Alex could bring me to where he normally sketched when it was warmer out. Our feet crunched in the snow that was slowly melting from the warmer climate.

We made it out to a clearing in the forest with a river running through it, a large tree trunk had fallen over it like a bridge. "I sometimes sit on that trunk and put my feet in the water during the summer. And sometimes I sit on this rock over here." He took my hands and brought me over to a large rock that was beside the water. "It's so peaceful out here. I can just forget about my responsibilities for a few hours."

"Is it hard being the alpha?" I asked.

"It's definitely not easy." He stared into my eyes. "Ultimately, I'm accountable for the pack—from the income that's generated by the dairy plant to the safety of all the pack members. Anything goes wrong, and the blame falls on me even when it's not my fault."

"Do you wish you didn't have to be alpha?"

"I've thought about it and, no, I don't wish that. When I look around the pack, I feel a lot of pride. My dad may have been a horrible person, but he did a good job maintaining and protecting the pack. He was ruthless when it came to enemies, and other packs knew not to mess with us. I want to be like that too, but I also want to be a good leader to my pack members and rule with respect instead of fear like my dad did."

"I think you'll do great." I smiled at him, believing it in my heart.

"And you'll be my luna. You'll help me lead."

"What does that entail?" I asked.

"Normally it means you'd help me run the pack and fight in battles. But I'm happy with you just being my mate if you don't want to do that."

"I'd like to help you. I just don't know anything about leading a pack."

"Don't worry. I'll train you." He kissed me on my forehead as I closed my eyes, imagining a future with him, enjoying the feeling of his strong arms around me.

He pulled away from me and said, "Sorry, Talia. I had a lot of coffee this morning, and I really need to pee. I'll go farther into the woods and be right back." He gave me a shy smile and walked away. I watched as he disappeared from view, beyond some shrubs. I turned back around to look at the river, seeing if I could spot any fish, inhaling the crisp winter air. Suddenly, a figure came into view under the water. At first, I thought it was a polar bear, confusing me, but as soon as it came to the surface, I realized it was a wolf.

The wolf leaped out of the water with a splash, some of the water spraying my pants and boots. I backed away and screamed as the wolf extended its claws. As it got closer, I recognized the smell and knew exactly who it was. She leaped toward me and got a deep slash across my face. The force of the strike caused me to fall over, my body slamming against the ground. I put my hand to my face, the contact stinging me as blood seeped from skin, torn as if it had been ripped to rags. A sharp pain emerged from my eyeball, now split by the deep cut, my sight in that eye gone. Acting on impulse, I quickly rolled and forced myself to shift, tearing my clothes. But I was barely trained and barely able to concentrate from the pain. She easily knocked me over again and pinned me down. I thrashed helplessly as she was about to snap her teeth around my neck. Before her canines connected with my skin, she unexpectedly froze and shifted into her human form.

I quickly pushed her off me and moved away as I saw Alex sprinting over in his human form. She was clearly immobilized, lying naked in the snow, looking up at Alex with the evilest look I'd ever seen. "Sara, you need to stop trying to kill my mate or I will kill you!" Alex shouted at her. "This is my final warning! I've only gone easy on you until now because you're my sister, but I am done."

"I, Sara Adalwolf, banish myself from the Pine Forest Pack and declare myself a rogue!" Alex's sister shouted in return. As soon as she said it, she was able to move again and shifted back into her wolf form.

"Fuck!" Alex yelled, instantly shifting into his wolf form as well, tearing his clothes. She was about to tackle me again when he pushed me forcefully out of the way, and I landed against the large rock, my body whipping against it like a rag doll. I was certain it had left a huge bruise, the pain severe. He was strong and it was even possible some of my bones were fractured from the force of his push. Tears dropped from my eyes from the aching, the saltiness stinging me.

I used my hands to push myself up off the ground, trying not to succumb to the pain. The two of them were standing off, hissing at each other, in fighting positions, circling as if in a boxing match. I watched as he made the first move and tried to slash her with his own claws, but she dodged the attack, opened her mouth, and bit his front right paw instead, pulling the digits clean off him, and spitting them into the water. A stream of blood covered the snow, but he continued fighting as if she hadn't just mutilated him.

She definitely put up a fair fight. She was much more skilled than me, and what she lacked in strength, she made up for in agility, dodging his attacks and landing her own. But Alex was stronger, and every blow he got in had a much bigger impact on her, clearly weakening her each time. I wasn't sure if she'd be able to keep going as the fight wore on. As she was becoming visibly more injured, Alex had his teeth bared, ready to bite down on her. But, before he could, she rolled away into the water and quickly swam upstream.

He followed the river up some of the way but eventually stopped, turning back around and running back to me, shifting into his human form once he got closer. "Talia, are you okay?" he shouted, coming toward me.

"Your hand!" I gasped, as soon as I shifted back into my human form so I could speak. "She bit off your fingers!" I looked in horror to where his hand was bleeding profusely and his fingers missing.

He looked down sadly at his hand—his hand that he drew with. "I'm just glad you're okay," he responded, but I could see the sorrow in his eyes as he quickly looked at me and then stared back down at his hand. "I still have my left hand," he said quietly but unconvincingly.

"No!" I cried. "We have to find your fingers! She spit them out!"

"The water is freezing, and they've probably been taken downstream by now. Sara's the only werewolf I know who can swim long distances in freezing water—long enough to find fingers in a huge river. And the water will have carried away the scent anyway." He looked defeated, tears brimming his eyes.

"I will find them," I said resolutely.

"No, you're injured!" He reached for me. Before he could stop me, I shifted back into my wolf form and dove into the river, ignoring all the pain on my face and body—adrenaline giving me strength to persist. It wasn't too bad at first. My inner layer of fur kept the water from reaching my skin. With enthusiasm, I searched the bottom of the river, weaving back and forth against the ground, coming up for air as needed. It wasn't long before I found one of the fingers stopped by a rock. I quickly grabbed it and brought it to the surface, leaving it at the side of the river, only to glance at Alex in his wolf form watching me before quickly diving back in.

I continued searching. The next one wasn't as easy to locate, and as time wore on while I searched, my fur slowly stopped shielding me, now fully penetrated by the water. But my urgent need to find his fingers gave me the strength to ignore the icy cold water.

I swam downstream with the current and, after more time searching, finally found the second one, now finding my ability to swim slowed and my paws numb. But I powered through. Although it wasn't perfect, I realized that I had an intuition to locate them, much like when my wolf had known where to go to find Alex previously. Something about our mate bond helped draw me to him, and in this case, his body parts. I followed the river farther down, becoming dizzier the farther I went, my breathing becoming more and more shallow. I could tell that the cold was defeating my body, but I wouldn't quit until I found every last finger, or died trying. It was too important to me that Alex could continue to sketch, especially after the heartbreaking story he'd told me.

By the time I found the third one, I could barely think straight, running only on instinct. At this point I had probably been swimming for over half an hour. I grabbed it in my mouth and brought it to the surface, depositing it on the side of the river again where Alex collected it in his own mouth. My breathing was becoming labored, and I felt the chill all the way to my bones.

After another several minutes, my vision began to go blurry. I was rapidly losing strength to stay in my wolf form. But I still hadn't found the last finger, so I pushed forward anyway. Was I hallucinating, or was my body becoming warmed again? And just like that, the world went black.

I woke to soothing sparks surrounding the top of my head and slowly opened my eyes to Alex staring down at me, blinking at him a few times as he came into focus. I looked around the unfamiliar room. "Where am I?" I asked.

"You're in the pack hospital. You passed out from hypothermia, but I was able to get you here, and you'll be fine. You just needed to heal. Your eye is looking much better now."

I blinked a few more times. I could feel there was still a cut on my eye, but it wasn't split anymore like it had been. And then I recalled everything that happened. "Your fingers!" I shouted.

He smiled, his whole face glowing. "I can't believe it, but you found them." He showed me his hand that was wrapped in a bandage. "They just had to stitch them back on and they're healing now. I can feel them reattaching themselves to my hand."

I let out a sigh of relief. But before I could get too comfortable, I thought back.

Had I found all of them?

"Wait, all of them?"

"Enough."

"But not all?" My throat and eyes burned and a dizziness came over me.

"You did amazing."

"But I didn't get all of them, did I?" I asked with desperation, my chest aching at the thought.

"Talia, look at me." He pulled my face into his hands. "You got the fingers I need to sketch. That's all that matters."

"But which ones are missing?"

"Just the pinky. But I don't care. You got most of them and tried until you passed out in the water. Luckily, I was right there to pull you out and you're alive. That's what really matters. And I can still sketch. I'll just have to live with one less finger."

"I still failed." A tear trickled down my cheek.

"Not even close," he gushed, giving me a huge smile. "I was blessed with the best mate in the world." He climbed into the bed with me, pulling me against him. I snuggled into the feeling of calm and sparks that engulfed my body. "You did more than I ever expected. I will always protect you."

"What will happen now that your sister is a rogue?"

He closed his eyes and let out a deep breath. "Well, unfortunately my alpha aura won't work on her anymore. But now she's an enemy of the pack, and she'll have more than just me to deal with if she ever tries to reenter the territory."

"What about your mom?" I asked.

"I don't know." He sighed. "I just wish there was a way to make her feel better. She's so depressed, and it will probably only get worse now that her daughter's been banished. All she does is talk about death and how she has nothing to live for anymore. I feel so helpless."

I brushed my hand through his soft hair and then rubbed my hand up and down his arm in a soothing gesture. He seemed to calm as I did this, his anxiety lessening. I kept doing it and he moved his face closer to me, kissed me, and then whispered, "Even if everything's a bit of a mess right now, I'm just glad I have you."

Chapter 53

Jasmine

"You know, you don't have to eat with me if you don't want," I said to Paige one day during lunch. "Don't get me wrong, I enjoy the company, but I feel bad taking you away from your other friends. I won't be offended if you go back to eating with them."

"Eating with them wasn't that much fun anyway. They mostly gossiped about other people all the time. That's not really my thing," Paige replied.

"It's not really my thing either. But my mom loves it. You should see her at temple every week. She's basically the president of the rumor mill." I laughed. "When I was in high school, she knew more about everyone I went to school with than I did!"

"She must love that you're engaged to the alpha then because she'll get to know all the really good stuff before everyone else."

"Ha, that's true! Maybe that's why she's so friendly with him." I smiled. "I kept wondering how Blake was able to get her to warm up to him."

"Blake's pretty suave though, isn't he? I mean, he has a really charming personality. Kind of like his dad. His dad was great at schmoozing. My mom was literally obsessed with him, like a teen girl with a crush." Paige laughed.

"That's true. His dad was that way, wasn't he? Like a politician almost."

"Yeah, that's a great analogy!" Paige agreed. "Blake must miss him a lot."

"Mm," I replied noncommittally. I didn't want to divulge to Paige that Blake didn't miss his dad at all because I didn't think it was something he'd want me sharing with other people. But Paige was right that Blake's dad was much different publicly than how Blake and Luke had known him. Prior to speaking to them, I'd always thought he was a good leader and nice guy. I still wondered if Blake was overly harsh about his dad. After all, his father had sacrificed his life to save Blake's. That didn't seem like something an evil person would do.

"Hey, would you want to come over one night maybe, to hang out? I have two sisters and we do potluck and game nights sometimes. You should join us this Friday! My parents will be having their date night, so it'll just be us girls in the house."

"I'd love that!" I smiled widely. It had been so long since I had girlfriends to hang out with.

"My twin sister, Ginger, is back home from school for the holidays, so you'll get to meet her too. Everyone calls her Gigi though."

"Oh, I didn't know you had a twin!"

"A lot of people don't. She went to boarding school during high school."

"Oh really? Why's that?"

Paige didn't answer right away, looking down. But then she looked back up at me and said, "I don't normally tell people the real reason. But you seem trustworthy."

"You don't have to tell me if you don't want to," I replied. "But I would never tell anyone. It's not like I have anyone to tell anyway."

"I trust you." She gave me a small smile. "Usually, I tell people she was really smart, so my parents wanted her to get a really good education. But the truth is that she was bullied a lot in middle school, so my parents thought she'd be better off at a human school."

"Oh, I'm sorry to hear that," I replied. "I can relate. I was kind of bullied in school too. Luckily, I had my friend Lucy who usually defended me."

"I tried to defend my sister too. But kids can be really mean." Paige sighed. "Anyway, it was for the best. She was much happier once she went away."

"Well, I'd love to meet her. And your other sister too."

"Oh, you'll love Heidi! She moved out a year ago after she got married."

"Great, I'm looking forward to it!"

"Yay! I'm so excited! Just bring a dish for the potluck. We're not picky eaters, so you can bring really anything!"

Since I had the day off from training on Friday, Tyler invited me to go over his house during the afternoon to keep him company while he worked and offered to help me put together my potluck dish.

"I still don't understand why you'd invite me over while you're working. Don't you have to actually, you know, *work*?" I asked him from the couch as I scrolled through my Instagram feed.

"The internet doesn't even work half the time this far out in the boonies," Tyler replied from his desk. "And my job hasn't caught on to how unproductive I am yet. So I don't think they'll notice If I spend more time socializing than working one day."

"You're crazy!"

"Plus, it's Friday! If I worked in an office, we'd all be having beers and playing ping pong today!"

"I'm not sure that's true."

"Sure it is! Tons of startups these days have beers on tap. Too bad we live in the middle of nowhere."

I looked up at Tyler and asked, "Are you going to stay here? Or are you and Jack planning to go back to your old pack?"

He sighed and looked a bit sad, his brows furrowed and his eyes heavy. I wasn't used to seeing Tyler so down. He was normally so positive and humorous. "I don't know. Jack wants to, big time. But I can't help but feel like that's just giving in to the bullies, you know?"

I nodded.

"Plus, Jack's whole family is here, and he's super close to all of them. And his family is great. They're so loud and fun. I'd hate to go back to my boring family." He laughed, but it sounded forced. "And you're not so bad." He gave me a sly smile. "Also, how can I say goodbye to my fantasy man, Blake?"

"Ha," I replied drily.

"Well, if we do leave, you better bring Blake onto FaceTime all the time. Especially when he's half naked. Or fully naked. Whatever he's comfortable with." Tyler smiled, back to his joking self.

"Oh my Goddess, Tyler!"

"How is my man, Blake, anyway? You haven't talked about him much lately."

I hesitated, not sure if I wanted to divulge all my dark thoughts to Tyler. The wedding was less than a week away, and I still felt anxiety at the pit of my stomach. It was so bad that I was now staying up late, having trouble sleeping, constantly waking in a state of panic. Everyone around me seemed so cheerful and happy about the event, so I played along, but I couldn't help all the toxic thoughts that poisoned my mind. I was feeling completely inadequate to become luna of the pack.

"Earth to Jasmine! Earth to Jasmine!" Tyler was standing in front of me waving his hand in my face.

"What?" I came out of a trance I didn't realize I was in.

"You were just majorly spaced out. Are you okay?" He sat down next to me.

"I'm fine. It's not a big deal. At least not compared to, you know . . ." I sighed.

"Compared to what happened to me?"

"Yeah, I feel so stupid even feeling this way when I think about how other people have it so much worse."

"Just because other people have worse problems doesn't mean your feelings aren't valid, Jasmine. Anyway, what happened to me is in the past now. I'd rather just forget it ever happened. Jack keeps talking about it, and I wish he'd stop. It's just so humiliating. I hate that that's how people know me now. Like people give me looks when they see me around the pack."

I touched his arm in understanding.

"You know, you look really tired. Have you been sleeping?" Tyler studied my face. "The bags under your eyes are really intense."

"Oh, that's probably just genetic." I waved off his worry.

"Jasmine, I'm your brother. Tell me what's bothering you." He put his hand on my knee in a friendly gesture. "If you don't tell me, I'm going to force-feed you alcohol, or truth serum as I like to call it, until you tell me. And we both know you're a very sloppy drunk who loves to blurt out anything and everything." He laughed. "So come on, what's it going to be? The easy way or the fun way?"

I took a deep breath, and said, "I just don't know if I should marry Blake."

"What! Jasmine! Why?" He widened his eyes and leaned forward.

"I just think he should be with someone that's more luna material. I don't think I can handle the responsibility." I looked down at my feet.

"You still feel that way? Have you talked to Blake about it?"

"Yes, but I don't know. I don't think Blake always looks at things logically."

"How does he look at things?"

"He acts on impulse a lot. I think us becoming mates is really impulsive and he hasn't really thought it through. And one day he's going to realize he made a huge mistake."

"I don't think you're giving yourself or Blake enough credit. First of all, when it comes to relationships, from what Jack's told me, Blake doesn't sound like he's impulsive at all. And second of all, why are you being so down on yourself?"

"Because . . ." I started, but left the word hanging, not sure how to answer.

"Because of the rejection, maybe?"

I sighed. "That's what Blake thinks."

"Well, maybe he's right. I mean, he hasn't marked you yet, so you'd still be affected, right?"

"I guess."

"Well, okay, at least answer this question before you do something completely stupid like dump the hottest man in the state, or possibly country. Do you love him?"

"Yes, I do but—"

"Well, that's all that matters then!" Tyler cut me off. "You love him and he loves you. Even if Blake found someone who's more quote, unquote 'luna material,' as doubtful as that is, that doesn't mean he's going to love her or want to be with her. And what's the point of even being with someone if you don't love them? Sounds pretty miserable to me, even if she can shoot wolfsbane bullets out of her nipples in battle."

I laughed. "I guess."

Tyler shook his head. "So, when are you leaving for the honeymoon?"

"We're leaving the night of the wedding to stay in a hotel in Montreal and flying out to Paris the next evening."

"So, marking before or during Paris?"

"That's a personal question!" I slapped Tyler's arm.

"Well, you didn't say no marking, so I can only assume the wedding and marking are still happening."

I sighed. "How are you and Jack doing?" I asked, wanting to change the subject now.

"Jack is great." He smiled, his whole face glowing. "I mean, I can kind of understand how you feel. There are days I think I don't deserve Jack because he's just *so* great. But that's love—believing you got the better end of the bargain. And hopefully, the person you're with feels the same way."

I sighed in reply. Sure, there was that, but Tyler didn't have a whole entire pack depending on him to lead them. How could he understand how I felt?

"Hey, Jasmine, if you're really feeling insecure about the whole luna thing, maybe you just need a way to build your confidence. And I know a group of people that could really use your help. As luna, you'll be in the perfect position to help them."

"Really? Who?" I asked, brightening, excited to have an opportunity to help someone and make up for how useless I'd been up until now.

"On Sundays, there's a group of us that meet at a pub in St. Albans. Maybe you can come this Sunday with Jack and me."

"Yes, I'd love to!" I nodded, smiling widely.

"Great, I'm so happy." Tyler gave me a hug.

Chapter 54

Jasmine

I arrived at Paige's house at seven with a Tupperware filled with honey barbecue wings and a plastic-wrapped meat and cheese board that Jack had put together after he got home from his warrior duty. I told him it was completely unnecessary, but both he and Tyler insisted, both probably a little too happy that I had made a friend.

Goddess, was I really that hopeless?

"Jasmine! Welcome! Come in!" Paige greeted me, taking the items from my hands as soon as I walked in. I followed her into the kitchen where she added what I brought to the spread. "Wow, this looks great! You didn't have to make so much food! There's only four of us!"

"I know. The meat and cheese board was actually my brother and his mate. I was at their house before I came here."

"Oh, how's Tyler doing?" Paige gave me a pitying look, and I instantly understood what Tyler meant. I'd also despise it if people looked at me like that. I hated feeling weak. I knew Paige meant it as a look of empathy, so I didn't let it bother me.

"He's great!" I replied, probably a little too enthusiastically.

"Oh, that's great! I'm so glad to hear."

"Fresh blood!" A girl that looked almost identical to Paige, except with a much curvier body, walked into the room. "I'm Gigi. Nice to meet you." She put out her hand for me to shake.

"Nice to meet you. I'm Jasmine," I replied, taking her hand.

Gigi turned to Paige and said, "Heidi just texted that she's on her way." She walked over to the table and remarked, "Someone's an overachiever. No wonder Paige likes you. That's okay, you can make up for the bowl of chips that I contributed as my portion of the potluck."

"Gigi calls me an overachiever, but she was always better at school and training than me. She just likes to pretend she's all cool and laid back." Paige rolled her eyes.

"Hey, don't be telling strangers all of my secrets!" Gigi responded. "Let's keep some of them in the family, okay?" On the surface, what Gigi said seemed lighthearted. But then I saw a look pass between the two of them, and I wondered if maybe there was something that Gigi didn't want me to know.

"Paige tells me you're in college?" I asked, changing the subject.

"Yep, my freshman year!" Gigi replied.

"Cool! What are you majoring in?"

"Biotechnology. But who cares about that! The social life is where it's at! I keep telling Paige she should live a little and go away to college too. Lots of parties and hot men. No one cares if you sleep around, and it would never get back to Mom and Dad."

"Gigi, you know I'm saving myself for my mate!" Paige exclaimed.

"So boring." Gigi rolled her eyes.

"There's nothing wrong with saving yourself for your mate!" I defended Paige. "I was planning to too."

"So what happened?" Gigi studied my face. "Let me guess. You met a really hot guy, and you realized it was a dumb idea."

"Well, not exactly." I blushed.

"Jasmine's going to be mates with the alpha. That's the wedding we're going to next week." Paige gloated on my behalf.

"Going to be?" Gigi looked at me again. "What does that mean?"

"We're not officially mates. My actual mate and I rejected each other about a year ago," I replied, not wanting to go into the whole story. "But it all worked out because Blake lost his mate in battle a few years ago."

"Well, damn. Alpha Blake is super hot! I'm jealous!" Gigi responded just as the doorbell rang. Both twins rushed to the entryway, and I followed.

"Hello, girls!" A slightly older version of Paige and Gigi entered the house. I looked her over, and I was pretty sure she had been a year above me in school. She was also strawberry blonde, with a curvy body like Gigi's. I silently wondered if people mistook Gigi and Heidi for being the twins instead. Although, I supposed, they could be triplets they all appeared so similar. "Don't worry, I come bearing wine! Lots of wine!"

"Yay! The fun sister has arrived!" Gigi wrapped her arms around Heidi.

"And, what, did Mom and Dad adopt another sister for us while I've been living away?" Heidi looked at me.

"This is Jasmine. She's our future luna—the one I was telling you about." Paige pushed me forward.

"Oh my Goddess! How exciting! We're friends with the luna now? Mom is going to die when she finds out. She was obsessed with Alpha James. Like fan club obsessed." She gave a hearty laugh. "Anyway, welcome to the family, Jasmine. So happy to meet you!" Heidi threw her arms around me.

"Nice to meet you too," I replied, smiling, overjoyed with the warm welcome. I silently hoped they would like me enough to invite me back. I had always wished for a sister and a big family, and it would be nice to pretend I had one with Paige and her sisters. I used to live vicariously through Lucy's family, but that was all in the past now.

"Come on, we're all too sober right now." Heidi marched toward the kitchen with a large tote bag. "Gigi, get the glasses ready!"

"I'm already on it," Gigi called as she pulled wine glasses from a cabinet.

"Paige, heat up this chorizo queso. We're going to need this once we get drunk!" Heidi handed Paige a large Pyrex dish. "I hope you like spicy food, Jasmine. Because my queso is hot!"

"I'll try it," I replied politely. I'd never really been one to handle super spicy food, but maybe it wouldn't be too bad.

Before long, we were all sitting on the living room floor, around a game of Clue, drinking wine. Although, we really weren't paying attention to the game much. I was more interested in the sisters and their conversation.

"So, come on, Gigi, spill." Heidi elbowed her sister. "You were so mysterious about this Adam guy before you came home. I'm dying to know what the deal is."

Gigi groaned. "He's such a fuckboy! But my Goddess, that dick. He knows what he's doing. He's like a drug. I didn't know humans could fuck so good!"

"Have you ever even been with a werewolf?" Paige raised her eyebrows. "How do you know which one is better?"

"How do you know I haven't been with a werewolf?"

"You've definitely never told me about any werewolves you've been with."

"It doesn't matter anyway. I don't do werewolves." Gigi narrowed her eyes at Paige.

"Why not?" I asked, curious, wondering why someone would choose to be with humans over their own kind.

All of the sisters looked at each other and didn't say anything. Finally, Heidi chimed in and said, "Gigi's just kidding, right?"

"Yeah," Gigi said, but she didn't sound convincing.

There was definitely something they were all hiding from me. I wondered what it was. Maybe if I got close enough to them they would tell me. I wondered if it had to do with Gigi getting bullied in school when she was younger.

"Jasmine!" Paige looked at me. "Why don't you tell us about the wedding? You must be so excited. It's less than a week away now. Or are you super nervous? The whole pack's going to be there, so I'd probably be afraid I'd trip in front of everyone walking down the aisle or something."

"What's the dress look like?" Heidi asked next.

"And how big's the groom's cock?" Gigi laughed. "I've heard alphas are huge!"

My face burned at the question, surprised at being asked something so personal.

"Don't ask Jasmine that!" Paige pushed her twin. "You're drunk. Go home."

"I think it's time to pull out all of the food," Heidi said, standing up.

"I'll help!" Paige got up and followed her sister. I was about to get up as well when Gigi pulled on my arm to keep me sitting.

"I'm glad Paige finally made a friend," she said to me.

"What do you mean? Paige has tons of friends." I looked at Gigi, confused by the statement.

"She has tons of acquaintances because she's super nice and friendly. But not any real friends. But don't tell her I told you that." She got up and I followed her into the kitchen. I wondered how it could be possible for someone to have tons of acquaintances but no friends.

We all loaded up our plates. I tried some of Paige's braised short ribs first. "Wow, this is impressive for a potluck!" I exclaimed.

"Paige is an overachiever too." Gigi snickered.

"Stop pretending you're not!" Paige retorted. She turned to me and said, "The two of us used to compete in everything."

"It was so funny to watch. Whoever got the better grade on a test would run home to show Mom first." Heidi laughed. "And they'd always play sports with the boys during recess in elementary school. On opposing teams. I bet if they went to high school together, they'd compete over who got the cutest guy."

"That's all Gigi!" Paige rolled her eyes. "I'm good with whomever the Moon Goddess sends me as a mate."

"That's the difference between us. I grew up and Paige is still competing." The way Gigi said it, there was an edge to it, as if it was not just a jest.

"Here, try some queso! It's good!" Heidi pushed the Tupperware toward me.

I put some on my plate, and dipped a chip into it, making sure I grabbed a generous amount. As soon as it hit my tongue, I realized that was a bad idea. "Holy shit! This is hot!" I yelled, my mouth burning, snot running out of my nose, and tears trailing my cheeks. I quickly grabbed a napkin to clean my face while my tongue was on fire.

"Drink!" Heidi lifted my wine glass for me. I grabbed it from her hand and swallowed it quickly. She instantly grabbed a bottle and refilled it. I drank more, realizing halfway that I probably shouldn't be drinking so much so quickly.

"Weak!" Gigi yelled.

"Not everyone has a high spice tolerance. It's okay. We'll break her in." Heidi smiled. "If you haven't noticed, we all love spicy."

"Sorry, Jasmine. I should have warned you." Paige patted my back. "I sometimes forget how spicy we eat compared to normal people."

"Have you guys always eaten this spicy?" I asked.

"It started as a competition." Gigi laughed.

"So, come on. Tell us more about the wedding and Blake," Paige said. "What's he like? What made you fall in love with him?" All three of them were now quietly staring at me waiting for me to speak.

I sighed, feeling drunk and all sorts of warm feelings began coming to the surface as I thought about Blake. "He's so loyal and sweet. He always knows the right thing to say and how to cheer me up. And he's always there for me. Whenever I have a problem, he always comes to the rescue. I know I can always depend on him no matter what. And being around him just feels comfortable. Like we don't have to be doing anything, just sitting around hanging out, and it just feels right." More tears began falling from my eyes, this time not because of spicy food. "He's too good for me. I don't deserve him!" Shit, I was really drunk and becoming overly emotional. I wiped the tears from my eyes, trying to force myself to stop crying.

"Aww! That's so sweet," Heidi exclaimed. "That's how I feel about my mate too." She gave a goofy smile.

"I can't wait to meet my mate," Paige said.

"Mates are overrated." Gigi huffed.

"Why so bitter, Gi?" Heidi asked.

"You know why," she said, and walked out of the kitchen.

"Is she okay?" I asked.

"Don't worry about her. She gets like that sometimes," Paige said. "Probably too much alcohol. Anyway, I'm so excited to go to your wedding next week. Especially now that I know more about your relationship."

"Yeah, Blake sounds like a really good guy. To be honest, I'd heard rumors about him. But they're obviously false," Heidi said.

I'd come to learn more about Blake's reputation over the past year. I was too young to have heard all the rumors when he left for Siberia. But I was now well aware of them, and that they were all basically true.

"He's a really good guy," I said, wanting others to think that about him as well.

After we finished eating, we began clearing the table, and Paige packed up to-go containers for all of us to take bits of the potluck home with us. "I'm really not good to drive. I might just sleep over," Heidi said. "Hunter has overnight patrol duty tonight, so he can't come get me."

"Yay, sister sleepover." Paige threw her arms around Heidi and they both laughed. She then looked at me and asked, "Are you okay to get home, Jasmine? Maybe you should call your parents to pick you up. You can just leave your car here and get it tomorrow."

"My parents don't know I drink," I replied, feeling anxious about the idea of calling them. I knew I was of legal drinking age and that they had lightened up over the past year. But I still felt weird about the idea of it. "I'll text Blake instead."

He arrived minutes later to pick me up. "You really are always there for Jasmine," Paige said while Blake waited for me to put my coat on and gather everything in the entryway.

"So does this mean we're VIPs in the pack now that we're friends with your mate?" Heidi winked at Blake. "Do we get front-row seats to the wedding?"

"That can be arranged." Blake chuckled. "A friend of Jasmine's is a friend of mine."

"How exciting!" Heidi exclaimed. "Mom will be so happy if it really does get arranged!"

"Well, if it makes Mom happy, then I'll have to arrange it," Blake replied, a friendly smile on his face. And suddenly I saw the resemblance between Blake and his dad—the way he was able to instantly turn his charm on. I wondered if Blake even realized it. He hated any time similarities between him and his dad were brought up.

Once we were in his car and driving, Blake said, "Can't lie, I didn't think you were the booty-calling type. But I am ready and willing to answer the call." He chuckled glancing my way.

"What makes you think this is a booty call?" I retorted.

"I'm pretty sure when someone sends a text at night that says, 'I'm drunk, can you pick me up?' that's exactly what it is." He took my hand in his as we drove in a different direction than I was expecting.

"Where are you going?" I asked.

"I thought we'd go to the party lake for you to sober up, for old time's sake. Just to hang out and talk." We drove in silence the rest of the way, with just the music on the radio keeping us company. When we arrived, at the edge of the woods leading to the lake, Blake pulled a blanket out of his trunk and we hiked over to the clearing where the lake was. Blake spread the blanket out and we both sat down on it. He pulled me against his body and kissed me on my head. I snuggled into him, enjoying being next to him, especially now that I was still feeling the effects of the wine.

"I can't lie, I've been worried." Blake looked down at me and I looked up to see his forehead was creased and his brows furrowed.

"Worried about what?" I asked.

"The conversation we had outside the gym the other week."

"When you wanted to take me in the back of my car?"

"Oh, I always want that." He snickered. "Back of the car, on the bed, in the lake, top of the laundry machine, middle of the woods. Anywhere and everywhere." He then looked at me seriously and said, "But that's not the part of the conversation I'm talking about, and you know it."

I sighed.

"Jasmine, I just want you to know that you are one of the best things that ever happened to me. When I proposed to you and you said yes, that was one of the happiest days of my life. And happiness isn't something that comes easily to me anymore. But you make me happy. I honestly didn't think it would be possible. I just assumed I was cursed to live in pain the rest of my life. But then you came into it and that changed. I'm telling you this because I want you to know there is no one better for me because no one else makes me happy. And I can't force you to be with me. But I really hope you'll choose to."

Feeling overwhelmed with emotion, I began crying—letting out both my despair and happiness simultaneously—the ceaseless depression that wouldn't leave me and the appreciation of Blake. I couldn't understand what he saw in me, but I was overjoyed with the fact that he saw something that was worth staying for.

"I'm hoping you're crying because you're staying with me and not because you're planning to jilt me at the altar."

"Blake, I love you," I whispered through my drunken tears.

"Thank the Goddess," he replied, kissing me.

Chapter 55

Talia

"Your coffee, beautiful." Alex kissed me on my cheek as he handed me a mug of coffee. We were standing side by side at the kitchen counter, cooking breakfast together, making pancakes.

"Merci beaucoup," I replied, smiling, taking the mug from him, and taking a sip. "It's perfect."

"Perfect coffee for my perfect mate." He winked. "Let me bring my mom her tea. I'll be right back."

"Maybe I should bring it to her instead this morning," I offered, my stomach quivering. But I needed to make things right and stop avoiding the situation, no matter how uncomfortable. It had been very awkward since I'd moved in, especially since she hadn't exactly been introduced to me in the best way. And things had only grown more awkward with the disappearance of his sister.

"Are you sure?" He pulled me toward him so I was facing him, his hands at my waist.

"She's your mom, and we'll be living together. I should make more of an effort to have a relationship with her."

"It would mean a lot to me." He sighed, bringing his forehead to mine, and I could feel that this was the right thing to do. I could sense his anxiety fading with my offer. This was something important that could make Alex happy. He said quietly, "But I also understand that it's a difficult situation."

"You shouldn't have to bear it alone," I replied. "That's what mates are for, right? Or at least, that's what I'm assuming they're for since I only recently learned about them." I gave him a small smile, masking how nervous I felt inside.

He squeezed my hand, and I could sense an affection from him. Yes, this was definitely the right thing to do. "I really appreciate it, Talia."

I took the teacup and saucer from the counter and headed toward the stairs. Before taking my first step, I turned my head to find Alex staring affectionately back at me. I took a deep breath and made my way to his mom's room. The door was open when I got there. A nurse sat next to her bed, chatting with her.

My heart was racing. I almost wondered if I could do it, but I knew I had endured much worse. I also owed this to Alex. Even when I was at my worst, he'd never given up on our mate bond, and now I couldn't imagine my life without him. I cleared my throat and both women in the room looked up at me.

"Good morning," I said, my voice a little shaky. "Mrs. Adalwolf, I have your tea. Can we talk, please?"

His mom nodded at the nurse and she walked out. I shut the door behind me and went over to her bedside.

"Put it on the table," she said, gesturing to the bedside table. I did as asked, careful not to spill. When she didn't say anything, I took another deep breath and sat down in the chair the nurse had just been occupying. She continued to look at me, not saying anything, which only made this more nerve-racking.

Finally, I spoke". "Mrs. Adalwolf."

"Please call me Luna Claire."

"Luna Claire," I repeated back. "I'm sorry about all the trouble I've caused you."

"You murdered my mate and caused my daughter to banish herself from my pack. Now I don't know if I'll ever see my daughter again. What makes you believe you are more worthy to be here than my daughter, who grew up in this pack and trained her whole life to defend it?" Tears began streaming down her face.

I felt attacked, wanted to lash out. But I clenched my hands into fists, doing my best not to, knowing this was Alex's mom—the woman who raised him. I wouldn't have wanted him to lash out at my mom if he were in my position.

I took a deep breath, trying to decide how to proceed. Finally, I said, "Luna Claire, I am sorry for the pain it has caused you that your daughter left the pack, but she left of her own free will. I didn't force her to leave. I've never harmed your daughter at all, even after she tortured me."

"My daughter tortured you?"

"Yes." I lifted my chin, keeping the tears that were threatening to fall at bay, recalling the horrible incident and how painful it was. I still sometimes had nightmares that stirred me from sleep.

"Alex didn't tell me."

"Probably because he knows how much you love her. He didn't want you to know what she's capable of."

For a moment, the look his mom was giving me shifted. Her features softened. But just as soon as they changed, they hardened again. "She had reason to. You murdered her father."

"He murdered my mom and her mate!" I yelled back. I didn't mean to, but I was feeling overly emotional, my loss still raw.

"Both?" she asked, blinking. "Alex told me about your mom, but her mate too?"

I nodded in response. My throat prickled, and all my feelings came to the surface. I still missed my mom terribly, and it was even worse knowing my mom and I could've had a better life had her mate never been murdered and she'd been allowed to be with him.

"I'm sorry about your mom and her mate," his mom said quietly, staring at the ceiling.

"Thank you," I replied. "I miss her. She wasn't perfect, but she was my mom, and she never hurt anyone."

"And your father?" His mom turned toward me, her eyes softer now.

"I never met my father. I only recently met my brother. He's the alpha of the Midnight Maple Pack in the US. He told me my father died in battle a year ago."

"And that was my mate's doing?"

"No, my father wasn't my mother's mate. My mother's mate was killed years ago because . . ." My voice trailed off. I couldn't bring myself to tell her. She was clearly in pain from losing her own mate, and as much as I wanted to tell her every evil thing he'd ever done, I couldn't kick her while she was down like that. It couldn't be easy to learn that your husband had been obsessed with another woman for the span of practically their entire marriage.

"Because why?" she asked in a shaky voice, her eyes intently on mine.

"He didn't want my mom to be with him," I finally replied, thinking that was probably the most tactful way to say it.

"I see," she responded, turning away from me. She most likely put two and two together.

"I also want you to know that your daughter tried to kill me after she tortured me. She tried to sneak into my brother's pack to find me. But they caught her. My brother offered to torture her to get back at her for what she did to me, and I didn't let him. Even though she hurt me, I still didn't hurt her back." My whole face was wet, soaked from my tears, my lips salty. I waited to see if his mom would respond but she didn't.

I wondered if she'd ever accept me as Alex's mate. At least I'd made an effort and a step in the right direction. I sighed, getting up, and went back downstairs where Alex had laid breakfast out on the table.

"Talia, are you okay?" He came over to me, pulling me tightly into a hug. "What happened?"

"I talked to your mom," I replied.

"And?"

"I still don't think she likes me, but I tried."

"Talia, it means so much to me that you tried," he whispered into my ear. I snuggled into him. I could sense his emotions as he hugged me against him, and it made me feel proud of myself for pushing past my fears and doing what I'd done.

Chapter 56

Jasmine

Jack and Tyler pulled into my driveway on Sunday afternoon. I ran out as soon as they arrived and hopped in the back of their SUV.

"Are you ready?" Tyler turned in his seat to look at me as Jack backed out of the driveway.

"I think so," I replied. "Why don't you tell me more about this group you're bringing me to?"

"Remember how I told you there are more gay people in the pack than just Jack and me?"

I nodded.

"Well, over the years, the queer people in the pack have found each other and formed a secret support group. We all meet on Sundays, and I'd like you to join us as an ally—our first ally actually."

"Your first ally?" I asked. "There are no others like me?"

"Since the LGBTQ+ community was so unwelcome in the pack for so long, most people are suspicious of outsiders. But Jack and I spoke with them and convinced everyone to let you come since you're going to have so much influence as our luna."

"But I don't know how to help," I replied, my anxiety brewing. "I didn't even know gay werewolves existed until a year ago."

"It's only the first time you're coming, Jaz. No one's going to expect you to make changes overnight. All you have to do is listen today. I'm sure they'll have some ideas and things to tell you." He squeezed my knee in a friendly gesture.

"They're good people. I've known them for years. They helped me through some hard times," Jack chimed in. "So don't be nervous."

"Have you always known?" I asked, curious to learn more about Jack. He never let Lucy and me hang out with his friends when we were younger, as much as Lucy always tried to.

"Honestly, I tried to deny it a long time. It's not easy to be different in this pack. I eventually met other people who were like me, and it made it easier to accept myself knowing I wasn't the only one. We were able to open up to each other without fear that we would out each other, you know?"

Tyler took Jack's hand in his in a really loving gesture and put his head on his arm. It was clear to see how much they loved and cared for each other, and I thought to myself, what a tragedy it would have been had they decided to reject each other to go along with the temple.

"And now look at you! First out gay werewolf in the Midnight Maple Pack." Tyler patted Jack's stomach. "Also the most delicious one."

Jack chuckled and ruffled Tyler's hair. "Not sure your sister needs to know that."

"Listen to Jack." I laughed. "Keep some things to yourself."

Tyler turned to the back to look at me. "Jasmine and I are tight. We're able to share everything with each other, right?" He winked.

"Tyler, I know what you want to share, and I'm not sharing, so stop asking."

"I didn't ask anything. Did I ask something?" Tyler asked innocently.

"The whole car knows what you were implying," Jack said.

"Okay, so I may have mentioned a certain alpha once or twice."

"Or a hundred times," I added.

"Okay, okay, I'll stop. I have the best man in the pack anyway. I was just trying to make Jasmine feel better about hers."

I sighed, relaxing into my seat. It was a bit of a drive to get to our destination, but Tyler and Jack kept it entertaining, bouncing jokes off each other. By the time we arrived, I was feeling much better and ready to enter the meeting. Tyler and Jack went ahead of me, and I followed them into a pub.

A group of about ten people were seated inside, taking up two tables, with appetizers and pitchers of beer laid out in front of them. As we approached, I was shocked to see my old coworker Liz. My eyes widened in surprise. Upon making eye contact with me, she instantly looked down, turning red. She had always been really shy and quiet. I gave her a small smile in greeting.

Everyone cheered as Jack and Tyler got closer. Tyler pushed me ahead of him. "Hey, all. This is my sister and our future luna, Jasmine. Go easy on her for today. You can start the hazing next meeting." Tyler chuckled.

"Hey, Jasmine, very nice to meet you! I'm Dana." A blonde woman in a turtleneck who appeared to be in her early thirties stood up and put out her hand for me to shake. "This is my mate, Jenny." A brunette woman wearing a scarf stood up and shook my hand.

"Mates?" I asked.

They looked to Tyler. "It's okay. Jasmine can be trusted," he said to them.

"Yes, we're mates, but we haven't told anyone. We pretend we're roommates," Dana said. "You know how the pack is." I nodded in understanding.

"Do your parents know?" I asked.

"I've told my parents, but they're in denial. They still call Jenny my roommate even though I correct them all the time."

"My parents don't really speak to me anymore." Jenny looked down at the ground.

"Oh, I'm really sorry," I replied, feeling a lot of empathy for Jenny. Even though I often struggled in my relationship with my parents, I couldn't conceive of not having any relationship with them at all, especially if it were due to something I couldn't change about myself. I could only imagine the internal struggle she went through when choosing to be with her mate to the detriment of her familial relationship.

"Hey, Jasmine." A guy named Tony who I'd gone to school with came over, giving me a hug. I hugged him back, surprised. Another person I'd known and never even suspected.

"Tony, I had no idea," I said.

He gave me a small smile. "I'm surprised. I thought it was obvious."

"She has the world's worst gaydar." Tyler chuckled. "It's okay, we still love you, Jasmine," he said, throwing his arm around me.

The rest of the group went around and introduced themselves to me one by one, and then we all sat down. "The reason Jack and I brought Jasmine today is that she's in a unique position to make changes around the pack. She's going to be our luna, so if any of you have ideas for how she can help, let's hear 'em."

At first everyone was quiet, but then finally Liz spoke. "Those signs," she said. We all looked at her. "I get it's freedom of speech, but the pack is on private land. Allowing pack members to post the Take Back Vermont signs in their yards sends a message that there are people who aren't welcome in the pack."

"Yeah, I agree," a guy named Matt chimed in. "If we put up rainbow flags, for example, we'd be ostracized. But the pack has no problem with sending such a hateful message to everyone."

Everyone responded in agreement.

"I've been thinking about something," Dana said. "I know we haven't been open to the idea of allies here in this group. But maybe, without us being outed, Jasmine could help with something."

I looked at her eagerly, waiting to hear what her idea was.

"Maybe we could start having our own flags, but not as obvious. Like maybe rainbow stickers that people could put onto the windows of their houses, so people could signal that they're allies and they support us in the pack. That could help others feel more comfortable coming out."

"I love that idea, Dana." Tyler tapped his glass against hers. "What do you think, Jasmine?" He looked at me meaningfully.

"I think it's a great idea," I agreed. "I'd be happy to put one of the stickers up on the packhouse." The gears in my head started spinning and I continued, "We could put it into the pack newsletter as an option and distribute them to pack members. We probably wouldn't be able to announce it at temple, but I'm sure there'd be other opportunities to encourage pack members to do their part."

Everyone smiled at me, and I began to feel a new energy surge through me. "And those signs! You're right. They're outdated and cruel. There's no reason we should accept them in the pack. I'll speak to Blake and have them banned."

"See, Jasmine's going help," Jack said to everyone, giving me an encouraging smile. "What else? Does anyone have more ideas?"

"Yes." A good-looking guy named Greg spoke up. "The stuff they teach at the pack school is messed up. Not only was I bullied by the other kids, but then the teachers just made me feel worse about myself in their sad excuse for health class. I mean, how many times do we need to hear about how being gay is a sin and unnatural? Why does our religion have to have so much influence in the school?"

"Plus, the stuff they're teaching is just plain false," Dana chimed in. "It's not unnatural. The Moon Goddess sends us mates who match our preferences. It's sick that the temple thinks we should reject who their deity sends us."

"And what about Leo?" Jenny asked the group. Everyone reacted solemnly, turning their eyes downward. It was as if a chill had swept the room.

"Who's Leo?" I asked.

Jack swallowed, furrowing his brows. "He used to be a part of our group, but he died by suicide. He was young—a senior in high school."

Suddenly I remembered there was a Leo who had passed away in our pack a few years back. His obituary had said that it was of natural causes. "He died by suicide?" I asked, my chest tight at the revelation.

"Yeah, he was severely bullied in school. And when he met his mate, his mate asked him to reject him because he didn't want to come out of the closet," Jack said quietly. "After the rejection, he couldn't find the will to live anymore, I guess. We all tried to be there for him, but it wasn't enough."

"Oh my Goddess," I practically whispered, sickened by the story. Then I felt the same energy from earlier pulse through me and I said, "We're removing that from the health program. The health program is outdated and needs to be updated."

"Thank Goddess. About time." Dana banged her hand against the table.

"We'll hire new teachers if we have to," I added. "Teachers who teach love and acceptance. If we're picking and choosing which of Artemis's scriptures we follow, it should be those ones."

"I agree, Luna." Greg clinked his glass against mine. I beamed at the mention of my soon-to-be title, and for the first time, I didn't feel too small to fill those shoes. I looked around and saw how much I'd be able to help my pack, even just by taking small steps. And this was only one group of people. There'd be others.

After the meeting, everyone was in good spirits. I hopped into the car feeling much better than I had in months, enthusiastic about how much I'd be able to help.

"So, what'd you think of everyone?" Tyler turned to look at me in the back seat.

"I loved them! I hope you'll bring me to more meetings. I like being an ally."

Tyler smiled widely at me and said, "Yeah, you can definitely come with us from now on."

"Thank you so much for bringing me." I sighed. "I guess I just never realized how much I could help. It's good to meet pack members like this and learn more about what they need. I really want to help as luna."

"See, you just needed to build your confidence. Soon you'll be taking over as our alpha." Tyler patted my knee. I smiled at him, so thankful he'd come into my life. He snickered and said, "There's a 'woman on top' joke somewhere in there."

I rolled my eyes. "Tyler, I'm trying to decide who's more obsessed with sex. You or Blake."

Chapter 57

Jasmine

"Oh my Goddess, Jasmine, you look beautiful." A tear trailed down my mom's face as I turned in my wedding dress for the photographer outside of our house, a white fur stole wrapped around my arms to keep me warm. This had to have been maybe the third time in my life I'd ever seen my mother cry. She was usually so cold, but today she was acting very motherly for once.

"She'll make a wonderful luna," my aunt said to my mom. "I remember the day I married your brother Lance. It was such an exciting day. You know, I saved myself completely for him. I was a virgin on my wedding night."

"You've already told me this, Julia." My mom lifted her eyes to the sky in a look of annoyance.

"Isn't it so nice to save yourself for marriage, Jasmine?" My aunt smiled at me. "I bet you're so excited for tonight and the wonderful gift you'll be giving your soon-to-be husband."

My entire body burned with embarrassment, and I had no idea how to respond, shocked she'd say that.

"Julia, don't talk to my daughter about her sex life. It's very inappropriate," my mom snapped at her sister-in-law.

After we finished taking pictures outside, we entered the house, which was filled with my mom's family. It was the most chaotic I'd ever seen my home.

"Look at the little luna. Isn't she precious?" my Grandmother Catherine said as soon as I entered the house. "Aren't alpha weddings wonderful, Bruce?" She turned to my grandfather. "Hopefully our Tyce will find his mate soon too."

"Maybe he would if he'd get off that fat bitch for a second," he replied.

"Bruce!" My grandmother gasped.

"Your son has been letting our grandson make a mockery of our pack, and I'm about to take matters into my own hands."

"Not tonight, Dad!" Uncle Lance walked into the room, clearly having overheard the conversation. "Can we get through one night without discussing Tyce?"

"I always said you weren't strict enough with him. That kid had it too easy."

"Dad, one night!"

"Fine, but this conversation isn't over."

"Trust me, I'm more than aware. This conversation has been going on for years now!"

"Because you still haven't straightened the kid out."

"The kid is the alpha. Now that he's taken title from me, there's not much left I can do. If you want to give it a try, old man, be my guest!"

"Who are you calling 'old man'?"

"Who do you think?"

"Do you want to take this outside. I'm ready to remove this suit, and then we'll see who the real alpha is!"

"Dad, please keep your suit on. No one wants to see your wrinkly ass."

"Lance, stop it!" my grandmother chastised my uncle. "Let's just enjoy the wedding. Look how beautiful your niece looks today."

"Yes, very beautiful. Miriam, you did good." He smiled at my mom.

"She's clearly kept up with her training. Look at those muscular arms," my grandmother remarked as I removed my stole now that I was in the house. Although my dress had long sleeves, they were sheer. I knew my grandma meant what she said as a compliment, but I felt weird about the way she commented, especially after she had been chastising my mom for putting on weight a few months earlier.

Once it was finally time to go to the temple for the ceremony, I was relieved. I was starting to reconsider my lifelong desire to have a big family. My mom's family was chaotic in the worst way possible. They were all constantly insulting each other, and even when they were being nice, it was more like a backhanded compliment. I was starting to understand why my mom never kept in contact with that side of the family.

When we arrived, they brought us to a private room in the temple. My dad stayed with me while everyone else went to take their seats. "How are you feeling? Nervous?" my dad asked me.

"I'm okay," I replied, although, in truth, I was freaking out on the inside, taking deep breaths to keep myself calm.

"I brought you something to help with the nerves." He winked at me and pulled a flask out of his jacket pocket. "Don't tell your mom, but the only way I got through our wedding ceremony was with the help of a little whiskey."

I widened my eyes in shock. It seemed like my dad was revealing something new about himself all the time now. He never drank while I was growing up. But, then again, he had also never smoked weed, and that had apparently been one of his pastimes as well.

"Here, take a sip or two." He handed me the flask.

I hesitated.

"It'll help with the long walk down the aisle," he encouraged me.

I began to think about all the eyes that would be on me, felt my chest tighten and the beginnings of a panic attack. I took a deep breath and tipped the flask back, feeling the liquid burn down the back of my throat.

"Better?" my dad asked, taking it back from me. "There's more if you need it." He gave it a little shake.

"I thought you were against drinking," I said.

"It's okay every once in a while. Sometimes everyone needs a little liquid courage. Plus, you're an adult now. Those rules were for when you were growing up. Now it's time for you to start making your own choices."

A tap sounded on the door. My dad got up to see who it was and cracked the door open.

"Can I come in?" Blake's mom asked.

"Of course," my dad replied, letting her in.

"Do you mind if I have a minute with Jasmine?"

"Sure." My dad stepped out of the room.

She sat down in the chair my dad had just abandoned. "Jasmine, I just want you to know how happy I am that you came into Blake's life. He had a very difficult upbringing, and after his mate died, he became closed off to everyone. I didn't know if my sweet little boy would ever return." A tear dropped down her cheek. "But after he found you, I see more and more of my little Blake returning. So thank you for making my son happy."

Tears brimmed my eyes at her words. She had so much tenderness and love for Blake, and my heart swelled. I sniffed, holding back the tears, afraid they would ruin my makeup. And then I realized this was the perfect opportunity to speak with his mom about what had been worrying me for months. "Dr. Luna," I started. "How did you feel on your own wedding day? How did it feel to know you were going to be the luna of the pack?"

She smiled at me. "Honestly, it was a bit overwhelming. Growing up I was always shy and studious. I never expected that I would be mated to an alpha and become a leader in the community. But sometimes the Moon Goddess sees things in us that we don't see in ourselves. I didn't know if I could handle the responsibility, but I just took it day by day. It was easier at the beginning too, because I loved James and being with him made me happy. With time, I grew older and with that came experience, maturity, and confidence. And, to be honest, us adults don't always know what we're doing. Sometimes we're just winging it and hoping for the best. You don't need to have it all figured out. Just do your best." She patted my hand.

"Thank you, Dr. Luna," I replied, reassured by her words.

"Jasmine, you remind me a lot of myself when I was younger. I know you'll do great as the new luna. So don't worry." She wrapped her arms around me. While the whiskey might have helped, that hug was ultimately what gave me the courage I needed.

Chapter 58

Jasmine

When my dad walked me down the aisle, the only thing I saw was Blake's handsome face as he smiled at me from the altar. My heart beat forcefully against my chest, and I returned his smile, feeling as if I were walking on clouds. The ceremony was long and tedious as we had to go through different chants, prayers, and meditations. I did glance over at the pews and notice that, true to his word, Blake had arranged for Paige and her family to be seated near the front.

Once the priest finally pronounced us husband and wife, my stomach fluttered as Blake kissed me, dipping me as he did. When he pulled away, he mindlinked me, *"Can't wait for the wedding night, Mrs. Alpha."* He gave me a mischievous smile, and then we finally marched out of the temple to head to the reception.

A limo was waiting for us outside, and we hopped in. "I figured if we're going to have sex in the back of a car, we should find one that's comfortable." Blake snickered.

"Stop!" I pushed on his arm, laughing.

"Maybe you just need some champagne to loosen up." Blake pulled out a bottle.

"We can't have sex in the back of a limo!" I whispered, not wanting the driver to hear, although I did notice the window that separated us from the driver was up. I wondered how soundproof it was, if at all.

"Okay, we'll play by your rules today." He grinned, putting the champagne bottle back and pulling me close to him, staring into my eyes. "You are so beautiful, Mrs. Alpha. I feel like the luckiest man in the world right now." He pulled me in for a kiss. "I know there's a lot of people here today. But soon it will be just the two of us." He kissed me again, and then smiled, continuing". "With a view of the Eiffel tower from our hotel window while I take you from behind."

"Do you ever think about anything else?" I shook my head, not able to keep myself from smiling.

"What could be more important to think about than pleasing my new wife in every sense of the word?" He brought his mouth closer, speaking in a low gravelly voice, his breath tickling my ear, and I really did start to reconsider my hesitation about going at it in the back of the limo.

When we arrived at the casino, we must have spent at least an hour taking pictures with our families. I didn't fail to notice my cousin Tyce being scolded by our grandfather for much of the time. I wondered what was going on.

"Reminds me of my father," Blake whispered to me at one point, looking over in that direction.

"How so?" I asked quietly.

"He was always on my case about everything. I know how your cousin feels. And he's got two former alphas on his ass. It's probably even worse. I never knew my grandfather."

I began to wonder what kind of father and husband Blake would be. Would he stay as sweet as he was now, or would he eventually transform to be like his own father? Hadn't his mom said Blake's dad made her happy in the early days? From what Blake had told me, that hadn't lasted forever. So what changed?

After we finished taking our thousands of pictures, Blake took my hand and led me to the ballroom. We waited outside until the DJ announced our entrance. "Introducing Alpha and Luna Wulfric of the Midnight Maple Pack." The room erupted in cheers as Blake held my hand tightly and led me to the dance floor.

The ballroom was packed with guests, the party spilling out into the hallway. I'd never seen so many people at one event. But I also shouldn't have been surprised as the entire pack was there, minus whatever warriors were unlucky enough to have to work that day. The decorations looked phenomenal. It must have cost a fortune, with a canopy of hundreds of small lightbulbs draped across the ceiling, candles and fresh flowers bordering the perimeter of the room giving it a cozy and romantic ambiance, the walls illuminated by blue LED lights, huge white floral centerpieces on the tables surrounded by more candles. I was in awe of how amazing it all looked. And in the front of the venue, next to the dance floor, was the biggest wedding cake I'd ever seen. Valerie and Lucy must have spent hours creating it.

Blake pulled me in for our first dance, holding me closely. "Wow, this is amazing!" I whispered to Blake as he swayed with me, his hand on my lower back.

"It was mostly Mariette. So you can thank her once we get back from our honeymoon."

"She did a great job." I smiled.

"Yes, she did. I'm so glad you love it."

After our first dance, Blake stayed close by me the entire reception, taking the lead, which was a huge relief. He led me from table to table so we could greet all the guests and thank them for coming. Blake was great at schmoozing. He easily joked and flattered the guests as they congratulated him. Had he always been like that or had his father taught him?

A sharp pain pierced me as we approached the table with Luke and Lucy's families. I muscled through it, not wanting it to ruin the evening which had gone so well thus far. Blake went from person to person, joking and laughing with everyone.

"Congratulations, Luna." Lucy's mom wrapped her arms around me.

"I'm so happy for you, Jasmine," Lucy's father said. Her younger brothers followed, giving me hugs. Then Kyle and Emma approached.

"You got a good guy, Jaz." Kyle hugged me.

"Congrats, Jasmine. We should hang out once you come back from your honeymoon," Emma said as she also hugged me. "It's been a while. And I have news." She gave me a sly smile. "Baby number two is on the way."

"Wow, Emma!" I exclaimed. "Congratulations!" I was a bit sad at the news, knowing I hadn't been there for her first baby and wasn't sure if I'd be there much for this one either. While we hadn't been super close in high school, she had been more Lucy's friend than mine, I had gone through all of her big life events with her at the time. It felt strange not to be a part of her life anymore.

"Thank you. I hate how our friend group got torn apart. I hope we can all be friends again," she said to me.

I nodded in agreement, making a silent promise to myself to reach out to both her and Madison once I got back from the honeymoon. Just because they were both Lucy's friends didn't mean they couldn't be mine too. After all, Emma was essentially now my family too, being mated to my brother's brother-in-law.

Lucy came over to me next, wearing a long dress that made her appear taller and more intimidating, looking beautiful in an ethereal way. "Congrats, Jasmine." She smiled, hugging me quickly and walking away, leaving me confused. And then I sighed, realizing we had a long-overdue conversation I'd been putting off for over a year. Why had I been expecting Lucy to be the one to initiate it? Why couldn't I? I, again, made a pledge to myself. I'd try to right things with Lucy, especially now that we'd be living together. We couldn't continue in the direction we were going.

I looked to Blake who was deep in conversation with Luke's parents and sisters, all of them laughing joyfully, when I felt a tap on my shoulder. I could smell him before I turned around to come face-to-face with Luke himself, a sharp pain piercing my chest again.

"Hey, Jasmine," he said, giving me a shy smile.

"Hi, Luke," I replied, feeling awkward in his presence.

"Congrats." He looked at me, not breaking eye contact. I wondered if he was going to say more as he stared into my eyes. I was about to say thank you and walk away when he continued. "You look beautiful today."

"Thanks," I replied, softening toward him.

"Blake's a good guy. I know I had my doubts about you being with him, but I can tell he loves you. I'm really glad that he was able to find someone after losing Ria and that things worked out." He shuffled his feet a little, looking down at the floor. Then he looked back up and continued. "I wish both of you nothing but the best." He squeezed my arm in a friendly gesture.

"Thanks, Luke," I replied, letting out a deep breath. He gave me an awkward hug, that I was too caught off guard to return, and walked back over to his family. Would things ever be normal between him and me?

Jack and Tyler approached me next, both of them throwing their arms around me and pulling me in for big hugs. "You better save a dance for me, Mrs. Luna," Tyler said. "I hope you won't forget about your li'l ol' brother now that you're a pack celebrity."

"Never!" I replied.

"So how does this work? Do I have to take a number, so I know when it's my turn?"

"You're number one." I smiled at him.

"I feel like a VIP now."

"You're a VIP to me. I always wanted a sibling, and now that I have one, you definitely exceed expectations. Thanks for being so good to me."

"Jasmine, you're such a mushy cornball!" He pushed on my arm. "Just kidding. You're making me tear up a little." He acted as if he was wiping a tear. "Best sister ever."

Blake suddenly wrapped his arms around me from behind and said, "Sorry, guys, but I'm going to have to take my new wife away for a bit." He then led me to the next table where Alpha Alex and Talia were seated. I noted that Talia looked much happier than she ever had while she was living in our pack. We made our way around the table greeting everyone. When we reached Alex and Talia, they both got up.

"Congrats, Wulfric." Alex put out his right hand to Blake to shake, and I had to do a double take when I noticed his pinky was missing and the skin was raised in pinkish-red rings around his other fingers, as if he'd been cut and the wound never fully healed. I didn't even know it was possible for a werewolf to scar.

"What happened to your hand?" Blake asked, clearly noticing the same thing right before he took it.

"Lost a finger." Alex gave a sheepish smile.

"I can clearly see that. But how?"

"Crazy family."

"I see." Blake cocked an eyebrow and finally took his hand to shake.

Toward the end of the night, Blake and I made our way to the bridal suite so I could change into my going-away dress. We were planning to have one final dance and then leave to begin our honeymoon.

"Can you help me undo the back of my dress?" I asked as we entered the suite.

"With pleasure," he replied, standing so close behind me I could feel his body heat. He lowered his mouth to the back of my neck, gently kissing it down to the buttons of my dress. He brushed his hands across my shoulders to find the top button. My breathing shallowed at the intimate gesture. "Do you think we have time for a quickie?" he whispered in my ear as he unbuttoned the back of my dress. My stomach fluttered at the thought.

"Not with how long you take," I replied playfully.

"If you prefer quickies, I can definitely make that happen for you. Fast, slow, medium speed. Your wish is my command. I can do them all."

I laughed. "I think I want it slow tonight. It's really special."

"I can guarantee you're going to regret saying that," he said mischievously as my wedding dress fell to the ground. I was about to step out of it and grab for the going-away dress that was hanging up when Blake pulled me against him, and his hand found its way inside the white G-string I had worn for the occasion—one of the pairs Lucy had forced me into purchasing during the Victoria's Secret shopping trip. His fingers slid down the front of my pelvis and made their way between my legs, feeling for my weak spot. I was ready to give into Blake and his quickie when a knock at the door interrupted us.

"One second!" Blake shouted, pulling his hand out. I quickly sprinted to the going-away dress and threw it on as Blake answered the door.

"We've just caught a couple members of the Bois Sombre Pack outside the casino." Luke and Alex were at the door.

"You've got to fucking be kidding me," Blake replied angrily, stepping out of the room. I followed him out to a group of people who were congregated in the hallway.

"I have some warriors holding them down in the casino back office," Luke explained. "We can bring them back to the pack cells for now."

"Happy to torture them for you," Alex offered. "After all, I'm sure you have better things to do."

"These motherfuckers showed up here on my wedding day. There's no fucking way I'm not going to torture them myself." Blake's eyes turned evil. "I want at least a few minutes with them. Then they're all yours, Adalwolf. Luke, find some warriors to sniff the rest of the place out to make sure there are no others."

"On it," Luke replied, heading back toward the wedding.

"Jasmine, go back into the suite. I'll come get you when I'm sure it's safe," Blake said to me, turning to go. "I won't be long. I can be quick when I have to." He winked at me.

I did as Blake said and slipped back into the room. But I was surprised that the window to the room was left wide open, the cold air blowing in. I knew that neither Blake nor I had opened it, and suddenly, I had a really bad feeling as the scent of the Bois Sombre Pack drifted into my nose. I remembered the scent clearly from a year earlier when I had rescued Blake and Luke in the cave. My heart raced as I walked over to the window to look outside. When I got closer, I realized something else—there was something very familiar about the scent.

I popped my head out of the window and looked around. We were at least three stories up, and there wasn't a clear easy way to climb up, although I also wasn't exactly an expert at scaling buildings. I brought my head back in and quickly shut the window, turning around to come face-to-face with Charlie. I gasped, jumping back.

"Didn't think you'd see me again, did you, PJ?" He smiled at me evilly. "Never really liked that nickname much, to be honest. I think Prissy Bitch has a much better ring to it."

I was about to shift into my wolf to attack him when he shoved something sharp into my neck. It almost instantly immobilized me. I fell to the ground, onto my hands and knees. As my limbs went limp, I succumbed to my weakness and fell to my stomach. He used his foot to forcefully roll me over, so I was facing up at him. The whole world faded as he said, "Payback's a bitch."

Chapter 59

Talia

Alex and I danced the whole night away on the crowded dance floor. I couldn't believe how many people showed up to Blake and Jasmine's wedding. I'd never seen so many people in one room before. I was pleasantly surprised to find out that Alex was actually a very good dancer. He spun me around until I was dizzy, dipped me low, swung with me to the beat of the music.

"My turn!" Lucy cut in at one point. "You're hogging my dance partner!" She playfully elbowed Alex out of the way.

He chuckled and gave my shoulder a squeeze, "Have fun. I'll go grab us some more drinks."

"No need, I have our tequila shots right here!" Lucy pushed one into my hand. "You've gotta love open bar! Now just follow what I do!" She put her shot glass out in front of her, and I did the same. Then I mimicked her movements as she shouted, "*Arriba, abajo, al centro, pa' dentro!*"

We both threw back our shots, and she grabbed the empty glass from me to put onto the empty tray of a waiter walking by. She then grabbed my hips and pulled me into a dance. Lucy was a lot of fun to hang out with, and I felt a bit sad that we wouldn't be living in the same pack anymore. It had been nice to have a friend, even if she was a little pushy sometimes.

When I made it back to the table, Alex had set out a piece of cake and cup of coffee for me. "So what do you think of the wedding?" he asked.

"I can't believe how many people are here," I replied.

"It'll be the same for our wedding. Bigger actually. My pack is bigger than Blake's."

I stared into his eyes, and they seemed to be sparkling. He really was in this all the way. Never having associated with many people, I'd never imagined myself having such a large wedding. But I liked the idea of it. It was so fun and lively, with everyone so happy and celebrating. He placed his hand on my thigh, and slowly inched it up under my dress, a mischievous smile on his face. The sparks from his touch danced up my leg and my breathing shallowed. We'd already gone at it a few times in the hotel room before the wedding, but I was ready for another round. It seemed like we couldn't keep our hands off each other, constantly drawn to one another, our bond magnetic.

"I have an idea," I said, returning his smile. Before he could respond, I quickly looked around to make sure no one was looking and dipped under the tablecloth.

"Holy shit, Talia." His voice sounded from above as he pushed himself into the table.

"Just act normal," I said, reaching for his belt, undoing it quickly, and unzipping his pants. I swiftly pulled out his massive erection and pushed it into my mouth, working rapidly to get him off, sucking it into my mouth, and moving up and down it with my hand trailing. Damn, he was so huge. But I loved how I could practically feel how good it was for him as I bobbed my head up and down, and his now-healed hand wove itself into my hair.

His grip tightened as I kept going, and soon his legs were shaking. I worked myself up and down his cock more vigorously until I heard his fist slam onto the table above and warm liquid filled my mouth. I quickly sucked it down, licking every last bit off him, and redid his pants for him.

"Holy shit, that was crazy," I heard him say. "I can't believe you just did that."

"Is the coast clear?" I asked.

A second later, he replied, "Clear," and I went to crawl out from under the table. Just as I pulled the tablecloth up, he put out his hand to stop me, but it was too late. I'd already peeked out of the table to come face-to-face with Lucy.

"Talia, I was looking all over for you!" she exclaimed. "You little ho you!" She snickered. She clearly meant that to be playful teasing, but I couldn't help but feel stung by her words, tears brimming my eyes, recalling why Alex had called me a similar name previously.

"Don't call her that!" Alex came to my defense. "Don't ever call my mate that again!" I looked up at him, and he was glaring evilly at Lucy. I suddenly felt so much affection for him, my chest warming.

"Goddess, calm down! I was just teasing. She's not doing any worse than I do to Luke regularly." She rolled her eyes and walked away.

Alex helped pull me up to my feet. "Want to go outside and get some air?" he asked. I nodded in response, and he put his arm around my shoulder, leading me toward an exit. As soon as we stepped outside, we were greeted by a cloud of smoke from everyone taking a cigarette break. We moved away, taking a walk toward the side of the building on the sidewalk that had been cleared of snow. Suddenly, a familiar scent entered my nostrils. I sniffed more deeply. I was now beginning to be able to distinguish the difference in scents of different packs and recognized that Blake's pack members and Alex's pack members each had distinct smells. This scent, that was currently clinging to the ground and drifting through the air, was very similar to the wolves that had arrived after the flying deer.

"Do you smell that?" Alex asked.

"It's those wolves. The ones that attacked you."

"Yes. Talia, this is very important. Can you go into the casino and go find Blake and Luke? I'm going to follow the scent and try to find the culprits."

"Okay," I replied, hurrying away, running as fast as I could in my heels. I knew I'd have to be fast because Alex might need backup. I couldn't find Blake anywhere, but I soon spotted Luke laughing with a group of some guys. Thank God he was tall. I hurried over to him.

"Talia? Are you okay?" He looked over at me as soon as I approached him.

"It's that bad pack. The ones that attacked Alex before. They're outside."

"The Bois Sombre Pack?" he promptly asked.

"Yes, that one!"

"Shit, fuck. Where?" He and the group of guys he was with all followed me as I led them outside to where Alex and I had smelled them. "Fuck, it is them. Come on, let's go find them," he said to the guys he was with, then turned to me and said, "Talia, go back inside. It's not safe out here." I watched as they stepped into the snow, following the footsteps that Alex had left behind.

I did as he said, deciding to look around to see if I could find Blake, but he was nowhere to be found. I took a seat at my table instead, finally digging into the piece of cake that had been left for me and sipping on my coffee that was now lukewarm.

When Alex didn't return after about twenty minutes, I began to worry, wondering where he was. I went back toward the door we had exited from to wait for him. Just as I approached, I spotted Luke looking a bit frantic. "Luke, where's Alex?" I asked.

"Follow me," he said, bringing me down the hallway to a secured door that he had a fob key to open. He took me down a long hallway beyond some offices to a closed door. "He's in there," he said, turning to go back where he came from.

I pushed the door open to see a group of people huddled around something. I couldn't see what it was as they were all huge, clearly warriors, blocking my view.

Alex instantly spotted me and got up. "Talia, you shouldn't be here," he said.

"What's going on?"

He seemed to hesitate but finally quietly told me, "Blake's torturing the culprits. Go to Jasmine's bridal suite for now. I'll go find you there once Blake is done. You know where that is, right?" I nodded, recalling where it was as we had gathered in that area earlier to take family portraits, and Blake had insisted that I be included.

I followed the hallway back to where I'd entered and made my way to Jasmine's suite. When I got to the hallway where it was, I couldn't remember if I had to take a left turn or right turn to get to the correct room. I tried going left first, and pushed open a door, gasping and practically falling backward from what I walked into. Jasmine's alpha cousin had his dress pants down around his ankles and a voluptuous waitress bent over a table, her very large, bare breasts hanging out the top of her unbuttoned uniform while he forcefully pounded into her from behind. Just as quickly as I had opened the door, I slammed it shut, and fell against the wall to catch my breath.

After shaking my head and the image from my mind, I headed back in the other direction. I reached the correct door, and this time I knocked, clearly having learned my lesson. But something didn't seem right. My instincts went into overdrive. I could smell that same scent very faintly. I pushed the door open to find the room empty. The smell was even stronger now that I had entered. I could smell it everywhere. And I realized something else. It also had a very distinct smell interwoven with it. I'd never forget that scent. It made me nauseous recalling how uncomfortable he had made me feel. It was that guy from the bar that I thought would force himself on me. Charlie.

I kicked off my heels and quickly ran to find Luke again, knowing I wouldn't be able to get back down that hallway without him. I finally found him, speaking with his father and two men I recognized to be Jasmine's alpha relatives from when we'd taken pictures earlier that day.

I ran up to the group of them and they all went quiet, staring at me. "Jasmine's missing. She's not in her suite. And it smells like the Bois Sombre Pack."

"What!" Jasmine's grandfather shouted. "Where is my granddaughter?"

"I'm sure it's fine, Dad. She's probably just somewhere else, right?" Jasmine's uncle turned to look at Luke and his father.

"Yes, I'm sure it's fine. Let's just find out where she went." Luke's father nodded. He turned to his son and said, "Luke, just mindlink Jasmine and ask where she went so we can all put our minds at ease."

Luke's eyes shot up toward the sky. He stayed like that for a few moments and then looked back at his father. "I . . . I can't."

"As in she's blocking you out?"

"No, like I can't link her at all. She's too out of range."

"Where the fuck is my granddaughter?" Jasmine's grandfather bellowed.

"We'll find her. Luke, just link the senior warriors and have them scent for Jasmine. I'm sure they'll track her down in no time." Even though Luke's dad said this calmly, it was clear that he was not calm at all, with his jaw tensed and his hands formed into fists.

Luke nodded, and I couldn't help but notice that they had both paled.

"Dad, let's go find Tyce. This could be serious. We need to get on this now," Jasmine's uncle said, grabbing his father's arm, a scowl on his face. Although the situation had turned grave, I couldn't help but cover my mouth to keep from snickering, recalling exactly where Tyce was.

"Where the fuck is her mate?" Jasmine's grandfather demanded.

"I'll go find him," Luke replied, and ran off down the hallway. Soon everyone was gone and I was left behind, wondering what I should do, wishing I could be more helpful.

Chapter 60

Alexander

My father and sister were both pretty fucked-up, but, damn, Blake was sick. Because we had to make do with what was available in the casino, which wasn't much, Blake had a bunch of his warriors holding the members of the Bois Sombre Pack down while he tortured them. They were both fully naked after being forced into their human forms. Chef's knives were brought in from the kitchen, and Blake tested each one of them out on the men's torsos until he figured out which one was the sharpest, their ensuing screams widening his smile, his eyes gleaming.

"You know what I should be doing right now instead of torturing you motherfuckers?" Blake asked menacingly. They both struggled against the men holding them down, expressions like deer in headlights. "I should be enjoying my wedding night. But since you assholes interrupted it, you'll just have to enact it for me." He laughed evilly. "Normally I wait a few hours until we get to the main event during my tortures. But I promised my new wife I'd be quick, so looks like we'll be getting to the good part right away."

He moved closer to them, standing over them. He tapped the back of his knife against his hand, staring at the two struggling men, both pale with bloodied torsos. "Okay, I guess a little foreplay is necessary." He squatted down, and before anyone could process his words, he shoved the knife into one of their chests and dragged it down the length of his torso while the man screamed in agony, more blood spilling out of the tearing in his chest. Blake laughed in a sick way and then turned to the other man, doing the same to him. "Not bad for a kitchen knife," Blake remarked, looking at the bloodied blade. He then gently glided the tip of the blade farther down the second man's body until he made it to the top of his thigh and then dragged it down to his knee and back up again, doing this several times on both legs, creating long bloody zig-zags, the skin practically falling off the man's legs from all the cuts. He turned to the other man and did the same thing. The screams were piercing, but Blake seemed completely unaffected as he continued his work, a sick smile on his face the entire time.

"I think you can both see where this is leading. I've got you all warmed up, and now it's time to suck some cock."

Everyone looked at Blake, wondering what he meant by his words until he swiftly cut one of their dicks off. I'm pretty sure every person in the room groaned while the unlucky bastard wailed. Blake then shoved it into the other guy's mouth, practically down his throat, while the man gagged before he finally spit it out.

"Holy fuck, Wulfric!" I exclaimed.

"What, you never witnessed that back at Grey Wolf?" He looked at me, smiling.

"I did, but I never did it myself," I replied. "And to be honest, never thought I'd witness it again."

"It goes great with my favorite Russian phrase." Blake had a glint in his eyes. He turned to the other poor bastard, who was convulsing uncontrollably in fear. As Blake's warriors struggled to hold him down, a puddle formed on the floor from him pissing himself. Blake just as swiftly sliced his dick off and yelled, *"Hui tebe'v rot!"* as he did the same thing again, shoving it into his companion's mouth.

"What does that mean?" one of the warriors asked, looking like he was about to gag.

"Dick in your mouth." Blake laughed. He dropped the knife, got up, and clapped his hands together in a gesture of cleaning them off. "Well, that was fun, but I have a new wife waiting for me. Adalwolf, take it away. And make sure you find out what the assholes' plans were."

I was just about to pick up the knife Blake dropped when his beta Luke ran into the room panicked. "Blake, Jasmine's missing."

"What do you mean she's missing?" He stared at Luke.

"Talia came to find me after she scented the Bois Sombre Pack in the bridal suite with Jasmine gone."

"Where the fuck did she go?"

"We don't know. The window was left open."

"And she's nowhere else?"

"No. We're tracking the whole place. Her family's involved now, looking for her. She just disappeared."

"Where's Talia? Is she okay?" I asked, panicked by the news. Not that I wasn't worried about Jasmine, but who was watching over my mate when this happened? What if they had kidnapped her too? When Luke didn't reply, I shouted more loudly, "Where's my mate? Where's Talia?"

"I don't know," Luke responded, clearly caught off guard.

Blake and I both sprinted out of the room we were in, heading straight to the bridal suite. Two blond men who were clearly brothers were in there when we arrived. "Blake, it smells like Charlie's scent mixed with the Bois Sombre Pack in here." One of them stepped forward.

"Fuck, I knew I should have killed him." Blake put his hands to his face.

"He must have joined the Bois Sombre Pack after you banished him." The blond man frowned, looking equally troubled. "It makes sense. Alpha Édouard would have welcomed him with open arms, especially with how much intel he has on our pack."

"Fuck," Blake said, his state clearly rapidly deteriorating as he kept running his hands through his hair, his mouth agape, his head shaking back and forth.

"Fucking Artemis," I said emphatically. "I didn't think he'd actually be able to go through with it."

"What the fuck do you mean?" Blake shouted, staring at me.

"He'd threatened me. Told me that he'd find my weakness," I said, becoming more anxious, wondering where Talia was.

"And you didn't think to tell me about these threats? You just let him blindside me and take *my* weakness?" Blake scrubbed his hands over his face.

"He might have taken mine too," I said, turning away, desperate to find where Talia had gone. I'd never made her a part of my pack, knowing that she'd automatically become one once we finally marked each other. But I couldn't mindlink her now. My heart raced. I'd make her a part of my pack immediately. I couldn't stand the fact that I couldn't get in touch with her right away when I needed desperately to know she was okay.

I sprinted to the ballroom and was relieved to find her in there alone, sitting at our table. I couldn't help but smile as I ran toward her, so happy she was okay and not in danger.

"Alex," she said, standing up. "Did they find Jasmine?"

"No, but I'm so glad you're okay." I pulled her against me. "Don't leave my side, okay? It's dangerous right now." I took her hand and led her back to the bridal suite where chaos had ensued.

We entered to find that Blake did not appear as if he was doing well at all. A small group had formed, staring at Blake in silence. He was collapsed onto the floor in a squatting position, practically pulling his hair out. I'd never seen him so distraught before. Luke squatted down next to him. "Blake?" he said, staring at him.

"Luke, I can't do this again. I can't do this," Blake cried out. He was clearly having a breakdown. We all watched on as he continued, "I can't fucking lose Jasmine too, Luke. I can't. I can't." He fell onto his knees and covered his head with his arms. "Goddess, why did I leave her alone? Why didn't I kill Charlie? I can't."

We all looked at each other, unsure how to react to an alpha becoming hysterical.

Luke suddenly pulled his hand back and slapped Blake across the face. "Pull yourself together, man!" he yelled. "Crying is not going to help the situation. We need to make a plan to find her and get her back. Now get up!"

Blake blinked a few times, coming to, and instantly stood up.

Once Blake seemed stable, Luke continued, "My dad called our warriors in Quebec to keep watch over the Bois Sombre Pack border and let us know who's entering and leaving. I was about to call the Lune Nordique Pack, but if you're done with your freak out, maybe you should be the one to do that."

"Yes, let me call Alpha Antoine." Blake nodded, still not appearing to be all there.

"As your ally, Pine Forest Pack is on standby to help as well." I stepped forward and patted Blake on the back, feeling terrible about the position he was in. I knew that if it were Talia who was taken, I wouldn't have been doing much better, desperate to get her back.

"Thanks, man." Blake looked at me, his eyes appearing haunted.

"Hey, are we making plans to go get Jasmine back yet?" Jasmine's cousin, whom I recognized from earlier when we'd taken family portraits, walked into the room. "Because I can get a flight chartered from Alaska and have a good number of my warriors here in less than twelve hours."

"Thanks, Alpha Tyce." Blake shook his hand.

"Hey, I didn't get a chance to introduce myself earlier. I'm Alpha Alex Adalwolf from Pine Forest Pack." I put my hand out to him, eager to make relationships with other alphas.

"Alpha Tyce Tikaani from Jade Moon Pack." He shook my hand.

I turned back to Blake, who had a pained, watery gaze, as if he was trying to figure out exactly where he was. "Wulfric, between us three alphas and the Lune Nordique Pack, that's four packs. We could easily eradicate the Bois Sombre Pack. As far as I know, they have no more allies. Alpha Édouard is completely insane to pull a move like this."

"Come on, Blake, let's go fuck them up and get your mate back." One of the blond men slapped Blake on the back.

Chapter 61

Blake

"We've got our warriors stalking the perimeter of the Bois Sombre Pack. But their territory is too big to cover every part of it." Beta Alfred walked into the bridal suite where I was now congregated with Luke, Jack, Kyle, Alex, Talia, and Tyce.

"Alpha Antoine is sending his warriors to join ours," I replied, barely able to move my mouth. I was trying desperately to hold it together, but I knew that if we made one wrong move, Alpha Édouard wouldn't hesitate to kill Jasmine. And, even if he didn't kill her, I could only imagine what else he might do to her. The man was completely unhinged. He'd beaten his own mate half to death even when he would have felt the pain as he did it; there was no reason he wouldn't do the same or worse to someone else's. The graphic thoughts wouldn't leave my mind.

The only thing that kept me half functioning was that I knew she wasn't dead yet. I would feel her death, same as I felt anyone in my pack when they died. No, she was still alive, but who knew how alive and for how much longer? I couldn't even sense the direction where she went, not having marked her yet. I was completely helpless and useless.

"I'm going to keep tabs on the warriors tracking her," Beta Alfred said as he was exiting the room. I nodded to him, feeling completely distracted and thankful he was taking charge.

"Shouldn't we head north?" Kyle asked.

"We don't know that's where she was taken. They could have taken her anywhere," I replied, thinking, *They could be torturing or raping her right now, just miles from where we are, and we'd be none the wiser.* This was all my fault. I should have killed Charlie. Why did I let Jasmine influence me? She hadn't been trained to be an alpha like I had. And why did I need to torture those assholes right then? I could have left it to Alex, just as he'd offered. And then I came to.

"Where did they take the dickless motherfuckers?" I asked, standing up.

"Do I even want to know?" Jack asked.

"Let's go get some answers out of them." I stood up. "Luke, get in contact with the warriors back at the pack, and have them bring me my good knives and some heavy chains." I smiled. It was time for round two, and this round would not be a quickie.

After torturing for hours, I was barely functioning anymore, hanging on by caffeine and desperation. Torture wasn't giving me the same enjoyment it normally did. Their screams echoed off the walls, but it may as well have just been static. The process was a means to an end. I mechanically cut off finger after finger, toe after toe, as if I was following a checklist.

I shoved a knife into one of the culprits' eye sockets, scooping his eye out as best I could. It was a messy job, with eyeball coming out in pieces as I cut bits of it out. "Sooner you tell me where my mate was taken, the sooner the torture stops," I said.

"I don't know," the asshole cried, wailing, begging for me to stop.

"Wrong answer." I shoved my blade into his stomach, reopening a wound that was healing.

He cried out in desperation as I stood above him. "I don't know, I swear!" he cried.

"I'm not stopping until one of you motherfuckers tell me where they took my wife."

"Blake," Alex said from behind me. Luke's mom and Lucy had taken Talia back to the packhouse with them, so she would be kept safe and wouldn't have to witness the torture.

"Yes?" I turned around.

"I just got a text from Alpha Édouard."

"What did that asshole say?" I asked both angrily and desperately, wishing he was the one I was currently torturing. Once I got Jasmine back, I wouldn't rest until he was dead.

"He says he'll return your mate unharmed if you bring him his."

"Even if I could, I would never give that piece of shit back his mate," I replied, disgusted by the idea of returning the woman he tortured for years back to him, or giving him anything that would make him happy for that matter.

"There's another text that just came in."

"What's it say?" He read it silently and took a deep breath. "Well?" I asked in anticipation.

"He says he's giving you twelve hours. After that, he no longer guarantees she's unharmed."

"Fucking Artemis," I said, flinging my knife against the wall angrily. "What the fuck am I supposed to do?"

"I've got the flight booked. My men will be landing in eight hours just outside Montreal," Tyce chimed in.

"I have my warriors on standby. I can have them loaded onto buses at a moment's notice," Alex offered.

"We also have Alpha Antoine on our team," Luke added.

"But we can't just attack the pack," I grumbled. "First of all, we don't even know if that's where he's keeping her. And second of all, he could easily just kill her if we attack." I was nauseous at the idea. Goddess, where did he have her? Was she okay? Was she scared? Was he threatening her? And what did he plan to do to her after twelve hours? Fuck, I had to find her before then. I pulled out my phone to take note of the time—just after two in the morning.

"Why don't we just pretend we'll agree to trade his mate back for Jasmine? Then at least he'll tell us where to meet him, and we can go there now," Luke offered.

"Great idea, Luke!" Alex replied. "Let me text him back right now and ask him where to meet him." We looked over his shoulder as the text conversation resumed.

> **Alex:** *Ok, we agree to the trade. Time and place?*
> **Alpha Édouard:** *I knew you'd be reasonable. Tell Antoine to bring my mate to my pack border and I'll tell you where you can find Blake's mate after. You have until 14:03 or I will torture.*
> **Alex:** *No, we trade mates at the same time, otherwise how do we know you'll keep your word?*
> **Alpha Édouard:** *My rules or no mate*

"Fuck, he's not stupid." Alex shook his head. "Crazy, but not stupid. Looks like we'll have to keep torturing and try to get it out of these poor bastards."

"May I?" Tyce asked, picking up one of the knives that had been brought in and were currently laid out on a table.

"Be my guest," I replied. He smiled menacingly, turning toward the two werewolves we'd captured. I watched as he picked up where I left off, carving the knife up and down one of the men's torsos while he screamed in agony. I nodded in approval. Clearly, my family and Jasmine's were not so different.

Jack pulled me aside. "Honestly, Blake. Don't beat yourself up over keeping Charlie alive. I also wasn't sure about killing him, even after what he did to my mate. I kept thinking, he could have killed Tyler so easily and he didn't. It seemed wrong at the time to take his life when he didn't take Tyler's."

"If Jasmine dies, I will spend the rest of my life regretting that one decision," I replied, anguished. "I should have known better. I was taught better."

"But you had no way of knowing he'd come back and steal your mate."

I took a deep breath". "I feel like a complete dipshit for not even considering it. If I had, I never would have let him live." I slumped down in a chair.

"We'll get her back. Don't worry, Blake." Jack patted me on the shoulder.

I shook my head. Jack was just trying to make me feel better. He couldn't guarantee we'd get Jasmine back any more than anyone else could. I was a complete failure as a mate and protector. This was now going to be the second time one of my mistakes got my mate killed. I put my head in my hands, feeling myself being pulled back into the darkness of my mind, a place I'd only recently escaped.

"Where the fuck is my granddaughter!" a man yelled from beyond the room. "I want to speak to her mate right now! I have a daughter who's hysterical, and I want some answers!"

My head shot up, and I stood. Jasmine's grandfather entered and approached me, his face red, nostrils flared, and eyes bulging. He stepped in front of me, apparently ready for a fight, and shoved me.

"Where the fuck were you when your mate was taken? Why weren't you with her? And why wasn't the pack protecting her? What kind of sad excuse for a pack are you running?"

I couldn't even find the words to answer, feeling myself retreating into myself, agreeing with all his words. I had no excuse. I was a failure as an alpha and a mate. And I'd have to answer to Jasmine's parents and family for my failure, for letting them down.

Fuck me.

"Grandpa, stop!" Tyce shouted. We both turned to look at him.

"And you, boy! Don't even get me started on you. Next thing I know, our pack is going to become some shithole like this one!"

Tyce approached his grandfather, his arms crossed and his brows furrowed in anger. "That's enough, Grandpa! If you aren't going to help, then you need to leave. We're trying to get answers out of these assholes." He gestured to the bloody bodies. "And you're just interrupting our work. We have less than twelve hours now until they hurt Jasmine. So if you don't have anything valuable to offer, then just go!"

"Give me that knife," he said. Tyce handed it to him, and he approached the chained men. "Okay, you scoundrels. What you've witnessed so far has been child's play. Let me show you how a real man does it." He smiled widely, his eyes cold and hard, reminding me very much of my father. I unexpectedly felt a bit nostalgic. Although I hated my father, one of the few activities we had been able to bond over had been torture. I suddenly found myself missing him a little.

Jasmine's grandfather didn't fuck around. He instantly went for the balls, shoving his knife into each nut and splitting them in half as he dragged his knife out of them.

"Fuck, Wulfric, and I thought my family was fucked-up." Alex stood next to me as we watched.

"My dad loves shoving knives into assholes, and I mean that literally." Tyce snickered. He turned to me and quietly said, "Sorry about my grandfather, by the way. In case you haven't noticed, he's kind of a dick."

"He reminds me of my dad," I replied. "He was the same."

"Torturing should keep him entertained for a while." Tyce and I shared a look and then he continued. "Between all of us, we should be able to figure out where they're keeping Jasmine."

I hoped to the Goddess he was right. I was barely hanging on, just a step from insanity, trying my best to hold it together and stay strong.

Chapter 62

Blake

At around five in the morning, we finally gave up on torturing the assholes and transported what was left of their bodies to the pack cells. All the alphas in Jasmine's family had gotten involved, taking turns. After Jasmine's grandfather began his work, it wasn't long before Jasmine's uncle also joined us. True to Tyce's words, he shoved the knife into their literal assholes. But even with so many people taking turns to find new and creative ways to torture, it ended uneventfully.

The pack members we held hostage either truly didn't know where Jasmine was or they were exceptionally good at keeping their mouths shut. I leaned toward the former. I didn't think it was possible anyone was that good. We'd tortured them in every way possible, they were begging for death, and they still didn't talk. It seemed futile to keep going, but we decided to keep them alive for now, with the small hope that if we resumed in a few hours, maybe they'd finally break. But it was doubtful at this point.

Luke drove me back to the packhouse, Alex following behind us in his car. Once the three of us were inside, Alex separated from us, heading upstairs to be with his mate. I watched him with envy, wishing I could be coming home to Jasmine.

"Blake, we'll find her," Luke tried to assure me.

"How do you know?" I narrowed my eyes at him.

"Because we've got four packs involved now. And Alpha Édouard has to come out of hiding at some point. I know he's unhinged, but he also has to know that if he kills Jasmine we'll take revenge on him, and his pack is far outnumbered. She's worth way more alive than dead."

"I don't know, Luke. I'm losing hope. And what's he going to do to her?" Tears were threatening to spill from my overtired eyes, my imagination once again replaying every gruesome scene possible. I could imagine all of it, being an expert in torture, and it didn't take too much creativity to imagine someone being raped. I was nauseous, walking into the living room and falling onto the couch.

"Baby, what's happening?" Lucy walked into the room in a robe.

"Baby, go to sleep. It's okay. We have a lot to deal with right now," Luke said to his mate.

"Did you find Jasmine? Is she going to be okay?" Lucy asked.

"She'll be fine. We're going to find her. Just go back upstairs."

"But I'm worried, baby. Jasmine's my best friend. I've known her since I was a kid. Can I help?"

"No, Lucy, I don't want you involved in this. Just go back upstairs, okay?"

She nodded and walked out of the room.

"Fuck, Luke, you were right." I groaned. "I was completely reckless, not protecting Jasmine, not even thinking about how valuable she is as a target."

"Hey, don't beat yourself up, man. We all make mistakes sometimes." He patted my shoulder. "That's why we have to work together, to keep each other in check."

Beta Alfred entered the living room, looking between the two of us. "What's the latest, Dad?" Luke asked.

"We've got everyone keeping watch outside of the Bois Sombre Pack territory. No sign yet of Jasmine being brought in. What about everyone scenting the area?"

Luke shook his head. "They tried for hours. They found where she was carried over the border through the woods. But once they got to Canada, her scent disappeared. They must have jumped into a car and drove away, leaving no trace. I asked them to check the whole thirty-mile radius where the scent ended and nothing."

"Still alive though, right?" Beta Alfred looked at me.

I nodded. Still alive, but for how much longer?

"Blake, I've kept Jasmine's parents informed. But they're getting anxious. You're going to have to talk to them at some point as both the alpha and her mate."

I nodded again, aware I had to be a man and own up to my stupidity.

"Dad, can't you hold them off longer?" Luke asked. "He's clearly not in a place to talk to them right now. And we were just with Jasmine's grandfather, uncle, and cousin."

"It's okay. I need to do the right thing," I said. "Are they awake now?"

"Your mom gave them some sedatives. Maybe go over to see them in a few hours."

I nodded, my stomach feeling as if it were filled with poison.

"Maybe you should get some sleep for now," Luke suggested.

"How am I supposed to sleep?" I asked. "My mate is gone, probably getting tortured. I can't fucking sleep! Would you be able to sleep if they took Lucy?"

"There's not much else we can do right now, Blake," Beta Alfred cut in. "At this point, it's a waiting game until we get more information about Jasmine's whereabouts. You're better off sleeping, so we're ready to fight once we know where Jasmine is. Now, come on, boys. Let's go upstairs and get some rest for now. We can reconvene in a few hours unless we hear something before then."

I reluctantly followed them upstairs and fell into my bed, thinking Jasmine should have been in it with me, my arms wrapped around her warm body. I felt so desperate and helpless, not knowing where she was or what was happening to her. I fell in and out of sleep, anxiety overtaking my entire body. My dreams haunted me—all of them about watching helplessly as Jasmine was tortured, her limbs being cut from her body as she screamed in agony, looking to me for help while I was stuck frozen just watching, blood draining from her. At one point, I couldn't even tell anymore if I were in a dream or reality, the horror of real-life mixing with my nightmares.

"Blake, are you okay?" Luke was standing over my bed, shaking me from sleep.

"What?" I looked at him, confused.

"You were just screaming as if someone were torturing you. You woke the whole house, and I ran up here to make sure you're okay. It reminded me of when you were a kid. You used to do the same thing."

"Fuck," I said in response.

"Blake, we'll find her, don't worry."

I got out of bed, checking the time. Just after nine in the morning. "I can't sleep. I need to do something. I'm going to talk to her parents."

"Are you sure you're okay to do that?" Luke looked at me with pity on his face. "I can ask my dad to hold them off longer. I just don't want you to . . ." Luke's voice trailed off.

"To what?" I asked, glaring at him.

"Never mind," he replied.

"Luke, tell me what you were going to say."

"I'm just worried. After what happened with Ria, you changed. And you finally seemed to be getting back to normal." He sighed.

"I'm not a fucking little kid that needs to be babied. I'm the alpha, and your dad is right. I have to take responsibility."

After I dressed and had some coffee, I drove over to Jasmine's parents' house. She wasn't dead yet—I kept repeating that to myself. I could at least tell them that with confidence. The rest—well, I could also own up to my stupidity and recklessness. It's not how I wanted her parents to look at me, but I had no choice.

I rang the doorbell and her father answered. "Blake!" He widened his eyes, the dark bags under them prominent. "Is there news? Come in. What's going on? How's Jasmine doing?" I followed him into the living room where Jasmine's extended family was already seated with her mom.

Everyone stared at me as I entered the living room, which was much more filled with people than I'd ever seen. I took deep breaths, forcing myself forward. Inside, I was shaking like a scared little puppy. But I couldn't present myself that way. I couldn't show weakness. I had to be a strong alpha for my pack and as Jasmine's mate.

"Good morning, everyone," I said with confidence. "I wanted to come here in person to give everyone an update. Jasmine is still alive, and we're doing our best to find her. We have warriors keeping watch over the border of the Bois Sombre Pack. My ally, Alpha Alexander of the Pine Forest Pack, is keeping contact with Alpha Édouard. He hasn't told us where she is yet, but hopefully soon we'll know so we can get her back."

"Why don't you tell my daughter where the fuck you were when her daughter was taken?" Jasmine's grandfather stood up, his amber eyes fierce with anger. "Why weren't you keeping her safe?"

I whimpered on the inside, but held my shoulders high. "I was torturing members of the Bois Sombre Pack after they interrupted the wedding. I left her in a place I thought was safe, but I will own up to my mistake. What I did was completely stupid and reckless."

"I hope this isn't a sign of how the future is going to go. It is your job to keep the luna of your pack protected, and I have absolutely no confidence you are capable of that. You are a sad fucking excuse for an alpha. You are delusional to think you are good enough to be Jasmine's mate. Even the Moon Goddess knew better than to mate her to you."

I stood there and took every blow as he dealt it.

"Dad, stop!" Jasmine's mom stood up. Her face was red and puffy as if she had been crying for hours. "There's no need for that. It's not helping the situation."

"Miriam, sit down. You've been too accepting of your daughter's out-of-line behavior. I am disgusted by the fact you allowed her to reject her real mate. And look what happened!"

"Dad, stop! Haven't we all suffered enough at the situation?" Jasmine's uncle stood up. "We get it already, okay? You don't need to rub salt in the wound. You lashing out at every single person in your vicinity is not going to bring Jasmine back. We need to work together so we can get her back safely." He turned to me and said, "Our men are landing in less than an hour. Let Tyce know where he should send them. We're ready to fight."

"I will. Give me some more time to figure out where she is. We should know soon." I said this with confidence, but the reality was that I had no idea if it were true or not.

"I trust you, Alpha." Jasmine's dad patted me on the back. "I know you'd never willingly let Jasmine get hurt."

This comment tortured me more than everything Jasmine's grandfather had said. I hated how much Jasmine's father trusted me when I didn't even trust myself. His confidence in me pierced my heart, a thick scar reopening.

All I could do was nod and say, "I'll keep you informed."

Jasmine's dad walked me out of the house, and I hopped back into my car, letting out a deep breath. I didn't know how much longer I'd be able to hold myself together. Luke wasn't wrong to be worried. Just as I was about to put my car into reverse to back out of the driveway, pain pierced my chest. Two warriors dropping dead. While I was not happy at the situation, I was relieved it wasn't Jasmine. Something had happened. I quickly backed out of the driveway to head back to the packhouse when I felt a third.

I mindlinked Luke, "*What's happening? Three warriors dead. Be home soon.*"

"*I'll find out,*" Luke mindlinked back.

I sped down the pack roads, rushing to get back, parked haphazardly, and ran into the packhouse. I entered to find Luke on his cell phone, his dad sitting at the dining room table as he paced the room. "What's happening?" I asked, desperate for news.

Luke finally hung up and said, "They found Jasmine. Charlie had her in a car. Some warriors tried to stop them before they were able to enter the pack, but their warriors shot ours down using wolfsbane darts. But we know she's in there now."

"Fuck!" I replied. "We need to head there right now! I'll inform all the alphas. Luke, get our passports ready and inform the warriors."

"On it," Luke replied, turning his eyes upward in a mindlink.

I quickly began dialing Tyce's number. I was ready to annihilate Alpha Édouard and his entire fucking pack!

Chapter 63

Talia

As soon as Blake knew Jasmine's whereabouts, Alex and I immediately jumped into his new car to head north to Quebec. I ran across the border in my wolf form and waited for Alex to pick me up at what was now becoming a landmark. I planned to get all my citizenships in order eventually, but it was still a work in progress.

"Maybe you should drive the rest of the way, eh?" Alex laughed when we were about an hour out from our destination. "With my terrible luck, I'm not sure if we'll make it, even being so close now. Especially with all these Quebecois drivers."

"I don't know how to drive," I replied.

"What? You can't be serious." He glanced at me, his eyebrows raised.

"I am serious. I never learned."

"Well, damn, there's something else I need to put on my list of things to teach you." He took my hand in his. His hand was fully healed now, although the incident had left scars around each of his fingers, like pinkish-red rings. The doctor believed the scars remained because his fingers had been detached for so long before we got to the hospital. They had to reopen the wounds before they stitched them back on. I liked to run my fingers along them. Alex told me it felt good when I did, so I constantly found myself doing it.

"Will your mom be okay while we're gone? I know we'll be gone longer than you were expecting." I turned to Alex while brushing my thumb against the raised skin on his fingers.

"I hope so. I have two nurses with her at all times." He smiled mischievously and said, "I can't lie though, except for all the shit that's gone down, it's been nice spending the time alone with you. That hot tub in our hotel room was very nice."

"Mmm, it was." I moaned as a graphic vision replayed in my mind of Alex's muscular naked body in the jacuzzi while I climbed on top of him. My whole body was becoming hot. I turned the seat warmer off and pulled off the winter coat Alex had bought me after I'd destroyed my old one in the woods when I'd shifted into my wolf form to fight his sister.

A sudden desperate need to have Alex right then and there came over me. I was already imagining how good it felt when he was inside me as I ran my fingers up his thigh, making my way to his belt buckle, ready to undo it to start the foreplay.

"Fuck!" Alex yelled as a loud honk resounded and he swerved, the screeching sound of tires waking me from my trance.

I practically fell out of my seat as the car shook, and we stopped. I whipped my head up to look around.

"Fuck, I almost caused an accident!" Alex was staring at me, his hands gripping the steering wheel. "You've gone into heat!"

"Oh, shit!" I exclaimed.

"It's okay. We'll just find an area to pull over. Hopefully, if we have sex, it will ease it for a little bit so we can make it the rest of the way. It's not much farther."

I nodded, trying to resist what I really wanted to do. I could feel that my panties were soaked with arousal, and my thighs were desperate, tingling to feel Alex between them. And I didn't fail to notice that he was sporting a huge boner, only making my desire for him that much worse.

I crossed my legs and sat on my hands while Alex drove until we found somewhere to pull off. He found a place to enter a wooded area in his SUV, clearly an area where cars weren't supposed to enter. But we were both desperate.

As soon as we parked, we both climbed into the back seat, stripping ourselves naked in no time at all.

"Goddess, I am so fucking horny right now." Alex moaned as I climbed onto his lap. He grabbed one of my breasts and pulled my face against his with his other hand as our tongues found each other, completely desperate, neither of us in the mood for foreplay. I wrapped my arms around his neck as he moved his body forward in his seat so I could comfortably lower myself onto his erection, an animalistic need to have it inside of me, not even caring that my long legs were in the world's most uncomfortable position at that moment. All that mattered was that Alex was inside me. Our bodies quickly synced, thrusting against each other desperately, as if we'd been possessed.

It had to have been the best sex I'd ever had in my life, a deep-seated need being fulfilled, transporting me to ecstasy. My whole body was soaked in arousal and desperation, the windows fogging as I screamed in pleasure, certain anybody driving by would hear without issue.

Alex groaned with each thrust, his body covered in sweat, his face appearing both pained and blissful simultaneously. "Goddess, you are so fucking wet. It feels so fucking good." He moaned into my ear.

"Fuck me harder," I cried, quickening my thrusts as Alex grabbed my hips and began pulling me up and down the length of his cock. God, it felt so good. Before long, we were both shaking, lost in each other, and orgasming. I could feel his semen spray forcefully inside me as I collapsed on top of him, panting against his body, my canines extending.

"Damn, that was amazing," I mumbled, my long teeth getting in the way of me speaking clearly.

"Goddess, I don't think I've ever felt anything so good before," he agreed, breathing heavily, his chest rising and falling beneath mine. We stayed together for a few moments until our teeth shrunk back down to normal size. Alex sighed and said, "Your heat is easing. Let's try to make it there before it starts up again. We have to help Blake get Jasmine back."

We disconnected from each other and pulled our clothes back on. As much as I wished we could just spend the rest of the day wrapped in each other, I knew we were on a mission. I still felt horny as we drove, but it wasn't quite the same desperation it had been. But as time wore on, I could feel the same yearning building up again. Five minutes out from where we were supposed to meet, we stopped again, fulfilling the need we had for each other. One thing about heat—there was nothing rational about it. When it came on, that was all that mattered, no matter how inappropriate the situation.

Chapter 64

Jasmine

When I woke, I found myself on cold, hard concrete. I groaned, my neck in pain from being in an awkward position while I slept. I tried to roll over and move my hands, only to find them very heavy. I could feel metal scraping against skin as I struggled to move my arms a little. I opened my eyes, looking around. At first, I couldn't process where I was, none of it made sense. I'd never seen surroundings like these before—a small room with a cold, hard concrete floor, and a barred metal door. A barred door like ones used for jail cells. I gasped as I realized that's exactly where I was—inside a jail cell.

I lifted my head to get a better look, moving it to find there was a toilet in the corner behind me—one that clearly hadn't been cleaned in a long time, possibly years. It didn't even have a seat, and the whole perimeter of it was stained yellow. I sat up, using my core strength to lift myself, and realized with horror that I had to pee. I would have no choice but to use that disgusting toilet. There wasn't even any true privacy. The door to the cell was see-through, and anyone walking by would be able to peek through it.

How did I end up in jail? I thought back, racking my brain. And then all the memories flooded back—my wedding, Blake leaving the bridal suite to torture members of the Bois Sombre Pack, and Charlie! He had shoved a sharp needle into my neck that caused me to pass out. And now I was here. My stomach ached, and I felt light-headed. Where had he brought me? Thinking harder, I recalled his scent—one of the last memories before I passed out. He had clearly joined the Bois Sombre Pack, and if I had to make an educated guess, this must have been their cells.

My bladder pulsed. The need to urinate was overwhelming. It must have been hours since I'd gone to the bathroom. I had no choice. I pulled myself up, the chains around my arms very heavy. Thank Goddess I was strong. If I hadn't trained as hard as I had, I wasn't sure I'd be able to get up. Metal was cuffed tightly around my wrists—so tight that it was practically cutting off my circulation. There was no way to slip my hands out.

I walked toward the toilet, practically gagging from how bad it looked and smelled. Pulling down my underwear was going to be a task in and of itself. Once I had the skirt of my dress lifted, I had to hold it up with the metal chains while I used my fingers to ease the thong I'd worn for Blake down my legs. Realizing I'd have to squat over the toilet, preferring not to sit, I let the panties fall down my legs so I could step out of them. Then I backed up over the toilet, doing my best to hold my dress up so I wouldn't get urine on it, and kept my legs from touching the filthy porcelain.

Once I was in the perfect position, I let it all flow out. I didn't think I'd ever felt more relief than at that moment, closing my eyes and sighing to myself. Goddess, I'd really had to pee. It was one of those times when so much had built up in my bladder that it was almost painful coming out, going slower than I would have preferred. I used my muscles to try to push it out faster, wanting to get out of the compromising position I was in, holding up my dress, my private parts exposed, my underwear abandoned.

"Hello there, Prissy Bitch," the most horrible voice said.

My eyes shot open to find Charlie staring at me peeing. I instantly dropped the skirt of my dress so I was covered. He had the most horrible smirk on his face.

"Looks like I finally got a glimpse of the magical pussy that's turned Blake into a bitch. Can't lie, doesn't seem so special to me. But maybe I should test drive it just to make sure."

I stared at him in horror Was he going to rape me?

He pulled out his cell phone and glanced at the screen. "Perfect timing too. I was told at 2:03 you'll be all mine."

My heart was racing and I was becoming dizzy. He pulled out a key and opened the door. I tried to shift into my wolf and an agonizing pain stabbed at my wrists as I tried. The metal was so heavy, my body couldn't tear through it to shift, leaving me helpless in my human form. I whimpered, terrified. He was really going to rape me, and I had no way out of this. I backed up as he entered the cell and closed the door behind him, locking it.

He undid his belt buckle. "Don't worry, I'll be quick." He grinned repulsively. "Just want to see what it feels like—why Blake's so pussy-whipped. I won't even hurt you if you just lie there and take it. Now go on, lie down like a good little bitch and spread your legs for me."

My eyes brimmed with tears as he got closer. I couldn't decide if it was worth trying to fight him when I was chained and he was clearly stronger than me. Would it be futile? Would it just anger him more, make him not only rape me but also do to me what he had to Tyler? I wondered if I really should just lie down and let him have his way with me—just close my eyes and wait for it to be over. The thought disgusted me, but maybe I could just pretend I was somewhere else and try my best to ignore his smell and the sounds of him moaning and coming. I became nauseous imagining it—how helpless I was trapped here, chained.

"Come on, Prissy. You're chained. Now, go on, sit like a good little bitch."

A tear escaped and ran down my cheek as I weighed my options. It seemed hopeless. He was going to have his way with me whether I went along with his instructions or not. Maybe if I did as he said, he really wouldn't hurt me. I sat down slowly, my leg and core muscles tensing from having to hold up my heavy chains while I did this. My bottom touched the cold concrete. Goddess, he was going to just fuck me on this hard ground.

"Good girl." He grinned and I thought I was going to vomit. He absolutely disgusted me, and I was now living one of my worst nightmares. "Now lie down, bitch. And spread your legs."

I whimpered. Why did he have to be so awful? And out of every person, why him? I did as asked, another tear falling down my face. I watched in agonizing terror as he undid his pants and pulled them down his legs, revealing an overgrowth of red pubic hair, that he was clearly fully aroused by the encounter, and that Blake had, in fact, removed both his balls.

At minimum, at least, I could feel secure in the fact I wouldn't end up pregnant by him. The thought flashed through my mind and gave me a small bit of relief.

He got down on his knees and fisted his disgusting penis, rubbing his hand up and down the shaft. Why hadn't Blake cut that off too?

"Like what you see, Prissy Bitch?" he sneered.

I wanted to give a snarky reply about him not having any balls but thought it might anger him. Now was not the time to anger him. I hoped to the Goddess he was maybe, at least, a two-pump chump. Maybe I wouldn't have to endure it for too long.

And then, just as I thought hope was lost, I realized, he might be stronger, but I had a clear weapon wrapped around my wrists. I smiled to myself at the quick plan I came up with. "Stop!" I bellowed.

And it worked!

It worked perfectly as he froze in place, his eyes bulging. Knowing I only had seconds to react, I quickly used the full force of my body to swing the chains against his skull as if I were swinging a baseball bat, making instant contact and cracking it while he watched, immobile and unable to do anything about it. His whole body fell over, blood pouring from his head. He was completely knocked out. Not wanting to risk any chance of him waking up and doing who knows what to me, I knew I had to kill him and complete the job Blake never did—because of me. I frowned at the thought. I had been the reason Charlie's life had been spared, and this is how he repaid me.

I got onto my knees, and used the heavy chains to smash his entire face in, obliterating his head. I kept smashing it until I could separate it from the rest of his body, leaving no chance for him to heal. Bone, brain, and blood were left splattered and smeared along the floor. I was partly disgusted but also partly in awe. Charlie was dead. Completely dead and unrecognizable. I sighed, thinking this was truly the most relieved I'd ever felt, beating out the feeling of emptying my full bladder.

I quickly ran back to where my thong was and shimmied it up my body. It really didn't cover much, but it was better than nothing. And then I wondered how long until someone else came to my cell? And would they find a way to rape, kill, or torture me?

Maybe this was the Moon Goddess realizing the same thing I had—that I shouldn't be with Blake, and he needed someone who was more luna material. After being too weak to break things off with Blake myself, being far too in love with him to just let him go for the greater good, the Moon Goddess did it for me. She found a way to take me away from him so he'd be free to find someone better. A tear dropped down my cheek. Would I never see Blake again? The thought broke me inside. He was the only reason I ever felt happy any more after having severed the mate bond with Luke.

I looked down at Charlie, remembering he had the key to the cell I was in. Okay, maybe I had been taken away from Blake for a good reason, but that didn't mean I had to just stay in this cell and await my fate. For all I knew, the alpha of the Bois Sombre Pack would come here next, and I wasn't sure that my alpha aura would work on him.

I quickly squatted over Charlie's corpse, digging my hand into his pocket, and I touched something that felt like a pen before pulling it out. A needle. I smelled it, and I instantly knew what it was. Tranquilizer. I was familiar with the smell as they had tried to treat my panic attacks with it in middle school after I started shifting into my wolf, to suppress it, so I wouldn't accidentally shift from my anxiety. But then I had to stop once we started training in our wolf forms. Clearly, Charlie had given me an extremely high dose, and that's what had caused me to pass out. It's possible he'd even reinjected me several times considering how long I'd been out.

I dug my hand back into his pocket and found what I'd originally been looking for. As soon as I clasped my hand around it, I pulled it out, a smile on my face. This had been almost too easy. I went to unlock my door only to find the chains around my arms were too thick, and they wouldn't fit through the bars of the door. I did everything I could to try to maneuver my hands, move my chains, getting into different angles, but it was useless. I was hopelessly stuck in this jail cell that they didn't even have the decency to put a bed inside.

I then recalled he had checked his cell phone, and I rummaged in his other pocket for it. I pulled it out, but it was locked, and I couldn't figure out how to make a phone call without unlocking it. There was no signal in the jail cell anyway. I walked the perimeter of it, hoping a bar would pop up, but it didn't. The phone may as well have been a brick. The only use it had to me was telling me the time. Just after two in the afternoon on a Thursday when I should have been with Blake in

Montreal, preparing to leave on our flight to Paris. Instead, I was stuck alone, in a windowless jail cell, hoping this wasn't my last day on earth.

Frustrated, I sat back down onto the concrete floor and began sobbing. I was alone, in jail, with only Charlie's headless body to keep me company, stuck waiting for someone else to come along and attempt to defile me.

Chapter 65

Talia

Alex and I arrived a mile outside the pack border at a quarter past two. As soon as we parked, Blake, Luke, and another man who looked to be in about his mid to late thirties slid into the back of our car.

"Adalwolf, you've met Alpha Antoine?" Blake introduced the man currently seated in the middle.

"We may have met briefly in the past. Alpha Alexander." Alex turned to face the man and shook his hand. "And this is my future luna, Talia." He gestured toward me.

I put out my hand to shake his. "Pleasure, Talia," he said in a French Canadian accent.

The sound of a text message receipt dinged, and Alpha Antoine pulled out his phone. After a moment, he spoke". "It's Alpha Édouard. He is asking where my sister Sofia is and says that we didn't meet our end up the deal. What deal is this?"

Blake groaned and replied, "We bluffed and said we would trade Sofia for Jasmine. With no intention to do so of course. We were hoping he would tell us where to meet for the trade. But he was too smart and said he'd tell us after we brought him Sofia."

"I see."

"Did he say what he planned to do to Jasmine?" Blake asked with desperation in his voice.

"No, he didn't. It's best not to imagine it."

I turned to look directly behind me at Blake who was clearly distraught, with his forehead creased and dark circles under his eyes. He normally looked so put together, but he couldn't hide his anxiety. I had seen how much he loved and cared for Jasmine when I stayed at the packhouse with him.

"We need to get her," Blake said, pained.

"His men all have guns with wolfsbane darts. Anyone crossing the border has no chance to get through alive," Luke said.

"Another text just came in," Alpha Antoine said, looking at his phone. A moment later, he looked up. "He says that if we try to attack his pack, he will instantly kill your mate."

"Fuck!" Blake cried out. "We need to think of a way to sneak in without him realizing."

"I know where his pack jail is located. Whoever sneaks in should try there first. That's the most logical place he'd be keeping her. Second is the packhouse."

"Let's think of a plan," Luke said.

"I'm pretty immune to wolfsbane. I think they can get about ten darts into me before I start feeling their effects. Adalwolf, you should be the same," Blake said, then turned to Alpha Antoine and explained, "We both built up a high tolerance in school."

At that moment, the intensity of the heat came on, arousing my body again, my thighs tingling and my mind penetrated with dirty thoughts, a desperate need to be filled by Alex. I was about to reach out for him, to feel his skin when I resisted, sitting onto my hands.

"Fuck!" Alex called out.

"What?" Blake leaned forward to look at Alex, and I noticed exactly where his eyes landed: on his lap. "Adalwolf, this is not exactly the most appropriate time to be getting a hard-on."

"I can't help it. I need to get out of the car." Alex threw the door open and stepped out, closing it behind him.

"I'm in heat," I practically whispered.

"Oh, shit," Blake said.

"I'm in heat!" I said more enthusiastically, an idea coming to me. "Blake, you said most men have a hard time resisting heat, right?"

"Unmated men, yes," Blake replied.

"You need a distraction, right?"

"Talia, you're a genius!" Blake exclaimed. "Did I ever tell you that you're my favorite sister?"

"I'm your only sister."

"Most likely not true, but definitely my favorite." Blake smiled. "Come on, guys, get out of the car! We have a plan!"

We all stepped out, and Blake had a huge smile on his face. "I just mindlinked my warriors. They're pulling up now," Alex said, clenching his fists. Then he looked at me and said, "Talia, get back in the car."

"No, we need her!" Blake said. "Luke, get our warriors to find a good place for us to penetrate."

"On it!" Luke said, sprinting away.

"What do you mean you need her?" Alex's faced reddened and he widened his stance, as if he were ready for a fight.

"I'm going to help!" I chimed in, wrapping my arms around Alex, my mind suddenly wandering to how nice his body felt against mine and the way his erection was throbbing against the front of me, only making me more aroused.

He groaned, clearly desiring the same thing I was at that moment, my heat making it difficult to concentrate on anything else. "What are you going to help with?" he asked, practically moaning.

"I'm going to distract the border guards with my heat."

"What!" he bellowed. "Whose idea was that?"

"Mine!" I replied.

"Fuck no! Wulfric, I am not involving Talia in this. She has close to zero training. She's practically human for Goddess's sake!" Alex shouted.

"I'm not human!" I retorted.

"We'll have our men on standby watching her, making sure nothing happens to her," Blake replied. "Do you have a better idea?"

"No. But we can think of something else that doesn't involve my mate. I know you're desperate to get yours back, but I'm not sacrificing mine. Sorry, my friendship only extends so far. *Druzhba druzhbai, a tabachok—vroz.*"

"What does that mean?" I asked.

Blake glared at Alex and replied, "It's a Russian proverb that essentially means we're friends, but not close enough to spare me some tobacco. Or, in this case, his mate."

"You wouldn't give me my mate either when you had her. And like you said, she's not just some object we pass around, and you get to use as some pawn to get your own mate back."

"If we attack, Alpha Édouard already threatened to kill Jasmine instantly. We need to find a way to get in without risking anyone's life, and this is perfect. The unmated warriors will be so distracted by Talia's heat that you and I can sneak in. As soon as we're in, Talia can run out in her wolf form, and we'll have my best men looking after her, making sure nothing happens to her."

"Nope. Wulfric, I'm willing to help, but not if my mate is involved."

"How does Talia feel? You just said she's not an object that gets passed around." Blake looked at me meaningfully.

"Alex, I want to help!" I responded, looking him in his eyes. "Blake and everyone else have helped me so much while I was down and out and so concentrated on my own problems. It's my turn to return the favor."

"Great, it's settled then." Blake clapped his hands together.

"No, I don't agree." Alex started to pull me toward his car.

"Stop, Alex! Let me do this, please. Blake would never let me get hurt. Right, Blake?" I looked toward Blake.

"Of course not. You're my sister. We're going to have all of my best mated warriors watching you and ready to intervene if necessary. But, trust me, the Bois Sombre warriors on patrol are not going to be thinking with their big heads anyway. Just look at Tyce." Blake smirked, gesturing at Jasmine's cousin who was currently clenching his fists, standing a few feet away, watching us.

"Wulfric, if anything happens to my mate, I just want you to know that I will behead you without hesitation." Alex scowled at Blake.

"Relax, Adalwolf. Nothing is going to happen. I'm going to gather all my best warriors to go with my beta to keep watch. And then you and I will sneak over the border."

"Why me?"

"Because we're the only two people I know who have a high tolerance to wolfsbane. So if we get shot, we're the most likely to survive."

"You know, you owe me big time for this."

"I know, and I will return whatever favor you ask of me. I promise," Blake said sincerely. "I'm a man of my word, and I take my relationships very seriously."

Alex shook his head and said, "I have to be fucking crazy to be going along with this."

Chapter 66

Talia

I was so horny, it was practically painful. I was ready to fuck the first dick that came along. Okay, not really, but every part of my body was hot and aroused. My nipples were erect, sensitive against the fabric of my bra as it brushed against them. My thighs were practically like jelly, tingling and desperate for someone to glide against them. And I could feel how swollen I was between my legs. Every thought consisted of Alex's muscular, naked body, and what I wanted him to be doing with it at that moment. I couldn't even concentrate on what I was actually supposed to be doing.

"I feel like I'm now Blake's official heat babysitter." Jack sighed.

"What does that mean?" Kyle asked, tilting his head at him.

He smirked and said, "Better that I keep my mouth shut."

"Goddess, I remember when Emma used to go into heat. She was like an animal." Kyle chuckled. "We were both living at home at the time, so we actually snuck into the high school one night and had sex on the gym mats. It was almost too easy to sneak in, and it may have happened more than once."

"Remind me to get better locks put onto the high school." Luke laughed. "And to make sure we have good cleaning standards for the gym area specifically."

"Poor high school kids. What will they do now that they won't have access to the excellent facilities our school has to offer?" Kyle responded.

"Do it in the back of their car or in the woods like everyone else." Jack snickered.

"Or wait until the parents are out," Luke added.

"Not so easy when there are seven people who live in your house!" Kyle rebuked.

"Just be very quiet. Just kidding." Jack smiled slyly.

"Dude, we shared a bedroom!" Kyle shook his head.

"Hey, guys, Blake just mindlinked me," Luke cut into the conversation. "He's giving us the go-ahead to send Talia in."

"Let's just hope none of these unmated guys are gay," Jack said.

"There are like fifty of us here ready to run in, so hopefully nothing bad will happen if it comes down to it," Luke said, glancing at us from the binoculars he was holding. I looked around at all of the warriors Blake, Alex, and Tyce had gathered together. Most of them were scattered behind trees and hidden. I was standing with Jack, Kyle, and Luke. Luke looked at me and nodded. I returned the nod and stripped myself naked, then shifted into my wolf form and ran down the hill we were on.

I approached the four warriors who all were stationed with large guns in their hands, ready to shoot wolfsbane darts. As soon as I approached, I noticed a change in their composure. Their pupils dilated as they stared at me, and I shifted into my human form, standing completely naked in front of them.

Something about that change brought a new feeling to me. After so many years of my body being sexualized by men, making me feel only as useful as the pleasure I could provide them—being poked and prodded against my will as an adolescent—I now suddenly felt powerful. These trained warriors were ready to shoot whomever came near their pack's border, and yet they were suddenly helpless against my heat, forgetting their duties instantly. For once, I saw my body not as a vulnerability but as a weapon.

The four border patrol warriors began speaking French to one another. While I wasn't sure what they were saying, the way they gestured, it was clear they were talking about me.

"Hey, beautiful!" one of them finally called out to me, winking.

I let out a deep breath and came closer. They were clearly not thinking with their big heads, just as Blake predicted. I could see by the bulges in their pants that they were all aroused. I smiled to myself in the knowledge that I was now *their* weakness.

I approached one of them and put my hand on his bicep, running it up and down his arm. He seemed powerless to stop me as he stared, looking pained. They all got closer to me, drawn in by my heat.

"Bonjour, hi," one of the others said to me.

"*Oh, bonjour, sexy*," I said, trying to sound as seductive as possible. "Those are some big guns you all have. And I don't mean the dart guns." I flirted, winking, touching the arm of the man who greeted me. He instantly put his gun down and brought his arm to my shoulder, brushing it down my own arm. Damn, that actually felt really nice. I was so horny that anyone touching my skin felt so good. But I did my best to concentrate on the task at hand and not get carried away. I just had to keep them distracted long enough for Blake and Alex to sneak by us.

"Where are you from?" one of them asked in a French Canadian accent.

"I'm from your dreams," I replied, almost laughing to myself at how corny that was.

They all snickered.

"*T'es ben chix*," the same man said, staring me up and down.

Even with my limited French knowledge, I knew he was telling me that I was hot, this being quite commonly heard where I grew up. I couldn't believe how well the plan was working. They were all completely focused on me, not paying attention to their surroundings at all.

"What do you like to do for fun?"

"*J'aime baiser,*" I replied, using another French phrase I'd learned living in the brothel.

They all moaned simultaneously, clearly delighted with my answer as I told them I liked to fuck in French.

"*Franchement?*" the man asked. "*En ce moment?*"

I knew he was ready to take me up on my offer, and I wondered if maybe I'd taken things too far.

"We can go into the woods," he said, smiling suggestively at me.

Shit! Maybe I had gotten myself into a really bad position. I suddenly wanted to flee, but I knew I had to wait for Blake to tell me to do so. I didn't want there to be a chance of them noticing my mate and brother and hurting either one of them. While Blake had said he and Alex had high tolerances to wolfsbane, I was sure there was a limit to how many hits their bodies could take before they succumbed to it like Alex's father had.

Desperate to keep them safe, I came up with an idea to keep the men distracted. "All of you, take your pants off and I'll decide which one I like best." I smiled at my cleverness.

They instantly put their guns down and began pulling down their pants. Damn, I couldn't believe the power I had and how eager they were. All of them were very hard and throbbing. I couldn't lie—I was now over the edge, very horny myself, but I kept my head in the game, acting as if I was inspecting them. Even with how cold it was, they stayed nice and erect.

"*Talia, leave!*" Blake finally mindlinked me. I was about to shift into my wolf when one of the men grabbed me, pulling me against his body.

Shit, this wasn't part of the plan. What am I going to do?

"No!" I yelled loudly, frantic, trying to get away from him. And he froze. Completely froze. "Everyone, stop!" I yelled again with the same passion, and they all couldn't move.

That's right!

Alex had told me someone with alpha blood could do that. I was delighted with my power as I was able to pull away from them and shift into my wolf, sprinting back into the woods from where I came.

As soon as I got close to the hill I'd been atop earlier, Luke mindlinked me to say, *"Talia, keep running. They're following your scent."*

I did as he said and sprinted past the hill deeper into the woods. I suddenly heard growls and howling behind me. Moments later, another mindlink from Luke came through and he said, *"Okay you can turn around now. We caught them."*

I sprinted back to where everyone was congregated. I quickly shifted back into my human form and threw my clothes that Luke had brought for me back on. They had the four men hostage, knocked out, and chained up.

"Nice job, Talia!" Luke hugged me. "That worked out better than expected!"

"Are you going to kill them?" I asked.

"No, we have to keep them alive or Alpha Édouard will feel that they died and know something is up. We've just knocked them out for now."

Chapter 67

Jasmine

Not even an hour after I killed Charlie, a man in either his later thirties or early forties with the sleeves of his shirt rolled up, tattoos covering his forearms, approached my cell. His distinct gray eyes scanned the entirety of the small room I was in. I could instantly sense this man was evil, a shiver traveling up my spine. My instincts were in full overdrive, my inner wolf howling with fear. I stood up, panicked.

"Hmm, not such a weak mate, I see." The man spoke with a French accent, scanning the room, smiling evilly at me. I stared at him, wondering what he was planning to do to me. After some time, he said, "I can't decide if I should cut you up or fuck you. Why not both?" He pulled out a switchblade, exposing the knife to me.

I began hyperventilating and the world was spinning around me as fur sprouted up my arms and legs. I was having a panic attack. As my body tried to force me to shift, agonizing pain shot up my arms. I cried in agony from the metal cutting into my skin, blood now dripping down my arms and hands.

"Yes, go ahead, cry. Only turns me on more." He smirked in a mocking way, opened the door to the cell, let himself in, and locked it behind him, same as Charlie had.

"Stop!" I cried out, using my alpha aura. But it was useless against him. He must have either been the alpha or someone else with alpha blood. To my dismay, he walked closer, taking his time. My heart pounded in my chest and my breathing shallowed with each painful step. Not knowing what else to do, and out of desperation, I clenched my fists and, with all the arm and core strength I could muster, I tried to swing my arm against his head as I did to Charlie. Clearly practiced at evading attacks all his life, he easily dodged and then grabbed one of the loose chains, pulling me toward him. Almost instantly, he yanked me upward so my feet were no longer touching the ground and then just as quickly shoved me down, my body crashing forcefully against the cement floor. I cried out in pain from the impact, my body instinctively curling for comfort.

I wasn't able to move too much as he promptly shoved me onto my back and pushed my chained hands over my head, holding them down with one of his hands as I struggled to get him to let go. I tried to kick him but he sat down on my legs, the full weight of his body practically crushing them.

"*Belle robe*," he mocked.

Even with my limited French knowledge from school, I knew that meant *beautiful dress*. I stared up at him.

He laughed and said in English, "It would look better off."

My whole body was convulsing with primal fear, my lips trembling, with the knowledge that it was probably over for me.

He put the blade he had in his other hand close to my face, taunting me, laughing like a maniac. Before I could even wonder what he had planned, he shoved his blade deep into my chest, ripping through my flesh and scraping against my rib cage. Before I could even process the sharp, agonizing, raw pain of metal slicing through me, he swiftly cut down my body, tearing my dress with his blade simultaneously. I cried out in excruciating pain, certain I would pass out from the torture of having my organs split, one of my lungs collapsing. He kept cutting down the entirety of my body until my dress was torn in half. I struggled and screamed, but it was useless. I was even weaker now that he had cut into my body. I sobbed uncontrollably as he used the tip of his blade to move the fabric of my dress, so I was completely exposed to him.

"*Petite*," he said, gawking at my chest. "Like a wall."

It was excruciating even to cry, my lung and stomach bubbling with blood as I did. My skin was soaked, and I could feel the wetness gathering onto the floor. He took the blade of his knife and first cut the sleeves of my dress and then the straps of my G-string with quick ease. I was now completely naked and helpless. I had avoided this with Charlie, but it seemed I couldn't escape my fate. He smirked at me.

Just as I closed my eyes to try to pretend I wasn't there anymore, knuckles cracked against my skull. I opened my eyes immediately to his fist speeding toward me. My eyes instinctively shut again. He continued to punch me across the face several times. I took the blows, waiting for him to finally stop. He must have punched me at least twenty times before he did. I was sure my whole face was bruised and swollen, as if I had been in a boxing match. I could taste the blood from my broken nose and split lip. When he finally ceased, he let go of my chained hands. I stayed still and opened my swollen eyes very slightly, so I was looking through my eyelashes. He must have thought I passed out. Why else would he be letting me go now?

He got up off me, and I continued to lie as still as possible and watched as he unbuckled his belt and undid his pants. I realized with horror that he was planning to rape me while I was unconscious. I was weak, very weak. But I was also a fighter. He'd already messed me up. What did I have to lose now? Quickly coming up with an idea, I waited until he was fully exposed, his substantial erection stiff and angry. He used his foot to push my legs apart. Then, just as he was kneeling down in position, I used the opportunity to get a good kick at his nuts and instantly sat up, ready to take advantage of his weakness.

He growled, and my stomach dropped. He hadn't cowered in pain. It didn't work like I was hoping. And he was clearly pissed now, his face red and nostrils flared. In seconds, he grabbed me, throwing me back onto the ground, knocking the wind out of me, and a sharp pain overtook my body from the impact to my open, bloody wound. *Fuck!*

"I love pain, *guidoune*." He moved between my legs and grasped my hips, tightening his hold and digging his fingers into me. I squeezed my eyes shut, tears freely falling from them. It was clearly over and there was nothing I could do about it. And then my heel touched something. I quickly glanced down to see the needle from Charlie's pocket was lying right next to my foot.

I wriggled my whole body, acting as if I were trying to get out of his hold, so it wouldn't be obvious what I was doing.

He laughed. "I love eating them alive and squirming. Makes my dick hard." He got closer, his mouth close to my ear. "Squirm, *guidoune*, squirm."

I made a show of being terrified as I grasped my toes around the needle and pulled my knees upward. I had it so close to his leg. I just had to angle it right. I pushed it down between my toes to get it to stick upright. *Yes!*

His eyes scanned my body. "Bloody. Sexy. And my dick is getting hard again." As he was busy repositioning himself to finally penetrate me, I used my leg to get a good shove of the needle into him. And then I prayed there was enough in there to knock him out. There had to be, right? Charlie had me knocked out for hours.

"*Mais pourquoi diable me fait ça?*" he bellowed. With my limited French, I had no idea what he said, but he was clearly pissed as he picked me up and flung me across the room, throwing me against the wall. I cried as the impact crushed my bones against concrete. Blood gushed out of my middle as the wound tore further. My pulse raced, and a dizziness came over me. I watched in terror while he pulled the needle out of his leg, smelling it.

He laughed again, a malicious smile on his face.

Fuck, it's really over isn't it?

He crawled toward me, evilly laughing. I cowered, tears freely flowing down my cheeks. He was going to rape and possibly kill me, and I was out of ideas and strength. I'd have to just give in.

And then—a miracle. He dropped to his hands. I blinked, wondering if that had really just happened. And then, I realized, yes, it did happen. He fell over, his body colliding with the floor. It worked! Adrenaline pumping through my body, I quickly gathered myself and got up onto my knees. Not wasting any time, I crawled over to him. I pulled my arm back in an overhead triceps extension and swung my chained wrists down on his head, crashing the heavy metal against his skull. I got a good two swings in when—

"Holy fuck! Jasmine?" I looked up and came face-to-face with Blake and Alex both staring at me. I quickly stopped what I was doing, attempting to cover my naked, bloody body, not that modesty was exactly the most important thing at that moment. Alex turned around to give me privacy, and Blake kept staring at me.

"Blake!" I cried tears of relief at seeing him.

"What did he do to you, Jasmine?" Tears were streaming down his face. I'd never seen him cry before and realized how terrible I must look for him to finally do so now. I was sure my face was bloodied and bruised from the beating I'd taken, and I knew blood was covering my body from the deep gash.

I swiftly located the key Charlie had left and then crawled over to hand it to Blake. He quickly opened the door and ran to me, pulling me against his body. "I killed Charlie," I sobbed. "And I think I killed him too."

"Alpha Édouard," Blake said, an evil glint in his eyes. "Holy fuck, that's the alpha. You just killed the alpha! And if you didn't, I'm going to finish him off now." Blake got up and stripped himself of all his clothes. He shifted into his wolf form and shoved his claws into the alpha's body, pulled out his heart, and smashed it onto the floor. He shifted back into his human form, a huge smile on his face. "Adalwolf, can you find the keys to the chains around Jasmine's hands?" he called out.

Alex disappeared, and Blake looked me up and down. "What the fuck did he do to you, Jasmine?" he asked with concern.

I sobbed uncontrollably as he wrapped his arms around me. I kept him far enough away so he wouldn't touch the cut on the front of my body, which stung any time it was touched.

"I found a few different keys. Try these," Alex said, staying turned with his back to us, presenting the keys to us with his hand outstretched. Blake swiftly grabbed them from him and began trying all of them on my chains. "They're not working!" he called out. Alex disappeared again.

He came back moments later and said, "Here, try this." Blake took the key and shoved it into the lock of my chains, it instantly clicking into place and the chains unlocking, falling from my hands. I sighed in relief, overcome with happiness to be able to move my arms freely again.

"Jasmine, lie down on my coat," Blake gently commanded, spreading his coat out on the ground. I looked at him, confused. His eyes locked with mine as he lifted his head, and I could see that he needed me to do this for some reason, so I didn't question it.

As I lay on my back, he shifted back into his wolf form and brought his muzzle to my wound. Then, very gently, he brushed his tongue against it. I thought the saliva would sting, but instead it soothed my torso as he slid it up the length of it, from my lower stomach to the top of my chest, lapping the blood from my body and sealing the wound.

"*You* are *my second-chance mate. It worked,*" Blake mindlinked me as he nuzzled his head against me, licking my cheeks. I had heard that mates could heal each other in this way, but I'd never thought it would work with Blake and me, at least not until we marked each other. I brought my hands to his head, rubbing him behind the ears as he made quiet whimpering noises.

Blake then shifted back, quickly grabbed the clothes he had stripped off, and threw his T-shirt over me as I got up. He handed me his boxer briefs, and I quickly stood up and pulled them up my legs, folding them over so the elastic band wouldn't touch my cut, which was no longer hanging open and hemorrhaging but still stung when touched. He pulled the rest of his clothes on himself and threw his coat over me.

"We're decent," he said to Alex who was still facing the other way.

Alex turned around and looked at the scene before him. "What the fuck happened?" Alex asked me, his eyes wide.

"And you said you're not luna material." Blake lightly punched my arm, shaking his head. "You didn't even need us to rescue you. It looks like you had it handled yourself."

Overcome with emotion, I fell against his chest, sobbing, so happy and relieved to be back with him, wondering why I ever doubted our future together.

"Come on, let's go. We have a honeymoon to go on." Blake put his arm around me and led me out of the jail.

"I've mindlinked my warriors. They've spread the word, and they're all ready to help us get back over the border. Shouldn't be hard now that this pack doesn't even have an alpha anymore," Alex said to Blake.

"Should have killed him years ago, but better late than never. And, of course, it's my Mrs. Alpha that's the one to do it." Blake beamed, kissing me on the head. He turned to Alex and, pride in his voice, said, "I told you my mate was a fighter."

Chapter 68

Talia

After I completed my portion of the mission, I went back into Alex's car, and Jack and Kyle followed me inside while some of Alex's men stood guard outside of it. I couldn't lie, my heat was unbearable. The longer I went without petting my cat, the more painful it became. Tears were brimming my eyes as I squirmed in my seat.

"Blake owes me big time," Jack said from the back.

"Goddess, this is awkward," Kyle replied.

"I can't help it," I cried out. "Can't you just go outside?"

"Can't, we have two alphas on our asses now," Kyle replied. I whimpered in response. I glanced in the rearview mirror as he turned to Jack and said, "I mean, maybe we should, Jack. Let her have some privacy."

"The last thing we need is to give her some privacy and then someone from Bois Sombre sweeps in when none of us are looking. Bad idea, Kyle."

"Just a thought, bro." He frowned.

"Consider yourself lucky. I had to go through over four hours of this before."

I grumbled, reminded of the last time, perturbed that they kept bringing it up.

I felt Jack's big hand squeeze my shoulder and he said, "Hey, it's not your fault. It's just really awkward, that's all. But hey, it's a story. We'll all look back and laugh at it one day."

I didn't feel like laughing at that moment, but I appreciated the sentiment.

"A pretty fucking awesome story at that!" Kyle added. "Distracting those guys with your heat—that was ingenious!"

"Total future luna." Jack beamed at me. I began to relax more, put at ease by their words.

"I just got a mindlink from Blake." Jack shot up. "They're heading back, ready to cross back over the border."

"Alex too?" I asked, desperate to see him and be with him, and to see that he was okay. Although it was hard to focus on anything past my heat, a nagging feeling of worry kept coming to the surface.

"Yep, Alex too," Jack said. I slunk back into my seat, forcing myself to hold on just a little bit longer. We all sat in silence and waited. Far too much time passed until I finally saw the sexiest goddamn man I'd ever seen in my life strutting toward the car—God, I loved that strut! He brushed his hand through his dirty-blond hair and then looked through the windshield of the car, locking eyes with me, a huge smile on his face. Jack and Kyle instantly exited the back seat, sprinting away. The warriors who were surrounding the car soon did the same.

Alex approached the car and I swung my door open, jumping into his arms.

"Hello, beautiful," he said just as our mouths collided. I pushed my tongue into his mouth, desperate to taste him, and he pushed me up against the car, his erection straining against his pants, pressed up against my crotch.

"Fuck, your heat is strong," he exclaimed. "I have to have you right now." Keeping me held in one of his muscular arms, he flung open the back door of the car and threw me onto the back seat, instantly ripping my pants and underwear off my legs. As he threw off his coat and undid his belt, I pulled off my own shirt and bra. I was completely soaked with arousal, certain the back of his car would need a full detail once we were through, my whole body shivering with desperate need.

I stared up at him as he hauled his shirt off, threw it to the ground, clearly not caring where it landed, and revealed his hot-as-hell shoulders, pecs, and abs. I barely had a chance to appreciate his amazing, Greek god-like body when he climbed on top of me, his left knee on the seat and right foot on the floor of the car. He forcefully pulled me toward him, grasping my hips tightly and bringing them to his own as I wrapped my legs around him.

Again, there was no need for foreplay. We were both desperate to get to the main event, both throbbing with desire, an animalistic need taking over us. He instantly had his cock inside me, vigorously thrusting in and out of me.

"Goddess, I fucking love you," he cried out, his face appearing both devilish and angelic simultaneously.

"I love you too," I replied, tears falling from my eyes.

He stopped suddenly and stared at me, our eyes locking for a moment, his mouth agape. "Wait, really?" he asked.

"Yeah." I nodded, smiling blissfully, realizing how true it was. "I love you." When he didn't continue, I said, "But, for the love of God, please don't stop fucking me."

He laughed heartily and pushed himself forcefully back inside me. But something shifted, and he changed his position, lowering himself down on top of me until our bodies were touching, weaving his hand into my hair, kissing me. The act felt so intimate that something else surprising left my lips.

"Mark me," I whispered into his ear. I wasn't sure if it was the heat or if I would have asked him to do it otherwise, but it felt right in that moment. Both our lives had just been in danger, and it only brought us closer together, allowing me to finally completely let go and be vulnerable with him—trust him fully, trust my wolf fully that she was leading me down the right path.

We stayed like that in the back seat for a long time, neither of us wanting the moment to end. Our noses brushed against each other, and our lips connected, as he nibbled gently on mine, and I pushed my fingernails into his back, wanting to have all of him. But it felt too good, and he knew how to position himself to hit exactly the right spot, and I soon found myself in the place of no return, my whole body on fire, shaking, my insides pulsing. Bliss spread from the center of my body to all of my limbs as Alex let out a guttural groan in my ear.

A trance came over me as my canines grew, tingling as they pushed out of my gums. I embraced the feeling. He looked at me and seemed to hesitate for a split second, searching my eyes. I nodded, silently coaxing him forward. He sighed and brought his teeth to where my neck met my collarbone, piercing them into me. A tear escaped my eye from the initial sharp pain, but then it just as quickly switched to pleasure as a second orgasm overtook my body. When the feeling passed, he withdrew his teeth and passed his tongue over the cut, soothing the mark.

I didn't even have to think as instinct took over, and I knew exactly what to do as if this were the most natural thing in the world. I found the same spot on his neck and pushed my canines into it, his blood entering my mouth. I pierced farther into him and a new sensation emerged, as if part of his soul were leaving through the cuts I'd created and entering into me through my canines. It was similar to the feeling I'd had when I joined Blake's pack but stronger and much more intimate. When it finally passed, I withdrew my teeth, panting as they retreated back into my gums. I quickly licked his wound same as he had done to me.

We both sat up slowly, and he pulled me toward his body, held me tightly against him, and brushed his hand through my hair. Everything I'd felt previously with Alex was now magnified. As he touched me, the sparks were that much more soothing, his scent that much sweeter. I no longer only sensed his emotions. They were a part of me. I relaxed into him as his bliss became my own.

"*Welcome to the pack, Luna Talia,*" Alex mindlinked me. I looked up at him in surprise. He smiled and continued, "*You should be able to mindlink in your human form too now that you're my luna.*"

"How?" I asked out loud.

"*Just concentrate on making a connection in your mind with me. You should feel it snap in place, and then you'll be able to do it.*"

I followed his instructions, and then I felt exactly what he'd describe as my mind connected with his. "*Does this work?*" I mindlinked him.

"*You did it!*" he mindlinked me back, throwing his arms around me and giving me a big kiss on my cheek.

"Wow, this is so cool!" I replied out loud, delighted that Alex and I could secretly communicate and no one would hear.

"You're very cool," Alex kissed my head. "What you did today was amazing. You risked your life to help Blake and Jasmine. I'm so proud to have such an amazing mate."

"I have a really amazing mate too," I replied.

Chapter 69

Jasmine

"All set, our flight's been rebooked for tomorrow night." Blake smiled as he plopped down on the hotel room bed—the one we were supposed to have slept in the previous night until, well, things didn't exactly go as planned. He stared into my eyes. "Your face is looking much better now. My only regret is that I didn't get a chance to torture that motherfucker for what he did to you."

"It's okay. It's over now," I whispered to Blake, wanting to forget what happened.

"You were amazing today, a true luna." He brushed his hand through my hair. "I can't believe you ever even doubted yourself."

I sighed. "I've actually realized a lot of things in the past week," I replied.

"Really? Like what?"

"Like I'm excited that I'll be able to use my influence as luna to make changes in the pack."

"What kind of changes?"

"Like Tyler and Jack took me to a secret pack LGBTQ+ meeting. And everyone came up with great ideas for how they could feel more welcomed in our pack. I want to help them. I want to help make those changes, so they don't have to live in secret anymore and reject their mates."

Blake beamed at me. "You'll be so great, and I'll help you however you need me to. We're a team now."

"I'm so glad you didn't listen to me when I told you I wasn't luna material and you shouldn't be with me."

"You'd have to work a lot harder than that to get rid of me. Even having a fated mate didn't keep me away." He chuckled softly, and then his expression turned more serious. "Let me see your cut." He'd been asking every hour, checking to make sure it was healing. I lifted my nightgown, and he pushed it up higher, giving him a full view of my breasts. "Does it still hurt?" he asked.

"No," I replied, sighing with relief.

"Thank Artemis. It looks much better—just a pink line now." He brought his face to my chest where the cut started, and planted soft kisses along it, traveling the length of the wound down between my breasts and kissing his way farther down my torso.

"I love you, Blake," I said, practically moaning from how nice his kisses felt. He kissed his way back up my body and pulled my nightgown completely off. He brushed the back of his hand gently down the length of the almost-healed cut and lowered his head back down to my body, kissing softly down my chest again. He made his way to my left breast, sucking it gently, tracing his tongue around it. I moaned in response, my body tingling with arousal. He kissed across to my other nipple, doing the same thing, bringing his hand to the first one, and using his thumb to rub it. I arched my back in response, losing myself in how good it felt, my whole body alive with longing.

Blake pulled his shirt off, and an almost electric feeling traveled up and down my body as I took in his strong, brawny frame. My eyes traced every muscular ripple, feeling so lucky to have him and to be able to call him mine. I brought my hands to his torso, running my fingers along the ridges of his abdominal muscles, tracing my hands down to the V-cuts on his lower body, and bringing my hands to the sweatpants slung low on his hips, easing them off. He finished the job, pulling them off completely, and his erection sprung free.

He then lowered himself onto his forearms and kissed me. I wove my hands into his hair and onto his neck, wrapping my legs around his hips. We rolled until we were both on our sides, and he pulled me against him, deepening the kiss. Our tongues intertwined with each other. We were unable to bring ourselves to separate, feeling more grateful for each other than we ever had. We must have lain there just kissing, enjoying the feeling of our lips and mouths connecting, for at least ten minutes, nibbling on each other's lips, our bodies rubbing against each other'.

Finally, Blake rolled me onto my back and asked, "Do you still want it slow?"

I nodded in response.

He smirked and kissed his way slowly to my ear, nibbling gently on it from top to bottom, then he kissed across my chin and down my neck, taking his time, lingering on every part his lips touched. He then kissed my shoulders and down each arm, very slowly.

"Okay, you can speed it up," I said, wanting him to get to the good part.

"You said slow though." He chuckled.

"Not that slow!" I replied.

"I know what you really want." He gave me a mischievous look, his eyes glistening.

"Oh really, what's that?"

"The alpha treatment."

"What's the alpha treatment?" Before I knew what was happening, he was pulling off my panties and placing his head between my legs After some quick kisses on my inner thighs, he had his mouth on my clit. I cried out as he did everything that I liked, tracing his tongue around it, then flicking it back and forth. He pushed his fingers inside me and continued what he was doing, bringing me to the edge of orgasm. I was shaking, on the edge of release, when he abruptly pulled away.

I stared at him as he went right back to kissing my body, kissing my left hip bone, and then kissing his way across my body to the other, kissing slowly down my pelvic bone. He looked up at me where I was glaring at him.

"What, that's not what you wanted?" he asked innocently.

"You know what you did," I responded.

"Alpha treatment again?" He laughed and went right back to where he left off, doing the same thing again until I was close to orgasm, and he pulled away again just as I was on the edge of letting go.

"Why do you keep doing that?" I asked.

"Doing what?"

"You know what!"

"Doing this?" He did it again, bringing his mouth to my clit, flicking his tongue against it until my body was convulsing, about to orgasm, and pulling away.

"You are torturing me!" I cried out.

"It is my expertise," he deadpanned, a glint in his eyes.

"I'm about to take matters into my own hands!" I said, exasperated.

"Now that is something I'd love to watch." Blake smiled staring down at me. I huffed and he laughed, pulling me against his body. "I love you, Mrs. Alpha," he said sweetly, kissing me gently. He then pulled a condom off the nightstand and rolled it onto himself. "Now it's time for the luna treatment," he said, kissing me again and positioning himself between my legs. We looked into each other's eyes as he hovered over me on his forearms. "I'd like to mark you tonight. Would that be okay?" he asked.

I nodded, a fluttering in my stomach.

He brought his lips back onto mine as he pushed his erection inside me, gently thrusting as we kissed each other. I moaned against his mouth as he sped up the movement, and his hips brushed against my inner thighs. My hands found their way to his back, and my hips lifted, syncing with his as we pushed and pulled against each other, our bodies as one.

As he sped up his movement, thrusting harder, he brought his fingers to my clit, rubbing them gently against it. I lost myself in the feeling, the whole lower half of my body heated, and my inner thighs and stomach were tingling, bliss building between my legs. As he thrust harder and rubbed more vigorously, my whole body began shaking beneath him, my legs trembling, until it all released in an intense orgasm that radiated up and down my entire body. He groaned as he also came before collapsing on top of me. My canines expanded, and before I even moved, I felt his hot breath on my neck and then his teeth piercing my skin just above my collarbone. It was a sharp pain at first, provoking a yelp in reaction, but that quickly turned into pleasure, and bliss spread across my body again, as if I were experiencing a second orgasm.

Once he pulled his teeth out of my neck, he quickly licked the wound, his warm saliva soothing the broken skin. I did the same thing, pushing my own canines into his skin, tasting his blood on my tongue as my sharp teeth pushed through the muscle, deep into him. Blake's life force flowed into me through my teeth, a warm feeling in my gums. Once the feeling passed, I pulled my teeth out of his neck and licked his cuts, feeling them seal as my tongue brushed against them.

As soon as I finished, Blake smiled at me from above, his piercing blue eyes so intense, as if they were staring into my soul. I returned his smile, the moment so special and intimate as Blake's body heat surrounded me, my body cocooned safely between his strong arms.

"Do you feel that?" Blake asked, brushing his hand up and down my arm.

"The sparks!" I exclaimed.

"I didn't think I'd ever feel them again." His eyes filled with emotion. He lay down and pulled me against his body, kissing me where he had just marked me. "It feels just as amazing as I remembered." And then I realized something. I could feel all of Blake's emotions. Not like I had with Luke, where it had been a sense of the emotion. No, I could feel them running alongside my own—both the happiness that he currently felt and a deep depression that hovered over him like a dark cloud.

"Blake," I whispered.

"Yes?" he asked, smiling at me.

"Do you always feel that?" I touched his chest over his heart. He nodded at me sadly. I kissed him on his forehead, overcome with emotion.

"I should get cleaned up," he said, sliding out of the bed. I rolled onto my back, feeling empathy for Blake. And then, another realization came to me. I no longer felt my own depression. The curse of the rejection was finally gone. I quickly thought about Luke and was relieved it no longer brought me a piercing in my chest. I smiled happily that marking each other had worked.

"What are you so happy about?" Blake grinned at me, climbing back into the bed, and snuggling me against him.

"I'm just so happy we finally marked each other," I said.

"Me too," he replied. "Now get some rest because tomorrow is day one of our honeymoon, and you're going to need a lot of stamina to keep up with what I have planned. I bought us a copy of the *Kama Sutra*, and I won't consider it a successful honeymoon unless we try every position at least once."

I laughed and snuggled into him. "What about seeing Paris?"

"Our hotel room has a view of the Eiffel tower."

"Shouldn't we experience some of the French culture?"

"How about I buy a copy of the *Kama Sutra* in French once we get there? Would that work?"

I slapped his shoulder gently. "Such a one-track mind."

"Oh please, you love it! Or as the French say it, *tu l'aimes*."

Chapter 70

Talia

"Good morning, beautiful." Alex placed a mug of coffee onto the bedside table early one morning and then instantly slid into the bed next to me. The connection between us was much stronger now that we had marked each other. It was almost as if we had become one, our emotions connected when we were near each other, his running beside my own. At that moment, Alex felt both content and worried. I was sure that the worry was for his mother.

"Is your mom okay today?" I asked, brushing my hand through his hair.

"She seems okay today. I brought her her morning tea and toast, and she seemed happy with the small gesture."

"You're such a good son." I kissed him on the forehead. He grabbed me, pulling me tight against his body, kissing me deeply.

"Ow!" I pulled away.

"What's wrong?" he asked, furrowing his brows.

"My boobs are just really sore." I rubbed one of them.

"Does that happen often?" he asked.

"No, not really. Sometimes when I get my period, but I don't know, they hurt more than usual."

"Maybe it's the mate bond taking effect." He chuckled. "Hormones for me taking over your body, making your boobs desire my touch more."

"Yeah, sure," I said playfully, grabbing for the coffee mug. As soon as I brought it to my mouth I almost gagged at the smell. I threw it onto the nightstand, coffee splashing everywhere, and sprinted to the toilet, barely making it in time to vomit what was left in my stomach from the previous night.

"Talia, are you okay?" Alex came rushing in behind me, pulling back my hair.

"What did you put in that coffee?" I asked, falling back onto my legs.

"I didn't put anything in it. I made it black, just the way you like it, same as always."

"It didn't smell right," I replied.

"Hmm, I'll check the expiration date." He put his hand out and helped me up.

I sniffed. "Ugh, this washroom smells awful. I need to clean it."

"Didn't you just clean it the other day?" he asked, looking at me funny.

"It definitely needs to be cleaned. I'm about to throw up again from how strong it smells." I wrinkled my nose, pulling open the washroom cabinet door to get some bleach.

Alex sniffed loudly and said, "It doesn't smell any different than usual. Are you sure you're not just smelling things?"

"No, it's awful!" I replied.

"Cleaning so early in the morning?" Alex's mom was at the door of our washroom, peeking in as I was pouring bleach into the toilet bowl and getting the cleaning brush out.

"Mom, what are you doing in here?" Alex asked.

"The door was open. Anyway, it's not like I haven't already seen what you two get up to."

"Please, let's not ever talk about that again!" Alex responded.

"This washroom smells horrible. It needs to be cleaned," I chimed in, certain his mom would agree.

She then looked at the two of us and began laughing.

"What's so funny?" Alex asked.

"I think it's pretty obvious," she replied. "I also thought the washroom smelled horrible in the early days. I almost considered going outside instead."

"The early days of what?" Alex asked as we both stared at her.

"Of being pregnant with you," she replied, a sly smile on her face.

"Pregnant?" I looked at Alex. And then I felt my face burn as I realized we had not been using protection at all, ever, not once, completely overtaken with lust for one another.

Alex blinked rapidly looking between his mom and me. She laughed again and said, "Alex, you must know where babies come from, eh? I'm sure I had your father give you the talk years ago."

He blushed and replied, "Yes, I'm well aware of where babies come from, Mom! I just didn't expect . . ." His voice trailed off. "I guess I should have expected."

"I'm pregnant?" I asked, feeling light-headed.

"Well, we did, you know"—he cleared his throat dramatically—"several times while you were in heat," Alex replied.

His mom laughed again, looking to be in much better spirits than she had during the entire time I'd known her. "That would do it! That's how I became pregnant myself! Things were a lot more conservative back then, and we had to rush a shotgun wedding. I'm pretty sure everyone did the math on that one."

"We're having a pup!" Alex smiled widely, wrapping his arms around me. "A little alpha heir."

"Ow!" I yelped.

"Oops, sorry, forgot to watch for the boobs." He repositioned how he was holding me. "I'm so happy, Talia. We're going to be a family now." He looked at his mom and said, "And you're going to be a grandma!"

"I suppose it was time for some happy news around here," she responded, giving a small smile.

"Does that mean you'll accept Talia as my mate now?"

"I'll think about it," she said, continuing to smile and turning around to walk out of the room.

I looked into Alex's eyes, and it was so difficult for his happiness and excitement not to influence me. It was infectious. "But I don't know anything about babies!" I exclaimed, my own hesitation and anxiety coming forward.

"It's okay. We'll figure it out. And if I have to, I'll hire nannies. Everything's going to be okay. No, it will be better than okay. It will be great! Now put that toilet brush down. I'm going to hire a full-time cleaner. You shouldn't be doing that in your condition."

"I'm not disabled! I'm just pregnant!"

"Nothing is more important to me than making sure you and my pup are spoiled rotten." He kissed me on the cheek. "Come on, let's lie down and enjoy the moment." He took my hand and led me to the bed, pulling me into it with him. He pulled up my shirt and kissed my stomach. "I love him already," he said.

"How do you know it's a *him*?" I asked.

"I just know. He was conceived during battle. He's going to be a tough alpha."

I shook my head. "You wouldn't have won that battle if it wasn't for Jasmine and me, and you know it! You were the one who was too scared to even let me help."

"I still think it's a *him*."

I rolled my eyes. "So what's going to happen to the Bois Sombre Pack anyway, now that they don't have an alpha?"

"They do have an alpha. His mate, the luna, returned to the pack with her pups. Her brother and father are helping her run the pack until her oldest son is old enough to take over the alpha title."

"Why her son and not her daughter?"

"Because that's tradition."

"I don't like it."

"Neither did my sister." Alex suddenly had a faraway look.

"Have you heard from her?" I asked.

"No, and it concerns me," he replied. I could feel the anxiety and overprotectiveness that came forward from his emotions as he wrapped his arms tightly around me, kissing my cheek. "Talia, I will always protect you and my family, so I don't want you to worry."

"Who says I need protection? I'll just beat her head into a pulp, Jasmine style." I chuckled, trying to lighten the mood.

He shook his head. "You should have seen it. It was sick. Blood, bones, and brains everywhere. I didn't think she had it in her. But I guess it's always the quiet ones!" He smiled and turned his attention to me. "You're pretty quiet too. I feel like I should be concerned that there's a stone-cold killer lurking somewhere in there."

I gave him an evil look. "Just stay on your best behavior. And maybe sleep with one eye open."

"Noted," he replied, smiling, and kissed me, placing his hand gently on my belly. "I wonder whose alpha eyes he'll get." He stared into my eyes.

"Alpha eyes?" I asked.

"Alphas all have distinct eyes that they pass down through the generations. Like your blue ones and Jasmine's amber ones."

"And your black ones," I added.

"Exactly. Since we both have alpha eyes, he could get them from either side. I can't decide which ones I want him to have more."

"You mean *her*!"

"No, it's definitely a *him*." He smirked.

"I guess we'll know for sure in nine months."

"Six actually."

"Six?"

"Werewolf pregnancies are only six months long. So we're going to have the whole summer to spend with our new son."

"Daughter."

Alex laughed and kissed me. "I can't wait to prove I'm right."

THE END

To be continued: Wolfborn, book 3 of the Wolfbane series

Author's Note

Thanks for reading *Wolfblood*!

If you enjoyed this book, please consider leaving me a review!
Honest, authentic reviews and feedback, written by real readers,
are invaluable to authors, especially indie ones such as myself.
If you have a few moments to spare, I'd really appreciate it, even
if it's only a quick sentence to say you enjoyed the book!

To stay informed of future book releases, please follow me on
Instagram: @celiahartauthor

About Celia Hart

Celia Hart is a boring accountant by day and a secret paranormal romance writer by night. Like Talia, she can be stupidly stubborn (thanks, Dad!). Unlike Talia, she is physically averse to tequila shots. She lives just outside of Boston, MA with her two miniature schnauzers. When she's not writing, her other hobbies include traveling, eating, cooking, and far too much shopping.